The Man Who Killed
Edgar Allan Poe

The Man Who Killed Edgar Allan Poe

by
J. R. Rada

AIM

PUBLISHING

A division of AIM Publishing Group

THE MAN WHO KILLED EDGAR ALLAN POE

Published by AIM Publishing, a division of AIM Publishing Group.
Gettysburg, Pennsylvania.
Copyright © 2016 by James Rada, Jr.
All rights reserved.
Printed in the United States of America.
First printing: January 2016.

ISBN 9780692598771

Cover design by Grace Eyler.

PUBLISHING

315 Oak Lane • Gettysburg, Pennsylvania 17325

Part I:
Alone

From childhood's hour I have not been as other's were
I have not seen as others saw
I could not bring my passions from a common spring
From the same source I have not taken my sorrow
I could not awaken my heart to the joy at the same tone
And all I lov'd
I lov'd alone.

Edgar Allan Poe
"Alone"

"He's not coming!" Tim Lawrence whispered angrily. Then realizing there was no need for his hushed tone, he said louder, "We've blown the whole night!"

His voice echoed slightly inside the old church, although it was no longer a holy building. Tim glared at the walls as if his gaze would silence the echo. The Westminster Presbyterian Church had been built in Baltimore in the late eighteenth century. It was a Gothic Revival building of brick and brownstone where Presbyterians had been able to worship God in their own way in a heavily Roman Catholic city. While the exterior of the building still appeared as it originally had, new owners converted the interior into a banquet hall in the 1980s.

Tim was sure that the tall stained-glass windows, pipe organ, and vaulted ceiling made a beautiful setting for a wedding, but at night, in the dark, it was just plain creepy. It didn't help that he and Brad Miles were here looking for a phantom or a myth.

Brad kept his face turned toward the stained-glass window, which was encased between two sheets of shatter-resistant plastic. The plastic served as both an insulator and a security measure, and given that this was downtown Baltimore, it helped protect the valuable window against damage from a vandal's thrown rock or gang member's stray bullet.

Brad's cheek nearly touched the cold glass pane as he stared out into the empty graveyard that not only surrounded but extended beneath the church. When the church had expanded in 1852, the new structure had been set upon brick piers that straddled gravestones on the cemetery. Tim was in a boat afloat in a sea of bodies.

The only light that touched the graveyard came from unseen streetlamps along Greene and Fayette Streets that were directed towards the streets and not the graves.

"Chill out, Tim," Brad whispered, his breath causing the window to fog slightly.

But Tim didn't want to be calmed down. He was cold. He was tired. He had had to pass up a date with his girlfriend to be here tonight.

"Chill out? If I chill out anymore, I'll turn into Frosty the Snowman! It must be thirty degrees in here. I think the old man is trying to freeze us out since there's no other way he can get rid of us."

Tim flipped up the collar of his ski jacket. Pulling his head closer to his shoulders, he looked like a turtle shrinking into its shell. He shoved his hands deeper into his pockets and paced back and forth from the window to the back door, passing in front of the old pipe organ as he did.

Tim's stomping sent vibrations through the carpeted floor that seemed to rattle the pipes of the organ. The resulting sound was an annoying mix of dull thuds and toneless echoes. He paused in front of the organ and looked toward the front of the church.

His car was parked two blocks away on Fayette Street. Tim could have it running and toasty warm inside before he pulled onto the Jones Falls Expressway.

If he left.

Tim turned from the door and stomped back to the window where Brad sat patiently watching out of the window. He stood on Brad's left alternately staring down at his friend, then out at the cemetery. In the darkness of the room, Brad's black ponytail looked like a snake curled around his shoulder. His face almost vanished beneath his beard and mustache. What little light did come through the window, reflected off his moist eyes giving them a slightly luminescent appearance.

Crossing his arms over his chest, Tim grunted. Not loudly, but loud enough so that Brad would hear him. He wanted to make sure that his photographer knew that he wasn't happy.

"Will you sit down?" Brad said without looking up from the window. "You're making me nervous. How many No-Doz did you pop tonight?"

Tim put his hands on his hips and said, "Just one."

Brad smiled. "Well then, it must have been the size of a golf ball."

The crackle of static through the walkie-talkie cut off any comeback Tim could have made. An angry and whispering voice followed behind the static. "What are you two doing back there! We can hear you all the way over here. So help me, if you two scare off the Toaster, I'll..."

Nelson Bennett was only at the other end of the building, but he didn't want to have to shout and risk the Toaster hearing.

Tim grabbed the walkie-talkie off the chair and keyed it. "Don't worry, Nelson," he said the church caretaker, "If he doesn't show, you can't blame it on us. To tell the truth, I think the whole thing is a sham. The Toaster hasn't been seen for years."

Nelson snorted as if he were getting ready to spit on the walkie-talkie. "Just the same..."

Tim shook his head. "Just the same, I'll shut up."

Tim tossed the walkie-talkie back onto the padded desk chair and leaned back against the window, feeling the outside chill through both the window and his coat. This assignment had been a mistake, but it wasn't in his nature to turn down writing jobs.

Brad still hadn't taken his eyes off the dark and silent graveyard. Tim should have been seated next to Brad relieving his friend every half hour, like they had agreed on, but he wasn't. Instead, he had been ranting for the past—he glanced at his watch—two hours about the cold and the boredom he had to endure waiting for this story to break.

Six hours of watching an empty graveyard waiting for a mysterious stranger to show up. Was it worth it? Not in Tim's mind.

Tim took a deep breath and leaned his head back against the window. The cold moved from his back up his neck. He turned his head to the side so that his cheek was resting against the window. Nothing was out there. Nothing alive, anyway.

So why didn't he leave?

Tim looked at Brad again and rubbed his eyes. Brad was determined to stay until morning. Pushing himself away from the window, Tim moved the walkie-talkie onto the window sill and took his seat next to Brad.

"It's three a.m.," he told Brad. "Take a break for an hour. I promise I'll watch the stupid grave for every second that you're away."

Tim thought he saw Brad smile, but in the dark of the small room, he couldn't be sure. He saw only a glimpse of white within the mass of black hair on Brad's face. Brad did sigh as he stood up and stretched, though. "Thanks, my bladder's going to burst. Those three coffees I had earlier are ready to move on."

"Fine, but if this guy doesn't show up, you owe me."

Brad laughed. "If this guy doesn't show up, we'll both owe *People*."

Brad's footsteps grew fainter as he walked away from the window. He wasn't nearly as loud as Tim's walking had sounded. There was no rumbling floor or rattling bottles in his wake. Tim finally heard the clack of the door latch as Brad closed the door behind himself.

He leaned back in the chair to get his face as far away from the glass as he could. He didn't want to have a frost-bitten nose and lips by the time the sun came up.

He took a couple of deep breaths and tried to calm himself down. Why was he so agitated tonight? It wasn't like him. Last year, he had sat for eighteen hours in his old Toyota Corolla watching the row home of a city councilman suspected of drug dealing. Because he couldn't leave his car, he had urinated into an empty two-liter Dr. Pepper bottle and poured it discreetly down a drain. That stakeout had lasted three times as long as this one had, and Tim had been alone then.

So why did this particular watch bother him?

He was a writer, so he was expected to dig for his facts. And he had done his share of stories about uncomfortable subjects. A year and a half ago, he had written an article for *The Baltimore Sun* that uncovered a prostitution ring. An unemployed East Baltimore steel worker had been selling his five daughters as prostitutes. The youngest one had been only thirteen.

But grave watching was different somehow. It reminded Tim too much of he would end up. His inescapable end. No matter how far up he went in the world, a six foot by three foot by six-foot hole in the ground was all that would be waiting for him.

Consider who was buried out there. Tim was standing vigil over the mortal remains of Edgar Allan Poe—horror writer, poet, detective writer, theorist, science-fiction writer, critic, and humorist. The finest writer America has ever produced reduced to dust beneath a thousand pounds of dirt and cement.

Yet, he was not waiting for Edgar Allan Poe to appear. No, Mr. Poe had rested quietly for 167 years. The person Tim was watching for was very much alive. He was one of Poe's drinking buddies.

Tim couldn't believe that he had been anxious to begin this assignment last Tuesday.

January 12, 2016

Tim gave his article for *Waste Age Magazine,* a waste-industry trade journal, one last proofread. Then he attached it to an e-mail and sent it off to his editor just as his telephone rang.

"Tim Lawrence and Associates." He smiled to himself. His associates were in his words, "Me, myself, and I", and all three of them worked out of his one-bedroom apartment in Baltimore's Little Italy.

"Cover story for *People* Magazine," Brad said.

The freelance photographer always had a way of getting Tim's attention. A thousand dollars for 1,000 words. *National Geographic* feature story. Super Bowl feature for *Sports Illustrated* that included box seats at the game. All of them were sure-fire ways to get Tim's undivided attention.

"Go ahead," Tim said.

"What do you know about Edgar Allan Poe?" Brad asked.

Tim fell back onto his sofa still holding his wireless phone to his ear. "His stories gave me nightmares when I was a kid, especially 'The Premature Burial.' I kept dreaming of waking up in a grave. My mother banned his books from the house. He and I both have the same talent for writing, and the same inability to make it pay. He died here in town, and to quote 'The Raven', 'Only this, and nothing more.'"

"Well, do you like a good mystery?"

Tim rubbed the back of his neck as he wondered why it seemed Brad was getting further and further away from *People*'s cover story.

"I occasionally read McBain's 87th Precinct or Parker's Spenser novels. I'm more of a Coben or Connelly fan, though."

"I'm not talking about books. I mean real mysteries."

"There are none," the cynic in Tim pronounced.

Brad responded with a short laugh. "You're wrong there, pal. There's one very valuable mystery to you and me right here in Baltimore."

Tim swung his feet to the floor and sat up on the couch. "Let me guess. Edgar Allan Poe."

"Bingo!" Brad shouted from his studio apartment across town.

"I know! His ghost is haunting the Enoch-Pratt Library on Cathedral Street. That's the sort of place where the ghost of a writer would hang out. Right?"

"Be serious, Tim."

Tim sighed and let his head nod slightly. "Listen, I just finished writing a piece of garbage about garbage, and it tears me apart inside knowing I'm getting paid for it while I can't make a dime off my really good stuff."

"Well, this could be one of your really good pieces if you would only listen to me," Brad told him.

Tim took a deep breath and picked up a pad and pencil from the coffee table so he could make notes on what Brad was about to tell him. "Okay. Let's hear it."

"Every January nineteenth since at least 1949, maybe longer, someone leaves three red roses and a half-filled bottle of cognac on

Edgar Allan Poe's grave. No one knows who this person is or why he does it."

Tim scribbled down what Brad had said then read his notes. "Why the nineteenth?"

"That's the easy part. It's Poe's birthday," Brad replied. "Supposedly that ended in 2009 on the bicentennial of Poe's birth."

"Supposedly?"

"After it had stopped for a few years, everyone assumed that the Poe Toaster had died. Some people tried to continue the tradition, but those who had seen the Toaster recognized them as frauds."

"How?"

"The guy apparently says something when he makes the toast and leaves the roses in a certain way. Since the Toaster started reappearing, it hasn't happened like that. The city started hiring someone to be the Toaster for the tourists, but last year after the paid Toaster left, another guy came by, and he did everything just the right way."

"So now everyone wants to know if it was the same guy from earlier," Tim guessed.

"Right, and they also want to know if he is going to come back this year."

Tim rolled his eyes although Brad could not see him. "Of course. What sort of article is *People* looking for?"

"Who is this man? Why does he visit Poe's grave? Why roses? Why cognac? People have written about this man before, but no one has ever definitively identified him."

A rendezvous between the living and the dead. Just the sort of thing to make an award-winning article.

"You're taking the pictures?" Tim guessed.

"None other. So how about it?"

Tim looked at his scribbled notes again. He had underlined Edgar Allan Poe's name three times as he stared at the piece of paper. There was something more to this story than exposing a dedicated Edgar Allan Poe fan.

Sixty-six years? Even if this person had started visiting Poe's grave when he was a teenager, he would be close to ninety-years old now. A lot happens in sixty-six years of a person's life, and yet, the Poe Toaster always managed to show up on the nineteenth. Could it even have been the same person for all those years?

"No one's seen this the Toaster before this? Sixty-six years is a long time," Tim commented.

"*Life* Magazine ran a photo that was supposed to be the Toaster in 1990. It was never authenticated, though. That's going to change this year." Brad paused. "Well, are Lawrence and Miles going to create another masterpiece for the reading and viewing public?"

Tim stared at his notes again. Something bothered him about the whole thing. Something he couldn't put his finger on, but it was making the hairs on the back of his neck start to itch. It was only a feeling, though, and a big check in the bank would certainly soothe that odd feeling. He couldn't pass up an assignment from *People*. It was the type of article that could lead to other high-paying jobs from them.

"We are doing it," he answered.

To begin the search for Poe's mysterious toaster, the first place Tim and Brad visited was the Westminster Church and Cemetery. They wanted to look over the grounds during the day to find the best place to hide from the mysterious fan's view but still see whoever showed up at Poe's grave.

Tim parked his car on Fayette Street in front of the church. The towering building stood as an anachronism in the West Baltimore neighborhood, more out of place than either Tim or Brad. Across the street from the church, the row homes had been renovated or replaced with tall office buildings and parking garages. It was not so with the neighborhood as it was part of the downtown business district. Either way, it was not a place where someone would want to walk alone in the dark, Tim thought. On the Greene Street side of the church, the VA hospital glowered. Behind the church was the University of Maryland School of Law.

The brick church with brownstone trim sat on the corner of its block as if the area had been frozen in time. It was imposing, but simple without a lot of ornamentation. The front of the church has three bays each with pointed-arch windows surrounded by projecting stone and lancet mullions. The steeple tower rose ten stories and in its time would have commanded a view of the area, but now was just one of many tall structures. A brick wall with iron grill work above it ran around the property separating the church from the rest of the city.

"Come, look at this," Brad called from inside the graveyard.

Tim locked the door to his Corolla and pocketed his keys. He stepped through the main gate to the church and walked into a garden of graves. Where most cemeteries had some order to their rows, Westminster Cemetery had none. Graves looked as if they had been fit together like pieces of a jigsaw puzzle.

"Let's walk around. I've got to get some shots of this place,"

Brad urged.

He raised his 35-mm camera to his right eye, but Tim put his hand over the lens before Brad could snap a shot.

"Hey!" Brad yelled, pulling the camera away. He took a piece of lens paper from his wallet and wiped the camera lens off. "What gives?

"Don't be morbid. Show some respect for the dead," Tim told him.

Brad's mouth dropped open slightly. "Morbid? Is it any less morbid than you writing a description of this place? These shots will help establish the mood for your article."

"That doesn't mean I have to like it."

Brad grunted and raised his camera again, but not before casting a warning glance in Tim's direction. He snapped off three quick shots and moved on. Tim winced as Brad leaned against a gravestone to get a particular angle he wanted in his shot of the church.

Nearly every inch of available space in the cemetery was used, which added to the illusion that the cemetery was a giant puzzle. Traditional gravestones marked the graves and foot markers betrayed the lengths of the bodies beneath. Snow, rain, and sun had battered the inscriptions so that many of them were unreadable and the names of the people buried below were known only to God. However, others showed names like Robinson, Henry, McCullough, and Lloyd. Revolutionary War martyrs, War of 1812 patriots, and Baltimore dignitaries lay beside ordinary people.

More noticeable than the graves were the burial vaults; semicircular mounds rising three feet out of the ground and running ten feet across. The small iron doors had rusted shut decades ago giving no one access to the inner remains. Other gravestones were not standing but lying flat, destined to become one with the walkway as were the four marble markers that bordered the brick walkway from Fayette Street to the main entrance of the church.

Tim found it odd that anyone would want to walk through a graveyard on their way to a wedding reception. It seemed like a bad omen.

Brad had no problem stepping onto the stones to get where he needed to stand in order to snap his pictures, but Tim couldn't make himself do it. The ground beneath his feet was someone's grave. It wasn't an actor's star on the Hollywood Walk of Fame. Six feet below the marker a body was laid out in his or her finest clothes.

Tim glanced at the name on the gravestone. Mary Holmes. Who had she been? All he could tell from the marker was that she had

13

died when she was thirty-six year old. Six years younger than him. Had she been married? Did she have children? Did she have descendants who still came by to visit her grave 155 years after her death? The marble beneath his feet was not a part of the walkway. It was the only remaining symbol of the woman's life.

"What's the matter?" Brad asked as he walked just as carelessly back across Mary's grave.

"I want to get inside where it's warm," Tim lied.

Brad nodded his agreement and tucked his bare hands under his armpits. "I know what you mean. It must be close to zero out here. Let's go inside."

They climbed the stone steps to the recessed doorway. The pair of doors that led into the church were lancet paneled with transoms. Brad pulled one open, and the two of them rushed inside. They quickly closed the door behind them to keep out the cold. The thud of the closing door echoed off the two-story arched ceiling, reminding Tim of a haunted house. The dull gray light filtering through the windows failed to warm the inside of the hall. It was one vast empty room. Tim could barely see light fixtures in the ceiling, but they either didn't work, or they weren't turned on. Although the temperature was comfortable, the church itself was cold. It was lifeless and filled with shadows.

An old man pushed a broom across the middle of the floor. Tim didn't understand how the man could see if he was cleaning the floor in the grayness of the church. When the man saw Brad and Tim, he stopped sweeping and stared.

"Next tour's not for another hour, gents," he told them as he leaned across the broom handle.

"We're not here for a tour. We're doing an article for *People* Magazine," Brad said. He started across the floor intending to shake the man's hand. He extended his hand, but his name dropping didn't have the same effect on the old man as it had had on Tim.

"Get out!" the old man yelled.

Brad glanced over his shoulder at Tim. Tim had moved away from the door and was looking at a display which showed an original copy of Edgar Allan Poe's *Al Aaraaf, Tamerlane, and Minor Poems* enclosed in a glass case. It had been published in Baltimore in 1829. At the sound of the old man's raised voice, Tim turned to see what was happening.

Brad tried to calm the man. "But sir, we only want to..."

"I know what you want." Raising his broom off the ground, the old man pointed it in Brad's direction like an old woman scaring away a cat.

Tim moved over behind Brad and said, "Let's go. He's not going to tell us anything even if we do stay. I'll give Conklin a call. He'll be able to arrange something."

Brad nodded. They retreated away from the man, reluctant to turn their backs in case the man charged at them with the broom. Before Tim slipped out the front door, he glanced back. The old man still held the broom like a bayoneted rifle as he waited for Tim and Brad to leave.

When Brad and Tim got back to Tim's apartment, Tim called David Conklin, the editor of *People*. David, in turn, called Harry Webster, president of the foundation that ran Westminster Hall. David quoted Webster an estimate of how much the free publicity in *People* would cost the foundation if it had been an advertisement and what they might mean in new revenue to the site. That was all it took. Webster called Nelson Bennett and told him in no uncertain terms he was to help the reporter and photographer from *People*, or he could start looking for a new job.

When Brad and Tim returned the next day, Nelson was unarmed. The old man wasn't holding so much as a whisk broom.

Brad extended his hand again, but Nelson still wouldn't shake it. His cheeks twitched, and his lips pressed tightly together as he stared unblinkingly at Tim's hand. Tim thought that Nelson looked as if he might spit on the hand, but he was probably just swallowing some angry words. As Tim explained the focus of the proposed article, the old man grumbled to himself. Nelson was silent when Tim finished his explanation, not volunteering any information.

He turned and led them out the front of the church to one of Edgar Allan Poe's graves. Tim hesitated as Brad again walked so carelessly across Mary Holmes' gravestone and two others that had long since become part of the walkway. Finally reconciling himself with the need to continue on, he jumped over the gravestone. Nelson saw him and nodded his approval.

"Why does Edgar Allan Poe have two graves, Mr. Bennett?" Tim asked.

"You can't fool me. You're trying to get me off track with your questions about the two graves, but it won't work," Nelson said without breaking his stride.

"I really am curious."

Nelson sighed and stopped walking. He faced Tim and Brad. "There's a gravestone out back here with Edgar's name on it. When he died in 1849, that's where he was buried. It wasn't very elaborate seein' how Edgar was broke when he died. Anyway, some school kids thought it was a shame that a great writer like Edgar Allan Poe should be buried in a pauper's grave. They began a collection, and in 1875, Edgar was reburied up front here where I'm tryin' to take you."

Nelson spun around and continued his walk. He led Tim and Brad to a large monument. Dominating the corner of the cemetery that bordered Fayette and Greene Streets, it stood six-feet high, two inches over Tim's head. Edgar Allan Poe's sad-looking face etched in the stone, stared out over the cemetery while his birth and death dates appeared on the opposite side of the monument. Sharing the stone marker with him were Maria Poe Clemm, his mother-in-law, and Virginia Poe Clemm, his wife. Their birth and death information were on the remaining two sides of the marker.

Tim looked down at the cement slabs he was standing on. Quickly, he backed off them when he realized he was probably standing on the grave of one of the Poes. It was so hard to tell what was actually a grave and what wasn't. The brick walkway around the church seemed to pass directly over at least three graves. The area around Edgar Allan Poe's monument was no exception. The cement base was very wide. It was impossible to tell where one grave started and another stopped.

Nelson stood in front of Tim with his hands shoved into the pockets of his coat. The old man stared at Poe's sad face for the longest time. At one point, it seemed to Tim, Nelson might actually be praying. His shoulders, which had remained straight while he walked, now sagged. When he turned around, the lines in his face appeared deeper, but his green eyes still held the same fire which had driven Brad and Tim from the church the day before.

"I know what you want," Nelson nearly whispered.

"We want to know about Edgar Allan Poe," Brad said.

Nelson stared at Brad and shook his head. "I'm not senile, Boy, and I'm not an idiot. You can find out about Edgar from 101 biographies. You want to know more about the Toaster."

Nelson shifted his stare to Tim. Tim nodded. "So the stories about the Toaster are true?"

2

January 19, 2016

Tim heard footsteps on the stairs from the main floor to the raised floor where he sat. He started to turn in that direction, but he had promised Brad that he wouldn't take his eyes off the grave. It was probably only Brad, and if he saw Tim looking somewhere other than the grave, he'd be mad.

So Tim continued staring out on the empty cemetery in back of the church. Here, too, the graves and burial vaults were arranged like pieces of a jigsaw puzzle. Edgar Allan Poe's smaller grave stood off to the left. It looked like any other gravestone except for the semicircular bulge at the top of the stone. In the extra space created by the bump, a raven had been sculpted in relief to honor Edgar Allan Poe's most-famous poem.

But there was no Toaster.

When the door shut, Tim said, "That was a quick pit stop, Brad, but as long as you're here, would you mind digging out a corned-beef sandwich from my bag?"

"I'm not Brad."

The voice was Nelson's.

Tim nearly turned around then, but he remembered his promise to Brad. Besides, even though he wouldn't admit it, he still hoped the Toaster would still show up, and he didn't want to miss him. He couldn't say the same about Nelson.

Nelson walked over and stood behind Tim. Tim squirmed uncomfortably in his seat but tried not to make it obvious. He didn't want to give Nelson the satisfaction that he had even the slightest worry. Still, he didn't like being an unaware target for a broom attack by Nelson.

Instead of attacking, Nelson lowered himself into the empty chair and stared at Tim. Tim concentrated on watching the grave, but there was nothing to see. His eyes kept drifting over to Nelson as he tried to watch the old man without being obvious about it.

The graveyard was just as empty as it had been all night. Even the cats refused to prowl through it. The corpses slept quietly in their coffins, and the neighborhood residents slept peacefully in their beds. Not even a passing car along Greene Street disturbed the peace.

"I don't think he will come," Nelson said finally.

"Why? If you had wanted to keep us away, you should have tried this earlier. It'll be dawn in four hours or so. I can wait it out."

Tim wasn't sure he had heard himself say that. Hadn't he wanted to leave only minutes ago? He just didn't want to agree with Nelson. Tim didn't like being threatened with a broom.

He had trouble watching Nelson from the corner of his eye, especially in the dark.

"I've watched him toast Edgar ever since I started working here twenty-three years ago. I've seen the real one and the fakes. The fakes always come early because they want to be seen and they want to get home and sleep. The real Toaster is different. This means something to him. He's never been this late before," Nelson said.

"Then why did he miss a few years?"

"I don't know, but he's back now."

"So you think he came last year."

Nelson nodded. "When I saw him last year, I thought he was another one of the fakes. I went out to chase him away because it was so late, but then I heard him toasting Poe."

"You know what the toast is?"

"I've heard him make it a couple of times in the past. It's always the same."

"What is it?

Nelson shook his head. "That's my secret. It's how I know the real from the fake."

Tim leaned his forehead against the cold window and took a deep breath. Nelson never made anything easy. "Maybe the Toaster went to the large grave while you're over here talking to me?"

"I left Roger watching, and he has the walkie-talkie. I also told your friend, Brad, to go out front when he's finished in the john."

Roger Davis was the curator of the Poe House in Baltimore. He had asked to be included in the watch when Nelson told him about it. Tim had agreed, saying that an extra pair of eyes never hurt.

"You think of everything, don't you?" Tim said.

"I couldn't think of a way to keep you and your friend away."

Tim smiled. "We're persistent."

"Yes, but it may be in vain." Nelson paused and took a deep breath, which sounded deafening in the quiet of the room. "A man died last month. A very old man named Mark Hammerstein. He visited this hall every other Wednesday and the Poe House on the Wednesdays he wasn't here."

"And you think since this guy was such a big fan of Edgar Allan Poe's, he was the Toaster?"

"Yes," Nelson said quietly. He looked at the floor.

"What about the people who say they are the Toaster?" Tim asked.

Nelson shook his head. "They aren't. Some are too young. Others I called in the dead of night while watching the Toaster at the grave. He might not even be Mark Hammerstein. If I was right, though, if the Toaster didn't show up this year, I was going to leave the cognac and roses myself to continue the tradition."

"I guess we spoiled that."

"Yes!" He almost spat the word.

"But the tradition had already ended," Tim said.

"No, it didn't."

"No one left anything on the grave for a few years. I read it was declared ended in 2012 after nothing had been left for three years."

"That's what people were told. It's just that nosy people like you didn't know about it." Nelson paused. "I've watched over this building for twenty-three years now. The Toaster has left his gifts every year. I've just been collecting them before dawn in recent years."

"Why?"

"Out of respect for Edgar Allan Poe and the Toaster. Why else? If the Toaster wanted his name known, he would have revealed himself. This is something private and solemn for him."

Tim's eyes stayed on the cemetery. A shadow shifted as a gust of wind blew through a tree.

"People were finally forgetting about the mystery," Nelson said. "You're going to start the speculation again, and Mr. Webster will let it happen to get his free publicity."

Tim watched as the trunk of a tree in the shadows seemed to bulge and then separate into two shadows. He rubbed his eyes and leaned forward to get a better view.

"I almost wish he wouldn't show up," Nelson continued. "I would rather the Toaster be forgotten than be exposed by the likes of you."

"I'm sorry to disappoint you, Nelson, but I think your toaster is here," Tim said as he pointed out the window.

A man had entered the cemetery. He must have come around the side of the church no one was watching and stayed close to the wall. Tim hadn't even been sure it was a man until he stepped away from the tree and limped across the yard towards Edgar Allan Poe's grave.

"So it's not Mark Hammerstein," Tim said.

"Good," Nelson muttered. "He should be a mystery."

Whoever he was, the man wore a dark overcoat and hat. The red scarf wrapped around his neck hid most of his face. He held a cane in his right hand, and a half-filled bottle of wine and three red roses in his left. He was definitely Nelson's Toaster, or rather, Edgar Allan Poe's Toaster.

Nelson watched from his side of the window, and Tim saw the old man smile. The mystery was still alive.

"Call the others," Nelson said with a sigh. "They'll want to see this, but tell them to come quietly."

"You call," Tim said as he handed Nelson the walkie-talkie. "I came here to interview this guy."

Tim started to stand, but Nelson grabbed his arm and pulled him back down.

"Don't be a fool. What right do you have to tell the world who this man is? He is paying his respects to the dead, for God's sake. If he wanted publicity, he would have told someone what he was doing. I don't see writers rushing out to tell everyone who's leaving what on Elvis' or Marilyn Monroe's graves. So why bother this man? Let him mourn in peace."

"I'm getting paid to do a story." Tim tried to shrug off the old man's hand. "If I want to get my questions answered for that story, then I need to talk to him."

Nelson squeezed Tim's arm even harder. "Don't. I saw you jump over the grave the other day. You have respect for the dead; the others don't. Leave this man alone. Please."

There was so much pleading in Nelson's voice that Tim almost agreed. Then he looked out the window. The man approaching the grave was leaning heavily on his cane. His legs shook as he lowered himself to his good knee in front of the gravestone.

Sixty-five years. What would drive a man to such a level of devotion?

Tim had to move quickly, or the man would leave in another minute.

"Nelson, you've watched this man now for twenty-three years. Aren't you the least bit curious as to who he is and why he leaves the roses and cognac? Haven't you ever wondered who this man is?"

The pressure on Tim's arm eased slightly. That was the answer to Tim's question. He pulled his arm free.

The Toaster was rising from his kneeling position when Tim slipped quietly out the unlocked back door. Luckily, the door didn't squeak on its hinges. He didn't want to spook the man. Not that it appeared as if he could move too quickly. He leaned heavily on the cane. Tim moved as quietly as he could as he approached the old man.

When he was about ten feet away, the man said, "I wouldn't come any closer if I were you."

Tim stopped. Not because of the warning, but this was Baltimore. The man might be armed. It was almost a requirement if you were going to be out in certain downtown neighborhoods at night. The man's voice was deep, melodic; almost hypnotizing. Tim thought he detected a slight accent, but he couldn't place it.

The Toaster put a hand on his back to straighten himself as he stood up. Tim still couldn't see his face in the darkness. He was staring at a huge shadow. He felt as if he was facing Lamont Cranston. *Who knows what evil lurks in the hearts of men? Only the Shadow knows.* The radio show had been years before his time, but he had read some reprints of *The Shadow* comics when he was a boy.

"I'd like to speak with you, sir. I'm doing an article for *People* Magazine and ..."

The Toaster cut him off. "Ah, another writer. How wonderful."

Tim took the friendly tone of his voice as an invitation and moved forward. The man quickly backed off three steps and held up his hand.

"Please, do not come any closer. For your own safety," the man warned.

"But I'd like to interview you and find out why you make this annual visit," Tim said.

The man was silent. Tim feared he might run off. Then the Toaster sighed and nodded his head.

"Perhaps, it is time that I told my story again. This is a new generation, more tolerant and believing than the ones before," he said finally.

He spoke more to himself than to Tim, but Tim turned on the small digital recorder he had in his coat pocket just the same. Again he tried to place the accent but was unable.

"Excuse me, young man, for talking to myself, but I haven't spoken to another person in years. I guess my ears have grown used to the sound of my own voice."

Years? Was the man a monk or someone similar?

"I will speak with you about my connection with Edgar Allan Poe, but there are conditions."

Here it comes. He wants money, Tim thought.

"First, you must tell my story as I tell it to you. There can be no embellishments. No editorial opinions from your pen."

Tim nodded, then realized the old man might not be able to see too well in the night. Although, apparently his age hadn't affected his hearing.

"I can do that," he said.

"Good. Second, you must maintain at least ten feet of space between us at all times."

"Why?"

"Let us say for now that I am diseased. You will understand better later," the old man answered.

Diseased? Did this guy have the plague or something?

Tim took a nervous step backward. "No problem there."

The Toaster chuckled. "I didn't think there would be. Third, you, and only you, will meet me tomorrow at three o'clock for your interview at my home in Western Maryland."

Tim looked at the windows in the church from where Nelson, and probably Brad and Roger, were watching. He moved to the side so that if Brad was shooting pictures, he would be able to get a clear shot of the Toaster. Brad and he were supposed to be working together. What would Brad think of this final condition? He'd hate it, of course, but Tim needed to talk to this man, though, or there wouldn't be a story. It wasn't much of a choice.

Brad would be mad, but at least he would get paid for the pictures he took of the cemetery and the Toaster.

"Fine. That will give me a chance to go home and get some shut-eye. It's been a long night. I'll need directions to your house, of course."

"Of course," the man replied. "I'll write them out for you."

Tim remembered he hadn't introduced himself except as a writer. "By the way, my name is Tim Lawrence." He held out his hand, but then quickly pulled it back when he remembered the second condition he had agreed to.

"I'm very pleased to meet you, Mr. Lawrence. You just may be the redemption my soul needs." The Toaster leaned toward Tim balancing his weight on his cane. "I am Alexander Reynolds, the man who killed Edgar Allan Poe."

3

Tim tapped his brake pedal to slow the car down. The speedometer needle fell back from 45 to 20 mph. The turnoff should be nearby. At least he thought it should be nearby.

He glanced at the hastily drawn map in his notebook. It obviously wasn't drawn to scale. The turnoff he was looking for seemed much closer to Frederick than Cumberland, and Tim knew that wasn't true. He was already an hour outside of Frederick and past Hagerstown for that matter.

Where was it?

He'd gotten off Interstate 68 at Hancock and headed up Sideling Hill on old Route 40 and then Staley Road halfway up the mountain. Now he was looking for an unnamed gravel road.

An impatient BMW driver honked his horn from behind Tim. Tim ignored him and continued scanning the right-hand side for the unmarked gravel road. The BMW crossed over the double yellow line and passed Tim's creeping Corolla. The BMW driver shook his fist at Tim as he passed.

"Jerk," Tim muttered.

Then he saw the road, although calling it a road was a generous description. The road was a gravel path scarcely six-feet wide. He turned onto the gravel road and followed it as Alexander Reynolds had instructed him.

Two miles from the Staley Road turn off, the path ended abruptly in front of an eight-foot high iron gate. Extending from either side of the gate was an equally high chain-link fence topped with barbed wire. The image of a prison flashed through Tim's mind. He expected to see armed guards with German shepherd attack dogs patrolling the grounds inside the fence.

He pulled out his smartphone and saw that he wasn't getting any service. He shook his head and shoved the phone into his jacket pocket.

Tim's hand rested on the gearshift. For a few moments, he put the car in reverse to back his car back onto Staley before he paused to think.

"Timothy Randall Lawrence, there's a crazy man in there," he murmured to himself.

Alexander Reynolds was crazy. How could he not think it after what Alexander had told him? The man who had killed Edgar Allan Poe? Not likely, unless Alexander had been alive 165 years ago. Alexander seemed to have no doubt that he was speaking the truth. He hadn't ranted about killing Edgar Allan Poe, and he hadn't gotten defensive about his story as Tim would have expected a crazy person to do. Tim hadn't seen Alexander's face in the dark, but the man had certainly spoken calmly enough.

What a story this could be, true or not!

Tim smiled to himself. *The Man Who Killed Edgar Allan Poe* by Tim Lawrence. It had a ring to it. And think of the publicity it would bring to his career!

Now sitting in front of the gate, he knew he had one more reason not to meet Alexander Reynolds for the interview.

He didn't want to die.

If he went through that gate, that is what he thought would happen to him. He would be trapped on an isolated piece of property with a crazy man. If Alexander thought he had killed Edgar Allan Poe, what was to keep him from killing another writer?

Brad had warned him not to come alone, but Tim had laughed him off.

"You know he's crazy, Tim. Look at the story he laid on you," Brad had said as they had left the Westminster Church shortly before sunrise.

Alexander had disappeared moments after he had written down the directions to his house in Tim's notebook. Tim was surprised the old man could move as fast as he did with his limp. Brad had only managed to get four photos of Alexander from inside the church. By the time he had gotten outside, Alexander had left.

"You're not jealous, are you?" Tim asked as he opened the door to his car. He was too happy about getting Alexander to agree to the interview to worry about anything else.

"Jealous? You're head's beginning to swell, Lawrence. I don't think you'll be able to fit it inside the car."

"Well, he did only invite me."

"Yes, but what did he invite you to?"

Tim put the car in park and reached down under his vinyl seat. After groping unsuccessfully twice, he found the holster and pulled it up.

He pulled the snub-nose .38 from its holster and checked the cylinder. Five chambers. One bullet pushed snugly into each chamber. He wasn't as foolish as Brad thought. He snapped the cylinder shut and slid the revolver back into the leather holster.

Would it be enough? With the short length of the barrel, the pistol's accuracy was good for only a few yards. He had test fired it at different ranges and knew, at best, he was fifty-percent accurate from twenty-five feet. Hopefully, he wouldn't have to use the pistol, but if he did, Alexander would certainly be closer than twenty-five feet.

Tim pulled his sweater up to his chest. He clipped the holster to his waistband so that it rested in the small of his back. Then he pulled the sweater down over the top of the holster. The inward curve of his lower back would hide any bulge the little holster would make.

He glanced at himself in the rear-view mirror paying particular attention to his eyes. Could he shoot a man in self-defense? Would he? Could he watch a man die?

He had watched the faces of killers before. Most of them had been death-row inmates around the country whom he had interviewed for an article on capital punishment three years ago. Each one of those six men and two women had had a certain hardness in their eyes. It was a blank look that came into their eyes when murder was mentioned. It was that hardness that Tim decided had given them the emotional distance to commit murder.

Tim looked again, wondering if that look lurked behind his blue eyes ready to be exposed.

He didn't look like a killer. Killers weren't supposed to look like California surfers. That's what he looked like, though. Blond hair. Blue eyes. Everything except the tan. His face was soft without any sharpness in his features that comes from hard living. Tim looked like a twenty-year-old boy-next-door.

He edged his car close to a control box next to the gate. When he rolled down the window, a cold blast of mountain air shocked him into alertness. He reached out through the window and pressed the "call" button on the console and imagined an electronic buzz sounding somewhere up the mountain in a huge stone mansion with turrets on each corner and a wooden door that was two-stories high. Frankenstein's castle.

He ducked back into the car and turned the heater all the way up. Tim hugged himself as his misting breath began to fog the windshield. With the window down, the cold was successfully fighting for control of the interior of the car.

He waited another minute until he toes went numb. "There's no one home, Tim, old boy. God has given you a reprieve," he muttered.

He should have been relieved, but he felt disappointed. Although Alexander had frightened him, he had wanted to interview him. Crazy or not, Alexander was still Edgar Allan Poe's annual visitor. What was the real connection between Alexander Reynolds and Edgar Allan Poe? Was Alexander simply an over-amorous fan performing some sort of ritual like John Hinckley shooting President Reagan to win the love of Jodie Foster? Tim wanted to know the truth even if it did involve danger.

But, if no one answered his call, he would never know. The old man could have lied to him and sent him on a wild-goose chase to protect his privacy. If that were the case, he'd be waiting at the grave next year and follow Alexander Reynolds home. He wouldn't be made a fool of, even by a crazy man.

Just as Tim was about to roll up his window and leave, a voice spoke from the console. "Hello."

Tim's doubts were forgotten as he bumped his head rushing to lean out his window. "Hello, Mr. Reynolds, it's me. Tim Lawrence," he said as he rubbed the sore spot on his head.

"Ah, Mr. Lawrence. Please, come in. I've been waiting for you."

Tim expected the line to be followed by a maniacal laugh, but there was only silence. The iron gate swung inward on unseen mechanical arms.

Tim rolled up his window and stared at the opening in the fence.

"'Come into my parlor,' said the spider to the fly," Tim muttered to himself.

He drove through the gate and paused long enough on the other side to see the gates swing closed. He wondered again if he had made a mistake. The small pistol resting in the small of his back didn't seem to be offering much assurance at the moment, but he was glad it was there.

The Corolla's speed on the gravel path hovered around fifteen miles an hour. As the car bounced over the gravel, Tim bounced around inside the car hoping his head wouldn't crash into the roof. He had doubts that his small car would make it over some of the larger stones further up the mountain. Tim could hear the smaller stones striking the windshields and sides of the car. Tim guessed he would find hundreds of little dings in the car body when he stopped and climbed out.

At one point on the path, he drove around a curve to find himself looking out over the valley to the next mountain. He tried to keep his attention on the road. His view over the valley extended for three miles at least and was a scene worthy of a painting. The road dipped, and for a half a mile, it seemed as if the car was flying. He couldn't see the road in front of him. On his left, all he could see was the valley, and on his right, the mountain seemed to push out against the car. His speed dropped to five miles an hour, and every second Tim thought the car would slide off the narrow path.

He sighed loudly when his car turned into another curve, and the ground rejoined the car. His hand cramped up, and he realized for the first time how hard he had been clutching the steering wheel. He stopped the car and worked the cramps out of his hand before continuing.

Tim kept a constant eye on his temperature gauge, which had begun to creep towards the red zone on his dashboard panel. He hoped the Corolla's old hoses would hold long enough to get him home again, and he promised the car he would change all its hoses when it got him home. The ground leveled off somewhat near the top of the mountain, and the temperature gauge dropped back slightly.

Why would anyone want to live alone on top of a mountain? There were no power lines he could see that would keep Alexander connected with the world. But that didn't seem to be a primary concern with Alexander Reynolds. From what Alexander had said the night before, apparently, he spent most of his time talking to himself.

What did Alexander do when it snowed? A few inches of snow or a sheet of ice on the road could trap him at the top of the mountain until the spring thaw. Certainly, no sane person would try to navigate a car down the mountain in conditions like that; especially when the path went onto that ledge, Tim had just driven over. If Alexander lost control on that ledge for only a second, he would go over the side. But then, a sane man didn't live on the top of the mountain, did he?

Tim eased his car over one final rise, and he saw the house.

Judging by the amount of land Alexander had fenced in, Tim assumed Alexander had money and lots of it. His house didn't show it. To begin with, it didn't stand out at all from the surrounding maple trees. In fact, during the summer, with the trees in full bloom, the house probably blended right in with the forest. It was constructed of wooden beams shaved to fit together with the precision of the stones of an Egyptian pyramid. The house had two floors and a two-car garage. A long porch ran along the front of the house from the front door to the garage. Essentially, the house was nothing more than a modified log cabin.

Quaint? Yes. Rich? No.

Tim had expected something more elaborate. Four floors. Twenty rooms. Greek columns supporting the porch. Or, maybe even Frankenstein's castle, which he had imagined at the gate. Almost anything would have been more acceptable in his mind than this. He pictured Alexander Reynolds closer to the mad scientist-type rather than the Grizzly Adams-type.

Tim parked the car in front of the garage, giving it a well-deserved rest. He hoped it would start when he was ready to leave.

Alexander Reynolds stood on the porch waiting for Tim. He wore blue jeans and a fur-lined buckskin jacket over a red-flannel shirt. This also shocked Tim since he had seen Alexander at the cemetery in a suit and top coat.

In the daylight, Alexander seemed younger than he had at the cemetery. His face wasn't as clouded by shadows. He appeared to be in his mid-sixties. That meant Alexander could not have been born when the Toaster first started visiting Edgar Allan Poe's grave. He was going to have a hard time proving that he was the original Toaster let along the man who killed Edgar Allan Poe.

Alexander had close-trimmed brown hair, and Tim wondered if he cut it himself. He seemed very healthy, except for his limp. Tim also noticed Alexander was thinner than he had first thought. The shadows and heavy overcoat Alexander had worn at the cemetery had given him the appearance of weighing about 180 pounds. That estimate now looked about twenty pounds too heavy.

Tim picked up his digital recorder and notebooks from the passenger seat. He put his hand on his lower back to make sure the pistol was still there. Even though he could feel it on his back, touching it with his hand somehow made it real. He wasn't going to give this crazy man an opportunity to stick an axe through his skull. Satisfied he was ready, Tim took a deep breath and got out of the car.

The wind blowing across the top of the mountain almost knocked him down.

"I'm surprised your car made it up here. This is Jeep country," Alexander noted.

Tim nodded vigorously. "It certainly is. How can you stand to live in such isolation?"

Alexander shrugged. "It's for the best."

Tim started forward holding out his hand to Alexander, but the older man quickly backed away.

"Remember our agreement," he said quickly.

Tim stopped off and lowered his hand. "I'm sorry. I forgot. Force of habit from my mother's manners lessons, I guess."

"It would be in your best interest not to do that again." The way he spoke the words sounded ominous, but then he smiled. "Let's go inside and get out of the cold. I've got a fire started."

Alexander turned from the railing on the porch and limped into his house. He still leaned heavily on his cane favoring his left leg. Even so, Tim was struck by the impression that Alexander was healthier than he had seemed in the cemetery.

After Alexander had gone in, Tim followed at a safe distance.

The house was spotlessly clean, but in complete disagreement. There was no single theme to the way Alexander had decorated the house. He seemed to have chosen the furnishings randomly. Colors clashed. The furniture was an odd mix of different eras and different countries. A six-panel, hand-painted Japanese screen covered one corner of the room. An English coat of arms for the Lightner family hung over the stone fireplace. Just as Alexander had promised, a huge fire burned in the fireplace heating the small house to a comfortable temperature. A small color television sat next to a vintage 1940's cathedral radio that was almost as large as the television. Bookshelves covered the opposite wall from ceiling to floor, and books crowded most of the space.

On the walls hung half a dozen different paintings of Alexander Reynolds at various ages from a young man of twenty or so to an older man. Tim glanced at Alexander, then back at the fourth painting. Alexander looked at least ten-years older in the painting, but the painting itself seemed to be at least eighty-years old. Tim could see minute cracks in the paint when he moved closer to it.

How could that be?

Had Alexander moved up into the mountains for health reasons? He certainly seemed in good health now.

The dining room connected without any division to the living room. A massive cherry-wood table surrounded by six equally large chairs filled the room. Alexander pointed to the table.

"That would be a good place for you to set up your recording equipment," he said. "When I speak, I sometimes feel the need to move around. That corner will provide you with safety without restricting my movements."

Tim looked into the corner. Cornered. There wasn't much room to move around in if Alexander did decide to attack him. He scanned the room again for a better place to set up. There was none. This corner would keep him far enough away from Alexander to honor their agreement while allowing him an unobstructed view of the room. He still didn't like it, but if he raised too much of a fuss, Alexander might cancel the interview.

He wished he had thought the consequences out more carefully before he had agreed to Alexander's terms. He hadn't imagined he would be placed in a situation like this, though. This certainly wasn't his usual type of interview. How often did he get cornered in an isolated house with a crazy man who thought he was a killer?

Tim set his tape recorder down on the table. He took the cellophane off an unused tape and inserted it into the machine. Then he took out his cell phone.

"You won't be able to use that up here," Alexander told him.

Tim nodded. "Yes, I already checked. I guess you have to use a landline to make calls."

"I don't have a telephone. I don't need one. I had this house built before cell phones were commonplace. Because of that, it happens to be in a dead spot."

"I can still use the camera app. Do you mind if I take pictures occasionally during the interview?"

Alexander shrugged. "That will be fine."

"The paintings on the wall. Are they of your father, grandfather, etcetera? They seem very old," Tim asked, trying to make small talk to break the ice.

He moved around to the back side of the table and sat down. Opening up one of his two notebooks, Tim jotted down the date and the subject of the interview.

"No. The paintings are all of me." Alexander turned to look at one of the portraits of himself in an old-fashioned broadcloth suit. It wasn't the painting that had attracted Tim's attention. This one showed Alexander at about thirty-years old standing in front of a window that looked out over a city with cobblestone streets.

"But how can they all be of you? Some of those are old paintings that show men who look older than you."

"That is part of my story. Shall we begin?"

Tim pushed the record button on the tape recorder.

Part II:
Romance

Of late, eternal condor years
So shake the very Heaven on high
With tumult as they thunder by,
I have no time for idle cares
Through gazing on the unquiet sky.

Edgar Allan Poe
"Romance"

4

"As I told you in the cemetery, my name is Alexander Reynolds. That is true, but in other countries, I have used other names. My name was Peter in Siberia. I was known as Zacchaeus in Greece. People called me Leonardo in Italy. Juan in Spain. Alexander is the name which I chose to use in America," the Toaster began.

"So what is your real name?" Tim asked as he settled into the wooden chair. It was comfortable, but it made him feel as if Alexander was interrogating him and not him interviewing Alexander.

Alexander took a deep breath and said, "I was born Lazarus, son of Jeremiah, in Bethany, which is a small village outside of Jerusalem or rather it was a small village long ago."

"Ah," Tim mumbled.

Alexander leaned forward. "Ah? The name means something to you then?"

Tim looked up from his notes and shook his head. "Not the name. The accent. I thought I recognized it when I spoke to you in the cemetery. It's Israeli."

Alexander laughed. "I sincerely doubt it. The accent you detect, if any, is a result of twelve languages and thirty-three different dialects all trying to express themselves in my words."

Tim's jaw dropped open slightly. "Twelve languages and thirty-three dialects? You speak them all?"

Alexander grinned. "You must understand, Mr. Lawrence. I am a man with much time on my hands."

Alexander paused, and Tim thought he had finished speaking. True to Alexander's expectations, he stood and began pacing the floor. Moving back and forth from one end of the living room to the other, Alexander alternated between holding his arms folded across his chest and letting them swing free. He stopped at a bookshelf and removed a thick volume from the many choices lining the wall.

In most homes, shelves full of books were mainly for show. However, Tim felt that Alexander had read every one of the volumes on the three-dozen shelves. Pieces of paper jutted up from between their pages and their spines were cracked. Tim saw at least a thousand various books. It must have been the way Alexander went directly to the book he was searching for and pulled it without hesitation from the shelf. Alexander was a man with much time on his hands.

Alexander set the book on the end of the table nearest the living room and moved away.

"Are you familiar with that book?" he asked, pointing to the volume.

Tim stretched across the table and pulled the book towards him. It was a leather-bound copy of the Bible. The cover was cracked, and the pages were dog-eared. It was a book that had seen many years use.

"It's the Bible," Tim answered nonchalantly.

Alexander sat down in a rocking chair across the room and slowly rocked. It made an odd rumbling sound like a bowling ball being flung down an alley as it made contact with the floor.

"Do you believe in it?" he asked.

The last time Tim had been to church was when he was fifteen years old. His mother had made him go to Sunday mass at Sacred Heart Catholic Church in Glyndon, every Sunday without fail. He hated listening to the priest talk. Everything sounded the same week after week, and the only thing that kept Tim from falling asleep was the constant kneeling and sitting. However, even though he hated church, he still believed in God.

"I suppose so. I'm not very religious, though" he answered.

The interview wasn't going the way Tim had pictured it going. Instead of talking to a man obsessed with Edgar Allan Poe, he was listening to a religious fanatic. Alexander was asking the questions instead of answering them.

Alexander crossed his arms over his chest. "I see. I assure you that the Bible is not a work of fiction, Mr. Lawrence. What is written in there, as much as it is translated correctly, is the truth spoken by the prophets of God. If you would open to the Gospel According to St. John, chapter eleven and read it, you will see what I mean."

Tim thought he had escaped Sunday mass fifteen years ago, but now it seemed like he was back in church again. He expected Alexander to start spouting Latin phrases at him any moment. Tim flipped through the New Testament, careful not to tear any of the yellowing pages until he found the gospel of John. Then he narrowed his search to find chapter eleven.

"'Now a certain man was sick, named Lazarus, of Bethany...'" Tim stopped reading and looked across the room. Alexander met his stare.

Alexander wasn't a religious fanatic. Tim was back to thinking of Alexander Reynolds as plain crazy. "You think you and this Lazarus are the same person," Tim said.

Alexander shook his head. "No, I don't. I know it to be true."

Tim stifled his laugh by coughing. Then he leaned back in his chair so that the holster pressed into his back. Tim felt reassured knowing it was there. He hoped he didn't need it.

"Well, this is fascinating, but how does being more than 2,000-years old connect you with the death of Edgar Allan Poe?" Tim asked, trying to get back on the subject and salvage the interview.

Alexander stood up and began pacing again. "You are too direct, Mr. Lawrence. You expect the answers to your questions to be short and easy ones, but they aren't. I can't compress 2,000 years of life into two quotes for your article. I need to tell my story in my way. You agreed to that. I can't jump around from century to century. I must begin at the beginning and finish at the end."

Century to century?

"Okay," Tim agreed reluctantly, "Tell me your story your way."

Alexander pointed to the Bible. "Please finish reading that chapter and then we will continue."

Tim sighed, but he turned his attention to the scriptures in front of him and finished reading chapter eleven and the story of Lazarus. He was already familiar with the story of the man raised from the dead by Christ, but he read it anyway. No use making the crazy man mad. Tim wanted to live to write the article.

When he had finished, he put the book down and said, "Lazarus is dead. He had to have died at least nineteen-hundred years ago."

Alexander slammed his fist against the wall. Tim jumped in his chair and almost drew his pistol. When he saw Alexander was not approaching him, he only scratched his side.

"No! I was dead, but by the command of Christ, I lived again!" he shouted.

Tim sat silently.

"Perhaps, I was wrong about your generation, Mr. Lawrence. You are not ready for what I have to say. Please leave me."

Alexander pointed to the door and waved Tim away. Tim looked at Alexander standing before him calm and unconcerned. The door to the front porch was close. Tim saw his chance to leave and be free of the crazy man. So why didn't he move? Why did he stay seated at the table?

The answer was easy. "I want to believe you, Mr. Reynolds. Really, I do, because telling your story would almost certainly win me a Pulitzer. I don't find it easy to believe in anything, though. If you can't convince me, how can I convince millions of readers who won't have the chance to meet you?" Tim thought it was a logical appeal to Alexander Reynold's craziness.

Alexander stood at the other end of the table massaging his chin with his hand. He opened his mouth to say something, but no sound exited. Then he turned just a bit so that he could see the portraits on the wall.

"So, you need proof." He nodded slowly. "People never change it seems. Just as Thomas needed to touch the wounds in Christ's hands, you need to see the marks of my age. My stigmata."

Alexander gently touched his face in a painting that showed him in a scholar's robes. He turned and limped off toward the staircase. At the foot of the stairs, he put his hand on the banister and paused.

"I will bring you the proof you need," he said. "Wait here if you would. If you'd like a drink, I have soda and juice in the refrigerator. Help yourself."

When Alexander had disappeared up the stairs, Tim reached back and touched his small revolver again. What would Alexander's proof be? A double-barreled shotgun shoved against his chest?

Tim glanced at the door. He could take the easy way out and stand up and walk right out of the house before Alexander came back down the stairs. Walk? It would be easy to *run*!

He had only one problem.

How would he get through the gate at the bottom of the mountain? He didn't know how to open it. There might not be any direct controls for it, and he didn't have any idea where to start looking for a remote control inside the house.

Tim also had to consider the nagging feeling at the center of his brain that whispered to him that Alexander was telling the truth, or at least telling the truth as Alexander knew it. The man was too at ease and friendly to be a liar. Tim knew the best liars often appeared that way, but in Alexander, the emotions seemed genuine. He reminded Tim of a grandfather sitting on the front porch during a warm summer afternoon and telling his grandkids about "the good old days."

Alexander limped down the stairs about five minutes later,

carrying a thick pile of papers. He laid them on the table in front of Tim and backed away. The pile leaned to the side and collapsed. Tim grabbed at the papers that were sliding toward the edge of the table.

"These are some of my wounds. Touch them, Mr. Lawrence, but be very careful. As you will see some of them are very old."

Tim stood up and gently looked at the pieces he had saved from falling to the floor. In his left hand was the deed to the 300 acres of the mountain that Alexander owned. The deed was dated August 21, 1851, in the name of Alexander Reynolds. The total cost of the property was $60,000.

Tim laid it aside and looked at the next piece. It was a yellowed copy of a speech given on November 3, 1809, at Harvard about how the stories of the Bible correlated with non-religious history. The signature at the end of the speech read Alexander Reynolds.

While Tim continued looking at each piece, Alexander sat quietly in his rocking chair. He let Tim draw his own conclusions about the material. Occasionally, Tim looked up from the pile to Alexander, but Alexander offered no comments. Otherwise, the writer was totally engrossed in the papers.

Tim read letters written from Edgar Allan Poe to Alexander. One letter written in 1829 seemed so condemning of Alexander that Tim wondered why the old man would want to keep it. Poe also wrote the second letter almost begging Alexander to come to Fordham, New York, to help Virginia Poe get over an ailment. Another letter was no more than a note from Elizabeth Poe filled with sentiment about a service that Alexander had provided her. The oldest piece in the pile was a love letter written from Catherine Lightner to Alexander Reynolds in 1621 from England.

Tim glanced at the coat of arms mounted over the fireplace. The shield was divided into four quadrants showing an eagle, a knight's helmet, an axe, and a hammer. It was the symbol of the Lightner family.

Tim could have discounted all of them as forgeries if he had wanted. *If.* That was the catch. He knew they were genuine. The paper felt old and delicate. One of the letters had almost crumbled to dust when he lifted it from the pile. The language in the letters and article flowed. It didn't seem jerky or methodic as a forger's words would sound trying to imitate the language of the era.

Then there was the photograph.

It was a daguerreotype of a slightly younger Alexander Reynolds standing on Fayette Street at the Westminster Church. However, it was not the Fayette Street Tim had seen last night. No VA hospital was being constructed across the street. He saw no law library connected to the church. No towering buildings in the background. Gas lamps replaced streetlights. The sepia tones of the photo seemed genuine, not doctored.

Tim wished Brad was with him to look at the picture. Brad could probably have pinpointed the date it was taken and its authenticity. Tim guessed it was at least 100 years old.

"I suppose you would let me take some of these pieces to have them authenticated?" Tim asked.

Alexander sighed. "You refuse to believe what you can see, Mr. Lawrence. I suppose if you must, you can take a piece of one of the articles or letters to authenticate, but only a small piece. I will not let any of those articles, letters, or pictures leave here entirely. I can't risk them being damaged or lost. They are too valuable to me."

"May I photograph you?" Tim asked.

"Certainly."

"He wouldn't be able to authenticate the documents with a photo, but he could read the language and study the picture for signs of authenticity or forgery.

Tim looked at the picture again. It was valuable to more than just Alexander. The article, letters, and photographs needed to be shown in the finished article. They would support Alexander's story. If Tim could get someone to certify the authenticity of the letters, the truth of the article would be verified.

He looked at the pile of documents spread out in front of him on the table.

Incredible.

Tim looked up from the picture to Alexander. Was he really nearly 2,000 years old? How could it be? But he had the proof. He didn't even have to get it authenticated for him to believe it. Alexander wouldn't have agreed to the idea if the pieces had been fakes.

"I believe you," he whispered.

5

January 20, 2016

Alexander leaned forward in the rocking chair and stared at Tim. Tim squirmed uneasily in his seat under the scrutiny of the mysterious man. The man's eyes were agates backlit so that they seemed to glow.

"You say, 'I believe you.' You say the words you think I want to hear, but do you really believe that I am telling you the truth?" Alexander asked.

Tim glanced at his notebook. He had written "Lazarus ???" Could he believe this man in front of him was more than 2,000-years old? Alexander didn't look more than fifty-six.

No!

Alexander couldn't be Lazarus. Humans could live to be 100-years old if they were lucky. Maybe even a few decades longer if they are extraordinary. But 2,000-years old? Never! Never! Never!

Yet, Tim had seen the proof. He had even held it in his hands. He couldn't believe Alexander would have gone to the trouble of creating false photographs and documents just to fool him. Alexander had even agreed to have the age of the papers verified. If they were fakes, it would show up in the tests. Besides, it had been less than a day since Alexander had talked to Tim at the cemetery. He couldn't have produced that pile of documents in that short amount of time. Not only would it have cost a fortune, but excellent forgeries took time.

Alexander was right. Tim had said he believed, but his statement had lacked any conviction. Despite Alexander's overwhelming proof, he still doubted.

Truly, he was like Jesus' apostle, Thomas. His nature was to doubt. His faith was small, and believing Alexander required a stronger faith. A faith Tim doubted he had.

"Do you believe in God?" Alexander asked suddenly.

"Of course!" Tim snapped.

Alexander drew back slightly from the outburst. "You seem

quite adamant in that belief."

"I'm sorry. It's just that I stopped going to church when I was a teenager, and my mother always asked me that question afterward." His voice rose to an imperfect falsetto in imitation of his mother. "'Do you still believe in God? Then why don't you go to church?' We had a lot of arguments about it."

"Then do you believe in the Bible? Do you believe that what is written is the words of apostles and prophets?"

Tim nodded.

"Then perhaps if the Bible were to say that there are eternal beings who haven't died, you would believe what I am telling you?"

"Does it?" Tim asked.

"Matthew 16:28, 'Verily I say unto you, There be some standing here, which shall not taste of death, till they see the Son of man in his kingdom.' Look it up if you would like.

Tim did, and he read exactly the same thing Alexander had recited to him.

"Who was Christ speaking about?" Tim asked when he had finished.

Alexander shrugged. "I don't know. I suppose no one alive knows, except of course, whoever he was speaking about. Common opinion says that one of the people is John the apostle. I would like to meet him. We would have many things to talk about. However, even though he will live forever, his life is entirely different from what I have experienced. I have known death, so my situation is different from John's and to whomever Christ was referring. Though the difference seems slight now, you will see its importance as we continue."

Tim sighed and rubbed his temples. A headache was working its way up the back of his skull ready to blow his head apart.

Alexander noticed and said, "It's not so hard to accept, Mr. Lawrence, if you have faith."

Tim gave him a half-hearted grin. "Well, faith has never been a strength of mine."

Alexander arched his eyebrows. "Perhaps it will be before the day is over."

Tim looked up, and Alexander smiled.

"Do you still believe I am crazy?" Alexander asked.

The hairs on the back of Tim's neck rose as they had at the gate. Could Alexander read his mind or had Tim simply been to obvious in his reaction to Alexander's comments?

"I never said you were."

Alexander was still smiling. "No. You've been quite polite in that respect. However, I am not ignorant of the enormity of what I am telling you. If you didn't think me crazy, I would think you were crazy."

Tim laughed and the hairs on his neck relaxed.

"Okay," Tim admitted, "I had my doubts at first, but now I don't think you're crazy. I do believe you have an interesting story to tell, though that doesn't mean that I'll buy it."

"Then perhaps, before we begin, you'll consider putting your pistol elsewhere. It can't be too comfortable for you to have it poking you in your back."

A knot formed in Tim's stomach and moved up into his throat so he couldn't speak. He tried to swallow it back down, but it refused to budge.

Seeing Tim's smile fall, Alexander said, "Don't worry. I'm not angry with you for bringing the pistol, but surely you must realize by now it would be useless against me. Though, I am concerned that you might use it. If you did, it would only harm you. I have lived through worse than bullet wounds."

The knot retreated slightly, and Tim said, "How?"

"How do I survive bullet wounds or how did I know you brought the pistol?"

Tim hesitated. "Both I guess."

"How I survive bullet wounds is a part of my story. We will get to it shortly if you wish to continue the interview.

"How I knew you had the pistol was simply a matter of observation. I have spent more than four mortal lifetimes living in the mountains. I have learned how to conceal weapons from enemies, and I know the signs of concealed weapons. When you bent over to position your recorder on the table, I saw the bulge against your lower back. It was too short to be a knife and too thick to be an automatic pistol. I assume it is a revolver.

"If it will make you feel better, I'll remove my concealed weapon also."

The knot tightened in Tim's throat again, and he could only nod. Alexander had a weapon! What had he been planning to do with it?

Alexander crossed his right leg over his injured left leg and pulled up the pants leg. Tim saw the knife haft protruding from the top of Alexander's workboot. Alexander pulled the knife from his boot and held it up to look at it. The steel blade appeared to be six inches long. It was double-edged and came to a very sharp point. The haft was also made of steel with ornate decorations carved into it.

Alexander smiled as he ran his hand over the haft.

"I bought this in Germany four centuries ago. I originally meant to use it only to shave. It was a waste of a good knife, but I had no other use for it. I wanted it from the moment I saw it. It is an exquisite piece of workmanship. The details in the haft are extraordinary. And look how sharp the edge is." Alexander rolled up his left shirt sleeve to the elbow. Then he ran the blade sideways along his bare arm. When he finished, he held up a handful of small hairs the knife had cut from his arm. "Don't look scared, Mr. Lawrence. I used to use it to skin animals when I lived in the mountains. Nothing, or rather, no one else."

The knot loosened, and Tim released a breath he hadn't realized he was holding.

Alexander pulled the sheath from his boot and slid the knife back into its home. Then he walked over to the table and laid the knife and sheath down.

"A gesture of good faith," he said.

Tim reached behind his back and unclipped his holster. He hoped he was doing the right thing, but he didn't have much of a choice. Alexander already knew about the pistol. If he didn't follow Alexander's example, he'd blow the greatest story of his life.

He wanted to slide the pistol across the table, but he thought it might scratch the finish on the dining room table. He leaned across the table and set it beside the knife.

"To good faith," he said.

Alexander smiled.

Tim turned on his digital recorder. Then he opened his notebook and waited. Alexander watched his preparations, took a deep breath and began telling his story.

6

Although my father was named Jeremiah after the prophet of the Old Testament, he was only a shepherd in Bethany. It was a lowly position for a man of his intelligence. He could read and write both Latin and Greek, as well as Hebrew, and he could have been a scholar if he had chosen to do so. It wasn't until I was twelve that I learned why he had become a shepherd.

My father knew of the prophecies of the coming of the Son of God written in the Old Testament. Nearly every prophet—Daniel, Ezekiel, Moses, Haggai, and even my father's namesake, Jeremiah—prophesied of the birth of the son of God. Before Christ's birth, my father was a wealthy scribe in Bethlehem. His excellent knowledge of languages caused him to be much in demand as a translator. His studies had told him of the signs that would mark the birth of the son of God, and he watched for them knowing the time was drawing near.

On the night of Christ's birth, my father saw the star in the sky and recognized it for what it was--a sign of the Savior's coming. He followed the light of the star deeper into Bethlehem, expecting it to lead him to a great house befitting the son of God. Instead, the light led him to a stable next to an inn. He went to knock on the door of the inn to inquire about the child when he heard a baby's cry from the stable. When my father walked into the stable, he saw a mother cradling her newborn baby. My father had found the Savior.

His surprise at the location of the birth was only surpassed by his amazement at seeing a group of shepherds already kneeling before the child. He wondered how these lowly shepherds could have discovered where the son of God lay before he had. He spoke with one of them and learned that an angel had appeared to them in the fields outside of Bethlehem and told them where the child could be found.

My father was shocked. He was a wealthy man and a knowledgeable man. He prayed to God regularly. And yet, the angel of the Lord had appeared to the shepherds, not him.

After considering why he had not received a vision and studying the words of the prophets for the answer, my father realized that man's standards to determine the worth of man are different from the Lord's. Wealth and knowledge did not necessarily make a man great in the eyes of the Lord.

My father then set out to become a great man in the eyes of the Lord. He devoted more of his time to studying the scriptures and teaching its lessons to those who could not read. He gave anonymous aid to Joseph and Mary and made sure they were provided with excellent lodgings in the finest inn in Bethlehem. When one of the eastern kings who came to pay tribute to Jesus, who was by then a toddler, told my father that King Herod wanted to know where the child lay, my father realized the reason behind King Herod's concern. Herod was afraid that Jesus, who had been heralded as the King of the Jews, would usurp his power. Herod didn't want to worship the child. He wanted to kill him. My father sold everything he had to buy safe and secret passage for Joseph and his family into Egypt so they would escape Herod's deadly wrath.

Once Joseph, Mary, and Jesus arrived safely in Egypt, my father left Bethlehem and returned to Bethany, which had been the land of his father. Instead of becoming a scribe again, he humbled himself and became a shepherd.

He married my mother, Ruth, four years later. They were very much in love, and when my mother died, my father never found another woman to replace her. The years they shared together were full of happiness.

A year after their marriage, my mother gave birth to a son named Matthias. I never knew my older brother. He died before he was a year old, through no fault of my parents. Infant mortality at that time in history was something with which nearly all parents had to deal.

My mother was already pregnant with me when Matthias died. However, the strain of having to bury her first child almost caused her to lose me.

After my birth, my parents took extra care with me. I drank only milk from my mother's breast. When I began eating solid food, I ate only the freshest vegetables. I was always kept warm in the winters, even if it meant my father did without a blanket. I was never out of my parents' sight because they were afraid I might hurt myself. Their fear that I might die lessened somewhat after my first birthday, but they were still careful.

Three years after my birth, my sister, Martha, was born. Martha delighted my mother because now she had someone to whom she could teach her skills. However, after Martha's birth, my mother spent three weeks in bed recovering from the stresses of giving birth. During the time, she never lost her smile. She always wanted to hold Martha, and when I came into the room, she would tell me stories of the prophets. I learned many of the same stories that children learn today. David battled and slew the giant Goliath. Noah built an ark and collected all the animals to be saved from the great flood, and Moses led his people out of Egypt to freedom.

Despite the fact that my mother had nearly lost her life giving birth to Martha, two years later, she became pregnant again. This time she was not as lucky. My sister, Mary, lived. My mother died.

I was only five years old at the time, but I can still remember my mother's screams as the contractions began. They were high-pitched and broken wails as if she were trying to inhale breaths amid the scream. I knew something was wrong, and I started toward my mother's room. As I did, my father rushed past me, sending me sprawling to the ground. My mother continued screaming, and soon her voice was joined by my father's panicked voice as he shouted my mother's name.

A curtain had been pulled across the doorway of my mother's room so no one could see what was happening. I pulled the curtain back slightly and looked inside. My mother was thrashing on the bed while my father tried to hold her still. Sweat drenched her head, and her eyes were clenched shut. A woman was at the foot of the bed, kneeling between my mother's legs.

"I felt a hand on my shoulder and looked up. My father's youngest brother, Simon, was standing behind me, holding Martha.

"Come, Lazarus," he said, "Let's go to my house. My wife has just made sweet cakes, and I'm sure you can convince her to let you have a large piece."

"Why is my mother yelling?" I asked.

I could see the worried look in his expression even though he was smiling, but I was too young to recognize it as such.

"She hurts, Lazarus," he answered.

"Can I kiss her and make her better like she does when I hurt?" I asked.

"No. All you can do is come with me. Your father will make her better," he told me in a whisper.

He took my hand and led me out of the house. His house was far enough away so Martha and I couldn't hear my mother's screams. I stopped worrying about her as soon as Simon's wife, Eve, brought a small, square sweet cake to the table. I didn't know that I would never see my mother again.

After her death, my father became our mother as well as our father. His cousins and brothers helped where they could, but they had their own families to care for. So my father had to learn how to cook and sew. As I grew older, he also became my teacher. I learned to read with the Old Testament as my primer, and I learned how to tend sheep. When I was ten, my father gave me my first flock to tend. It was small, just a dozen sheep, but they were my responsibility.

By the time Martha was ten, she had taken over the cleaning and most of the cooking from my father. It relieved him of some of the burdens he had shouldered after my mother's death.

I made only one trip outside of Bethany during my childhood. When I was sixteen, my father took Mary, Martha, and I north to Galilee to the shore. We traveled for five days until we came to the sea. It was the first time in my life I had seen such a large body of water as the Sea of Galilee. I couldn't see the opposite shore, and I wondered if there was one. My father assured me that there was and that there were even larger bodies of water than this one to the west.

I wanted my father to take us out on the sea in a boat, but he told me we were not in Galilee to sail on the water.

"He pointed toward a man by the shore. The man was dark-skinned with piercing blue eyes. His brown hair hung to his shoulders and a beard and a mustache covered his face. As we watched him, he planed the sides of a fishing boat.

"He's handsome," Martha whispered to Mary.

My father turned to her and said, "I would say this of no other man, Martha, but he is too good for you. That man is the son of God."

Martha put her hand to her mouth as if she was trying to pull back the words she had just spoken.

I know we were too far away from him to have heard us, but the man stopped his work and stared at the four of us. He waved to us to come to him, and my father urged us to go.

As we approached, he stood up and dusted the sawdust from his robe. "I am Jesus," he said.

We introduced ourselves, and then I said, "My father says you are the son of God."

Jesus smiled and put his hand on my shoulder. "Your father is right."

"You don't look any different from us," Martha said.

"The difference is not easily seen. It is in here." Jesus touched his hand to his forehead. "My time on earth must be spent in a mortal body, but I have retained the memory and knowledge of who I am and where I came from. Because of this, I act according to the wishes of my Father and not of man."

"Why do you do carpentry then if you are the son of God?" I asked.

"A wise man must always remain humble to have the Spirit accompany him. Service to others is no sin. Ask your father."

"I looked around and saw my father still standing where we had been when he pointed out Jesus to us. He was kneeling in the sand, staring intently at Jesus.

"Please join us, Jeremiah," Jesus said.

"You know my name," my father said as he walked over.

"Of course, you are the man who sold his goods to help my family escape into Egypt. I owe you a great deal."

My father shook his head. "No. It is I who owe you. Because of you, I live, and I am happy."

Tears slid down the side of my father's face as he knelt to kiss Christ's hand. It embarrassed me to see such a display of emotion from him. Christ gently pulled his hand away and raised my father to his feet.

"You are a good man, Jeremiah. Father is pleased in the direction you have chosen to follow. Even as we speak, He is preparing to receive you. Ruth awaits you also."

My father began to cry again at the mention of my mother's name.

As we took our leave from Christ, my father told us, "Trust in him, for he is the Savior of mankind. Never forget that." My sisters and I told him we would not forget.

Five weeks later, my father died in his sleep. We placed his body alongside my mother's in the sepulchre. As we rolled the massive stone back into place, I wondered about Christ's words to my father. *Even as we speak, He is preparing to receive you. Ruth awaits you also.* Had Jesus known my father was dying? Even in a mortal body was the son of God a seer? Or had he simply been speaking in general terms?

Not that it mattered. The outcome was the same. My father was dead, and I had become the head of my family. I was the guardian of my two sisters. Martha was thirteen, and Mary was eleven. I was only sixteen years old, scarcely more than a boy myself, but the responsibility fell to me to watch over them as I did my sheep.

I took over my father's flocks and tended them with what I hoped was the same intelligence and care he had. I made sure my sisters continued to study the Old Testament because my father had little tolerance for ignorance. I began considering what I could give as a dowry. As part of my responsibility as the head of the family, when my sisters' times came to marry, I had to provide a dowry to the bridegroom.

The new responsibilities overwhelmed me. I hadn't realized how much my father had done for us. I rose each morning two hours before the sun and went to bed four hours after sundown. My sleep seemed more like a series of all-too-short naps. Because of the increased size of the flocks I tended, I had little time to rest during the day. Financial obligations had to be met. Food had to be gathered. And in all this, I was not caring for only myself, but for Martha and Mary as well.

In the first months, the weariness overcame me. Dark circles formed under my eyes, my skin sagged as I lost weight. On three separate occasions, I climbed to the top of a hill far from town and screamed until I was hoarse. Then I would fall in a heap and cry. I came home those nights with red, swollen eyes and only able to speak in whispers. Martha and Mary showed extra kindness to me on these nights, but it did not ease the burden.

After five months, I no longer cried myself to sleep. I began to accept the responsibilities and deal with them. I had become a man, and I was treated as such when I walked through the town.

By the time I was twenty years old, the word of Christ's ministry had reached Bethany. Stories of the healings he performed, the wisdom he spoke, and the lessons he taught were much talked about where men gathered. People argued over the legitimacy to his claim to be the son of God. The Pharisees and Sadducees, in particular, seemed critical of him.

I remembered what my father had told my sisters and me at the Sea of Galilee, and I defended Jesus. I pointed out the miracles he performed among the people and asked how could anyone not of God do such things.

Two months before I turned twenty-one, sickness began to show itself in me. I woke up each morning with a heavy congestion in my lungs. It took fifteen minutes of coughing before they cleared enough for me to breathe easily. My energy also began to wane. I woke up later and later each day and still felt tired. I tried my best to hide these symptoms from my sisters, but I suspect they knew. Though to their credit, they said nothing.

In the fields, my legs shook as I walked among my flocks. My staff became more of a cane that I would rest my weight, holding onto it with both hands as I sagged against it so that I could continue walking without falling.

I thought the sickness would eventually pass until one night on my return home, I collapsed and passed out. Finding me outside, my sisters carried me into the house. They put me in bed and revived me.

After that, the congestion in my lungs got so bad that I never seemed entirely free from it. I was breathing in short gulps of air instead of deep breaths, and even that pained me. If I exerted myself, I felt dizzy and collapsed. I felt cold even though it was the end of the planting season and the air was quite warm. At times, I wasn't unable to feel one of my feet and a hand. Other times, my body itched as if a million ants were swarming over it.

My sisters were in a panic. They were still so young. Even after having experienced the death of our father—they couldn't remember our mother—they were unprepared to deal with death. Our father had died quietly in the night. The bonds had been cut quickly to lessen the pain. With me, it was different. I was fighting to live even though I was losing the fight. The bonds were being stretched to their limit, but they weren't breaking. I wasn't going to give up my life as easily as my father had. I wanted to live.

I still had much I wanted to do. I had yet to know the love of a woman and to hear the laugh of my child. I wanted to visit Egypt and cities further south where it was said that the people were as black as night. I wanted to visit the lands in the east where the people had flat faces and narrow eyes. I admit my reasons were selfish, but in the last moments before death, I was not considering what those around me were losing. I was only concerned with what I was losing. Others still possessed life which meant they still possessed the time to recapture whatever they would lose with my death.

My usual fatherly demeanor with my sisters changed in the last weeks when I realized death would win the battle we were fighting. I made unreasonable requests of my sisters and criticized them harshly when they tried their best to meet them. I once demanded of Mary that she cook my meat to a blackened crisp. When she brought in my meal, and I saw the burnt meat I threw the plate at her. Mary, who was the gentlest of my two sisters, fell to the floor and cried. I would dirty myself so that I could see the grimaces on their faces as they had to change my blankets. And if they were near enough to me, I would try to vomit on them.

I hated them. Why should my sisters enjoy life when I was dying? They were alive, and they had their health. They would live after I had died. Why? I had given up years of my own pleasure to provide for them. Why should I not have the chance to enjoy life?

One morning, I awoke and felt the warm flow of urine between my legs without realizing I needed to go. It had happened without warning. Oddly enough, I didn't feel glee that Martha or Mary would have to clean up after me.

Martha walked into the room carrying a pitcher of water she used to bathe me. Mary never came into the room anymore. I had scared her off with my screaming and unreasonable demands. She still assisted Martha with the cooking and cleaning, but she never entered my room. Once or twice, I had seen her peering in at me from the doorway, and I had made a choking sound. She had screamed and backed off.

Martha had found her own way of dealing with me. She had stopped heating the water in which she bathed me. The sharp bite of the ice-cold water always made my joints ache. I never gave her pleasure by revealing my discomfort, but she knew how I felt. It was her way of punishing me for my childish behavior.

Martha saw the wet spot on my bed and shook her head. She set the pitcher down next to the bed so she would be able to roll me onto my side to clean me and pull the blankets from the bed.

Martha leaned over my bed and said, 'Good morning, brother.' Her voice echoed in my head as if she were talking to me within a large cavern.

I looked at her smiling face and smiled back. Then her smile faltered. Her brow wrinkled as she examined my face. She placed her hand under my nose and quickly pulled it away.

What was wrong, I wondered.

I saw a tear creep from the corner of her eye, and suddenly she was crying harder than I had ever seen even Mary cry. I would expect to see Mary cry but never Martha.

What was wrong?

I tried to reach up and touch her cheek and wipe away the tears, but my right hand wouldn't move. I couldn't move my left hand, either. That was unusual. I was used to one side or the other of my body feeling numb, but never both sides at once.

Martha continued crying until finally, Mary came to the doorway to my room wondering what was wrong.

"Lazarus is dead!" she said through her sobs."

7

January 20, 2016

Tim shifted uneasily in his chair. He kept his eyes on the pistol. It was just out of his reach, but he could reach it quickly enough if he needed it. The story was just too much to believe. It couldn't be true. Alexander had to be crazy.

When Alexander stopped talking, Tim looked up and saw Alexander was staring at him.

"Were you really dead?" Tim asked, trying his best to conceal his suspicions.

Alexander nodded and walked over to the opposite end of the table. "Yes. Quite dead, though I didn't realize at the time."

He sat down and brought his hands together in front of his face. He leaned back and began speaking again:

33 A.D.

At first, I didn't understand what Martha had said. Her echoing words overlapped each other, and I had to decipher them.

How could I be dead? Me?

I tried to laugh at her and call her a foolish child, but no sound came from my mouth. Thinking my chest was congested again, I tried to cough. I couldn't. I couldn't clear the congestion!

Now, both Martha and Mary were crying as they stood over me. Martha hugged Mary as she cried into Martha's shoulder. I wanted to tell them I was all right. I wasn't dead. I was just sick. Mary pulled away from her sister and knelt down beside me. She grabbed my hand and held it to her cheek, but I couldn't feel the warmth of her skin on mine.

I was sick. That was all. Nothing else.

As I watched Mary cry, my vision blurred. The images doubled, and one set of images faded to black. The second set rose, but my body remained on the bed.

I was watching the scene as if I were not a part of it. I suppose, in a sense, I wasn't. I could still see my sisters crying over my body.

Martha pulled herself away from my bedside and staggered out of the room. Mary stayed behind, kneeling at my side and crying.

Remembering all the unkindnesses I had dealt my sisters in the past weeks, I knew I didn't deserve their tears. I was ashamed of myself for coveting their lives and for taking my anger out on them.

I reached out to touch Mary, but I couldn't feel my hand or any other part of my body. I wasn't even on the bed anymore. I was standing next to my sisters and staring at myself laying on the bed.

Something rushed past me from above. Although I didn't see it or feel it, I somehow sensed it as it moved past me. The essence passed through my fingers like water. Then I saw it above my body. At least, I think I saw it. A shiny, pulsing area of light hovered over my chest. It looked like a reflection, but of what or off what, I couldn't say.

"It touched my body and disappeared. Suddenly, my body began convulsing. My arms and legs jittered with quick spasms. My eyes opened, but I was not seeing through them. I was still only an observer.

"Mary looked up and screamed. She backed away from the bed until her back was against the wall.

"It's not me, Mary! It's not me! I'm here! Look at me!" I screamed at her from above her head.

She gave no response that she had heard me. She only covered her face with her arms and screamed.

My entire body appeared to me to be shimmering like sunlight reflected off of water. Then the shimmering collected into the small area of light I had originally seen and flew off. Had Mary even seen the light on my body? Was that why she had screamed?

Whatever had caused the shimmer rushed past me again. No, this time it was three collections of light. Instead of entering my body, they seemed to hit it and bounce off. They were unable to animate my body like the first shimmer had done, and for reasons unknown to me, I was glad.

What were they?

Mary cowered in the corner. Where was Martha? Martha shouldn't have left her alone. I reached out to touch my sister, but again, I couldn't feel my hand. I cursed at my helplessness. I could see her fear. It was so intense I could almost feel it, but I couldn't help her.

"I'm sorry, Mary," I said. "There was so much more I needed to do for you."

Martha had always been strong. She was a survivor. She would handle my death as she had our father's, keeping her tears inside until she was alone. Besides, she was eighteen. She would be wed before too long.

But Mary, little Mary... She had used up her strength it seemed just managing to survive her birth. She cried on rainy days, sunsets, and the onset of winter. She was so gentle and frail. How would she survive without someone to watch over her?

"I'm sorry. I failed you, sister, but not because you weren't loved. Please remember me well as I was in the past and not as I have been. I would help you if I could, but it is too late for me," I whispered to her.

I began rising until I had passed through the roof of our home as if it were only a shadow. I could see all of Bethany from two-hundred feet above the ground. I saw Martha rushing back to the house with Simon. She had hold of his arm and was pulling him along behind her as she hurried toward the house. She hadn't run off from Mary. She had only gone to seek help.

"Goodbye to you, too, Martha. Be strong. Be wise."

I continued rising until suddenly I was cast into utter darkness. But I continued to rise. I could feel it. I could not feel my body, but I could feel the sensation of rising. Eventually, the darkness yielded to gray, then to white.

When my vision returned, I was in Heaven. It was not the Heaven that you hear about when someone writes of near-death experiences or goes on a talk show to say they traveled through a tunnel with a bright, white light at the end of it. Those are merely quick, fleeting glimpses that are more often than not confused. Someone dead for ten minutes or even an hour has no notion of what Heaven is. At an hour after death, the spirit is just beginning to prepare to release its claim on the body. A thin strand of mortality still connects it to the body.

This was not the case with me. I spent four days in Heaven. They seem like only four seconds now, but those moments are more time than anyone has spent there since before their birth.

I had a body in Heaven. I was not the disembodied consciousness I had been upon my death. I don't remember entering my new body like I remember leaving the old one. At times, I have wondered if my heavenly body was a true body of flesh and blood or if passing through the veil of light had given my consciousness the ability to form matter into a body so that I would have a sense of touch again.

Upon entering what I assumed was Heaven, I saw a man and a

woman beside me. They hugged and kissed me and told me how happy they were that we were together again. Until they spoke, I didn't recognize them. This couple was my parents, but they looked as they had looked when I was a baby. Younger, without the stress of life showing itself in the lines on their faces.

As they embraced me, I cried. It had been nearly five years since I had last seen my father, and sixteen years since my mother had died. I could barely remember her, but when I saw her, I wondered how I could have ever forgotten her. She looked so beautiful. Her black hair flowed over her shoulders making her smooth dark skin seem radiant. Then I noticed the tears in her brown eyes. I think the tears were both a mixture of happiness and sadness at seeing me again.

They were as happy to see me as I was them, but they were saddened by the fact that I had lost my life so early. I was only twenty years old, almost twenty-one. I had just begun my life. I hadn't yet had the chance to travel outside of Bethany, except the journey with my father and sisters to Galilee. I hadn't taken a wife or fathered children. I had not lived my life yet.

These were the things that had caused my anger while I was sick, and to my surprise, they still caused anger in me in Heaven. I suppose part of the reason that my parents were there with me was to help me accept my death. It was their job to introduce me to my new home.

If only my words could paint a picture one-tenth of the beauty and happiness of the place. I walked among endless gardens filled with an endless variety of flowers I have not seen since, and I have traveled all over the world. The air was sweet and clear like the air in the western mountains. I could see for miles on end and without a road or billboard to disturb the view. The animals weren't afraid of me, either. I walked right up to grizzly bears and lions and petted them like they were puppies. There were none of the trappings of civilization. Buildings, cars, airplanes, smog, landfills. All missing.

I was quite happy there. Despite the fact I had lost my sisters and friends, I had regained my parents. I also experienced a peace of mind and spirit I have yet to regain on earth. Even my anger at dying so young left me as I explored my new world with my parents. I witnessed the birth of the world and met the ancient prophets.

Then just as suddenly as I had left my body, I returned. Heaven faded from my view like a ghost image, and I was forced into my body, a body I could not control. After feeling the freedom of existence without the physical restrictions of a body, being thrust back into mortality was like being thrown into solitary confinement in prison. I saw my body laying in a sepulcher and wrapped in linen as my spirit entered it. I was alone and cut off from everyone by my physical being. The sense of intimacy I had felt when I was free from my body was unmatched by mortality. Even the most intimate moments between a man and a woman are shadows in comparison to the intimacy I felt simply standing in Heaven without a physical body. I was free! Truly free! How could anything come close to that when there is always a barrier of flesh between you and the world? To experience such intimacy, only to lose it, is almost maddening. I still cry at times when I think of it.

As I lay unable to move in the sepulchre, I could feel my body repairing the decomposition from four days of death. The feeling was a cross between the pins-and-needles sensation you feel when your arm or leg falls asleep and the twitching of a muscle spasm.

I wanted to scratch or rub my body, but I was still unable to command even the slightest movement of myself. I was trapped in a shell. Only after the irritating regeneration had faded was I able to move. Even so, it was only a gradual returning of sensation.

When I was able to hear again, I heard a voice say, "Lazarus, come forth." The odd thing was even though I knew someone was speaking; I didn't hear the voice with my ears. His voice spoke to me from inside my head. I managed to stand, which was a miracle in itself, considering the constricting burial bandages wrapped around me. I guess I shouldn't complain, though, without those bandages wrapped around my legs, my knees probably would have buckled within a few steps.

I couldn't see the entrance to the sepulchre because the bandages also covered my face. I only saw the brighter areas of cloth where the sun shone into the sepulchre and onto the bandages.

I wobbled toward the sunlight trying not to stumble and fall. I stopped on the hill outside and waited. Without the contrast between the darkness of my burial chamber and the daylight, I had no sense of direction.

I heard the murmurs of people around me wondering what sort of man stood beneath the burial cloths. Was I deformed or crazy? Others loudly proclaimed Jesus Christ's divinity, while some still refused to accept Christ as the son of God. They claimed he was a heretic and worked with the devil.

I heard the voice, more gently this time, say, "Loose him, and let him go."

Sandal-clad feet ran almost silently over stones as I heard people rush toward me. A pair of arms surrounded me in an embrace while another pair of hands fumbled for the cloth around my head trying to untie it quicker than it would unwind.

I squinted at the bright light of day as the final layer of cloth fell from my eyes. Once my eyes adjusted to the light, I opened them and saw my sister, Mary. Her brown eyes were wide with amazement at seeing me alive again. She unwound the cloth even faster. I smiled as she finished unwrapping my head.

"Mary," I said.

She began to cry. Martha, who had been hugging me, stood up.

"Lazarus. I knew it! I knew if anyone could do it he could," she said.

I glanced over her shoulder and saw Jesus standing midway up the hill. His expression seemed one of regret rather than happiness.

"Mary. Martha. Please help me over to Jesus," I asked my sisters.

"They grabbed hold of my arms and slowly led me to Christ. I stumbled twice, but my sisters managed to keep me upright. When we stood in front of him, they released me and stepped away. I fell to my knees and bowed my head in front of him.

"Thank you, my Lord," I said.

He squatted beside me, put his hand under my chin, and raised my head. I looked into his eyes and, I saw the peace that I had just lost. For a moment, I was jealous of him.

He smiled, and said, "You know not what you say, Lazarus, but to the extent that you do know, you are welcome." Then he rose and helped me to my feet. He beckoned to my sisters. "Help your brother to the house. Allow him to dress and clean himself, and tonight we shall celebrate his return."

The banquet my sisters threw turned out to be a grand affair. Most of Bethany came to see the results of Christ's latest miracle. Three lambs from our flocks were slaughtered and roasted. Other families brought baskets of fruits and vegetables and casks of wine.

After the meal, Christ pulled me aside and said, "Lazarus, I have done you a great injustice. I am sure you realize that."

I suppose I did know what he meant at least regarding how Heaven compares to earth, but that didn't mean I wasn't happy to be back with my sisters and friends. "How so, my Lord?" I asked him. "You have brought me back to the ones I love."

He laid his hand on my shoulder, and I thought he was going to bless me. "I have also taken you from them," he said.

"You know?" I don't know why his knowing what had happened

to me surprised me. I was talking with the Son of God. Of course, he would know. I guess I thought that only someone who had died and returned to life as I had should know of Heaven. It was prideful of me to think that I was the only one who remembered Heaven, but I am not a perfect man.

Jesus smiled. "Yes, I remember my father's home, too," he said in his calm voice.

"My Lord, my life on earth is short; I realize that now. It is better that I enjoy it while I am able. I will have an eternity to spend with my family. I will rejoin them again, and it will seem as if I had just left them."

Christ nodded, but the smile left his face. "Yes, you will rejoin them, but that time will not be as soon as you hope."

I shrugged. "Another thirty or forty years, perhaps? It is a mere second in the span of eternity."

Christ put his other hand on my shoulder and faced me directly. "No, my friend. It will be another two millennia before you see them again."

Just then Mary walked by on her way into the house. She smiled when she saw me talking with Christ. He released his grip on my shoulders and smiled at her. Mary threw her arms around my chest in a tight embrace.

"Oh, Lazarus, it's so good to have you back among us," she said.

Then she grabbed Christ's hand and began kissing it. "And thank you, Lord. You are the one who has made this possible."

Christ nodded without saying anything. Then Mary noticed the surprised expression on my face and decided it would be better to leave us alone.

When she had gone, I said, "What do you mean *another two millennia before I see them again?*"

"The body is intended to die but once. When the spirit leaves the body, the body is left to decay because there is no soul to nourish it. Only at the Resurrection will the body and spirit once again be one. Once a body is vacated, it is not meant to be used again except to wait for its reunion with the spirit.

"I altered that with you. I commanded your soul to return from Paradise and reenter your body. In doing this, the damages from decomposition were repaired, and you were resurrected.

"However, there are certain eternal laws to which even I must adhere. The Law of Resurrection is one of them. Because I have rejoined your body and soul now, you cannot die again. Your body will refuse to release your spirit until I return to this earth again at my second coming."

January 20, 2016

"So Christ made you an immortal," Tim said.

Alexander chuckled and smiled his broad smile. It was a friendly smile that reinforced Tim's feeling that the man was telling the truth.

"I assure you, Mr. Lawrence, I am not a true immortal. My time to die again will come. Nor am I the only one who has been given an extended life through resurrection. Christ, on separate occasions, performed similar miracles. I was the third, and undoubtedly, the most impressive."

Tim glanced up from his notes. Nothing in Alexander's tone of voice had seemed boastful. He was quite relaxed as he spoke.

"Christ also resurrected the daughter of Jairus and a widow's son from Nain," Alexander said.

"Are they also alive?" Tim asked.

Alexander hesitated just long enough to make Tim believe what he was about to hear was not the entire truth.

"I don't know. I doubt I would even recognize them if I saw them today. However, there were distinct differences in each of our resurrections that must be noted. Jairus' daughter had been dead scarcely more than an hour before Christ brought her back to life. The widow's son had been dead longer. His body had already been prepared for burial when Christ stepped in. I, on the other hand, had been dead four days. Four days!" He held his right hand out with his thumb tucked into the palm to emphasize his point. "Do you know what happens to a body that is dead that long? Decomposition sets in. The blood begins to pool at the lowest points in the body, usually discoloring the back and buttocks. The joints stiffen. The body is only a vessel, which when empty, is discarded like a paper cup. I had no more need for my body. My spirit had left it, and the spirit is the glue which binds the body together. When the spirit leaves, decomposition begins."

"So you're saying Christ made a mistake when he resurrected you?" Tim asked.

Alexander spun around and nearly rushed the table. His eyes were wide and glaring. Tim reached behind his back for his pistol and remembered he had set it on the table out of his reach.

"Of course not! The Son of God is perfect! I was part of his plan to achieve the desired effect among the people to convince them of his divinity. To most effectively make his point, my death had to be postponed."

"For 2,000 years or so?" Tim said in a slightly sarcastic tone.

Alexander nodded. He backed himself up to a wall and leaned against it. "It has been a long wait. Everyone I have ever loved or cared for is dead and waiting for me to join them. Loneliness is what makes my life cursed, not the length of it. But with every day, my time grows shorter. I look forward to an end to the killing I have done."

At the mention of killing, Tim shifted forward in his chair and wished for his pistol. He kept hoping Alexander wasn't planning on adding him to his list of victims, however long that might be.

"You continually refer to yourself as a killer. Who have you killed?" Tim asked hoping to get a confession on tape.

Alexander's body sagged forward, and he took a deep breath. "Many, Mr. Lawrence. I have killed everyone who was ever close to me. I have outlived ten wives. Each one I loved completely, and each one I killed.

A tear rolled down his cheeks. Alexander wiped it away. He stared blankly at nothing, blinked, and began again.

47 A.D.

As I grew older after my resurrection, I aged like any other person. Jesus was martyred three years after my resurrection, so I had no one to remind me of what he had said. I remember the day of his death. When I heard he had been arrested as a heretic, I rushed to Jerusalem. I arrived too late to do anything but kneel at the foot of Jesus's cross and cry. He had just committed his soul into his father's hands and allowed his spirit to leave his body. His head fell forward. The crown of thorns that the soldiers had placed on his head would have fallen off except that it had tangled itself in his hair. It hung loosely in front of his face like a picture frame. The blood from the wounds in his feet continued to run down his feet and drip off the tips of his toes. A small pool of his blood had formed in front of where I kneeled.

Beside me, Mary Magdalene was also crying. I put my arm around her shoulders and tried to lead her away.

"No. Let me stay," she said through her tears as she pulled away from me.

"It's over," I told her. "His body is dead."

The sky blackened suddenly, and the Roman guards who had been laughing only moments before fell silent. Thunder rumbled louder than any waterfall I have ever heard. The ground trembled, knocking over some people who had been standing. A jagged yellow bolt of lightning lit up the sky, followed by another almost immediately after it.

As I looked around at the upheaval that was beginning, I saw a black-haired teenager. He stood, unswayed by the trembling ground, a few feet behind me. His legs were spread wide to brace himself against the tremors, and his gaze fixed unwaveringly on the body of Christ. His hands hung awkwardly at his sides, and his expression was impossible to read.

He yelled at the dead body of Christ, "You tricked me! You trapped me in this shell! But I'll conquer you yet! You can't control me! I will win! You can't beat me!"

Another bolt of lightning tore open the sky throwing shadows across his face and causing his gray eyes to change momentarily to yellow.

"Who is that?" I asked Mary.

She turned toward the young man and studied his face. "He is Matthew of Nain. Christ brought him back from the dead."

Then this would be another person who remembered the joys of Heaven, I thought. We were brothers in spirit.

I stared at him until he tilted his head downward to look at me. He was a handsome man, but his features were hard as if his face had been chiseled from stone.

"Who are you?" he asked me.

I told him. At the sound of my name his eyes widened, and he cocked his head to the side.

"Why do you curse him?" I asked Matthew.

"Because he has cursed me, and until my death comes upon me, I will cause him to regret what he has done to me."

I remembered the sadness I had felt when Jesus returned my spirit to my body. At the time, I had not wanted to live again. I assumed Matthew still felt this way. I glanced over my shoulder at Christ's body. I might be disappointed at regaining my life, but the son of God had made the choice for me, and I knew it was the correct one.

I turned back to tell Matthew this, but he was gone. I looked down the hill to see if I could see him; he was nowhere to be seen. The day had returned to normal, and there was a crowd of people gathered at the base of the hill looking up at the body of Christ. I could not see Matthew among them.

I was tempted to try and find him so that we might talk, but Mary clutched my arm. "I am ready to leave," she said.

As I walked down the hill with Mary, I wondered what Matthew had meant when he said he would make Christ regret resurrecting him. I would not realize the answer to the question for many centuries to come.

8

73 A.D.

As I grew older, Matthew's words faded from my mind, as sometimes happens with older people. My body had reached the point where it was simply a fragile shell like a cicada's and just as useless. As my friends died, I thought I would, too.

In the year 73 A.D., I was sixty-four years old. That was quite old for a man in my time. Christ had been dead for forty years and forgotten by most, except the faithful. His original church had splintered into segments and disappeared from the earth. The apostles were all dead, many of them dying as martyrs as Christ had. They had been stoned, crucified, and attacked. This was the way of my world.

At the time, I didn't think things could get much worse. I truly believed it was time for Christ's second coming.

I was walking home from the open market with my first wife, Rebecca, when the pain began. It started near my heart, and I thought my life was about to end. I was thrilled at the thought of seeing my parents again. Then the pain rippled through my body.

Imagine a still pond. Throw a rock into the center of it. The waves caused by the rock expand in circles ever outward covering a greater and greater amount of area on the surface. When one of the waves strikes an obstacle, such as the shore, it is reflected and sent back toward the center.

That is the way of my body. The pain begins in my heart; I imagine it feels much like a heart attack. It seems to be the signal of the onset of death, the end of that phase of my life. However, instead of stopping, the pain turns into the rippling sensation. I used to react dramatically to the pain, but after having it occur so many times, I barely even flinch when it happens now. The rippling moves outward from my body. I can feel it leaving me as if an unseen cord still connected it to me. When the ripples come in contact with another person, they return to my body and rejuvenate me with most of that person's life force.

January 20, 2016

"That's why you don't want me too close!" Tim shouted.

Alexander nodded slowly. "Even with that precaution, your life may be in danger. I have never been able to determine the effective range of the rippling, but I believe it to be no more than ten feet. Also, there is no way to predict when it will occur. If this bothers you, we could, perhaps, find another way to conduct the interview."

Alexander was offering Tim another chance to leave, but he still hesitated. The old man was obviously lonely. Once Alexander started talking, it was hard to get a word in edgewise.

So there was danger involved with the story. He had been shot at while on a story riding on patrol with a police officer and even stabbed once during a fight when a gang member he was interviewing thought Tim was going to turn him into the police. Besides, watching Alexander's reactions at various points in his story gave Tim a better sense of who Alexander Reynolds actually was.

"We've already started," Tim said. "I'll stay."

Alexander smiled broadly. "I was hoping you would. Despite my best attempts at isolation, loneliness gets the better of me sometimes. Can I get you something to drink or eat?"

Tim shook his head. "Not right now. I'm more interested in what you have to say."

Alexander laughed. It reminded Tim of the Pillsbury Dough Boy's laugh in the Pillsbury television commercials. He moved his hand across his mouth to hide his smile at Alexander's reaction.

"I'm sorry. I'm just happy I'm finally going to be able to tell my story. Now where was I? "Alexander said.

"Your first attack."

Alexander nodded as he gathered his thoughts.

73 A.D.

At the start of the pain, I clutched my chest and fell to my knees. Silently, I gave thanks to the Lord that my time had finally come. I was an old man, and old men seldom like to see change in their life when they become old. I was no different. Having seen all the persecutions and murders of the apostles, I was scared for the future of mankind.

I didn't die as I had expected, though. The pain left me with the rippling feeling. All the while Rebecca stood by my side holding me; trying to help me. As quickly as it had begun, the pain ended. I was fine.

Lying still in the dirt for a few minutes after the pain ended, I wondered what had happened. When I finally realized I wasn't going to die, I stood up and hugged my wife.

"It is not yet my time," I told her.

She was silent, but I saw tears in her eyes. I assumed that they were tears of happiness that I hadn't died.

We finished our walk home in silence. Rebecca continually stared at me as if I somehow looked different to her. She stewed some vegetables for our dinner, and we went to bed without ever having said another word about my attack on the road.

The next morning I woke up feeling better than I had felt in years. The aches and creaks that had become constant companions to me in my old age were gone. You wouldn't know the feeling of living with pain for years then suddenly being freed from it. It was a miracle! At least, I thought so at the time. Now I know it was part of my curse.

Not long after I rose, Rebecca woke up. This was unusual because she generally woke about an hour before me to prepare the morning meal. As she sat up in bed, she groaned quite loudly.

I found it hard to believe I was staring at my wife. The wrinkles in the corners of her eyes had deepened into valleys. Her long hair had lost its dark luster. Her skin, especially on her hands, seemed to have thinned so much that I could see many of her blood vessels showing through her skin. When I looked into her eyes, I saw only weariness. She tried to hide it with a smile, but after thirty-two years of marriage, it was quite impossible.

"Lazarus," she said. "You look so much younger."

"It is from the happiness which you bring me," I told her.

She smiled weakly and shook her head. "No, I mean you really do appear younger." She touched my face with her cold hand, and I almost pulled away. I didn't want to offend her, so I grabbed her hand in my own and kissed her fingertips. I touched my hand to her cheek, and she began to cry.

"What's wrong, my love?" I asked as I wiped away the tears from her cheeks.

"I will miss you when I am gone. Will you remember me?"

I laughed and hugged her gently. "That is foolish talk. I know we will die, but why dwell on it? We still have time left together."

Rebecca nodded in agreement, but she still continued crying.

The next morning I awoke. Rebecca did not.

At her burial, people stared at me. When I met their stares, they looked away. They whispered quietly and avoided contact with me. Soon after, the rumors began circulating through Bethany about my appearance and condition.

One day, as I walked through the marketplace, the crowd parted before me. They were afraid to be near me. All except for one man. He was a tall man with black hair that was graying at the temples. He stared at me with his gray eyes and said, "You are the spawn of the devil." I was so taken aback by the comment I didn't know what to say. "You were brought into this world by the blasphemer who the Romans crucified. And now you bring the power of the devil back into the world by stealing your wife's life." The man held his arms above his head and turned to the others in the market. "Brothers, do not let this evil live among you. Cleanse yourselves, or you will face the wrath of God!"

The people in the marketplace started to murmur. The man who had pronounced me devil spawn crossed his arms over his chest and smiled. At that moment, he looked familiar, and I thought I recognized him.

Then people I had known for all their lives began to close in on me. Some grabbed fruit and vegetables from the stands and threw them at me. A shepherd used his staff to club me across my back.

I first, I tried to argue my innocence, but I feared for my life and ran.

I assumed the man had been a member of one of the new religions appearing over the land. All manner of wild beliefs were replacing Christ's church at the time of Rebecca's death. Superstitions were taking over the lessons of the Bible. All the love and goodness Christ had given his life to try and bring about was fading as the older people who remembered him died.

Although I think I would have welcomed death so that I might once again be with my parents and Rebecca, I had no intention of dying at the hands of people who so quickly embraced false religion and refused to accept the truth that Rebecca had simply died of old age. I packed all of my belongings on a donkey and left Bethany for Egypt.

I intended to travel west to Gaza, then south along the coast into Avaris. I rode about twenty-five miles the first day and made my camp in the Valley of Ajalon. It was not the wisest decision on my part. Stories of thieves robbing and beating travelers were well known in Bethany, but I didn't care. It had been hard enough for me to lose Rebecca, but then to have the town I had spent my entire life in turn against me was almost unbearable. Still, by some miracle of

God, I was not attacked.

The next morning I went to the river to drink, and I was shocked at what I saw. Up until that moment, I had forgotten about what Christ had told me the night of my resurrection. But as I bent to drink, the proof stared me in the face.

I was younger. My face no longer showed the signs of old age. My reflection in the water was that of myself as I had been thirty years earlier. I touched my fingers to my face and watched my reflection do the same thing.

Then I remembered what Rebecca had said about my appearance the morning after my attack. I wondered if I had looked so young then or if the change had taken place over the past week. No wonder my friends had been afraid of me and thought I was in league with the devil! I grabbed a lock of my hair and tried to pull it down in front of my eyes so that I might see it.

I had brown hair again. It was no longer dull gray. I hadn't had brown hair for at least twenty years.

I think I laughed then...or cried. I truly had a new life waiting for me. I pushed myself to a kneeling position and prayed to Christ asking him to forgive me for forgetting his warning to me.

When I finally reached Egypt a week later, I took a position as a scribe as my father had been in Bethlehem. I translated Hebrew writings and epistles into Egyptian so that scholars could study the Jews. Two years after I entered the city, I married again. My wife's name was Callames. She had been married to a merchant whose ship was lost at sea a few months earlier. I came to know her because her father was one of the scholars who frequently read my translated works.

Callames and I were married for twenty-three years. Then one night I had another attack while I lay in our bed. It happened the same way with pain rippling out from my body and then rushing back to crash like a wave upon me. When I awoke the next morning, Callames was dead.

And so, I buried my second wife.

The nature of man, I have found, is very similar no matter what nationality or race is involved. The Egyptians were no different from the Jews. After Callames' death, the rumors began that I had somehow traded her life for an extension of my own. The rumors were aided by the fact that I suddenly appeared twenty years younger. Though Callames' parents had died twelve years earlier, her brothers and sisters still lived, and we had always gotten along. Yet, from the moment of Callames' burial, they began to disassociate themselves from me as my sisters had done at Rebecca's funeral.

Three days after Callames' death, two men whom I did not recognize dragged me from my bed and took to the edge of town. They pushed me into a steep-sided pit about ten-feet deep. I scrambled to climb out, but the ground crumbled beneath my fingers. I only slid back down. The one time I did near the top, a man kicked me in the face and sent me tumbled to the bottom of the hole. Others appeared at the edge of the pit pulling heavy bags. When I saw the bags, I realized what they intended to do.

I argued my innocence, but it was no use. The crowd refused to believe me. I knew when I saw Callames' brothers among the crowd that any cries for mercy would fall on deaf ears. As if by telepathic command, they silently opened their bags.

I scrambled up the edge of the pit again, and this time I thought I would make it. Then I saw the gray-eyed man who had turned my home town against me. He didn't look any older than he had that day in Bethany, but he had to be at least seventy- or eighty-years old.

"Die, Lazarus," he said as he kicked me in my face.

I lost my grip and slid back to the bottom of the pit. I grabbed at my bleeding nose and looked up at the man. Who was he and why did he hate me so much that he would follow me to Egypt? The first stone hit me on the shoulder, and I saw him smile. I screamed. Other people in the crowd laughed at my cry, and I vowed not to give them the satisfaction again. I tried to avoid the stones, but with at least a dozen people throwing stones at me, it was impossible. The pit had little room to maneuver in.

A rock struck me on the side of the head, and I fell to my knees. I felt the rippling go out from me and return. I also felt a tingling on the side of my head where the rock had struck. I didn't have much time to consider it because another rock smashed me in the chest, knocking the breath from me. I tucked my head under my arms and curled myself into a ball. Another rock hit me on the side, and I grunted. More rocks hit me, and I stopped feeling any pain as I passed out.

When I awoke, I was alone. The sun had set, and I was shivering in the cold night air. I was surprised that I awoke. It was unusual for a stoning victim to survive. I sat up checking myself for wounds. Surprisingly, I saw none. I didn't even feel any pain. When I looked at my shoulder, there wasn't even a bruise where the first stone had hit it.

Something was wrong. I knew the rocks had hit me, and they had hurt when they hit. They had even drawn blood. I could see the stains on my robes. So why wasn't there any pain? Why was I still alive?

I finally realized the connection between the rippling feeling and my good health. Every time I had felt the rippling, I had felt better soon after, but someone near me when I had felt it died soon after. Because my body refused to die, it stole other people's lives to compensate.

It was not old age that had killed my two wives, but me.

9

Tim thought he had found the flaw in the old man's logic that he had been looking for since Alexander had started talking. He was quick to point it out.

"That's a gigantic jump for you to make, especially at that point in time," Tim said, "I mean you had just been attacked. You were probably beginning to believe their talk about you aiding the devil. Even now, when you're living proof of what you're saying, it's a large jump in logic," Tim said.

"Perhaps, but whatever led me to make that assumption certainly was right, wouldn't you say?" Alexander countered. "I was ninety-two years old, but I looked only thirty. Something had to be causing the change, and the only time people ever noticed a change in my appearance was after one of the attacks. Otherwise, I aged naturally. I connected the two incidents. Both my wives had died, and I'm sure some of the people who stoned me died within a week after I felt the rippling. Again, this could have only been a coincidence, but the years have proven me out. If my original assumption had proven wrong, I would have developed another one. But this theory has always held true. I am a murderer."

"But what you couldn't control what happened," Tim noted.

"True, but that doesn't change the outcome or who caused that outcome."

Alexander was silent for a minute as he rocked in his chair. Tim glanced at his tape recorder and saw the red recording light blink out. The recorder was voice-activated and wouldn't start recording again until someone said something. Finally, Alexander broke the silence.

97 A.D.

Needless to say, I could not return to live in Avaris. I snuck back to my house under cover of darkness and gathered up as much as I could carry. Food, money, clothes, and a few books. I went east, finally settling in India. I took the time to learn the language, and then

I took up my former position as a scribe and translator. Eventually, I even took another wife. Her name was Asuka. Our marriage lasted forty-one years before she died.

This time I did not wait for the accusations to begin after Asuka's death, I left India and continued east.

I had learned one more thing about myself by this time. I was sterile. In my marriage with Rebecca, I had fooled myself by saying she was the barren one. My pride had once again betrayed me. I had even continued thinking that with Callames, though my conviction had weakened considerably. But after Asuka's death, I could no longer deny the fact that I was the sterile one. I had been married for nearly a century to three different women, and I had not fathered a single child. Certainly, I could not continue to place the blame on my wives. That left only me.

From India, I crossed over the Himalayan mountains into the Chinese empire. China was going through many changes at this time. The Han Dynasty had just fallen after a revolt in 221 A.D., and warlords were struggling for control of each of the provinces.

I did not marry during my time here, but I did fall in love. I fell in love with the beauty of their character language. I never tired of looking at it, not reading it, just looking at it.

I heard talk of Gautama Buddha. He had been thought of as a god in India, and his religion had spread over the mountains and was just taking hold in China. From what I understood, Buddha taught that life was suffering and that a spirit would suffer through endless reincarnations until it could rid itself of earthly desires and attachments. Then the spirit would reach Nirvana. With the talk of ridding the soul of earthly desires, I wondered if Christ had perhaps visited these people upon leaving Israel.

I left China after three more people died because of my curse, including a very close friend named Chang Ti. By the year 349, I had reached the Pacific coast and could go no further east, so I turned north and moved into Siberia.

I lived in the cold wilderness of that land for over a century. I enjoyed the isolation that the cold weather brought. I didn't have to look at everyone I passed and wonder, *Will you be the next to die because of me?*

I did manage to marry two more times again while I lived there. My first Siberian wife was Ilya. We were married for thirty-one years before she died. Fifteen years after she died, I married Dora. We were happy for thirty-six years. Neither marriage bore any children, and both Ilya and Dora each died within a week after I had a regenerative attack.

After having so much sorrow associated with Siberia, I finally decided to move on. I made my way over what eventually would become the Bering Strait. Though when I crossed it, it was simply a huge ice bridge between two continents. I saw little vegetation throughout the land except in isolated areas and even less animal life. I must have been over 500-years old at that time, but I looked as if I were only twenty.

I wandered from the strait down the continent following the path of the Rocky Mountains. On that journey, I saw a history of this continent that very few people know. I saw the civilizations of the Anasazi, the Mayans, and the Incas at the peaks of their power. Once, as I was journeying through what is now the Canada-Alaska border, I even saw a living wooly mammoth! However, nature forced me to stop at the tip of South America near the Magellan Strait.

I had taken two more wives in that 200-year period I spent wandering. Again, I outlived each one of them with no children to remind me of the good years we had spent together.

How can I make you understand the pain that each one of their deaths caused me? When you give yourself to someone and make a lifelong commitment... How can I make you understand the guilt and sense of failure I felt when that lifelong commitment didn't last my lifetime?

January 20, 2016

Alexander sat on the bottom step of the staircase and cried. Tim felt such pity for him that he was tempted to try and comfort him. He held back partly because of their agreement and partly because he was afraid of Alexander. He didn't want to feed Alexander's hungry life.

Alexander's tears ended after a few minutes, but he still continued to hold his head cradled in his arms. When he finally looked up, his eyes were red and slightly swollen.

"Please forgive my outburst," he said.

He stood up and smoothed out his flannel shirt and wiped his eyes with the cuff of his sleeve.

"I wish I could tell you that I understand, but I can't. Despite what you feel, Alexander, you have found many times what many people, including me, are still searching for just once," Tim said.

"And I have experienced many times the hurt from the loss, too," Alexander added.

"You found that one person with whom you were willing to

spend your life. Even though you might not have spent your entire life with her, you did spend her entire life together, which adds up to quite a few years. I think you should consider yourself lucky."

With narrowed eyes, Alexander stared at Tim silently. He thought Alexander was going to order him out of the house. Instead, Alexander smiled.

"I see I am not the only one who has given time to philosophizing."

Tim shrugged.

"Suppose I get on with my ramblings?" Alexander suggested.

"Please do."

1358 A.D.

After reaching the tip of South America, I decided to journey back up through the continent this time on the eastern side of the mountains. I had no purpose in doing it. It was simply something to occupy the overabundance of time that I had. Besides, I had found it hard to stay in one area for too long. When my regenerative attacks occurred, someone always died, and I always looked younger. It didn't take even the most-primitive people long to decide that I was the cause of the mysterious death.

Along the gulf coast, I met a group of Spaniards exploring Central America. I convinced them to take me on as a guide, and I showed them the cities of the Mayans and Aztecs. When they returned to Spain, I sailed with them. The voyage on the *Maria* took nearly a month. It seemed short to me, but to the soldiers who weren't used to being out of sight of land, it dragged on for an eternity. If they had asked me, I could have told them how long an eternity actually is.

I lived in Madrid for a half a century. I had a comfortable life there. It was at this time I began to invest my money so that I might always have an income in case I was not able to work at some point in the future. I might have stayed longer, but I began to see a religious zealousness among the people that disturbed me. It bordered on the fanatical, and I knew that if a regenerative attack occurred during this time, I would be persecuted and more innocent people would have died because of me.

I traveled Europe, visiting France, Portugal, Sweden, Germany, Bohemia, and Italy. It wasn't until I reached England that I stopped roaming. It was also then I took the name Alexander Reynolds.

Up to that point, I had been changing my name to fit with whatever land I was in at the time. During my time in America, I saw people so infrequently that I didn't even worry about a name. However, I knew I would need an English name for London. I happened to meet a man named Alexander Reynolds as I walked along the road into London. We talked for quite some time, and when he turned off the road toward his village, I took his name with me.

In London, I developed an interest in the theater after seeing *Romeo and Juliet*. Shakespeare was still alive at this time so his plays were exciting and new to everyone and not yet considered the classics they are today. He also directed his plays to make sure the productions carried his original intent.

The saying, "Misery loves company," is quite true, at least in my case. I found Shakespeare's dialogue a pure delight to my ear. The poetic conversations would lull me into a trance as I listened. However, I took my greatest joy from the subjects of his plays. I am ashamed to admit it, but it made me feel better to see others in such tragic circumstances. Romeo, King Lear, Othello, and Hamlet. I identified with them all. We became friends, and they made me feel more comfortable about my position in life.

Shakespeare's plays inspired me to make a few half-hearted attempts at playwriting, but I found it harder to do than I had imagined. So much needed to be said in such a short time. I lived in a longer time frame, and my writing reflected that with plays that were so long some people may have grown old watching them.

Despite that failure, I was quite happy in England. I even opened myself up enough to fall in love with another woman. I appeared to be in my mid-twenties, and the beautiful woman I married was five years my junior. Or so she thought. Her name was Catherine Lightner.

Catherine loved everything with such intensity. When she wanted to learn to fire a rifle, she practiced shooting daily until she was a crack shot. When she set out to make a ball gown, she worked until her gown rivaled the gowns of the richest women in England. I loved that intensity in her because she was so opposite me. She knew her life on this earth was finite, so she made the most of her time here. I, on the other hand, had lived for over 1,600 years accomplishing very little. Life enamored her more than me.

I regret that we only had nine years together. And, of course, it was my fault that Catherine died. We were out riding one day when my mount threw me. I had not adapted well to horseback riding after so many centuries of walking. Catherine, of course, was an expert. She had pursued horseback riding with the vigor she pursued everything else.

When I hit the ground, my head smashed against a rock, fracturing my skull and snapping my neck. I heard a loud crack as it snapped. I should have died instantly, but my body clung to my spirit. I was a prisoner in my own body!

I lay helpless on the ground not seeing a thing because my broken neck left my head nearly lying on my chest. I tried to move, but I felt as I had in the tomb. I was in my body, but I was not in control of it.

"Then I felt the familiar pain in my heart and tried to wish it away. Catherine was too close. I could not even call out to her to run away. The rippling began.

Catherine cried out in pain. I thought it was from the shock of seeing me lying mangled on the ground.

My head and neck tingled, marking the beginning of the regeneration. I could actually feel the fragments in my skull reattaching themselves and knitting back together. The trickle of blood down the back of my neck stopped.

After five minutes or so, I was fine. Better than fine, even. I sat up and looked over at Catherine. I thought I would have to make up a good excuse for what had just happened to me.

She had collapsed. She must have fainted when she saw all the blood surrounding me. I patted her cheeks trying to revive her. When she came around, she had a confused look in her eyes.

She stared at me for a long time, then said, "Alexander?"

"Thank God, you're all right, Catherine," I told her as I pulled her closer and hugged her tightly. I was afraid my regeneration had killed her.

Catherine pushed herself away from me. "Alexander, I saw you on the ground. I thought you were dead. All the blood."

I shook my head as I lied to her. "A bad scrape, nothing more."

She knew I was lying, but she said nothing. As I think back on it, I almost wish my regeneration had killed her immediately. It would have been more merciful than what happened.

Catherine was not herself during the next three days. Instead of wanting to go to a play, read a new book, or learn some new past time, she sat in front of the fireplace with a blanket over her. She was always cold even though it was the middle of the summer. This woman was a shell of my Catherine.

In the three short days after my accident, I actually grew to hate this woman who looked like my Catherine. I was certain that she was somehow an imposter. She *looked* like Catherine, but she didn't *act* like Catherine.

When I found her dead in her favorite chair, it was a relief, but it still affected me. Falling to the floor at her feet, I cried. I had killed her. I deserved to die, not her. I considered killing myself, but any attempt I would have made would have only caused someone else to die. I was the man who couldn't die, the man who would live forever.

I booked passage for the New World the next day. I wanted to be as far away from England and her people as was possible. I remembered North America from my journey a century earlier. All the open space and mountains would give me a way to avoid people.

When the ship arrived in Jamestown, I bought a smaller boat and loaded it with supplies, things like blankets, flints, flour, and salt. I thought these things would help make my life easier wherever I decided to settle. Then I sailed the boat deeper inland pushing as far away from civilization as the river allowed me. When I could no longer take the river any further, I stopped and made my home.

For 124 years, I lived in the Appalachian Mountains. I supplemented my supplies with venison and bear that I hunted. Even so, my supplies eventually ran out, but by then I had cultivated a small vegetable garden of corn, tomatoes, cucumbers, and potatoes with seeds I had included with my supplies. My blankets fell to pieces after seventy-five years, so I hunted bears and skinned their hides.

The Indians left me alone, except for a little bit of petty thievery, about which I didn't make a big deal.

I was attacked by a band of Senecas once. The meeting was purely accidental. I was absent-mindedly walking along a trail enjoying the scent of the honeysuckles and the warmth of the sun on my face. The war party of Senecas had been on their way to rejoin their tribe after an unsuccessful raid further south.

Three arrows hit me almost at the same time. One of them lodged in my neck. The other two stuck in my side and my chest. I screamed and fell to the ground. I fell on the arrow that was in my side and drove it through my stomach. That turned out to be the easiest arrow to dislodge. I simply had to finish pulling it through. Pulling the other two arrows out of my body was an experience in pain. The notched arrowheads tore gaping holes in my flesh as I pulled them out, screaming in pain as I did. I know that pulling them out only increased the bleeding, but I was afraid to leave them in my body. I didn't want my flesh healing around them.

The Seneca warriors stood around me ready to release another barrage of arrows into me if necessary. Since they didn't, I assumed they thought I was dying.

The pain started more severely than usual. I shook from the spasms the rippling sent through me. The war party must have thought I was in my death spasms. They lowered their bows and waited for me to die.

The nearest brave to me suddenly screamed. He quickly looked around until his stare met mine. Screaming again, he dropped his bow and ran off into the woods.

I have since come to believe that when the rippling effect makes contact with someone, they can feel it just as I can feel it leave my body. The person may not be able to identify what is happening, but they can feel the intrusion by the ripples into their body. Rebecca was oddly silent after my first attack. Ilya, my fourth wife, called me a spirit man. Catherine had screamed in pain, and then the Indian had screamed and ran. There are other similar incidents, but I think you understand.

After the one brave ran from me, the remaining Indians stood by, still waiting for me to die. But I didn't die. My wounds knitted themselves closed. When the tingling stopped, I stood up and wiped the blood on my neck away. They saw no wound on my neck and became nervous, and they backed away from me. I jumped up and down yelling in Chinese. They turned and ran, thinking I had cursed them.

Another time, an Iroquois actually buried a tomahawk in my head. To his surprise, I stood up and pulled the weapon from my head so that my wounds could heal properly.

During my time in the mountains, I gathered occasional bits of news from different sources. The white settlers had established themselves as a nation in the lowlands. Though I wasn't affected by the war that was fought, I knew of it. I heard thunder when there wasn't a cloud in the sky and realized I was hearing cannon fire. I saw the English soldiers in bright-red coats marching in their columns, and I even witnessed the battle at Fort Duquesne.

The settlers continued pushing further and further inland. Where I had been one of a handful of whites in the mountains a century earlier, I now ran into other white trappers every other month or so. Towns were being established within a day's ride of my homes. My original home, which I had set up when I sailed inland, had become part of a small settlement on the river a decade earlier.

I considered traveling further inland myself to try and maintain the distance between myself and the settlers. I thought I might return and explore the Rocky Mountains again. I even started journeying across the plains when I realized I didn't want to go. I hadn't seen another person, Indian or white, for three months. I had grown accustomed to seeing them and knowing they were nearby.

I wanted to see people. I didn't want to be alone anymore.

It had been five years since my last regeneration. I thought I would be safe among people for at least another twenty years, but I can never tell how long the effects of a regeneration will last, though. You never know when an Iroquois will sink an axe in your head or a brigand will knife you in a dark alley.

I spent the next year trapping beavers and skinning them. Beaver hats were in style among the Americans, and beaver pelts brought a lot of money on the coast. If I was going to live among the Americans, I wanted to have money so I would be able to enjoy myself without using the money I had already invested. I wanted to be able to dress properly, eat well, and see how far modern theater had progressed.

I came down from the mountains into Pittsburgh, then a small community surrounding Fort Pitt. I sold my pelts to a trader there for less than they would have brought in a coastal town, but after 124 years of self-imposed exile, I was anxious to be among people again.

The first thing I did was buy myself new clothes. The deer-pelt clothing I had stitched together with thin strips of hide was not fashionable in the towns. I bought anything that was considered stylish at the time which was not necessarily what I felt comfortable wearing. The European styles during Shakespeare's time had been quite tight fitting with lots of laces and buckles. They also tended toward useless designs and bows. The American fashions were quite similar, except that the men's styles tended toward more subdued colors like black, gray, and brown.

I rented a room above a quiet tavern and took a hot bath to wash the wilderness off of me. It was the first time I had used soap in fifteen years and the first time I had bathed in hot water since exiling myself into the mountains. I soaked until the water turned my fingertips into raisins and raised the gooseflesh all over my body. Yelling for the innkeeper, I had him refill the tub with hot water, and I soaked some more.

After the soothing warmth of the bath, I retired to my room where I slept for nearly a day. The wilderness had taught me to be a light sleeper and an early riser, so I was surprised I slept so long. Yet, when I laid down on that feather mattress, my body told my head, "This is the way a man should sleep." I still keep a feather mattress on my bed to this day.

On that first morning after rising from a very sound sleep, I continued getting to know civilization. I knew much would have changed in over a century, especially since the colonies had recently established themselves as an independent country.

I gorged myself a huge breakfast of fried eggs, porridge, and fresh bread with butter. I ate so much I thought I might not be able to fit into the clothes I had bought the day before. The clothes fit fine, though. I chose to wear black pants with black silk hose, a white vest, and a pea-green coat. After wearing loose-fitting furs for over a century, I was uncomfortable, but I looked like a man of culture and wealth, which was how I wanted to appear. My final conformity to civilization was to gather my overgrown hair in a tail and tie it behind my head. Tails and wigs were still common among men. Some men even went so far as to attach false tails to the back of their heads. I did not have a problem with short hair. Even tied in a tail, I still had to have the innkeeper cut off four inches to make my tail a stylish length. When I stepped out into the streets of Pittsburgh, I was a new man.

I spent the morning finding a sturdy mare that I could buy. I purchased a chestnut at a fair price and spent the next week riding to Baltimore. Needless to say, I was awed by the changes happening throughout the land. It had been over a century since I had been into a city, and the architecture of the buildings, the dress of the people, and the small luxuries of life had all changed drastically. I saw many more wood dwellings in America than in England, and the American roofs were more sharply angled than their English counterparts. Homes in the rural areas were almost entirely constructed of wood. In the city, I would guess there was an even division between stone and wood houses. The stone houses, of course, were owned by the wealthy. Most of the everyday clothing styles had found common ground between the rich and the poor. Men's styles had more subdued colors, as I said. Some men, I noticed, were also wearing pants that came down to their shoes so that their silk hose were not visible.

I walked around Baltimore enjoying the sound of human voices and the company of many people. I stopped into a tavern on Light Street near the waterfront and had a lunch of broiled fish and apple pie. I wanted to study the mannerisms of the people so that my actions wouldn't betray that I was a stranger. I am, by nature, an extrovert. I enjoy talking with people and listening to their lives, and there's no better place to talk to people than in a tavern. However, it is my condition...my curse, which has caused me to become an introvert. So when I do experience those rare instances of being among people, I enjoy them to the fullest.

That evening I bought a box ticket for a dollar and went to the Baltimore Theater. It was not nearly as elaborate as the three-story, open-air Globe Theater in England. Baltimore Theater was relatively small, seating only 500 people. It only had one tier of box seats, but quite a large gallery for the poorer theater-goers. Unlike the Globe, the Baltimore was enclosed and lit by chandeliers. I was surprised to learn that the theater was relatively a new form of entertainment in Baltimore, having been in the city only since 1782. It seemed the Americans had learned quickly from the English the proper way to present a show.

To my delight, Placide's Acting Company performed *Romeo and Juliet* that night. It brought back fond memories of the first time I had seen it performed in England. It also brought back a few sad memories of Catherine.

Juliet, or the actress who portrayed her, outshone all of the other performers. She was so natural in the role that she made even the artificial props seem real. I watched her every move, enthralled by the fluidity in her motion. Her voice nearly sang each line of dialogue. Her death scene brought tears to my eyes.

At the end of the performance, I am sure I was the one who clapped the loudest. The cast took their bows in front of the audience. When Juliet rose from her curtsy, she glanced up into my box. Our eyes met and locked. She smiled broadly as I continued to clap.

I leaned over to the man next to me and asked, "Who plays Juliet?"

"She's good, isn't she?" he said. "She's a favorite here in town. Her name is Elizabeth Poe."

Part III:
The Masque of Red Death

And now was acknowledged the presence of the Red Death.
He had come like a thief in the night. And one by one
dropped the revellers in the blood-bedewed halls of their
revel, and died each in the despairing posture of his fall.

Edgar Allan Poe
"The Masque of Red Death"

10

"That's Edgar Allan Poe's mother!" Tim shouted. He jumped up from the table excited that Alexander had finally mentioned someone related to Edgar Allan Poe. He had been beginning to wonder if Alexander's ramblings would ever connect with Edgar Allan Poe.

Alexander nodded as he continued speaking. "Elizabeth was a beautiful woman, perhaps the most-beautiful woman I have ever known. She wasn't sensual. Her beauty came from her frailty, like a dried flower that crumbles if it is handled too roughly. People wanted to protect her and to be her friend. I was no exception, I guess."

He fell into the silence of some lost memory, smiled slightly, and gently shook his head. Then he blinked and focused on Tim.

1808 A.D.

After the crowd had emptied into the streets after the performance, I slipped over the side of my box and snuck backstage. What I did was not uncommon, but it was frowned upon. Still, no one standing on the stage tried to stop me.

Everyone backstage was in motion. Stage hands were resetting scenery for Thursday night's performance. Women and men stood behind canvas panels changing out of their costumes. Others were seated in front of mirrors illuminated by lanterns removing their stage make-up. The smell of greasepaint and coal oil was thick in the air.

Elizabeth sat in front of the mirrors. She had pulled her hair back and tied it in a bun on top of her head so that it was easier to remove her make-up. As I watched, she dipped a face cloth in the basin, wrung it out, and began scrubbing her face. She lathered up a bar of soap, wiped it on her face, and scrubbed again. It made her face glow with healthy color. Without her make-up, I could see she was barely a woman. She couldn't have been any older than twenty.

I felt so ashamed at myself at staring at someone that young that I blushed. A child! A child had caught my eye! But on stage she had seemed so much older. She carried herself with poise and grace not usually associated with the young.

I walked up to a rack of costumes a few feet behind her and tried to nonchalantly watch her in the mirror. I would stare at her for a few moments then look around to see if anyone was watching me. She caught me watching her when she happened to look up while I was staring one time.

Turning in her chair, she smiled at me. I was so stunned by the beauty of her smile that I forgot what I wanted to say. I stood in front of her gawking with my mouth hanging open!

Me!

Need I remind you, I was not some awestruck schoolboy. I was a man nearly 1,800 years old. I had seen the most-beautiful women the world had to offer, and I had married ten of them. And yet, there I stood unable to say even the simplest greeting to this young woman!

I think I finally managed to stutter my name. She must have thought I was an imbecile that had wandered backstage. Forcing my mouth to work, I said, "I thought your performance tonight was out-standing."

Her smile never faltered. If anything, it grew larger. "Thank you, it did feel like a particularly good night,' she said with genuine modesty.' The audience certainly seemed happy, and the gallery was quiet. Sometimes they can be so distracting."

Her continuing smile gave me the confidence to say more. "I've seen many performances in many cities throughout the world. Your's certainly ranks among the top."

She arched her eyebrows. "Oh, do you travel around the world?"

I nodded vigorously, again acting like a child. "Yes, I've lived in just about any place you could mention."

She put down her face cloth and leaned forward. "Really? Have you ever been over the mountains? Ever since I was a little girl, I've wondered what lay beyond the mountains."

I sat down in the chair next to her as I tried to gather my thoughts. "On the other side of the mountains, there are plains. Hundreds upon hundreds of miles upon miles of wide-open flatland covered with tall grasses. When the wind blows, it looks like a green wave blowing across the plain.

"Most of the animals on this side of the mountains have been driven into hiding. They've learned to fear men. But on the other side of the mountains, the animals still rule, and man is the intruder. The king of the animals is a huge beast with coarse fur. It stands as high as a man and resembles a bull, except no bull ever had horns the size of this beast. The fur around the shoulders and head is even thicker than on its body which makes it appear even bigger. The beasts run in herds that must number in the hundreds of thousands, and when they stampede nothing stands in the way of the herd. A stampede will turn a path through the plains into a strip of plowed dirt."

"After the plains, there is another mountain range even larger than these mountains. Many of the peaks will stay covered..."

I stopped speaking because Elizabeth was looking across the room toward a young man who had entered the backstage area through the rear doors of the theater. He was a handsome man with dark hair and a strong build, but Elizabeth wasn't looking at him. She was staring at the squirming infant he held.

The man smiled at Elizabeth and let the child stand on his own. Then he whispered something in the boy's ear and pointed to Elizabeth. The young boy rubbed both his eyes with his small fists. It looked like he had just awakened. He looked around the theater in wide-eyed amazement until his eyes fixed on Elizabeth.

"Mama. Mama," he said as he waddled toward Elizabeth. With each step, he looked as if he would fall over.

As soon as the toddler neared Elizabeth, she snatched him up and swung him into the air. He giggled and kicked his bare, chubby legs. Elizabeth lowered him and set him on her lap."

January 20, 2016

"Was that Edgar?" Tim asked.

Alexander looked up from his thoughts and shook his head. "No, no. Edgar wasn't even born at the time. This young boy was William, Edgar's older brother. It was also the point when I realized Elizabeth was married."

The tape recorder clicked off as the tape ended. Tim opened it, turned the tape over, and restarted the recorder. "Certainly you weren't thinking of romancing her after what had happened with your other wives, were you?"

Alexander rubbed his chin as he walked over to stand in front of a painting of an attractive young woman. Though Alexander didn't say who was pictured in the portrait, Tim guessed the brunette was Elizabeth, and he agreed with Alexander that she was quite lovely.

"I can't say. When I first met Elizabeth, I'm not sure if what I felt for her was love or simply the happiness of having someone around to talk with for the first time in over a century. As my thoughts became clearer, and our time together grew, I did realize how I felt about her."

"Which was?"

Alexander shook his head. "That would be jumping ahead of my story."

Tim waved his hand in a small, circular motion. "Well then, please continue."

1808 A.D.

I looked at the child, a handsome boy no older than two, and smiled. He looked up at me and pronounced in his hesitant English, "You old."

His words surprised me. Not because I was embarrassed that he thought I was old. For a moment, I thought the child might be able to see how old I actually was. I know the thought was foolish, but it scared me nonetheless.

Elizabeth was quick to interrupt when she saw the surprise on my face. "William!" Elizabeth said, "This is Mister..." She turned back to me." I'm sorry, I don't even know your name."

"Alexander Reynolds, ma'am," I said, using the name I had chosen in England centuries ago.

She turned back to William and said," Mr. Reynolds was telling your mommy what a good job she did tonight. What do you think?"

"Mommy good," the boy answered.

Elizabeth hugged him and said, "My biggest fan."

"I wouldn't say that," a voice spoke from behind me.

"I turned around and saw the man who had carried Elizabeth's son into the theater. He was a striking man with dark hair and almost-sad eyes. The clothes he wore were very plain and threadbare. His white shirt was almost worn through at the elbows. I recognized him from the play. He had played one of the Huguenots, a small part.

He walked around me and kissed Elizabeth on the forehead. "I think I may be your biggest fan."

Elizabeth giggled much the way a schoolgirl would. I had to remind myself she was not much more than a school girl. She glanced away and said, "Mr. Reynolds, this is my husband."

The man held out his hand. "David Poe," he announced.

I stood up from the chair I was sitting on, wishing I was taller. I'm five-foot-six in my bare feet. It was considered tall when I was born, but over the centuries a sort of natural selection had occurred favoring the tall. So, in essence, I grew shorter through the years. Knowing that didn't stop me from wishing I was one or two inches taller when I stood up, though.

I introduced myself as I shook his hand.

"Mr. Reynolds was just telling me about all the places he has been," Elizabeth said.

"Well, I'm sure it's not as many as we've been to," David said with a certain air of superiority that instantly irked me.

"He's visited many more places. We've been around the country. He's been around the world," Elizabeth said in my defense.

David crossed his arms over his chest. "Oh? So what brings you to Baltimore, Mr. Reynolds?"

"I've just finished an extended stay in the mountains," I told him.

He looked me over from head to toe. "You don't look like a mountain man. And you certainly don't *smell* like one.'

I smiled at his faint jest. "I'm not. I'm a language and history scholar, except for the past years when I've been living in the mountains," I said.

"He says beyond the mountains are flatlands with great, shaggy, bull-like beasts," Elizabeth added.

David laughed. "He's only teasing you, Elizabeth, because he knows you are a gullible female."

"I told her the truth," I said.

"David turned to me. "You expect us to believe that on the other side of the mountains are creatures unlike anything we have ever seen?"

"Have you ever seen a lion, an elephant, a giraffe or a camel? I doubt it, but you know they exist from what sailors who have been to Africa and India say. This is no different," I explained.

David held up his hands in surrender. "I'm sorry if I have offended you, Mr. Reynolds. I didn't mean to. However, my wife and I must be going. My mother is expecting us. She will have dinner waiting."

Elizabeth stood up holding William in one arm. At least she wasn't taller than me. She held out her hand to me. I took it and kissed it lightly. Her skin smelled faintly of soap. She thanked me for visiting her. I assured her that the pleasure had been mine. It had been quite some time since I had enjoyed a conversation. I asked if it would be possible to continue our conversation at a later date.

Instead of Elizabeth answering, David did. "I'm sure Elizabeth would enjoy it, but we're moving on after tomorrow's performance," he said.

He took William from Elizabeth so she could put on her coat.

His comment struck me as odd. With Elizabeth's popularity in

Baltimore, I couldn't understand why she would want to leave. I eventually learned that actors of that time were nomadic. They traveled a circuit through the country from Boston to Philadelphia to Baltimore to Richmond. There was also a smaller southern route that went from Richmond to Charleston to Norfolk. The acting companies would move from town to town, spending a few months in each city depending on how well their current play was received. After completing their circuit, the company would begin a new play.

After the Poes had left me to return to David's parents' home, I stood alone in the empty theater looking out on the hundreds of chairs hidden in the darkness. Loneliness was not a new feeling to me. Except, I was in a city with more people than I had seen in years. I couldn't understand how I could feel so alone.

For this, I must blame Elizabeth. I had sensed something in her. I think, perhaps, it was empathy for our shared condition.

January 20, 2016

"You mean she could live forever, too? "Tim interrupted.

"No." Alexander paused and allowed his head to droop. When he raised it again, I could see tears welling up in his eyes. "She was quite mortal, and her death brought great sadness once again into my life. When I speak of our shared condition, I speak of our loneliness."

"How could she be lonely? She had her family."

"That is what I thought at first. I knew that a family was all that kept me from feeling fulfilled. I wondered how I could even begin to think that she was lonely when she had all that I desired. Yet, the notion continued to nag at me. Elizabeth was lonely. That feeling joined us together in a common need that was somehow unanswered in the both of us."

"You went to Richmond," Tim guessed.

Alexander nodded.

1808 A.D.

I wanted to be around people, and there was nothing to hold me in Baltimore. I saddled my horse and rode for Richmond the next morning. It was a three-day ride. I was struck by the different feel of the city compared to Baltimore. Baltimore had been a large port city, but this city was far smaller and relied more on road travel. The people spoke with a different accent, which seemed to fit the more-relaxed feel of the place.

When I arrived, I took a room at the Swan Tavern on Broad

Street. It was twelve-years old and considered one of the nicest places to stay in Richmond. The reason I chose to stay there was that the Richmond Theater was only four blocks away on Broad Street.

I probably got to Richmond a day or two before the acting company. They were traveling in wagons loaded down with props, scenery, and the earthly possessions of all the players.

It amazes me now that I think about it, how few possessions I had actually accumulated up until then. There was so little that I had wanted to keep from life to life. I had a few things stored away in a cave in China, but everything else I owned I could pack on my horse. Items like clothes and many of my written records deteriorated with time. I had no need to save furniture, but I did save other bulky items, such as the paintings that now hang on my walls, the Japanese screens, and some of the documents I showed you earlier. Mainly what I kept were portraits, letters and things of sentimental value to me. The main reason I stored most of my possessions was that they would have been inappropriate in different countries and eras.

Picture the customary robes worn by men in Christ's time being worn in colonial America. Or better yet, seeing how the colonists had only recently come through a war with England, imagine what would have happened if I had worn the finery of an English gentleman?

I waited until Placide's Acting Company had been in Richmond a week before I announced myself to Elizabeth. However, before that meeting, I attended each evening performance up until that point. My entire day revolved around being at the Richmond Theater by six o'clock. I sat tucked away in my box seat in the darkest corner of the theater away from any windows or lanterns, which might betray my presence before I was ready to make myself known.

Elizabeth's talent was unparalleled by any of the other actresses in the company and most of the actors, too. In fact, when two actresses were sick and couldn't perform, I saw Elizabeth play three separate roles in one performance. She played each role to perfection without mixing up the dialogue of her characters. She was on the stage as Juliet first. She finished her scene and left the stage only to appear minutes later as Juliet's mother. Then she appeared later in another scene as one of Juliet's cousin's. If she had lived longer, Elizabeth would have become a theater legend. Of that, I had no doubt.

I decided to reintroduce myself to Elizabeth on a Monday night. As before, I walked behind the stage after she had finished her performance. I didn't see her, though, and to my sadness, I thought she might have hurried off to wherever she was staying.

Then I saw David standing in front of one of the changing screens. At the same time, he saw me. He seemed to say something into the air when he saw me, but I was too far away to hear. I saw a hand drape a petticoat over the top of the screen, and I knew it must be Elizabeth.

As I approached, David shifted from his slouching position against the screen so that he was standing at his full height. I pretended not to notice, even though I straightened my own posture to make myself appear taller.

Elizabeth stepped from behind the screen about the same time I reached David. She smiled her beautiful smile, and I tried not to look as awestruck as I must have looked the week before. I invited them both to dinner at the restaurant on Twelfth Street where I had been eating most of my meals since I had arrived in Richmond. David started to say "no," but Elizabeth spoke first and accepted.

The restaurant was not one of the finer establishments in Richmond, but it was far from a dockside tavern. The food was well prepared, and the staff was friendly. The dinner conversation was quite cheerful as we talked about acting and travel. Then I made a mistake and asked about William.

Elizabeth fell silent and directed her gaze to her lap. David took her hand in his and patted it.

"William is in Baltimore with his grandfather," David said.

"Is he ill?" I asked.

"No, he's not!" David snapped.

"David!" Elizabeth scolded in the same tone of voice she had used to scold
William. "He's only asking a question."

"Well, it's none of his business," David nearly yelled, turning his anger on his wife.

Elizabeth drew back slightly at his sharp tone, then turned to me and said, "We can't afford to keep William with us, Mr. Reynolds. Actors and actresses don't make much money. David gets upset about it because his father was a soldier and has always looked down on acting as unmanly. He agreed to care for William, but David had to nearly beg to get him to agree."

I told her I was sorry, and she assured me it was not my fault. Then I said, "I pity those people who scorn acting. They are so grounded in reality that they are afraid to let go of it even for a little while. They are afraid they might dream of grander things that are impossible for them to reach. They don't realize that if they stretch and fall short, they will still be further along than if they hadn't reached at all. Those are the sort of people who hate acting. Acting creates a dream and pulls them into it, and they don't want that."

"That's a wonderful speech, but it doesn't provide much of an answer to our problem. Do you know what it's like to be separated from your children, Mr. Reynolds?" David asked me.

"No." I wanted to cry out, "I only wish I could have children, but when you're immortal, there's no need to have someone carry on the family name. You do it yourself!"

January 20, 2016

"Have you ever thought about why you can't have children?" Tim asked unexpectedly.

Alexander nodded. "Not that it has given me any answers. It's simply one more way this gift of life has turned into a curse. My body is selfish. It hoards its own life and takes that of others. Where it could bring new life into the world with only a few drops of its life essence, it refuses."

Tim stood up and stretched. Sitting in one place for so long had begun to tire him out.

"You talk as if you and your body are two separate entities," he commented as he readjusted himself in the chair.

"At times, I believe they are. I, who am Lazarus, am a spirit that has seen the glories of Heaven. I am the same. I possess much more knowledge, yes, but essentially, I act the same as I did before my resurrection. My spirit is that of a mortal.

"But my body!" Alexander's rocking motion in his chair quickened. "It has changed. It was given properties not meant for a mortal body. The body that was mine died. It ceased to function when my spirit left it. The body that I am in now, though it appears the same, is not. It has been touched by the hand of God. My body is immortal, but my spirit is mortal. The two do not belong together.

"I am not a killer!"

Alexander slammed his hands against the arms of the rocking chair and gripped it until his knuckles turned white. Tim tensed. He thought Alexander was about to explode, and he didn't want to be the focus of that explosion.

"My body kills and forces me into complicity! Nightly, I hear their cries. In my dreams, I see their faces. Although I didn't know all of them, I still grieve for each one, save one. Him, I do not grieve for. His soul burns in Hell, as mine undoubtedly will do for killing him."

January 20, 2016

Alexander clenched his eyes shut and rubbed his forehead as he tried to separate himself from the deaths he had caused. As Tim listened to the shakiness in Alexander's voice, he understood what role he played in this interview. Alexander was the sinner, and Tim was the father confessor. Through Tim, Alexander intended to cleanse his soul, to confess two millennia of sins. He would ask for mankind's forgiveness through Tim's story.

"Who don't you grieve for?" Tim asked. "It certainly isn't Edgar Allan Poe. If you hated him, you wouldn't visit his grave every year to leave the roses and cognac. You've already shown that."

Alexander dismissed the idea with a casual flip of his hand in Tim's direction.

"Of course not Edgar!"

"Then who?" Tim persisted.

"His name would mean nothing to you now. Thankfully, I killed him before he had achieved his goal. He was an evil man in a shroud of righteousness, more evil than some of the people Edgar wrote about," Alexander said as he began pacing again.

"You seem to be almost gloating that you stole his life force."

Alexander spun around to face Tim. "Do I? It's good he is dead, but it is not something I take pride in doing. And," Alexander shook a threatening finger in Tim's direction, "I did not steal his life force. I would not want such a corrupted essence sustaining me. I killed him with purpose and no need."

The uneasy feeling that had caused Tim to bring his pistol into the house returned. Even if Alexander Reynolds was immortal, it didn't necessarily make him sane. He could still be a very dangerous man. He could just as easily turn his anger on Tim. How could he defend himself if Alexander turned violent? He had set his pistol out of reach on the table. Besides, you can't kill an immortal.

"Do you have anything to drink?" Tim asked, trying to divert Alexander's attention from thinking about a man he so obviously hated.

Alexander smiled broadly. "I'm sorry. I've been a poor host. I have an excellent selection from all corners of the globe. Gin from England, Amaretto from Italy, Sake from Japan, and Vodka from Russia. What would you like?"

He stood up and limped toward the kitchen.

"I was thinking more along the lines of water. I need to keep my wits about me, especially concerning the things you're telling me. If I came down off this mountain telling your story with alcohol on my breath, I'd be laughed out of the state."

Alexander snorted. "You must handle your liquor as poorly as Edgar did. I'm able to drink a considerable amount before I begin to feel the hindering effects. Fortunately, it is rare that I drink to that point."

He disappeared into another room that Tim assumed was the kitchen, but he continued to talk.

"It's quite fortunate I was not drunk later that night after my dinner with the Poes, or Edgar might never have been born. What a loss to the world that would have been."

Alexander stepped back into the living room holding two glasses of ice water. He set the glass on the table and slid it across to Tim to keep from getting too close to him. Tim quickly caught it before it slipped off the edge. A little water sloshed over the side of the glass, but Alexander hadn't filled it to the top. Tim took a sip and was surprised to find the water tasted sweet. It was so cold that it actually made his teeth hurt.

"Spring water," Alexander said when he saw Tim wince. "You had better let it warm up a bit if your teeth are sensitive to cold."

Tim nodded and set the glass on one of his notebooks so it wouldn't leave a ring on the dining room table.

1808 A.D.

Alexander continued speaking. "When I returned to my room that night, I was restless and unable to lay down and sleep. I found myself pacing back and forth only stopping for a few moments to stare out the window at Broad Street, which was nearly empty at that hour. I don't know why I felt this way. Perhaps, there were so many thoughts trying to get my attention inside my head that I wasn't able to relax. I may have been angry with myself for bringing up the subject of William and upsetting Elizabeth so much. Whatever the reason, it won out over my fatigue. I gave up trying to sleep. I redressed and went outside for a walk.

I walked briskly along Broad Street hoping to tire myself out. Then I saw him, or at least, I thought I saw him.

He passed me as I turned onto Ninth Street. His head was tilted down so that I only glimpsed shadows flickering across his face from the oil lamps. Something in his appearance jostled a memory I had nearly forgotten. Almost two millennia separated the instances, but the man who yelled at Christ as he died on the cross and the man I saw on Broad Street looked the same.

The man hurried by me, trying to keep his head turned away. I stopped and turned to face his retreating back.

"Matthew?" I murmured.

The man stopped as if he had run into an invisible wall. He stood with his back to me for an instant, then broke into a run.

I chased after him calling his name. He never acknowledged my calls other than widening the gap between the two of us. I am not a slow runner. At least I wasn't at that time. Yet, he managed to escape me. He turned into an alleyway, and when I ran into the alley after him, he was gone. I hurried to the other side of the alley and looked around, but I saw nothing. He had disappeared as if he were only a figment of my imaginings. I didn't even hear the rapid clicking of running footsteps on the cobblestones. He had vanished.

January 20, 2016

"Matthew? The widow's son from Nain?" Tim asked anxiously.

Alexander sighed. "Yes, and a very dangerous man."

"How so? He certainly couldn't harm you."

Alexander cocked his head to the side. "No? I wish I could have been as sure."

"But you told me you can't be killed."

He held up his finger to correct me. "No. What I told you is that I won't die again until the Second Coming of Christ."

"It's the same thing," Tim argued.

Alexander raised an eyebrow. "Is it?"

Tim slammed his hand against the table. "You're playing games with me,

Alexander! If you want me to be your confessor, fine! I'll listen to your story. But tell the truth. Don't dance around it."

Alexander looked hurt that Tim had accused him of deceit. "I assure you I'm not avoiding telling you the truth."

"Then you're saying you can be killed."

"Yes."

Tim's mouth dropped open slightly. "But how?"

"Fire, definitely." He cocked his head to one side and seemed to be considering something. "Dismemberment, maybe. If I am burned to ashes, my soul certainly can't remain within the ashes. It would be released because the body would no longer be a structure that could hold it. As an extension of that thought, if I were beheaded, I don't believe my soul would be able to animate a body without a head. I might be able to regrow an appendage, but I don't think I could regrow a head. The separation of my heart and my brain would release my spirit."

Tim nodded his agreement. "I suppose it's possible. So Matthew wanted to kill you?"

"No. Not at first. At first, I believe Matthew wanted to make me dependent on him so that he could control me. I would have been useful to him."

"Did he feel the need to try and kill you once he found out you were immortal?"

Alexander shook his head. "No. He knew of my extended life from the very beginning. I really did see Matthew at the foot of Christ's cross those many centuries ago and again in Richmond. He was also the man who turned the villagers of Bethany against me after Rebecca's death and he cast the first stone when the Egyptian's stoned me after Callames' death."

Tim felt like he was ten years old again, and he had just found out there was no tooth fairy. He still got fifty cents for each tooth he lost, but he also lost part of his ability to believe by faith because his mom and dad had lied to him. Mom and dad weren't supposed to lie to him and let him believe in something that wasn't true. They were his defense in school when Joey Braddock told him there was no tooth fairy. *Well, my dad says there is, and my dad wouldn't lie, he had told Joey.*

Now Alexander had lied to him in the same way. Telling him only partial truths and allowing Tim to believe them because it was easier than explaining the entire truth. Alexander was baiting him with a trail of crumbs that he wanted Tim to follow to the end of the story. The trouble was, Tim had a large appetite, and he didn't want to settle for crumbs.

"But you said you didn't think either he or the girl had been affected the way you had," Tim reminded him.

Alexander shrugged unperturbed by Tim's agitation at his half-truths. "I'm not sure the same power that has extended my life prolonged Matthew's. I did not know Matthew as a boy before he died the first time, so I really have nothing on which to make my comparison. My feeling is perhaps the spirit that returned to Matthew's body upon his resurrection was not his own, or at least, not entirely his own. The man I met was not a holy man. I cannot even call him a good man. So why would Christ have resurrected him? The boy Christ would have resurrected would have been someone who had faith in Christ, who loved him. Matthew certainly did not. That is why I think something happened to his soul before it could return to his body."

"You're talking about Satan, aren't you?" Tim asked.

Alexander saw the skeptical look on Tim's face and said, "Of course. Knowing that there had been a son of God on the earth, did you doubt the existence of Satan? According to the Bible, Satan and one-third of the angels of Heaven gave up their right to be given bodies when they were banished from Heaven. That did not stop them from possessing bodies, though. Suppose two spirits entered Matthew's body when he was resurrected? Matthew's spirit and another one?"

Tim looked up from his notes. "I wouldn't know," he said.

"I suppose not. I didn't even give it much thought myself that night. By the time I returned to the hotel, I had forgotten about the incident.

1808 A.D.

I continued my walk admiring the stone and brick rowhomes as I did. I passed a night watch and stopped for a few minutes to talk with him. When we parted, he directed me to a tavern on College Street called The Corner Stop.

I looked through a side window and saw about two dozen men and women inside enjoying themselves. Most of them were men. Half of the men were strung out along a wooden bar against the back wall. Four were alone and seemed to be oblivious to everything except the drink in their hands. The other six were paired off in three couples talking to each other. Two fair-looking women wandered among the men seated at the tables urging them to buy another drink or to buy the women a drink. I could hear someone banging harshly at a piano that I couldn't see off to my right. His poor playing drowned out most of the voices so I couldn't hear any of what was being said.

As I watched, I realized this was how I had spent most of my life. An observer. Other people lived their lives while I stood back and watched. Sometimes, I feel that I actually did die those many years ago. What was resurrected was only a ghost thinking of himself as human.

January 20, 2016

"Did you say something?"

Tim felt like a boy who had just been caught passing a note in class and was now being forced to read that note in front of the class. He hadn't meant for Alexander to hear him as he mumbled to himself.

"It's not important," Tim said and then turned his attention to his notebook to jot down a useless piece of information so he wouldn't have to meet Alexander's gaze.

Alexander walked to the table but stopped at the invisible barrier he had set for himself. He rested his hands on the edge of the table too near the pistol and knife for Tim's liking.

"Please, don't be afraid to speak your mind with me. I appreciate honesty...even if it is unfavorable to me."

Tim unconsciously sucked on his lower lip as he considered his choices. To tell Alexander what he had mumbled would put the interview at risk by hurting Alexander's feelings. However, not telling what he had said would put him at risk by making a man who called himself a murderer angry.

"Self-pity," Tim said finally barely louder than he had mumbled it.

Alexander drew back. "What?"

"Self-pity," Tim said more firmly. "You wallow in it. It drips from nearly every sentence you speak. You must have really taken Buddhism to heart to believe that you have spent your entire life suffering. With your immortality, you could have been the greatest historian the world has ever known. You have seen things and done things that are lost to everyone else because there was no record of the events except what you saw."

Alexander leaned over the opposite end of the table, allowing himself to come as close as he ever had to Tim.

"That is part of the reason I brought you here, don't you see?"

Tim pushed himself back against the chair trying to keep as much distance between himself and Alexander as possible.

"I suppose I do, but I listen to you talk, and all I can think of is all the years you lost by isolating yourself from the world. It makes me sick. As you have said, people died to give you life, and you wasted it. You could have made their deaths have some importance if you hadn't."

Alexander turned away from the table toward one of the

bookshelves. Tim hadn't meant to say all that he had, but once he started talking everything had spilled out. Alexander paused at the bookshelves. He held his hands behind his back and stared at the books.

"You are right, you know," he said without turning around.

He pulled a thick book from the second shelf and tossed it on the table next to Tim. Tim turned the book toward him so he could read the title. *The Mayans and the Aztecs: A Global Perspective.*

"Leaf through it," Alexander urged him.

He did. At first, he wasn't sure what Alexander wanted him to see. He didn't understand how the central American Indians fit into the interview. Then he noticed the handwritten notes in the margins surrounding the text. In other parts of the book, words had been crossed out and new ones added. Drawings and diagrams had been altered. In most instances, the notes and deletions only had a minor impact on the meaning of the text. However, there were a few points, that if correct, significantly altered what was considered the truth.

Alexander wrote that certain sects of both the Mayans and Aztecs worshiped Christ as Quetzalcoatl. That, in fact, Christ had visited them after he had left his disciples following his resurrection. This completely dispelled the belief of the Indians worshipping multiple gods like the Romans and the Greeks. In another area, Alexander gave support to the theory that a mass war between the two tribes leads them to extinction. He even listed dates and the names of key people in the war.

Tim looked up from the book. "All of this is true?"

Alexander nodded.

"Then why haven't you published it?"

"To be published, *and accepted*, I would need to support my work with personal credentials and sources for my conclusions. Those alterations are things I know of from my journeys through Central America. To support those changes by saying 'I am a man almost 2,000-years old, and this is what I know to be true because I was there when it happened.' would discredit this account."

Alexander waved his hand across the library. "Many of the books you see here are much like that one. I know differences between the truth and history about colonial America, the Chinese Empire, the ancient Egyptians, and even the Bible, but their information shall never be known to the public. The time to publish these facts was in the past. They would have been accepted more readily then."

"But you wasted those years."

Alexander nodded. "Yes. But I must point out that I am a different man now. I have changed."

Tim let out a skeptical "Humph!"

"You don't believe me?" Alexander asked.

"Well, you are living alone on the top of a mountain. How can I believe that you're still not wasting your life?"

"My reasons for my isolation are no longer because of self-pity."

"Then why do you stay here alone when you have so much to offer the world?"

"Fear. I can only offer the world death. In my anger, I committed the second-greatest sin against God. I don't want that to happen again. I live in fear that it might. You may consider this weakness. If it is, I am guilty just as I was concerning self-pity. Yet, I am not a particularly strong-willed man. Having committed the sin once, I may not be able to resist again.

"You see, I do know myself, Mr. Lawrence, and in doing so, I know the limitations of my spirit," Alexander confessed.

"But now that you know the truth about yourself, you can take steps to change. Do you want to spend your remaining years on this mountain waiting for Christ to come and save you?"

Alexander thought for a moment and shook his head. "No, I don't. Still, I must. The last person who died because of me was a hitchhiker. He was just a teenage boy who had at least a half a century of life to look forward to. That was twenty years ago. Though there should be more than enough time to venture among people, I can't be sure. The length each regeneration lasts varies. It doesn't seem to be based on the amount of time the person who died had left to live. Someone else could die if I were too careless. I don't want to kill anyone else."

Alexander fell silent. Tim looked up from his notes and saw him staring off into the air. The red recording light on the tape recorder blinked off.

"We can stop the interview if you want," Tim offered.

As Alexander focused his gaze on Tim, he ran his hand through his thick, brown hair. It was beginning to gray slightly at the temples.

"No. I need to tell these things that I've kept inside of me for so long. Time is growing short."

"How can time grow short for an immortal?" Tim asked.

"Christ is coming."

1808 A.D.

I decided to have a drink in the tavern. I hoped it would take the edge off whatever was causing my restlessness.

I walked in the front door almost unnoticed. Only a few heads turned in my direction as I made my way between the tables to an open spot at the end of the wooden bar that had seen better days. I propped myself up against the bar and ordered rum. When it came, I drank half of it quickly before I even set the mug down. The rum was watered down, of course,--this was not the finest bar in Richmond by any stretch of the imagination--but it served its purpose and calmed me down somewhat.

Then I saw David Poe.

He sat alone at a table in the corner of the tavern opposite the piano. His back was to the front wall, and a half-filled mug of beer sat between his forearms. I tried to turn back to the bar when I saw him, but he saw me and waved me over to his table. His arm motion was wild and exaggerated. I knew without even having to smell his breath or listen to him talk, he was drunk.

I stood across the table from him and said hello.

He gestured to the chair nearest him and said, "Sit down, Mr. Reynolds. Join me in a drink."

"I think you may have already had too much to drink," I told him.

He tilted his head to look at his glass. "This is only my second." He held up his mug and said, "Alas, poor beer. I knew it well. He laughed a very hoarse, throaty laugh at his own pun.

It amazed me that he had had only two drinks. As I told you earlier, I have an incredible tolerance for alcohol. I had naturally assumed everyone did. I was obviously wrong because David was definitely beyond his polite limit.

Taking the seat he had pointed out to me, I sat down across the table from him. I still had my own drink in my hand, so I didn't bother to order another, but he did.

He leaned across the table toward me. I thought he was reaching for my drink, and I pulled it away. He waved to me to come closer. He wanted to whisper something to me that he didn't want anyone else to hear.

I leaned in closer. David cupped his hand to my ear and said, "You like Liz, don't you?"

At the mention of Elizabeth's name, I was cautious. I pulled away and looked at him. I didn't want to cause trouble for Elizabeth, and at the same time, I didn't want a jealous husband trying to defend himself against some imagined offense.

"Your wife is a very talented actress," I told him. "I appreciate such talent as I'm sure you do."

David smiled a lopsided smile and giggled. I smelled the beer on his breath and blinked my eyes to try and keep them from tearing.

"I'm an actor, too," David said. I told him I knew that. "Then why doesn't anyone tell me how good an actor I am. Dad calls acting another form of begging and says I should be ashamed of myself. The best thing the newspapers say about me is that I'm "adequate." Most of the time they don't even mention me at all, only Liz, but I'm good!' So I told him he was a good actor, which was stretching the truth. "That's right!" he nearly shouted, "But try telling that to Louis Placide. I wanted to play Romeo, opposite Liz, but he gave the part to Payne. Payne is a pain!"

He giggled again this time, spraying a mouthful of beer across the table. "I'm twice the actor Payne is!"

"I'm sure you are," I lied.

"Liz is good, too," he repeated.

"Elizabeth is a wonderful actress, as I've said."

David shook his head with a drunk's exaggerated motion. "No, no. That's not what I mean." Then he whispered, "She knows how to please a man."

I stiffened at the implication, and I hoped I had imagined what he meant.

David noticed my reaction. He pulled back slightly and patted my arm. He said, "Come now. I know you like her. It's quite obvious. You've had to wonder."

"Even if I did, and I'm not saying I have, mind you. She's married and in love with you," I explained to him.

"But if you have five dollars and a bottle of rum, she can be yours tonight," David told me.

I jumped to my feet so quickly that I almost turned the table over. My first impulse was to backhand the perverted wretch and knock him out of his chair. I stayed my hand, though. Starting a fight in which someone might be injured or killed would not have been a good idea. I already had too many deaths claiming pieces of my soul.

I stared at him as intensely as I could. So intense was my concentration that I began to think I could see the back of the chair through his body. I wanted to say so much to him, to tell him what I thought of what he was doing, but the words wouldn't come. My mind was holding my mouth, as well as my body, in check.

"Come on, Mr. Reynolds," David said as he gestured for me to sit down. "We're both adults. We can surely discuss this and come to a suitable agreement."

I looked around and saw that many of the people had directed their attention to us with my abrupt jump to my feet. The piano had stopped playing so that people would be able to hear our conversation. Again, I felt like lashing out at the man. How could he attempt to sell his wife as a whore?

"There is nothing to discuss," I said slowly struggling to keep all the other comments I wanted to say from slipping out.

"I know you have money, and you like Liz. Why else would you have followed us from Baltimore? We need the money," David told me.

"Then stop drinking and save that money," I said.

He shook his head in wide arcs back and forth. "I couldn't do that. I enjoy it too much." He smiled a lopsided grin.

By then, my body was shaking from rage I could barely contain. I kept telling myself I wasn't talking with David Poe. I was talking with the beer he was drinking. David Poe, the actor, would never have offered his wife to another man. He was too proud. David Poe, the alcoholic, would. His only desire in life was to continue drinking. The problem was that with each failure of David Poe, the actor, David Poe, the alcoholic's appearances grew more frequent. Sooner or later, he would offer his wife to someone who would accept. What would that do to Elizabeth?

"Come on, Mr. Reynolds," David urged me. "Five dollars will buy you enough pleasure to last you a lifetime."

"Not my lifetime," I told him, but, of course, he didn't understand what I meant. I turned and walked out of the tavern as fast as I could without breaking into a run.

That same night I packed my bags and left Richmond. Perhaps, I should have warned Elizabeth about her husband's behavior, but I believed it would only make matters worse. I was the cause of the problems. My presence and David's insecurities. I couldn't do much to alter his insecurities, but I could do something about my presence. I figured if I weren't around, David would stop trying to make a whore out of his wife.

I had originally intended to head back into the mountains, to isolate myself again. But as I left Richmond on my horse, I realized how much I hated the loneliness of those towering hills. I wanted to be among people. To hear them laugh, to see them move, to taste the delicacies prepared in the restaurants. That is what I wanted, and I couldn't get it in the mountains. The happiest times of my life had been the times I shared with others.

People talk nowadays of how they want to escape from the hassles of the city to the solitude of the country.

Not me.

Loneliness is my Hell. What I remember most about Heaven are the individuals who I met there. I was surrounded by people, but not crowded by them. I knew my entire lineage back to Adam. Misery may love company, but happiness does, too. It was impossible to be sad among such happy people. It was like a contagious disease. I tried to hold onto my anger at having died so young, but I felt it slipping away with each person I met.

The ancient Greeks believed that everyone created their own personal Hell by the things they did while they were alive. Sisyphus eternally pushed a huge boulder up a hill only to have it roll down the other side. Tantalus, starving, was placed in a pit with food just out of his reach. And me, I'll be in a black void. Completely alone.

January 20, 2016

"What is your personal Hell?"

Tim sat quietly for a moment until he realized Alexander had directed the final question to him. He returned Alexander's question with a blank stare and then shrugged.

Alexander sat in the chair at the opposite end of the table from Tim. "There must be something," Alexander persisted. "Please tell me. I'm curious. I think in viewing our personal Hells, we discover our true personalities."

"I've never thought much about Hell," Tim said.

Alexander smiled. "Well, think about it now. What will be your stone to push forever up a hill?"

Tim set his notebook aside and sighed. He rested his chin against his hands as he considered Alexander's question.

What was his personal Hell?

What would cause him the greatest frustration or fear?

"Nothingness," he answered.

Alexander's eyes widened as if he hadn't expected the answer. "So your Hell would be the same as mine?"

Tim shook his head. "No. You fear the world being nothing and being alone in it. I am afraid of me being nothing. My Hell would be being forgotten, of not leaving my mark upon the world. I want to be remembered. I want my life to mean something."

Alexander was silent.

"I envy you," Tim said suddenly.

Alexander's face turned red as he jumped up from the table. "Envy! Are you a fool! I am cursed!"

Tim leaned back in his chair away from Alexander. "But you are not forgotten. You are immortalized in the Bible because of your association with Christ. Just about every Christian in the world knows your story. The thoughts and feelings that are associated with your story are intense. Your death made Jesus weep. Your life set an example for others and proved Christ's power."

Alexander cast his eyes to the floor and shook his head slowly. "If not me, there would have been another. I would have preferred to live my life unknown and to have died at the end of my natural life. If this is what it takes to leave my mark on the world, I would not wish it on my enemies. Do you know what it is to grow close to someone only to have them die and know it will be centuries before you meet again? Worse yet, do you know what it feels like to kill someone you love?"

Tim shook his head silently.

"I do, and I have to live with those feelings for every second of my extended life. Is that the type of memories you want people to have of you? That you were their killer?"

Again, Tim shook his head.

"I dream of Heaven every night. The vision is so vivid I can remember every detail as if it were a reality. My father, in his mortal years, had broken his leg when a boulder he and two others were trying to remove from a field rolled back onto his leg. The two other men freed my father who was pinned beneath the boulder, then set and splinted his leg. Despite their good intentions, they did a poor job of setting the bones, and after that, my father walked with a limp. He does not have that limp in Heaven. Not from I have seen. He walks as straight and as tall as any other man there.

"Heaven frees us from the deformities and restrictions of a mortal body. It is the ultimate freedom!"

Alexander stopped speaking and turned back to Tim.

"Don't envy me. You know nothing of what my life has been. It is not enviable."

"I'm sorry," Tim said.

Alexander shook his head and smiled again. "Of what? Speaking your mind? Don't be. Better to talk about it now before you become fascinated with the thought of immortality.

"Let's continue my tirade, shall we? I've nearly reached a point that you'll be very interested in. Now where was I..."

"You had just left Richmond after your argument with David Poe."

Alexander nodded.

1808 A.D.

I thought about returning to the mountains, but I couldn't impose that isolation on myself after such a short time amid civilization. Instead, I rode north, stopping for a week or so in each town I passed through trying to find one in which I felt comfortable and at home. By the time I reached Boston, I wanted to stop for more than a week.

I secured a position as an instructor of history at Harvard. It was much easier to do such a thing at that time than it would be now. There were no reference checks, no searching for transcripts, or parading diplomas. I told Professor Smith, who was in charge of the history studies that I was also a professor, and I demonstrated the depth of my knowledge of history by answering Professor Smith's historical questions and relating bits of history that I knew from my own experiences. He was impressed with my knowledge of the American continents and the native people.

During my time at Harvard, I expanded my own knowledge as well as those of my students. I studied a variety of subjects in my free time from religion to chemistry. I discovered that part of my need to be among others lie rooted in my thirst for knowledge. I enjoyed studying and hearing other people's thoughts and ideas. Most importantly, for once in my life, I was learning through active participation.

One evening, after an unusually lengthy discussion about the intelligence of the American Indians with Professors Jackson and Whiting, Professor Whiting invited Professor Jackson and myself to attend a performance of *King Lear* in Boston with him. As you know, Shakespeare is a favorite of mine, so I accepted, as did Professor Jackson.

I was quite impressed with the Federal Street Theater. It had been open since 1794, but it had only been completed for four years.

The designer had incorporated many aspects of Greek architecture into it. Even though it was constructed of red brick, there was a central Palladian window and a colonnaded entry.

The three of us walked into a lobby decorated in gray and gold. The theater sat twice as many people as the Baltimore Theater. There were two tiers of box seats and a large gallery surrounding the semicircular pit. I was surprised that the builder hadn't used any columns to support the boxes. However, there were other decorative columns and moldings within the theater itself.

We had purchased box seats on the first tier that gave us an excellent view of the stage. I must admit that I was quite anxious to see the play. I hadn't had the opportunity to see it while I lived in London. When the curtains parted to reveal King Lear's palace as Kent, Edmund, and Gloucester entered, I was enthralled. Then Cordelia, dressed in her royal finery, made her entrance to the sounds of a trumpet.

I let my breath out in a loud sigh. I hadn't even realized I'd been holding it. I had hoped, but not expected that Cordelia would be Elizabeth. I hadn't been able to fully get her out of my mind. Not that I had made a conscious effort to do so. My work and studies had taken up much of my time leaving very little to think about anything or anyone else, but being back in a theater had reminded me of the beauty of Elizabeth's Juliet.

Professor Whiting noticed my reaction to Cordelia and said, "Sarah Montrose is her name. She's not bad, but she's only the understudy. I was here two weeks ago and saw a woman named Elizabeth Poe playing Cordelia. She was magnificent!"

I turned to him suddenly oblivious to the play. "Elizabeth Poe? Are you sure?"

"Yes, quite sure. Check the program. I'm sure you'll see her name," Whiting said, looking at me as if I was a raving madman.

I opened the folded sheet of paper in my hand. I hadn't bothered to look at it when the doorman gave it to me at the beginning of the performance. Now I scanned the cast list hungrily looking for her name. It was listed second, under John Hathaway who played King Lear. Her named had been scratched out and under it was written 'Sarah Montrose.'

"What happened to Elizabeth Poe?" I asked.

Whiting shrugged. "How the devil should I know? Now sit back and enjoy the show."

How could I enjoy the play? All I could think about was that Elizabeth was in town. It was one thing to try and forget about her when she was several hundred miles away, but it was quite another thing when she was probably less than a mile away.

The remainder of the play was a blur to me. I couldn't concentrate on it. I kept wondering about Elizabeth. Why wasn't she on the stage? Was she sick? Had she been in an accident? Had David finally sold her to someone? Had David beaten her in drunken anger? All I had were questions with no answers. It was maddening!

After the performance, a doorman at the front of the theater told me that the Poes had rented a house on Carver Street. He checked a list he had and gave me the correct address of 62 Carver Street.

Jackson and Whiting wanted to go to a tavern to drink and discuss the effect Thomas Jefferson's massive land purchase from France five years ago was having throughout the country today. I excused myself, claiming a headache and went directly to Carver Street. The house was not much more than a wooden shack in bad need of repairs.

My knock on the door was answered by a huge man missing one of his front teeth. I almost cried. Had David finally succeeded in selling his wife as a whore to this brute? Was I looking at the man who had bought Elizabeth for a bottle of rum? My face flushed with anger. I clenched my fists but kept them at my side.

"I'm looking for the Poes," I said.

"He's gone out," the man told me as he blocked the doorway.

"I would actually prefer to see Mrs. Poe," I said.

He squinted trying to get a better look at me in the dark. "Why, are you a doctor or something?"

"No, is Mrs. Poe ill?" I asked anxiously trying to look past him into the house, but his bulk blocked my view.

He laughed a throaty chuckle. "Not too many people would call a pregnant woman ill."

"Pregnant?"

The man nodded. "My wife says her time is coming. She wants me to go get a doctor for the woman, but I'll be damned if I will. They owe me two weeks worth of room and board. He tells me they don't have any money since Elizabeth isn't working right now, but he seems to have money to go off drinking."

Elizabeth was pregnant. It must have happened shortly after I left Richmond. I hoped it meant things were better between her and David, but he was still drinking. Then I wondered if they would send this child to live with David's parents in Baltimore as they had William.

"Elizabeth is due now?"

"That's what my wife says, and she should know."

A horrible thought crossed my mind as I stood there. Had David found some wealthy admirer of Elizabeth's to buy his wife for a night? Was this pregnancy the result of such an encounter?

Suddenly, I heard a woman cry out in pain, and I knew it must be Elizabeth. I started to push past him into the house.

He grabbed hold of my shoulder and said, "Wait a minute."

"She needs help," I said as I pushed my way past the man.

Her room was at the end of the downstairs hallway. Elizabeth was lying on a double bed holding her stomach. A woman, I assumed the big man's wife, was mopping her sweat drenched forehead with a damp cloth. Elizabeth's breaths were coming quickly, so quickly, I thought she might hyperventilate.

"Are you the doctor?" the woman asked. She tried to smile at Elizabeth, but her eyes betrayed her fear.

I shook my head, and the woman went into a panic. "Nelson! I don't care how mad you are at them! Mrs. Poe needs a doctor."

Nelson cringed at his wife's yells and backed out of the room.

Even though I haven't been blessed enough to have a child of my own, I have seen more births than any doctor. Quite a few of them were in the most desolate stretches of Siberia. If you want to see a miracle, watch a woman give birth. The creation of life is a miracle. Envy that, not me.

So I did have some idea of how the birthing process worked. Apparently, more than anyone else in the house.

"Where's her husband?" I asked the woman.

"He left about four hours ago. Hasn't been back since." She cast a worried glance in Elizabeth's direction.

"Find her husband. He should be here," I told Nelson.

He didn't move. He just murmured to himself about the Poes owing him his money. Then Elizabeth screamed, and he shut up.

"Go find David Poe!" I ordered Nelson.

Then I heard something I wish I hadn't heard. The woman said, "Check the taverns, Nelson. That's the most likely place you'll find him."

Nelson turned and stomped off down the hall grumbling to himself. His heavy steps shook the small house, and I thought for a moment the roof would fall in on me.

"And find the doctor, too," the woman yelled as her husband went out the front door.

"So David was still drinking. My leaving Richmond hadn't helped in that respect at all. He had only found other excuses to drink once I had gone.

"Mr. Reynolds?" someone said. I looked down. Elizabeth had finally noticed me. "Mr. Reynolds, help me." Her voice was weak, almost a whisper, and I wondered how long she had been in labor.

She reached her hand out to me, but as she did, a contraction began, and she screamed. Her hand dropped to the edge of the bed, and she squeezed. "It's coming! It's coming! I can feel it! Help me!" she cried out.

There was such fear in her voice. I couldn't understand why. I can identify with fear. I have lived with it my entire life, but I have never known a pain so great that it made me afraid. My life before my first death was relatively pain-free, and after my resurrection, the pain-causing injuries had always healed themselves before the shock of being injured wore off. I have known mental anguish, yes, but never physical pain, at least to the extent Elizabeth felt.

I pulled a chair up beside the bed and sat down next to her. She grasped my hand and squeezed. She squeezed so hard her fingernails pierced my skin and drew blood in a small line across the back of my hand.

Where was the doctor, I wondered. It certainly shouldn't be so hard to find a doctor in Boston.

Elizabeth squeezed my hand as another contraction began. For a small woman, she had quite a powerful grip. Her pain must have been quite intense to lend her so much strength.

The woman dabbed at Elizabeth's forehead with the damp washcloth.

Elizabeth smiled up at me and said, "I'm sorry I'm hurting you."

"Quite understandable under the circumstances," I assured her, "but now I have some work to do." I turned to the woman and asked, "What's your name, ma'am?"

"Lorna Engels," she said.

I gently pulled Elizabeth's hand free from mine and moved my chair to the foot of the bed.

"I'm going to need a clean blanket, Mrs. Engels," I said.

"These blankets are clean. I washed them myself," she said indignantly.

I nodded my head. "Yes, I'm sure they are, ma'am. What I mean is I need a fresh blanket to wrap the baby in once it is born," I explained.

She didn't move. She just stared silently back at me. "You're going to deliver the baby?"

"This baby's not going to wait for a doctor or a midwife. Now please get me a blanket."

"Mrs. Engels nodded and left the room. I took a deep breath and prayed I knew enough about births to deliver a child.

I flipped back Elizabeth's damp skirt over her knees. The top of the baby's head had already appeared. I spread her legs open further to allow the baby more room to push free.

"You've got to push hard the next time you feel the pain, Elizabeth. I can see the baby's head, but you've got to push," I told her.

"I'll try, but...agh-h-h!" she screamed as the contraction began.

"Push, Elizabeth! Push!" I yelled.

I wasn't sure she could hear me over her own screams, but more of the baby's head appeared. She had pushed. Good for her!

I reached down to help ease the baby out, and my hands started shaking. I took a deep breath and forced my hands to be still. I reached between Elizabeth's legs and turned the baby perpendicular to the floor.

"Push, Elizabeth! Just a little bit more and it will all be over," I urged her.

"I looked over her legs at her, and she tried to smile. Another contraction began, and her smile turned into an expression of agony.

"Push, Elizabeth!" I told her.

The baby's shoulders appeared. I gently grabbed him by the shoulders and pulled him free of his mother. With my boot knife, I cut the umbilical cord and tied it off. I held the baby upside down so that the fluid in his lungs would drain. He hiccupped a cough, then he began to cry.

"It's a boy, Elizabeth," I told her, with just a little bit of pride.

Mrs. Engels handed me a clean blanket. I hadn't even noticed her coming back into the room. My entire concentration had been focused on Elizabeth and the baby. I wiped the baby off with a corner of the blanket. Then I wrapped the newborn in the blanket and handed him to his mother. Elizabeth reached out with shaky arms to take hold of him.

She brought him up close to her face so that she could see him. His cries had diminished to whimpers. Elizabeth smiled at him, then looked up at me. "Thank you," she said in a voice hoarse from screaming.

"What are you going to name him?" I asked her.

"I don't know. What are we going to call him, David?" Elizabeth said.

Had she called me David? I thought she might be delirious. I had enough sense to look behind me before I said anything, though. David was leaning against the side wall looking at his son. I wondered how long he had been there and how much he had seen.

"Edgar," he said.

13

January 20. 2016

"Edgar Allan Poe," Tim whispered.

Alexander sat down in his rocking chair, leaned back, and closed his eyes. The edges of his mouth curled into a smile as he remembered the event.

"No, not Allan," he said. "That came later. At the time, he was simply Edgar Poe. A baby delivered by the forever man, who could have been a character out of one of Edgar's future stories. In fact, his experiences with me were the basis for some of the ideas he used."

"Which stories?" Tim asked quickly.

Alexander opened his eyes and leaned forward. "You can't guess?"

"A lot of Edgar's stories involved very unique characters, but I don't remember any immortals."

"Though he never actually told me so, I have always assumed 'Ligeia,' which dealt with death and reincarnation, was based on information I gave him. I also think he patterned the character in 'The Masque of Red Death' after me."

Tim remembered the story as one where Death was the uninvited guest at a party thrown by a king. The king had sealed himself and his friends in his castle to escape the Red Death that was killing people throughout the land. Death couldn't be escaped, though. It appeared as another costumed partier, but when it came to close to a person, the person would die from the Red Death.

From only his nearness.

Just like...

"Then Edgar Poe feared you?" Tim asked.

Alexander shrugged and stood up. "At times, but at the time of his birth, he only saw me as his deliverer. I should have left Boston after he was born, but I couldn't bring myself to do it. It didn't matter to me that my presence might make things difficult between Elizabeth and David again. I only knew the complete joy I felt at the time, and I wanted it to continue. Can you understand how I felt,

Timothy?"

Tim noted Alexander's use of his first name, but he said nothing about it. He only shook his head.

"All my life I have caused death. Not just to strangers, either. I have killed the ones I have loved dearly, also.

"But this!

"This was so different.

"In delivering Edgar, I brought a life into this world rather than removing it. Because I was there, Edgar was gently and lovingly brought into the world. What would have happened to him if I hadn't been at the house when I was? Could Mrs. Engels have delivered him? I don't know."

1809 A. D.

It was incredible, almost as if God had brought me to Elizabeth's home that night and at that moment simply for the purpose of delivering Edgar. Elizabeth had been having contractions all through the day, but she thought she still had time before the birth. I truly don't think David would have left her side if he had known the baby would come so soon. He had to go and perform his small part in the play, though. Without Elizabeth working, they needed every penny they could earn just to get by.

I left Elizabeth to the care of the doctor who arrived fifteen minutes after Edgar made his appearance in the world. I wanted to stay, to hold the baby, but Elizabeth and David did not appear willing to share their son with anyone.

On the walk home, I was happier than I had been in two centuries since I had spent those few wonderful years with Catherine. I even found myself humming as I walked. I had done something good! My selfish body hadn't destroyed another innocent life.

The next day I found my thoughts completely consumed by the baby I had delivered. I was so absorbed that when a student of mine asked a question on the rites of human sacrifice by the Mayans, I accidentally called him "Edgar." Questions continually formed in my mind and crowded out all my other thoughts. How was Elizabeth feeling? Was Edgar doing well? How had David reacted after seeing me deliver his second son?

Knowing I not educating my students, I left early and headed for the Poes' house to see baby Edgar. Instead of taking the long way down Center Street to Fourth Street, then out to Carver Street, I took a more-direct side road which connected directly with Carver Street about four blocks from the Poes.

As I stepped into a narrow alley that led from the building where my office was to the side street, I saw a man standing halfway along the length of the alley. He was a large man wearing multiple layers of shabby clothes that only added to his size. His cap was pulled down low on his head so that his eyes were hidden in shadows. He looked out of place in the alley. His clothes suggested he was the type of man who hung around the wharf taking on odd jobs. I thought he might be staring at me, but I couldn't be sure.

I continued forward and attempted to pass the stranger on his left. He stepped to his right and blocked me. I moved to my right to pass him on the opposite side, and he blocked me again.

I suddenly felt very uneasy walking alone in the alley with this stranger. It wasn't that I feared for my life. All sense of fear connected with my death and dying had long ago left me. I did fear for his life, though. I did not want to be responsible for killing another human just to continue my own life. Especially not so soon after having brought a new life into the world.

I backed away from the stranger a step and started to turn back the way I had come into the alley. I would take the long way to Carver Street if it meant avoiding a fight. I wasn't above swallowing my pride to avoid killing a man.

He grabbed me by the shoulder and spun me around to face him. "Where do you think you're going?" he whispered in a gravelly voice.

"I don't know you, sir," I told him. "You must have me mistaken with someone else. I don't want any trouble."

The stranger grabbed the front of my coat and pulled me close to him so that my face was only inches from his. I could smell his rancid breath.

"But you have trouble," he whispered, "and you have something I want."

"I couldn't possibly have anything you could want...no money, no valuables," I said to him.

"That's not what I've been told. I want them now!" He drew a knife from behind his back and poked it into the fleshy part of my chin. "And I do mean now," he added.

I didn't know what to do. If I told my attacker the truth, he wouldn't believe me. More than likely, he would try to kill me, then search my body for what he wanted. I didn't have it, whatever it was.

I tried to explain to him. "I don't know who told you I have these things you want, but they were wrong. I'm just a teacher at Harvard. I don't..."

"No!" he shouted.

He slammed me back against the stone wall of one of the buildings that bordered the alley. I hit the wall so hard that I thought my spine might have been broken. I almost collapsed onto the ground, but I managed to brace myself against the wall and keep my balance. My eyes watered from the pain.

My attacker moved closer to me again. I think he wanted to see if there was any fear in my eyes. "Give me what I want, or I'll kill you," he threatened.

I knew he would, too, or at least he would try. He had a cold look in his eyes that told me he placed little value on human life. I had seen the same look in many pairs of eyes in Siberia where survival was everyone's number-one priority above all else. I felt fear again. Not a fear of dying. I had no doubt he would die if he attempted to kill me. I feared the pain. Though I never actually felt physical pain to the extent Elizabeth had felt when she gave birth to Edgar, the anticipation of pain always caused me great anguish. In my case, shock and my body's regenerative ability always removed the pain before I ever felt it.

I knew that I couldn't give the man what he wanted so I gave him what he wasn't expecting. I straightened both of my arms like battering rams against his chest. He released me and staggered backward a few steps. Bolting for the entrance to the alley, I hoped that if I could reach the street, he wouldn't pursue me any further for fear of being seen.

Even before I had taken a half a dozen steps away from him, I felt his fingers entangle themselves in my hair. He yanked hard, pulling me back. My feet flew out from under me, and I fell hard onto the ground.

With his handful of hair, he pulled me to my feet and drove his knife into my side. The shock of feeling the knife in my side, of knowing he had actually carried out his threat overcame any fear I might have felt at the moment. I found myself hoping for the regeneration to begin.

Though I wasn't sure, I felt my wound wasn't fatal. It felt different than a fatal injury. There was no tingling. The rippling didn't begin. The wound might have had to heal naturally.

I dropped to my knees holding my side. I could feel the area around the wound throbbing as my blood ran between my fingers making them slick.

The stranger kept his grip on my hair, yanking it back, so I was staring at the afternoon sky between the buildings forming the alley.

He pressed the tip of his knife blade under my right ear just hard enough so that it would draw blood. I smelled the hot, metallic scent of my own blood on his knife.

"One more time, Professor. Where is it?" he asked.

I still had no idea what he was talking about. What did he want from me? I had already told him I didn't have what he wanted. Did he expect me to somehow materialize it out of thin air simply because he wanted it?

I tried to tell him. "I don't know what you mean. Please leave me alone."

He grunted his disgust and dug the knife deep into the side of my throat and drew it across to the other side of my throat. My protests came out as gurgling cries. My hands seemed floundered uselessly in the air.

He released his hold on my head and almost immediately began going through my pockets in search of whatever he thought I had. Because there was no connected muscle left in front of my neck to hold it upright, my head fell backward at an unnatural angle.

I knew it was the end for my attacker. The ripple left me with a surge; almost immediately it returned. When he stood up, his eyes widened as he stared at me with a look of horror. You might have thought I was some sort of monster, rather than the victim in the situation.

The edges of my wound tingled. I felt my flesh knitting itself together. As my flesh healed, my head was gradually pulled forward to its original upright position. After a minute, the regeneration had almost stopped, and I was staring at my attacker.

"A devil," he muttered. "You're a devil."

I would have denied his accusation, but my voice had not yet returned. I could only shake my head, but he took my silence as a confirmation of what he thought.

He backed away from me never taking his eyes from mine. I think he expected me to cast some sort of spell on him before he could leave. The spell, if you could call it that, had already been cast when he cut my throat.

I held out my hand beckoning him to wait. I wanted to know things that he could tell me. What did he think I had that he wanted bad enough that he was willing to kill me for it? More importantly, who told him I had what he wanted?

He continued to back away, and I attempted to speak to tell him to wait. My words came out as a gurgle, which he must have taken as some sort of curse. The color rushed from his face, and he turned and ran out of the alley.

He left me kneeling in a muddied pool of my own blood. Taking my handkerchief from my pocket, I wiped the remaining blood from my throat. From experience, I knew there would be no tell-tale scar on my neck or side, but my shirt was ruined, stained with my own blood. I turned the collar of my coat up and hoped no one would notice the blood stains.

The man had tried to kill me and had only succeeded in ending his own life. I knew his body would be found dead in the next few days, and no one would be able to say what had killed him.

But someone else who had had a hand in the man's death. Someone had told the man to seek me out. Someone had lied to the man about what I possessed so that he would attack me. That person would certainly be as responsible for the man's death as I. Who would have told him such a lie? And why? I didn't have any enemies that I knew of.

As I stood up, my legs shook slightly, and I swayed like a drunkard. Physically, I was fine, but the whole ordeal had left me emotionally shaken.

I laughed at myself. I was shaking from a fear of pain never realized. Meanwhile, Elizabeth had experienced real pain last night and could still smile afterward. I straightened myself up and smoothed down my hair.

Having no reason not to, I continued on to the Poe home. Mrs. Engels' seemed hesitant to let me inside. I think she glimpsed the bloody shirt beneath my coat and thought I would bring trouble into the house. She should have trusted her instincts, but instead, she let me in. I walked myself back to the bedroom while she went back to the kitchen to finish preparing the meal she was working on.

As I approached the bedroom, I saw the door was slightly ajar. I peeked inside before knocking. Elizabeth sat on the bed, cradling Edgar as he took milk from her breast. David was there, too. He sat on top of the blankets next to Elizabeth. His arm was around her as he watched his son.

What a beautiful child, I thought as I watched Edgar. I wondered how I could have brought such a beautiful life into the world without destroying it as I had done with so much else.

I watched the three of them for a few moments more. Then I turned away not wanting to intrude. They were together, and they were happy, which is how it should have been. They were a family, joined by common bonds, and I was only a stranger who had come in and disrupted those bonds.

I left the house and wandered through town. I was in no mood to return to the university and try to teach, but I also didn't want to be alone in my house, either. But, the wind was blowing in off the harbor making the day colder than most. I finally gave ground to the elements and returned home.

How empty the house seemed as I walked in. The sound of my footsteps on the floor echoed loudly. There were no greetings as I stepped through the doorway, only the echo.

I had intended to cook myself dinner, and maybe drink myself into oblivion. I didn't drink much, I still don't, but there are some times when I need that temporary escape from the world. After all, I've been in the world for nearly two millennia. I deserve to step out of it every once in a while.

As I walked past my study on the way to the kitchen, something caught my attention, and I stopped. A fire was burning in the fireplace. Someone had been in my house while I was gone. Then I noticed that my high-backed armchair was turned away from my desk so that it faced the fireplace.

Someone was sitting in that chair. I knew it without even seeing him.

I didn't know what to do so I stood at the entrance to the study waiting for some movement to give away his presence. Was this the man who had attacked me in the alley waiting to make another attempt? Or was it simply some frozen traveler seeking warmth from the January chill?

Then I heard three words which totally changed my outlook on my life. They told me I was not alone in my situation. I was not as unique as I had thought.

"Come in, Lazarus."

14

1809 A.D.

Hearing my true name after so many centuries numbed me. I almost didn't recognize it. That was how unfamiliar the name was to me. What's more, I recognized the voice that spoke, although it had been centuries since I had heard him speak. You tend not to forget the voice of someone who tried to kill you.

I moved into the den without even realizing I had started walking. I circled around the edge of the room staying close to the wall to keep as much distance between myself and the chair as possible. I knew who was sitting in there, but I didn't want it to be true. I kept telling myself that it was impossible. He was dead. He was dust on the ground as was everyone else from his time.

I saw his straight, triangular nose first as the side of the chair came into my view. Then I saw his jet-black hair, which was graying at the temples, and one of his piercing gray eyes that refused to look in my direction. The light from the fire alternately threw shadows and light across his face. If not for the fire, I might not have immediately recognized him. The fire imitated the effects the lightning had had on his face when Christ had died.

Matthew was alive! Maybe I hadn't imagined seeing him on the streets of Richmond the previous year or in Egypt seventeen-hundred years ago or in Bethany 1,800-years ago.

Matthew, I said. It came out as a whisper. I had wanted to speak in a voice that was even and unafraid, but it sounded like a child's frail voice.

He turned his head only slightly toward me and smiled. It wasn't the warm, open smile of reunited friends, but the knowing smile of someone who held the upper hand.

How long had he known I was alive? I thought of all the times I needed to share my experiences with someone, to talk about how my feelings, and I never had the slightest notion that he was alive.

"Hello, Lazarus," he said. "It's been a long time."

"Only ten months or so. That is not so long for us," I reminded

116

him. My voice sounded stronger, and I was pleased.

"You're speaking of the night I ran away from you in Richmond, of course," he said.

I nodded. "So it really was you."

Matthew smiled slyly. "Yes, it was. You were quite observant. I was following you that night. Normally, I wouldn't have been so careless, but you seemed so absorbed in your thoughts I thought it was safe to follow more closely."

"Why were you following me? How long have you known that I was alive?" I asked.

"I have always known you lived. It was logical. If I was still alive after being dead only a matter of two days, then you who were dead four days and resurrected must certainly be alive. I was following you because I wanted to talk with you."

"They why did you run from me when I called your name?" I asked.

Matthew shrugged. "Once the decision was forced upon me, I wasn't as sure I wanted to speak with you."

"Why?" I wanted to know.

"We are 1,800-years old, Lazarus. Much has changed in our lives. I didn't know how you would react to my presence."

"Especially since you tried to have me killed in Bethany and helped stone me in Avaris," I commented. "How long have you been following me?"

Matthew rubbed his chin with his hand. "Living in your shadow has not been my lifelong pursuit if that is what you are concerned with. I wanted to test your ability in Bethany, but your people would only talk, not act, against you."

His smile reminded me of a bad child grinning because he had gotten away with some prank.

Matthew continued speaking. "I went my own way from there and chanced to hear about you again while I was in Egypt. Later, I happened across you again in Spain, I followed you from there until you reached England. The next time, you were in Baltimore at the theater."

"And since Egypt, you chose not to reveal yourself to me until now. Why?" I asked.

"As I said, I wasn't sure how you would react to me. I had to make sure that you had experienced some of the similar things I had."

"What things would those be?" I asked.

He shifted his position in the chair and turned to face me.

"Murder," he said.

Murder. So I was not alone. Yes, I had committed murder. I had committed the second-greatest sin against the Lord. And now I knew I was not the only one who had had to endure the agony of continual killing simply to survive.

Matthew stood up and walked to the fireplace mantle. He was very careful to stand off to the side of the hearth where the flames could not reach out to touch him. He stared at the landscape painting hanging above the mantle, then stooped slightly to read the artist's signature. It was a lesser-known work by Benjamin West.

"I see you have been...surviving," he said.

He put such an emphasis on the word, *surviving*, that I felt guilty I had been.

"I'm a teacher," I told him.

Matthew chuckled. "A teacher? How fitting. And I suppose you teach history? It's almost comical. You're not teaching. You're simply telling about what you've seen through the centuries, Professor Reynolds."

Professor Reynolds. He already knew I was a teacher. He even knew the name I was using now. He knew much more about me than I did about him.

"What name are you living under now?" I asked.

Matthew waved his hand in the air. "Names are not important. I've had too many of them to remember. Power. Wealth. Those are the important things in life."

It seemed Matthew had already achieved a certain degree of wealth. He wore a red-velvet coat over a satin shirt. His pants were black velvet, and his stockings were made of silk. It was not the outfit of a poor man.

I looked at my own clothes. I still had my fancier outfits that I had bought when I first came down from the mountains, but they were looking slightly shabby now. Most of my clothes were made of broadcloth except for my wool shirts.

"Can I get you something to eat or drink?" I offered Matthew.

He glanced at the bottles of liquor I had sitting on a small table off to the side of the room. "May I?" he said.

I nodded, and he walked over to the table. He picked up each bottle, uncorked it, and smelled it. I had an assortment of rum, sherry, and wine. He smelled one bottle and started to cough. He held the bottle toward the fire.

"What is this?" he asked.

"Blackberry wine," I told him.

"More blackberry than wine, I would venture. You should shoot the man who sold it to you."

"I made it myself," I said.

During my time in the mountains, I had experimented with crushing and fermenting various fruits. Even though none of the variations were particularly well-made, I had developed a taste for the blackberry wine and continued to make my own in my free time.

Matthew looked at me as if he were seeing me for the first time. Finally, he said, "I guess that explains the pulp and seeds I can see in the juice."

He poured himself a small glass and sipped it. He started to cough, but he still managed to swallow the mouthful.

"I'll stick to an excellent chardonnay," he said as he put the glass down. "I guess I will skip the drink. Besides, I'm not here for a social call to talk over old times. I'm here for business."

He sat back down in my armchair and directed me to another chair as if it were his den we were in. Rather than taking control of the situation right there, as I should have, I sat where he directed me. I think I was so delighted to have the company of someone who understood what I was going through, I would have done anything he asked. Well, almost anything.

"Business?" I said. "What sort of business could you have with me?"

Matthew smiled that smug smile that I quickly grew to hate. "While you have been eking out a living, I have been making my fortune. Through the centuries, I have been a baron, a mason, a highwayman, a knight, a mercenary, and to certain ignorant tribes, a god."

A god, I thought. How could he equate himself with the Lord? We were closer to Satan in our present states than the Lord.

He continued speaking. "I made as much money as I could in each of my ventures, then took the money and reinvested it in another venture. I had the patience to wait for the right opportunities. I had all the time in the world!" Matthew laughed at his own joke. I remained silent but smiled to be polite. "Now I am an importer. Up to a few years ago, while this infant country was at war, I was called a smuggler."

"I'm sorry, Matthew," I said. "I have little or no knowledge about the professions you've mentioned, even importing. I don't see how I could be of much use to you."

Actually, I didn't want to work with Matthew. Someone who worked only in what he could make money at, even when it was unethical, was not someone I wanted to have as a partner. It surprised me he would even want a partner considering how proud he sounded when he told me some people worshiped him as a god.

"You're foolish, Lazarus," Matthew said raising his voice a little. "We have the time to become anything we want. That is why I am rich. I have patience. I can outwait anyone. I can go almost anywhere, do almost anything without the fears that bind mortals."

"We are also mortals, not gods," I reminded him.

He laughed. "No, we are not mortals. We are the bastard sons of mortality and immortality. Eventually, we will die, but before that, we will live through hundreds of human lifetimes."

"So what business do you want to enter now?" I asked.

He waved his hands in circles in the air. "It doesn't matter. We could be the world's greatest thieves if we wanted."

"Matthew," I corrected him.

He gave me an angry look then shook his head. "I'm just saying with our ability we can be the greatest at anything we choose to do."

"Why me?" I asked him. "Why do you want to work with me? I don't share your passion for wealth and power."

"I have seen what my own efforts can do. How rich they have made me. I'm not satisfied with that. However, if the two of us combine our efforts, nothing could stop us. We could become the richest and most-powerful men in the world for the rest of this planet's life," he explained.

"What if I don't want to rule the world? What if I just want to teach people?" I asked.

He stood up from the armchair and approached me. "Then you're a fool! I tested you today. Did you know that? I tested you to see if you have the same gift I have."

I thought in silence for a moment until I realized what Matthew's test had been. "The man in the alley. You sent him to steal something from me, knowing I didn't have it." Matthew nodded. "Then you have killed him almost as surely as I have."

Matthew waved his hand off to the side. "He was human waste. I gave him a meal and a few coins, and he was ready to do anything I asked. But you, Lazarus, you pitied him even after he had attacked you. You did not defend yourself properly. You waited until there was no possible alternative but to use your gift. You use it like a miser. You waste it."

I was quick to anger. "A gift! You call what I did to that man a gift? You sent him to his death!" I yelled.

Matthew crossed his arms over his chest and frowned. "You are such a child, Lazarus. Don't tell me the killing disturbs you."

"Of course it disturbs me," I told him. "It's a sin."

Matthew sighed as he sat back down. "It is not a sin. We live because of an act of the son of God. How can the results of an act of a perfect man be a sin? How many times have you read in the Bible, and I do assume you read the Bible?" I nodded. "How many times have you read passages where God has ordered men to kill other men; where God has ordered nations to war; where God has killed a man because he spoke heresy? So if killing is a sin, wouldn't that mean God is contradicting himself?"

I didn't want to agree with him. I felt it was still wrong, but I didn't know how to argue with his logic.

"Lazarus," Matthew continued, "Can't you see we are only doing what our bodies were redesigned to do? It's like breathing or eating. Doing what we need to live is no more a sin than those things."

"Have you ever loved a woman?" I asked him.

"I've loved many women in my lifetime. What does it have to do with killing?" he wanted to know.

"Have you caused the death of any of those women?" I continued with my questions.

Matthew shrugged. "On occasion."

I moved next to the armchair and dropped to one knee so I could look Matthew in the eyes. "And how did you feel?"

He hesitated and couldn't meet my stare. Instead, he looked into the fire. "At first...at first, I felt something. Pity or regret. I don't know which. But I learned, Lazarus. I learned to live with it."

I stood up. "Did you learn or did your heart grow harder?"

"And I suppose idolizing a married woman is the safe way to live?" Matthew shouted as he stood up. "You are afraid of life. You are afraid to take part in what goes on around you. You're willing to waste the most valuable gift you've been given as an observer." Matthew shook his head in frustration. "This is getting nowhere. Do you want to be a part of life and work with me or not?"

"I don't think so," I answered. "I have enough to meet my needs, and I don't need to be in control of the world to be a part of life."

"So you choose to swoon over some mortal woman who will grow old and die long before you ever do," Matthew taunted.

"I know she will die eventually. That is part of her beauty. She is like a fragile flower that can only survive a few days after it is taken from the ground. I only wish I could die as well."

"You can die," Matthew said.

"How?" I asked quickly.

Smiling, Matthew shook his head. "That is something you need to find out on your own just as I did. Then, perhaps, your perfect view of the world will change. And know this, if you're not with me, you're against me. And all the people that have been against me are dead."

15

1809 A.D.

I watched from behind the curtains in my front window as Matthew left my house. He never once turned around to look back as he walked away, but I felt he knew I was watching him. He walked to the edge of the street and stopped. Then he held up his hand with a slight wave.

An enclosed carriage that was parked across the street a block from my house started rolling as the driver whipped the horses. The carriage was wooden with a leather roof and a small door on either side to allow the passenger to enter it. It was pulled by a pair of beautiful white mares. One horse should have been enough to pull the carriage unless the additional speed or strength of a second horse was needed in some way.

The carriage driver, a wiry black man, reined in the horses in front of Matthew. He looped the reins over the handbrake and then jumped from his seat. Matthew said something to him I couldn't hear. The black man looked over Matthew's shoulder at the window where I was standing and nodded. He grabbed a small stool from under his seat and put it on the ground to help Matthew into the carriage.

After he had closed the door behind Matthew, the driver glanced once more at the window and at me, then climbed on top of his seat and drove off. When the sound of the clopping hooves of Matthew's matched white mares had faded into the afternoon, I stepped back from the window.

I looked at the chair where Matthew had sat, and I imagined I could still feel his presence in the room. It was a thick, slightly metallic smell that I automatically associated with Matthew. I moved closer to the chair, wondering if the smell would grow stronger. It didn't.

What was I smelling?

I took off my overcoat and draped it over the chair I had been sitting in. I still had on my bloodied shirt. The red blood had dried into a muddy brown patch making the fabric stiff. On an impulse, I smelled the stain. It was the same smell, though much fainter than the one Matthew had left behind.

My throat filled with vomit, but I managed to keep it down. Had Matthew killed someone before he had come into my house? Had he let himself be attacked only to steal his attacker's life? I hadn't seen any blood stains on his expensive clothes. Why did I smell blood?

I rushed back to the window and raised it as quickly as I could. Sticking my head out into the ten-degree air, I gulped in deep breaths of air not tainted with the scent of blood.

A bearded man passing my house on the street looked up at me and said, "You're daft, mister. You'll catch your death of cold opening a window in weather like this."

I pulled back inside but left the window open. I wanted the scent of blood out of my house. I tore my shirt off and threw it into the fire. As the flames caught, and the shirt disappeared, I smiled.

My teeth started chattering, and I moved closer to the fire, trying to keep warm. I could still smell blood in the room, and I wasn't closing the window until it had vanished. My flesh started to pimple from the cold, but I waited. What did I have to worry about? If a man could cut my neck and not kill me, the cold of the winter wasn't going to hurt me.

My head began to spin, and I thought I might faint. I reached out a hand and braced myself against the mantle.

Matthew was alive!

Knowing that another person existed with the same condition I was tormented with sent a surge of relief through me. I was not alone in the world. Someone else shared my misery. However, knowing Matthew was alive also angered me. He had known of my existence since the beginning, but he had withheld his existence from me. And Matthew enjoyed the killing! He had even tried to kill me. Why? How could a man who had felt Christ's power and then seen him die, enjoy taking another man's life? We had both started from the same point but were now totally opposite each other.

He reveled in the power he felt with each kill. To control life as we could was a temptation that was hard to resist. Matthew and I could change the power structure in countries by killing kings and czars. We could go anywhere and do anything without fearing that we would lose our lives. We were invulnerable...to an extent.

I admit, I have skirted the edges of the abyss that Matthew had fallen into. I had been tempted at times to kill those who opposed me. I have wanted to dare someone to attack me so that they could see my power and run from me. I had always realized the consequences that would follow, though. I was not willing to live with those deaths on my soul.

When the smell of blood finally left the room, I took the Bible from my bookshelf and sat down next to the fire to read it. I tried to read the story of Job, but I found myself continually rereading the same passage. My thoughts drifted away, and I thought about Matthew. I refocused my attention on the passage, but it was no use. Eventually, the words ran together and blurred so that I couldn't read the passage at all.

If you're not with me, you're against me, and all the people that were against me are dead.

The words echoed through my mind. Matthew had threatened to kill me. He had even alluded to the fact that he knew how to kill me.

What could he do to harm me? I was an immortal, or as close to one as a person could get. How do you kill an immortal? Did Matthew know something I didn't about our condition? Had he learned how to die by living so close to the edge while I, who had been observing life, learned nothing?

I needed to know. Was there yet a way to escape this eternal misery I was experiencing? Could I die and return to my family and wives? I needed to know the answer one way or the other.

I put the Bible back on the shelf and left the house. St. Timothy's, a Roman Catholic church, was on Front Street. I didn't belong to any particular denomination because I had seen all of the different churches veer from the original teachings of Christ over the centuries. It didn't take an immortal to see this happening, either. That was the reason there were so many different denominations. A person in one faith would become dissatisfied with his particular church and break away with a group of other unhappy people to form a new church that was supposedly closer to God. Many of them even started out in the right direction, but they all seemed to eventually give into the weaknesses of man, and their faiths reflected it.

I stopped in front of the church and considered going inside. Would there be any remnants of God inside? The last time I had been in a church was when I married Catherine. That had been a Protestant church, though. Was this a place to start looking for answers I needed?

I passed through the vestibule, which was actually the base of the three-story bell tower. The church was made of stone and mortar. The stone clung to the cold and made the inside of the church even colder than the outside. Wondering if the priests had decided, like the

Buddhists, that a person must suffer to draw closer to God, I went inside.

St. Timothy's was a local church with the capacity to hold, perhaps, 300 worshippers. On this particular evening, only eight or nine people sat scattered among the pews.

I paused at the back of the chapel and allowed my eyes time to adjust to the dim light inside. Four large windows on either side of the chapel let in plenty of light during the day, but the sun had just set. The amount of light available for the windows to let in was very little.

I moved forward, up the center aisle between the two sections of pews. The flickering flames from the lanterns cast shadows over the small alcoves where statues of the saints stood. They jumped out at me like mythical imps. I thought I could see their heads turning as they watched me pass on my way to the front of the chapel. I knew it was only my eyes playing tricks with my brain, but considering what I had been through that day, you can see how it disturbed me.

Rows of candles were lit at the front of the church. Not being Catholic, their significance escaped me. The candles did provide better lighting for the front of the church, though. It was an ideal place for me to escape the shadow creatures that waited for me at the rear of the church.

I sat down in the first pew and marveled at the gold candlesticks mounted to the plaster walls. That a small church could have such wealth amazed me. A life-size statue of Christ on the cross stood at the very front of the church. It drew my attention away from the candlesticks. Staring at the statue, I realized any suffering I might be feeling was nothing compared to what Christ had felt with the weight of the world's sins blackening his soul.

I kneeled down on the floor and began to pray.

"Dear Lord, I try not to burden you with my complaints. You have done so much for me I know it is unfair to ask for more, but I need your help. I continually find myself doing that which I don't want to do. Is my life so important that others must give their own lives for mine to continue? And if my life does have an importance that warrants its continuance, what is its purpose? How can I perform my role in life if I don't know what that role is? And what about Matthew? You extended his life just as you did mine. Our present lives are so different from one another that one of us must be living the wrong way. Is it me? Should I enjoy the regeneration of my life as much as Matthew enjoys his regenerations? Please help me understand, Lord. Direct me. Point me in the right direction. Just don't leave me floating through life as a victim of the prevailing current."

I sat there afterward staring at the plaster statue of Christ on the cross. I must have rested there for a half an hour waiting for a response. I don't mean that I expected Christ to descend from Heaven to speak with me or to whisper the answers to life inside my head. I had hoped for a feeling, though. I hoped he would bless me with the insight about what to do. I thought that since he had been the cause of my predicament, he would be there to assist me through the tough moments.

I was wrong. I was on my own.

I was cut off from the world and alone. Elizabeth was happy with her family. My family and friends were long dead and dust in their graves. Matthew, someone I thought I could identify with, had let me down and disappointed me, and now my Lord had failed to respond to my prayers.

I leaned my head against the rail in front of me and cried. The tears dripped from my eyes, and I watched them make small spots on the stone floor.

"It's a heavy heart that has burst such as your's, son," someone said.

I looked up. I wiped my tears away with the back of my hand so that I might see who had spoken to me. Standing in front of me was a priest. His black robes nearly touched the floor. He had a large, round belly that stretched the fabric of his robe in the middle. His face was as equally as round as his stomach. Although he was fat, in his case, it wasn't a hindrance. The softness of his features gave him a friendly appearance that put me immediately at ease.

"What sort of sorrows could cause a man to cry like you are doing?" he asked, speaking slowly to control his Irish accent.

I looked around the church. As far as I could see, it was empty now except for the two of us.

"Father, I don't think you would believe me if I tried to explain my problem to you," I told him.

The priest sighed and shook his head. "It's that sort of trouble, is it?"

I nodded.

He sat down beside me and said, "I'm here to listen to you, no matter what you have to say. I've heard a lot through the curtain in the confessional. You'd be surprised at how readily people talk once they're inside there and the things they talk about." He rolled his eyes in disbelief.

I couldn't help but smile at his reaction. "I suppose that with the curtain closed, they feel like they're talking to themselves," I added.

The priest nodded silently. "I guess they do." Holding out his hand, he said "I'm Father Halloran, and I'd like to try and help you. Would you like to step inside the confessional?"

I chuckled, and Father Halloran looked confused.

"You make a good argument, Father, but I'm not Catholic," I told him.

Father Halloran arched his eyebrows. But the Lord has brought you into St. Timothy's, and St. Timothy's is my church. Let me help you. Compassion doesn't recognize a denomination."

I stared at him without saying a word. He just smiled and looked right back at me. I knew he was sincere in wanting to help me, but I didn't know if he would be able to help me. More importantly, I didn't know if he would believe me.

I decided to trust him with the truth because I needed to talk.

"Father, do you believe that John the Apostle is still alive today?" I asked.

He thought for a moment before he answered. "I honestly don't know. I suppose you are talking about the comment Jesus made near the end of the Gospel of St. John?" When I nodded, he said, "I believe there is at least one apostle still alive today, maybe more. But who they are, I can't say."

"There are others besides the apostles who haven't died," I said.

"Is this what is bothering you?" he asked.

"Yes. Lazarus of Bethany and the widow's son from Nain are also alive."

As Father Halloran shook his head, his flabby jowls shook slightly. "I don't believe there's any doctrinal support for that. Where did you hear it?"

"Someone once told me that a body can only be resurrected once. Is that true?" I continued.

Father Halloran nodded. "Yes, the body and the spirit will be reunited at the Second Coming of Jesus Christ. The apostles who are still alive will never know death because their bodies and spirits will never be separated."

"Since Lazarus and the widow's son were both resurrected before the Second Coming, wouldn't that mean that they wouldn't be able to ascend into Heaven until then?" I asked.

Father Halloran's forehead wrinkled into layers of fat. "As I said, I really don't know. And since there is no doctrinal evidence to support your theory about Lazarus, it really doesn't matter."

Father Halloran stood up. "I really don't see what this has to do with you. I thought you needed to talk to someone. I really..."

"Father, I am Lazarus of Bethany," I said.

Father Halloran's mouth hung open in a large "O". He stared at me, and I met his stare without flinching.

"You can see the point I'm trying to make is quite valid," I said.

"You can't be Lazarus," he insisted.

"Why not? You said there is no proof in the scriptures that he continued to live. There is also no proof in the scriptures that he died because I didn't," I pointed out.

Father Halloran shook his head, jiggling his jowls more fiercely. "Impossible. Impossible. His accent returned as he began to speak more rapidly.

"No, it's not, Father."

"Why did you come here?" he asked.

"I need answers, Father. You said you wanted to help me find the answers I need," I said.

"I can't help you find answers when you insist on lying to me." He laid his hands on his broad hips.

I stood up and grabbed him by the shoulders and shook him. The flesh of his shoulders felt like dough that I could squeeze between my fingers. "I am not lying to you! Shoot me! Drown me! Stab me! I have a knife in my boot if you want to use it." I reached down and pulled the knife out of my boot. I held it out for him to take. He backed away, shaking his head. "Take it. It doesn't matter what you do. I won't die, but someone else will. I don't want other people to have to die so that I might live. I want to die!" I let go of him and sat down in the pew. "I want to die," I said more softly.

Father Halloran took a tentative step toward me. He waited there, staring at me, unsure of what to do. He glanced at the statue of Christ, then he overcame his hesitation and put a hand on my shoulder.

"Calm yourself, my son. Suicide is never the answer," he whispered.

I shook my head and slid the knife back into my boot. "I don't want to kill myself. I just want to die as I should have all those centuries ago. I miss my family. I'm so alone, Father. Anyone I've ever been close to has died. Good men, better men than me, have died. Why do I go on living when I don't want to? I'm sure my life has a purpose. Jesus had to have had a reason to extend my life. What is it?"

Father Halloran didn't reply.

"I'm not crazy, Father. Really, I'm not," I told him.

Father Halloran sat down beside me and put his arm around my shoulders. It was the first time I had been touched so gently in years. It had been a long time since I had felt the warmth of another body near mine. His touch reminded me of the gentle way my father had of talking to my sisters and me when we were troubled. My body trembled, and I wondered if Father Halloran noticed it.

"I wish I could tell you the meaning of life, but I don't have the answer to that question. I suspect that it is different for every person. My role is to simply guide those people who come to me hopefully in the proper direction."

I grabbed his hand. "Then guide me, Father. What should I do?"

"What is your name, son?" he asked.

It sounded odd to hear him continually refer to me as son. I may have looked only thirty-five, but I was actually about 1,750-years older than him.

"For the past 200 years, it's been Alexander Reynolds."

Father Halloran nodded. "Alexander, I can't begin to point you in the right direction until I know from which direction you came."

We sat there quietly for a few minutes. When I looked over at him his eyes were closed, and his lips were moving slightly as he recited a prayer.

I looked up at the statue of Christ hanging from the cross. His head was tilted back, and his eyes turned to Heaven. *Did you feel as I feel when God forsook you at the end?* I wondered.

And so I told my story to Father Halloran much the same way I'm telling it to you now. I told him small pieces of my history trying to touch on the areas that I viewed as important. My father. Jesus. My wives. Delivering Edgar. I was surprised at how easily everything came out. I was also amazed that I remembered in so much detail incidents that were truly ancient history. As he listened, I could see skepticism in his expressions at various times, but he said nothing.

When I mentioned my encounters with Jesus, he leaned forward and listened carefully. I thought he would say something, but he didn't. He stared at the plaster statue when I described the crucifixion, and I watched him cry.

I spoke to him for over two hours. When I finished, I was exhausted, and my throat was dry.

"So you believe Matthew is the widow's son?" he asked when I had finished speaking. It was his first words in over two hours.

I noticed his use of the phrase "you believe." Meaning, he didn't. He still couldn't accept what I was telling him as the truth. The fact that he was still willing to sit next to me supported that.

"He is," I replied.

"He doesn't sound like a righteous man. Not at all like the sort of man our Lord would resurrect."

"Am I that sort of man?" I asked.

He hesitated. "I would say so."

"But I have killed," I reminded him.

"You mean the lives that your body has stolen?" He laid his hands on his round belly and thought. "I don't believe you really killed all the people you say you have, but for the sake of easing your sorrows, I'll go along with your story. You speak of your body as being separate from you. It is. You didn't kill those people. Your body did. It was not done as a conscious effort on your part. In a way, I think Matthew was right in one respect. If this "rippling," as you call it, happens as part of your bodily functions, you can't be held responsible for it."

"That doesn't relieve me from the pain of knowing that if I had been elsewhere that person would have lived," I told him.

"I suppose not, but then either would my absolution," he said.

Father Halloran was right. Any prayer he could have said would not have given me a dreamless sleep, and I knew that. Still, hearing him actually say it somehow made it final. It was a seal on my misery.

I stood up. "Thank you for hearing me out, Father. You were quite kind and understanding," I said.

He pulled on my arm trying to get me to sit back down. "Wait. There is still a lot we need to talk about. You have some very deep problems."

"No, Father. It's time I left."

And I did.

That night a new face was added to my dreams. Matthew's. I saw him standing before multitudes of people. He was wearing a white robe and holding a golden scepter as the people kneeled down and prayed to him.

Two men, supporting a woman between them, approached Matthew. They set the woman on the ground in front of Matthew. The woman said nothing. She sat and stared at Matthew.

Matthew raised his scepter above his head with both hands. He tilted the pointed end toward himself. With a swift stroke, he plunged the scepter into his stomach and pulled it free. Again, he held the scepter above his head so that all of the people praying to him could see his blood dripping from the end.

He pointed to the gaping black hole in his white robe. Even as he pointed it out to his followers, the blood flow stopped, and the wound healed itself.

Matthew looked down at the woman in front of him. Nothing was left of her but a withered husk of a woman who had had her life force drained from her. Matthew grabbed her face between his hands and kissed her on the lips. Then he crushed her head into powder.

I woke up screaming, "No, Matthew! No!"

I had tossed my blanket and top sheet onto the floor. The room temperature was barely above freezing, but I was sweating as if I were lying in the summer sun. I sat on my bed shaking from fear, not cold.

Matthew wanted to be worshiped as a god. That was his ultimate goal. My dream might not have been a prophecy or a vision of the future, but the point it tried to make was accurate. Matthew thought he was a god, and he wanted to be worshiped as such.

After all, money was too easy for either I or Matthew to get. In my case, all I had to do was make a few small investments during one lifetime, then wait for them to accrue during another lifetime. Even a small investment with a small annual return would amount to a fortune after a hundred years. I'm sure Matthew did similar things, but he had moved onto killing and stealing to gain money.

Power was another thing Matthew craved. He enjoyed the taking of life as he saw fit. He enjoyed being in control of the situation. That is why he never revealed himself to me until he wanted me to know. If I was never aware of his presence, his control over the situation never changed. Something had prompted him to reveal himself to me, but he had to do it on his own terms, not mine. That is why he ran away from me that night in Richmond when I saw him.

His hunger for that power evolved into his need to be considered a god. He had taken considerable pride in telling me he was worshiped as a god by certain tribes. That feeling of ultimate power delighted him. After 1,800 years of extended life, of bold raids, of a growing base of authority and wealth, Matthew had come to think of himself as a god.

I knew he wouldn't be satisfied with just a few tribes worshipping him. Those tribes more than likely had many gods, and he became one in a long list of different gods.

No, Matthew wanted to be a solitary god. He wanted to be worshiped by people who worshiped only one god. He wanted to steal that god's worshippers and turn their attentions to him. He wanted to be the god of his people.

I climbed out of my bed and stoked the still-glowing embers in the fireplace. I fed the small fire another log and watched as the fire tasted it. Then I wiped the sweat off my hands and face as I began to feel the cold.

My assumptions stunned me. I had only talked to Matthew for fifteen minutes. Yet, the impressions he had left with me were so strong, I knew they were true. The dream had opened avenues of thought I hadn't considered earlier.

The question remained, however, why had Jesus resurrected an unrighteous man?

16

1809 A.D.

My office at Harvard was in Washington Hall, a cramped space no better than most professors have today. The next day I spent an hour between two of my classes in my office drafting three letters to wealthy men in Boston that I knew socially from various university-related meetings. I asked each of them if they knew of a wealthy man in the city who had arrived approximately nine months ago. I described Matthew by appearance and by the fact that he was particularly ambitious. I asked them to tell me the man's name and any current activities he might be involved in. I also asked for their discretion in the matter. I didn't want Matthew to know I was trying to uncover his identity.

After I addressed and sealed the envelopes, I walked down the hall to add them to a pile of university mail that was to be posted that day.

Walking back to my office, I saw a woman standing in front of my door. Though her back was toward me, I knew by her size and hair style it was Elizabeth. My pace quickened. She must have heard the click of my heels on the floor because she turned in my direction. When she saw me, she smiled that wonderful smile she had; warmth and friendliness flowed from it. The bundle in her arms squirmed. She had brought Edgar, too.

"Mr. Reynolds, I'm glad you're here. I thought that I might have missed you," she said as I approached.

I shook my head. "I'm glad you didn't. I was posting a few letters down the hall. How are you?"

"I'm still feeling weak, but I don't have a reason not to get back to the stage. I need to start working again. We need the money, especially now with the baby," she told me, glancing at the baby.

"How is Edgar?" I asked.

She tilted the blanket bundle so that I could see his tiny face. "He's fine. He looks like he will be a very happy baby. William was always so grouchy and crying all the time, but so far, Edgar has been

134

very quiet. He's been very little trouble at all."

"You're not going to send Edgar to Baltimore to be raised by David's parents, are you?" The thought of the one good thing my life has ever allowed me to do being sent away scared me. I didn't want Edgar to be taken from my life forever.

Elizabeth clutched the bundle tighter. "Of course not!" She hesitated. "Well, we don't plan to send him away. Mrs. Engels said she would watch Edgar at night when David and I are working. She's such a wonderful woman. She doesn't have any children of her own, and she really wants to help us take care of Edgar."

I opened the door to my office and motioned her to go in. "Let's go inside, shall we? I have an extra chair you can sit down on and rest a bit."

I moved a pile of graded reports from the wooden chair to my already full desk. Elizabeth sat down and rested Edgar in her lap. She smiled at her son, then opened the blanket somewhat since my office was quite warm.

"I just wanted to thank you for all you did the other night," she said once I had sat down. "I don't think Mrs. Engels would have been able to deliver the baby on her own, and the doctor obviously wouldn't have gotten there in time."

I shrugged off the compliment. "I did what I could. Thankfully, it was enough. I've never delivered a baby before."

She seemed surprised. "What you did was a lot, and I wanted you to know that I appreciate you being there and taking charge. I thought from the way you handled everything that you might have been a doctor at one time."

I shook my head. "I've just seen a lot of births, and I worked from my memory of what the real doctors and midwives do," I explained.

"Oh." She looked like she wanted to say something else, but she didn't.

"I'm just glad everything went well and that both you and Edgar are fine," I said.

Her smile returned.

Then she dropped her eyes away from mine. "David and I don't have the money to pay you..."

I held up my hand. "I'm not asking for any payment."

"I know." Her face was red with embarrassment. "But David feels we owe you for your service. I know you like the theater, so I made arrangements for you to have a box seat at the Federal Street Theater whenever our performing company is in Boston."

"That's very kind of you. Thank you." I accepted in order to try and ease her obvious embarrassment at not being able to offer me money.

She glanced up at me, then back at the baby. "I'd also like to invite you to the house for dinner today."

"I thought you had gone back to acting?" I said.

"I have. Dinner will be at three o'clock. That will give me time to get home and prepare it after rehearsal."

I nodded eagerly. "Thank you again. May I request one small thing, though?" I asked.

Elizabeth looked up. "Certainly."

"May I hold Edgar for a while?" I asked.

She smiled a mother's proud smile. "Of course."

I took the small boy gently into my arms. His dark eyes were wide open and quite large. He seemed to be staring at an unknown point behind my head. I touched his small, button nose, and he shook his head. He raised his little arms free from the blanket. I put my finger near his hand so he could grab it. His skin was so smooth and soft compared to my dry, callused hands.

"He's beautiful, Elizabeth. Just like his mother," I told her.

Elizabeth blushed. "Thank you." She stood up. "I've enjoyed talking with you, Mr. Reynolds."

"Alexander, please," I insisted.

She nodded. "I've enjoyed talking with you, Alexander, but I must be going. I'll be expected at rehearsal today."

I stood up and handed Edgar back to her. "Please come again. I would like to talk with you some more."

"I think I would like that," she said.

I held the door open for her as she left, and I watched her walk down the hall. As she turned a corner, she saw me watching and waved. I waved back and went inside my office.

Dinner that afternoon was enjoyable but tense at times. Elizabeth cooked a duck with peas and carrots on the side. She also served fresh-baked rolls. I brought a bottle of mild wine hoping David wouldn't be able to get drunk on it.

Conversation at the dinner table was minimal. The moment David saw me at the front door, he was quiet. I don't think he had known Elizabeth had invited me to dinner. I'm sure if he had, he would have made her cancel it.

Elizabeth had on an attractive calico dress. I hadn't noticed earlier at my office because she had kept her coat on, but she appeared to have returned to her normal size. It was hard to imagine she had been nine-months pregnant only a few days earlier.

All through dinner, David kept glancing at me from across the table. I tried to ignore him and concentrate on Elizabeth's questions.

"So Alexander, you must be quite a fan of the theater?" Elizabeth asked at one point.

I took a sip of my wine and saw David glowering at me from across the table. I nodded my response to Elizabeth's question and said, "I love the theater. My joy at watching an excellently produced play could only be surpassed if I had the skill to be an actor.

"Who is your favorite playwright?" she asked.

"Shakespeare. His writing is poetic as well as tragic. Such a duality is hard to accomplish, but he not only accomplished it, but mastered it. In fact, the first play I saw you in was *Romeo and Juliet*. I saw you play Juliet in both Baltimore and Richmond. You were masterful."

Elizabeth smiled. "I remember that play. David almost got the part of Romeo, but Louis gave it John Payne. Do you remember that David?"

I looked at David, and he was blushing with embarrassment. I wondered if he was remembering our conversation about John Payne that had led him to offer his wife to me.

"I remember," he said curtly.

Elizabeth stared at him. I think she expected him to say more. Instead, the blush faded from his cheeks, and he refilled his wine glass.

"Well, can't remember when I've enjoyed a meal more. Do you always cook such delicious meals, Elizabeth?" I asked.

Elizabeth turned away from David and said, "No." She hesitated. "We can't always afford it."

I cursed myself for bringing up another sensitive area. I had already learned that talking about William upset her. Now I could add her financial situation to the growing list.

Just before dessert, Edgar began crying. He was lying in a small crib in one corner the kitchen with the rest of us because it was the warmest room in the house. The cooking fires had been burning nearly all day. Elizabeth picked up the baby and held him in her arms as she whispered to him in his small ear.

"Can't you shut him up?" David snapped.

"I think he's hungry," Elizabeth told him.

"Then feed him."

After she had left the kitchen, David turned to me. "Why did you come here tonight?"

"It was your idea," I answered.

"The hell it was!"

"Didn't you tell Elizabeth to offer this dinner to me as part of my payment for delivering your son?" I asked.

David laughed. "I told her you would <u>want</u> money for delivering Edgar, not that we should offer you any."

"I didn't want any money," I said.

"No, you want my wife," he said, stabbing his fork into a piece of duck in the center of the table and lifting it over to his plate.

I leaned back in my chair and crossed my arms over my chest. "You of all people should know I don't. You've already offered her to me, and I turned you down. I almost beat the life out of you for that, too."

David's face blushed red with embarrassment.

"I was drunk," he said weakly.

"You get drunk quite often. You should watch what you say. Next time, someone may say 'yes' to your offer."

Elizabeth came back in with Edgar, and David quieted down. He still continued glaring at me, though. I stood up and thanked Elizabeth for the meal. She tried to get me to stay for the pie she had made, but I refused. I said I still had many research reports to read. Since she had seen my office earlier, she knew I had a lot of paperwork and dropped the subject.

As I passed by an open alleyway on my way home, I thought I heard someone fall into step behind me. Was Matthew following me again? I turned around, but there was no one there. I stood still and waited a few minutes. No one approached me. I was alone on the street. I laughed at myself for being so foolish and resumed my walk.

I wondered where Matthew was and what he was doing. I was sure that he had some sort of grand plan in mind that he wanted to set in motion in the near future. That was the only reason I could think of to explain why he had chosen to reveal himself to me after eighteen-hundred years. He wanted to gauge my personality to see if I would help or hinder his plan. Now that he had met me, what would he do? He must have surely realized I would not help him.

I soon discovered I wasn't the only one who was thinking of Matthew. When I reached my house, Father Halloran was pacing back and forth in front of my front door trying to keep warm. He looked like a large, black steam engine as each breath he exhaled became visible in the cold night air.

I didn't want to talk to him. I had other things to worry about. I had made a mistake in confiding in him the previous night. Now he would watch me looking for other signs that told him I was crazy. He could cause me to lose my position at Harvard if he told the president what I had told him in the church.

"We must talk, Alexander," he said as soon as he recognized me.

I shook my head and headed for the door. "I appreciate you coming, Father. I'm really sorry for what I said yesterday at the church. I've been grading so many reports these past few days, I suppose I got carried away and thought I was part of history," I lied. "How did you even know where I lived."

"I asked some of my parishioners about a man who looked like you. You may live a life of solitude, Alexander, but you are not invisible."

Father Halloran grabbed my arm and pulled me back to him. His strength surprised me. I had assumed there was little strength in his softness.

"You weren't tired when you spoke to me, Alexander. You were upset, but you weren't imagining things." I was silent. "If you won't talk to me, at least let me talk to you. Please."

There was a desperate look in his face that even the dark shadows and the softness of his features couldn't hide.

"Come inside, then. Let's get some tea into you, and a fire burning. You must be freezing," I conceded.

Father Halloran nodded his agreement and followed me inside. He gratefully accepted the steaming mug of tea I prepared and drank it down quickly. As he drank, he stared over the top of his mug at me.

"I don't mind telling you, you've been in my thoughts and my prayers all day," he said to me.

"Why?" I asked.

"Your story that you told me last night was quite convincing, but to accept that you are the Lazarus of the Bible would mean that I would have to accept that horrid man you described as the widow's son from Nain. Why would Christ have resurrected an unholy man?"

"I haven't been to church myself in quite some time, Father," I said.

Father Halloran set down his empty mug and shook his head. "I don't mean unholy as in not attending church. I mean unholy as in basic personality. You regret the deaths your body has caused. You have even tried to avoid causing them. This other man...Matthew enjoys the killing like a common street thug. That is unholy."

"Maybe he was different when Christ resurrected him." I don't know why I was trying to find excuses for Matthew's behavior. I think I was afraid that whatever had caused him to become too bitter and unrighteous was an effect of his resurrection rather than his personality. If so, it might still affect me. After all, I had already begun to feel bitter about my extended life. How far away was I from taking out my frustration on innocent people?

"I am sure he must have been. So what happened? Why did a resurrection, which had such a profound effect on you, have the opposite effect on him?" Father Halloran asked.

A silence fell between us. Neither one knew how to answer the question. I waited for him to venture a guess at what had changed Matthew. Then I saw him staring at me waiting for me to voice a theory.

"I don't know," I said, shaking my head. "I didn't even know he was alive until I found him in my house last night."

Father Halloran stood up and began pacing the room. He held his hands clasped behind his back as he walked. His stomach bounced up and down slightly with each step. Sweat beaded on his forehead, and his breaths came faster.

"There must have been something," he insisted.

"Father, why are you so worried? You said you didn't really believe I was Lazarus yesterday."

"That was yesterday."

"So what changed your mind?" I asked.

Father Halloran stopped pacing. "I had a dream last night."

I stood up quickly and moved closer to him. "A dream. What sort of dream? Describe it to me."

"I usually place little faith in the prophecy of dreams. I can barely even remember them the next morning most of the time, but this dream was different. I can remember it as if I just saw it. There was a man in it who matched your description of Matthew. He had very dark black hair, hypnotic eyes, and a sharp nose. People were kneeling in front of him worshipping him like a god. Thousands of people. Maybe millions. There were just too many to count."

"Did the man in your dream stab himself in the stomach and let the wound heal by itself while everyone watched?" Father Halloran nodded. "Was there a girl sitting in front of him that withered away as he stole her life force?" I said quickly.

Father Halloran covered his mouth with his hand. His eyes were wide with fright. "Yes, that is what I dreamed." He lowered himself slowly into the armchair. After staring into the fire for a few moments, he finally turned away and looked at me. "You had the same dream, didn't you?"

I nodded. "It appears so."

"What does it mean?"

I shrugged. "Until you said what you just said, I thought it was a dream based on my personal impressions of Matthew."

"And now?"

"Now, I'm not so sure." Father Halloran looked scared. "I don't think it's literal, though," I told him.

"Who is Matthew now?"

"I don't know. I asked him, but he wouldn't say," I said.

"We need to know. Matthew can't be allowed to continue unstopped if there is a chance of something similar to this dream happening."

"I agree, but how would you stop him? We don't even know for certain that he needs to be stopped," I said.

"I was thinking about that also. The pools of light you saw around your body when you died, could they have been spirits?"

I rubbed my chin, reminding myself that I needed to shave, as I thought about his theory. "I suppose. I have considered that possibility before, but there was no way to prove it, one way or the other. Besides, if that were the case, what were they doing to my body?"

Father Halloran nodded vigorously. "My point exactly. What were they doing? If we assume the pools of light were spirits, then apparently the first spirit was able to enter your body and give it life, but the three spirits that attempted the same thing after the first spirit left only bounced off your body. Why?"

I thought for a moment then said, "Maybe a body can only be entered once by a spirit?"

Father Halloran shook his head. "That wouldn't make sense. If it was true, how could your soul have reentered your body, or how could the first spirit have entered your body since your soul was the first one to live in your body?"

I shrugged. "Then the first spirit did something to my body that kept the other three spirits out," I said.

"That is what I think," he said quickly.

"It's an interesting theory, but how does what happened to my body when I died relate to Matthew's behavior?" I asked.

"Suppose the first spirit that entered your body tried to enter Matthew's body when he died, but for some reason, it didn't get there fast enough. One of the other spirits that only bounced off your body was able to enter Matthew's body first." I nodded my agreement. "This spirit would have had possession of Matthew's body when Jesus recalled Matthew's spirit to his body. Once Matthew's spirit reentered his body, both spirits were trapped inside the body."

"You're assuming the spirit in Matthew is evil, then?"

"One of them, the stronger one is. Good spirits don't need to possess bodies. They are given them by the Lord."

"So what was the first spirit that protected my body by possessing it? Since it helped me, I doubt it was evil," I said.

"You're right. The first spirit you saw was probably an angel. It didn't attempt to stay in possession of your body. It only entered it for a few moments and then left, so it probably wasn't evil. Also, your sisters had already sent for Christ. He hadn't arrived yet, but he knew you were sick. He could have sent an angel to protect and prepare your body for his miracle."

An image popped into my mind, and I started laughing. Father Halloran looked at me like I truly was crazy.

"What's so funny?" he asked.

"I thought Catholics believed in angels with halos and wings. There's a statue of that sort of angel in your church."

Father Halloran looked indignant. He leaned close to me and said, "That is just someone's idea of what angels look like. We really don't know, though, since we've never seen one." He paused and pulled back. "Alexander, I'm being quite serious now. If there is a spirit possessing Matthew's body, it can't be exorcised. According to what you have told me, the body clings to the soul and will not release it. That means that a soul that should have never been given a body now has one. He can be very dangerous."

"He is very dangerous. He knows that he will live for many more years, and he can do anything he wants to do," I reminded him.

"Matthew must be stopped before he can complete whatever plan he has in mind. Certainly no good could ever come of it."

"How would you do that? He and I haven't lived for 1,800 years because we die easily," I said.

"Don't you know of a way?" Father Halloran asked.

I shook my head. "Matthew mentioned a way we could die, but he didn't say what it was. He could have only been trying to frighten me, though."

"We need to find out what that method is. We may need to use it," Father Halloran said.

17

1809 A.D.

Father Halloran and I met for dinner several times over the next few weeks. Occasionally, I would eat with him, Father D'Armand, and Father Davis at the rectory. Other times, when our conversation was more private, Father Halloran and I would eat at a busy tavern where we could go unnoticed. During these times, we compared our information in our search for Matthew's true identity.

I traced each of the leads my letters brought me, which wasn't very many. One letter referenced a banker named John Caldwell. He was exactly that, a banker with no resemblance to Matthew. The second letter mentioned Brian Hearns and Mark Tanner. Both of these men turned out to be the letter writer's opposition in a land-buying deal. I didn't even receive a reply to the third letter. Father Halloran tracked his leads from sources through his clerical grapevine without any luck, either. No one recognized Matthew by the description Father Halloran gave them.

I enjoyed my dinner talk with Father Halloran. It was hard not to like him. For the most part, he was a friendly and open man. I even attended Mass at St. Timothy's four different times to watch him work. He was very kind and patient with anyone who wanted to speak with him. The people attending the service were really interested in what he had to tell them about God and religion.

The only time he seemed impatient and tense was when we spoke about Matthew. I wasn't sure Father Halloran's theory about angels and evil spirits was correct. If he wasn't right, we could have been misjudging Matthew. Maybe I was wrong about him. Maybe Matthew hadn't threatened me. He could have meant he outwaited everyone he knew until they grew old and died. I was no theologian so I couldn't be sure, but Father Halloran was adamant that Matthew should be stopped. To hear such strong feelings coming from such a gentle man disturbed me. I wondered if he saw something in Matthew that I failed to see, or if I had painted too biased a picture of Matthew when I described him to Father Halloran. I wanted to watch

Matthew until his motives could be determined. Then I would make my decision.

As long as we couldn't find Matthew, the decision as to what to do about him could be put off.

Also, during those weeks, I was at the theater nearly every night. I used the free tickets the Poes, or rather Elizabeth had offered me for delivering Edgar. I even took Father Halloran along with me once and introduced him to Elizabeth after the performance. He thoroughly enjoyed the play, and I saw what he was like when he wasn't on a witch hunt, a gentleman just as quick to laugh as to cry.

Elizabeth easily slipped back into her role as Cordelia and was once again the favorite actress of the Bostonians. David played the part of Gloucester. The part of Edmund went to John Payne. I'm sure that the situation continued to fuel David's drinking.

I had dinner with Elizabeth on two occasions. David was conspicuously absent from both. I wondered if it was Elizabeth's planning or David's drinking that contributed to his absence. I never asked about it, though. I enjoyed the time with Elizabeth too much to chance spoiling it. We talked about the places we had traveled. She told me about Philadelphia, New York, and Charleston, and I told her about Jerusalem, Paris, and London.

She particularly liked hearing about England. Although she had been born there, she remembered almost nothing about the country. She and her mother had come to America when Elizabeth was just a girl.

"Have you ever been married, Alexander?" she asked me once while we were eating dinner.

It was an inevitable question. Somehow, I knew Elizabeth would ask it eventually, and I had gone to great lengths to avoid bringing my romantic life into our conversations. It was a too hard to talk about. If I said "yes," she would surely want to know the details of my past loves. How could I explain to her how I had had ten wives already when I only appeared to be thirty-years old? That would have shocked her. She would have thought I was lying, or worse yet, crazy. I didn't want to lie about my wives either. By denying their existence, I would have been betraying them.

"Yes," I answered.

As I had guessed, she wanted more details. "What happened to her, if I may ask?"

"She died when a horse she was riding threw her," I lied. I couldn't tell her I had taken Catherine's life, so I told her how I had died during my marriage to Catherine. I hoped Catherine would forgive the betrayal of her memory. I also hoped revealing one of my wives to Elizabeth would be enough, and she wouldn't ask if I had had any other wives.

"I'm sorry," Elizabeth said, her voice filled with sorrow that I knew was sincere.

"So am I. We only had nine years together."

"My first husband and I only had three years," she said.

I had been getting ready to take a bite of applesauce, but my hand stopped midway to my mouth. "*Your* first husband?" I asked.

Elizabeth nodded solemnly, then smiled at my reaction. "You seem so shocked, Alexander."

I ran a hand through my hair to brush it from my face. "It's just that you appear too young to be able to claim two husbands."

"I know, but it wasn't by choice. Charles died of consumption when I was eighteen. He was an actor, too. David actually joined the company to fill the spot Charles had left open, and I suppose, he filled the open spot in my heart, too."

"Two husbands," I said. "Why, I was..." I caught myself in time. I was about to say how old I was before I married my second wife, Callames. That would have opened the way to more questions than I wanted to answer.

"What were you going to say?" Elizabeth asked.

"I started to say I was only twenty-eight when my wife died, and that seemed a young age to me to lose a lifelong companion." I hated lying to her, but what else could I do?

I changed the subject to more pleasant topics as quickly as I could. I didn't like being reminded how I had killed the women in my life.

Two days after that dinner, I was awakened early in the morning by someone pounding on my front door. I glanced at the clock on the mantle above the fireplace in my room. It was five o'clock in the morning. I pulled on a pair of pants and went downstairs.

As soon as I opened the front door, Father Halloran rushed inside. He hurried toward the study, then stopped and faced me.

"His name is Peter Cromwell," he said without even greeting me.

He walked into the study and began making a fire in the fireplace. I followed him in still in a slight daze from being awakened so early.

"Who's name?" I asked.

He placed a handful of kindling under the logs. "The devil's." When he saw the confusion on my face, he added, "Matthew's name."

"How do you know?"

Father Halloran touched a match to the kindling and then backed away as it caught. When he was satisfied the flame wouldn't go out, he turned to me.

"A man came to me while I was hearing confessions yesterday. He was hysterical and begged me to cleanse him of his sins so God wouldn't take revenge on him. When I finally managed to calm him down, I asked him to explain his fears. He told me that he and a friend had gotten drunk three nights ago at O'Malley's Tavern on the wharf. I didn't believe it, but I think he told me that to help justify what he did later. Anyway, as he and his friend started home, thoroughly drunk, they saw a very well-dressed man walking completely alone. They could see his gold watch chain hanging against his vest, and hear coins rattling in his pockets. In Boston, especially at the waterfront, that's asking to be attacked. So these two men, in their drunkenness, decided to rob this man and teach him a lesson. They stopped the man on the street and pulled him into an alley. The confessor's friend pulled a knife on the man while the confessor began searching through the man's pockets. According to the confessor, the rich man suddenly jumped away from him and right onto the knife the other man was holding. Instead of screaming as a typical person would do, the rich man laughed. The two friends didn't care to wait around after that to see the rich man die, so they ran off.

"Two nights ago, the confessor's friend died in his sleep. The confessor was certain it was God's way of punishing the man for holding the knife that killed the rich man. The confessor was afraid God would kill him, too. He came to me seeking forgiveness."

"And you think the rich man they attacked was Matthew?" I asked.

He nodded vigorously and shook his hands in front of his face. "Yes. Yes. When I asked the confessor what the rich man looked like, he described Matthew to me the same way you did. Why else would the one attacker die in his sleep so soon after attacking the rich man? Both attackers were quite robust men."

The time to avoid making a decision about how to handle Matthew was slipping away fast, and I did not want to face it.

"Maybe the rich man was Matthew," I admitted. "But how do we find him?" I was hoping there wouldn't be a way to find him. I really didn't want to meet with him again. I was happy to live my life without seeing what I might become.

Father Halloran smiled proudly and tapped his chest. "I found him. Yesterday, I spent the day at the wharf searching for him. I started by asking people who lived around the area about a rich man that had been attacked, but no one knew anything. At least they didn't say anything to me. I went from there to O'Malley's, the tavern the confessor had gotten drunk in. I talked to the owner, a good Catholic, about Matthew saying I had heard a man along the waterfront had been attacked and required a blessing. When I described Matthew to him, he recognized him as someone he had seen along the waterfront. O'Malley remembered him because Matthew wasn't the usual sort of customer he had in his tavern. O'Malley had seen Matthew the night before, though, and he didn't look to be in need of a blessing. That was all he could tell me about Matthew. He had never heard his name or where he lived or worked.

"I was very disappointed by all of this. Luckily, the feeling didn't last long. As I left the tavern, I saw the carriage you said you had seen drive away from your house, complete with the matched white horses and the black driver. I was so excited at stumbling onto the carriage that I almost cheered out loud.

I walked over to the carriage. The black driver was brushing the horses when I walked up to him.

"Who owns this carriage?" I asked him.

He stared at me for a long time without saying anything. He just ran his eyes over me from head to toe only pausing to pay extra attention to my gold cross. I thought he might not understand English, and I would have to wait to see who owned the carriage myself.

"Mr. Peter Cromwell owns this rig," he said finally when I started to turn away from him.

I turned back. "Mr. Peter Cromwell must be a very wealthy man," I commented.

"The driver nodded. "Mr. Cromwell is a magic man."

"A magic man?"

"The driver continued to nod. "He can't be hurt. All the time I sees blood on his shirts and rips like he was cut real bad, but there's no cuts on his body. It's magic, I think."

"I described Matthew to the driver, and he nodded. "That's him. He'll be comin' back in a little while if you wants to talk with him."

"Where is he now?" I asked.

"The driver pointed to a large ship anchored in the harbor. "He's on that there boat talking with Mr. Arthur Gordon."

"I thanked him for his time and assured him I would get in touch with Mr. Cromwell at a later date, and I left after that."

Father Halloran stopped talking and waited for my response. From the grin on his face, I could tell he was proud of what he had accomplished.

"That was a foolish thing to do," I said. Father Halloran's smile fell. "What if the slave tells Matthew you were asking questions about him?"

"The slave doesn't know me, and I never told him my name. How would Matthew be able to find out?" Father Halloran replied.

"I don't know," I conceded, "but if anyone could find out, it would be Matthew. He found me again after centuries."

Father Halloran pulled a chair up next to me and sat down in it. "I think you're giving him too much power."

"Me!" I said. I pointed to Father Halloran. "You're the one who told me that Matthew is probably an evil spirit in a human body. You even called him the devil tonight."

Father Halloran put his hand on my arm. "I still believe that. Even though he is a spirit from Satan's dominion, he is still held to the restrictions being in a human body brings. What I found out yesterday is a great opening for us. We now know who Matthew is and what he is doing. That puts us on equal footing with him."

"What is he doing?" I asked.

Father Halloran buried his face in one hand and sighed. When he looked up, he said, "Do you never read the newspapers, Alexander? Arthur Gordon owns Atlantic Importers, an importing business which has twenty-eight ships making voyages all over the world. Didn't you say Matthew called himself an importer?" I nodded. "Can't you see that Matthew is trying to buy Atlantic Importers from Mr. Gordon? It would be an important investment on his part. Because he supplies such a large quantity of goods to the states, he could influence prices by choosing to sell or not. Atlantic Importers is also quite a profitable business for Mr. Gordon. Matthew would have to make him a sizeable offer to convince him to sell."

"I suppose that's possible. It's also legal, and there doesn't seem to be anything evil about wanting to make money," I said.

"But we can't let Matthew expand his power base. It will only make him that much harder to stop when he does reveal his ultimate plan." Father Halloran saw the doubtful expression on my face and added, "You know he has a plan. You had the dream yourself."

I had dreamed of Matthew. That was the problem. I hadn't been able to forget my dream, especially the expression on the woman's face as Matthew crushed it between his hands. I couldn't forget it, and I so desperately wanted to forget.

"How can we stop him?" I asked.

Father Halloran faltered. He didn't have the answer to that question, either. "We could tell Arthur Gordon who Peter Cromwell really is," he suggested.

I laughed a quick, hard laugh. "Arthur Gordon wouldn't believe my story any more than you did. The only reason you believe me is because you had the same dream I had about Matthew. Why are you so against him, Father? He may not be a righteous man, but Christ himself resurrected him. That must mean there is some good in him. Why do you hate him so much?"

"I believe Matthew is the Antichrist," Father Halloran said without meeting my gaze.

I wanted to laugh again, but I could see he was serious about what he had told me.

"If Matthew were the Antichrist, he would have been the Antichrist all along, even before the first resurrection. The true Antichrist is not supposed to come until before the Second Coming. Matthew's been alive since before the First Resurrection. Am I right?"

Father Halloran was silent as he stared at the yellow flames in the fireplace.

"You're right, but Matthew is still evil. You may wonder if he actually threatened you, but you can't doubt that he tried to kill you. If we let his wealth grow, his power will grow, too. It may get to the point where only God can stop him. We can't allow that, Alexander."

"No, I suppose not." I don't know why I felt so uneasy about facing Matthew, but I wanted to avoid a direct confrontation with him. I think I was afraid of what I might discover about myself if I confronted him.

"You are the only one who can stop him, you know. You are the only one he can't kill," Father Halloran said.

"That is only if he was lying about knowing a way for us to die," I replied.

"How could he know? The only way for him to know would be if one of you or someone like you had already died by that method. Since, as far as you know, you and he are the only ones living that Christ resurrected, how could he know how to kill you? You are both alive."

"I can't kill him, either, which means we may not be able to stop him. Perhaps, the best we could do would be to slow his progress."

Father Halloran's eyes widened, and he looked alarmed. "I'm

not asking you to kill him, Alexander. I am not that fanatical, though, I may sound it at sometimes. As a priest, I believe the right to decide life and death does not lie with my decision of good and evil, but with God's. I'm just saying we can't sit back and allow his evil to grow. It is our duty, mine because I am a priest, and yours because Christ blessed you with life, that we fight Matthew's evil."

I nodded my agreement without saying anything. I knew Father Halloran was right, but I couldn't stop being afraid.

"Think about what can possibly be done to prevent the purchase. I will do the same. Whatever we decide must be done no later than tomorrow night. Mr. Gordon's ship is scheduled to return to Charleston. Whatever dealings he has with Matthew will be completed before then."

"I'll come by the church after my classes today with my ideas," I answered.

Father Halloran put his hands on my shoulders. "God bless you, Alexander."

"I wish he would," I mumbled to myself.

After Father Halloran had left, I went back into the study. I already knew what I could do to prevent Matthew from purchasing Atlantic Importers. It would work, in theory, at least. One question nagged at me: Would preventing this purchase really stop Matthew, or would it only cause him to be more secretive? If he became more secretive, it would be impossible to stop him in the future.

I went back up to my bedroom to dress for the day. I opened my armoire to pick out a shirt, and I saw my good black coat.

I could pull it off, I told myself. I'd been living other people's lives for centuries, I could certainly do it for a few hours.

I took out the coat and brushed it off. It was still in excellent shape. Next, I took out my best ruffled white shirt, my red-velvet vest with gold trim, and red knee breeches. Finally, I chose my cleanest silk stockings and my new leather shoes.

I usually walked almost everywhere I went unless the distance was more than a few miles. I never quite trusted horses after being thrown by my horse in England. This day, I realized I would need a more impressive form of transportation than either my feet or a horse. I walked down to Marshall Street to the livery and hired a fancy carriage and driver for the day.

The driver took me to the wharf. Arthur Gordon's ship was docked in the harbor. It was the flagship of his fleet, a huge three-masted vessel with at least five decks that was capable of carrying large cargoes across the ocean.

I asked a seaman standing at the base of the gangplank to take me to Arthur Gordon. At first, he refused. I handed him a dollar, and he agreed readily enough.

Arthur Gordon's cabin was below the main deck at the very front of the ship. The ship's officers" quarters hugged the hull on either side of the ship toward the bow. Each cabin was scarcely more than six feet by ten feet in size. They looked more like jail cells than officers" quarters, but at least they had quarters. Most of the crew slept in hammocks they strung up on the main deck at night. There were no windows in the any of the cabins except in the doors. Even those weren't really windows. They were more like open holes covered with bars which added to the image that the cabins were jail cells.

I walked to the very front cabin and rapped on the door. Through the barred window, I saw a man sitting at a desk look up.

"Yes, who is it?" he asked.

"My name is Alexander Reynolds, sir. I'm here on behalf of Mr. Peter Cromwell," I said.

At the mention of Matthew's new name, the man stood up and opened the door. He was about fifty-five years old, but his face was very weathered, and he appeared older. He was one of the few men left who still preferred to wear powdered wigs. He was also clean shaven, so there was no way to tell what his natural hair color was.

"Come in, please," he said.

I stepped into a room that was scarcely bigger than the officers" quarters. The cabin was triangular in shape with no one wall being over fifteen feet in length. The bunk was built into the apex of the hull. A sea chest sat at the foot of the bed. Next to it, against the wall, was a small cabinet with a door that could be closed to keep the books, papers, and liquor bottles from falling out if the seas got too rough. On the opposite wall, there was an armoire and a small desk and chair. Unlike the other rooms surrounding it, this room had a porthole on each wall facing the outside.

"This is my traveling office," Arthur Gordon said as he saw me studying the cabin. "My home is in Charleston, but I find myself needing to travel to different ports to protect my interests and negotiate deals."

"I understand," I told him.

"Can I get you something to drink?" He started toward an array of bottles on one of the shelves in the cabinet.

"I held up my hand and hoped he didn't notice it shaking. "No, thank you, I only came to complete Mr. Cromwell's business."

Gordon's face brightened. "Then he agreed to my terms?"

I nodded. How much could I say without giving myself away? I needed to know what Arthur Gordon's conditions of sale were.

"I have been authorized to sign the contract in his place, and I will issue a bank draft for the discussed amount."

Gordon's smile broadened. The thought of all the money he was about to be handed blinded him to the fact that I was an imposter. He opened the top drawer of his desk and removed a small packet of papers wrapped in oilcloth.

I took the papers and moved closer to one of the portholes where there was more light to read by.

"Mr. Cromwell read them all yesterday," he said nervously. Was he beginning to suspect I was not working with Peter Cromwell?

I nodded, but I kept on reading. "I am only rechecking to make sure the negotiated points were written in and initialed."

According to the papers, Matthew, or rather Peter Cromwell, had agreed to purchase all twenty-eight ships, five warehouses, and 300,000 dollars of inventory from Atlantic Importers and Arthur Gordon. The packet also included a very detailed list of the inventory owned by Atlantic Importers. According to the contract, the company traded with France, Italy, Greece, Spain, Egypt, and India.

"I must say I am a little confused, Mr. Reynolds. I was expecting Mr. Cromwell himself to show up in another hour. This is quite a large investment. It should be handled personally by him," Gordon said.

My head snapped up. Another hour! Matthew was coming here in another hour. I couldn't let him catch me on the ship. I had to get off quickly!

"Mr. Cromwell trusts me implicitly," I told Gordon and hoped he didn't hear the falseness in my voice.

I took my bank book from my coat pocket. Alexander Gordon seemed prepared to say something, but the sight of my bank book shut him up. I laid the book down and wrote out the draft for the amount listed in the contract. I handed the slip of paper to him.

He read the bank draft and frowned. "Shouldn't Mr. Cromwell's signature be on this? After all, he is the one purchasing the business."

"My signature is accepted on bank drafts as long as it has been approved in advance by Mr. Cromwell. This draft has. There should be no problem, but if there is, have the bank contact Mr. Cromwell, and he will gladly sign the draft," I lied.

I knew there wouldn't be any trouble transferring the money to

Gordon's account because I had already drawn on the account to purchase my home in town. I had transferred half of the funds from the Bank of England to the City Bank of New York when I passed through New York City on my journey up the east coast. There was enough money in either account to easily cover the cost of Atlantic Importers.

Matthew had made a sound choice in attempting to buy the company. Atlantic Importers was a healthy company with contacts in a dozen countries. The profits earned didn't depend on one country's economy, and the company gave Matthew an extensive international network of contacts.

Arthur Gordon signed the ownership transfer papers, and I signed my name below his. I refolded the packet of papers and placed them in my coat.

I'll file the ownership papers with the Hall of Records here in Boston," I told Gordon.

"I can do that for you if you prefer," he offered.

I didn't want to leave the papers on the ship where Matthew could tear them up when he discovered he did not own an importing company.

I held up my hand and smiled. "No, no. I'll do it. You can retire to Charleston like a prince now."

"I look forward to it," he said and grinned himself.

I shook his hand, and he insisted on leading me back to the gangplank. My heart was beating so fast I thought Gordon would hear it as we walked. My blood pounded in my ears. I couldn't believe I had pulled it off.

At the gangplank, Gordon shook my hand once more. "I wish Mr. Cromwell were here, I'd like to thank him, too, but do tell him he's made an excellent deal."

"He knows that I'm sure," I said.

I walked down the gangplank to my waiting carriage. I was glad I had decided to rent the carriage instead of walking. What would Gordon have thought if he had seen Mr. Cromwell's assistant walking down the street? As I stepped into the carriage, I looked back at the ship. Arthur Gordon waved.

Inside the carriage, I collapsed onto the bench and sighed. Then I smiled to myself and patted my coat pocket.

Matthew's plans had hit a snag. Whether it was a permanent hindrance or not remained to be seen, but it was an obstacle in his path, nonetheless.

And as for me. I owned an importing company.

18

1809 A.D.

I had the driver take me straight from Arthur Gordon's ship, actually my ship, to St. Timothy's. After not finding Father Halloran in the chapel, I searched for him in the rectory.

"It's done, Father," I said when he opened the door to his room.

He stared at me blankly for a few moments until he realized what I was talking about. I could tell when he realized what I meant. His huge body, which filled the doorway, shook slightly and actually seemed to shrink.

"You mean Matthew? You stopped him? Really? How did you do it so quickly?" he asked.

I expected him to be excited, but his voice was weak and monotone. I saw no signs of excitement, only relief.

"I bought Atlantic Importers before Matthew could," I told him.

He took a step backward to allow space for me to enter the small room. "However did you manage that?"

"I have my own money, Father," I said.

"That much? Atlantic Importers must have cost a small fortune, and you are only a professor."

I nodded. "I have not always been a professor, though." I paused. "Arthur Gordon did make out quite well in the bargain, but I was in no place to argue with him over prices. He was expecting Matthew within the hour."

Father Halloran sat down on his bed. The thin mattress sagged beneath his weight.

He looked up at me. "Amazing. You've done it," he said.

"You sound disappointed," I said.

I was feeling exactly the opposite. Despite my initial hesitance and fear, I was now excited at the thought of stopping Matthew from increasing his wealth and power. It was my way of showing him that he should be careful of whom he considered his inferior.

Father Halloran shook his head slowly and reached out and patted my thigh. "I'm not, but I had hoped to participate."

"But you did," I assured him. "You gave me the information I needed to do what I had to do. I would not have done this without your support. You helped me realize what I had seen when I died and what probably happened to Matthew when he died."

He nodded slightly and attempted a half-hearted smile. "Thank you for saying that. What will happen now?"

I shrugged as I sat down in the chair by Father Halloran's small writing desk. I wondered if, with his size, he was able to sit in it. "I truly don't know. I do wish I could have used a false name with Arthur Gordon, but I still would have had to use my current name to sign my bank draft. He would have noticed the difference between the two names."

"What are you going to do with an importing business? Do you know how to run a business? You've taken on an enormous responsibility," Father Halloran asked me.

I rolled my eyes and threw up my hands. "I really haven't given it much thought. I came right here from the wharf. I suppose I will hire the best manager available, and let him run the business as he sees fit."

"You're going to continue teaching, then?" He seemed surprised that I would consider it.

"I don't see why not. I enjoy it," I replied.

He pushed himself slowly to his feet and put his arm around my shoulders. "You've done well, son. You should be proud of yourself."

"I'd feel a lot more at ease if I knew what Matthew was going to do now," I admitted. "I don't imagine he will treat this casually."

"I guess we won't know that until it happens."

"I guess so," I said.

For the rest of the day, I tried to continue as if nothing had changed. I returned to Harvard, taught my afternoon classes, and graded reports afterward. Things had changed, though. The balance between Matthew and myself had shifted. I now knew more than I had the day before. Matthew and I were equals. I had taken from him, and in doing so, added to my own knowledge.

I went to the theater, as usual, at six o'clock. Elizabeth gave a wonderful performance. I searched for David among the cast, but Louis Hatter was playing the role of Gloucester. I watched the play through different eyes that night. I could feel the excitement the players felt performing for a crowd. I had felt the same way playing out my role in front of Arthur Gordon. While they were concerned with whether the audience would appreciate their performance, I had worried about whether Arthur Gordon would believe me. It was a stressful position to be in, and I appreciated the performers all the more for putting their feelings in jeopardy every night.

After the performance, I went backstage. David was still nowhere to be seen so I felt it would be safe to talk with Elizabeth. She was nearly ready to leave when I saw her at the rear door.

When she saw me, she said, "Hello, Alexander. Did you enjoy tonight's performance?"

"As always, but I noticed David was missing. He's not ill, is he?" I asked.

She frowned as she tied her hat strings under her chin. "He is, but not in a way that you would think. He's gone off drinking somewhere again. He just can't stop. I thought he had finally quit right after you left Richmond last year. He didn't have a drink for at least a month, at least not that I noticed. Then one night he staggered into our tenement house at four in the morning. After that, he didn't even try to stop or even hide his drinking.

"I had hoped he would at least show up to walk me home tonight. He knows how much I hate walking through town by myself. Some of the neighborhoods I must walk through are not too safe at night. I guess it was just too much to expect from him," Elizabeth said.

I saw my chance and took it. "May I walk you home?" I offered.

She smiled demurely. "Thank you, Alexander. You are always the gentleman. I would like that very much. It really isn't wise for a woman to walk the streets alone."

"No, it isn't," I agreed, smiling.

I put on my topcoat, which I had been carrying, and held the back door open for Elizabeth. A breeze blew into the theater carrying with it a few flakes of snow. Elizabeth shivered and pulled her coat tighter around her shoulders.

As we walked down Federal Street, Elizabeth asked, "Alexander, have you ever thought of becoming an actor?"

The questioned surprised me especially after what I had done that afternoon. Becoming an actor? I was already an actor. My audience was the world as I acted my way through my different lives.

"You love to watch plays so much, you might make an excellent actor," she added.

I laughed when I realized she was serious. "I once tried to write a play because I enjoyed watching them so much. It was much harder than it looked, and I never completed it."

"Acting is not the same as writing," she said.

"Maybe not, but my playwriting experience taught me one thing, and that is I had no place in the theater except as a grateful spectator. Besides, I don't need another profession. I've found one I already enjoy."

"Teaching?" she asked.

I nodded. "Teaching."

"Are you a good teacher, Alexander?"

I thought about that question. Just how successful was I at communicating my thoughts and ideas to others? Did my students remember what I told them after they left my classroom?

"I suppose that depends on who you are talking to. Some students respond better than others."

Elizabeth sighed. "I wish I had more schooling. Sometimes, I think if I were only a little bit smarter, I would be able to make better decisions."

It was unusual to hear such a self-pitying remark come from Elizabeth. She was usually the cheerful one. Self-pity was my forte´.

"Perhaps, but then again, maybe not. In my life, I have seen two types of intelligence. There is school-taught intelligence, and there is common-sense intelligence. School-taught intelligence can be impressive, but it is common-sense intelligence that helps us make our decisions about life. I think you have a lot of common-sense intelligence," I told her.

She grinned. "Thank you, Alexander."

She touched my arm and applied just the slightest amount of pressure. Her touch, even one so light, sent a jolt through my body. My heart accelerated, and I felt dizzy.

We stopped at the house. "May I see Edgar?" I asked her at the door.

Elizabeth nodded. I followed her through the house to the bedroom. Edgar was asleep, but she bundled him up in his blanket and picked him up without waking him. I took him and held him close to my body, hoping my body heat would help to keep him warm in the chilly room. Such a small body. Such a frail life. But I had helped this life live. I had been the first person in the world to see him. Not even his mother had seen him before me. God had placed Edgar's life in my hands, and I had not killed him.

I smiled down at the small, sleeping face.

"Do you have any children, Alexander?" Elizabeth asked.

"I only wish I had, but I was not blessed in that regard," I told her.

"It's a shame. I think you would make a wonderful father. Of course, you're still a young man, I'm sure you'll have many children, once you find the right woman."

I didn't offer a comment. Talking about my sterility would have only led to subjects that I couldn't talk to Elizabeth about, no matter how much I would have wanted to do so.

I handed Edgar back to her and said goodnight. She thanked me for walking her home with a kiss on my cheek. I almost fainted! I went home that night a happy man. Not only had I stopped Matthew, but I had been kissed by Elizabeth!

I kept telling myself that I wasn't in love with her. We were simply friends with an interest in the theater. I knew I was lying, though, and it's a terrible liar who can't even convince himself of the lie. Originally, Elizabeth and I had only been friends, but my feelings had crossed over the line between friendship and love. I'm not sure when it happened. All I knew was that it had happened. I had denied the truth for so long, I couldn't say when the precise time I fell in love with Elizabeth was, but on the walk home that night, I finally admitted the truth to myself.

I was in love with Elizabeth Poe.

The trouble was, what could I do about it? Elizabeth was a married woman who was in love with her husband and her two sons. I wouldn't purposely try to split them up, especially for my own selfish reasons. So I was left with living with the pain. I thought I could endure it as long as she stayed in my life even if it was only as a friend, but what would I do when the acting company moved on to the next city?

Oddly enough, my cursed life was what allowed me to accept my circumstances so easily. It had taught me that nothing in my life would ever last. Even if I had been able to marry Elizabeth, how long would I have had with her? Twenty or thirty years? That was only a week in my life. I could live with being friends with her. Why should I change it? I was happy.

When I fell asleep that night, I dreamed about Elizabeth. I was holding her small body in my arms. I moved one hand from around her waist to stroke her cheek and brush a wisp of brown hair from her eyes. She smiled at me, and I kissed her.

I saw something completely different when I woke up.

I don't know what time it happened. I went to bed at ten o'clock, so it was sometime after that. I'm not sure what caused me to wake up. I think my senses were barraged at the same time. I smelled oil and attributed it to a leftover scent from a lantern that I had extinguished. I heard the "whoosh" as a flame caught, and I wondered why the fire in the fireplace still burned so strongly. Until I felt the heat on my face, I didn't know anything was wrong.

I opened my eyes, and I was blinded by the brightness of the room. Matthew was standing at the side of my bed, holding a burning torch. The yellow flame illuminated his face. His lips were drawn back in a dog-like snarl. At first, I thought I was having a nightmare, but then I realized I could feel the heat from the torch. This was real. Matthew was in my room!

I tried to move, but my movements seemed too slow to actually be called movement. His snarl turned into a smile. The fire reflected off his teeth giving them a luminescent glow. At the same time, his hand that was holding the torch dropped. His mouth opened wider, and he laughed.

I rolled from the bed taking the top blanket with me. My elbow hit the top of an exposed floor nail, but I barely noticed the sharp pain that shot through my arm. The nail snagged my night shirt and ripped it to the shoulder.

Behind me, the torch touched my mattress and turned it into an inferno. Matthew jumped back from the growing flames but held onto his torch.

What was he trying to do? Didn't he know he couldn't kill me?

But he had said there was a way.

Fire!

Death!

I saw the flames creeping up the side of my blanket. I flung it at Matthew before the flames reached my legs. He jumped out of the way, and the blanket landed on the floor beyond the bed.

Matthew laughed at me from the other side of the room. "Did you think you were stopping me or did you hope to hurt me by stealing my wealth?"

I was too busy searching for a way out of the room to bother answering him. I had backed myself up against the wall. I was about to make a dash for the door when Matthew moved around the bed, blocking my way.

The room brightened with the light from the burning bed. Flaming feathers from the burning mattress floated in the air like a thousand stars in the night. Some burned out before they touched the floor. Others went out as they hit the floor. A few continued to burn until small wisps of smoke started to rise from the wooden planks.

Matthew lunged forward and swung the torch. Rolling along the wall in the opposite direction, I hoped he would miss me. I felt the heat of the flame as it passed close to my head.

I still wasn't convinced that fire would kill me, but I wasn't willing to gamble my life on it. For the first time in many years, I wanted to live. I wanted to see the next sunrise, and the one after that, and the one after that. I wanted to go to the theater again and see the new plays of William Dunlap and James Nelson Barker. I wanted to see Elizabeth and hold her in my arms.

"You wanted to know how to die, Lazarus. Let me show you how," Matthew taunted as he tried to move closer to me.

He jabbed the torch at my chest. I ducked under the flame and scrambled along the floor. I heard the torch strike the wall with a dull thud. A few pieces of loose, burning canvas fell on my back, and I quickly shook them off. I tried to get around Matthew, but he stepped back and to the side blocking my way out of the room.

The floor finally caught fire and small flames burned in several places around the room. My left hand accidentally grazed one edge of the flame. Pain as hot as a molten nail shot through my hand, and I winced. Even after I jerked my hand away, I could still feel the pain. The heat from the fire had entered my hand and stayed there.

From above me, Matthew screamed, "I will prevail, Lazarus! Nothing in this world can stop me! I will conquer it, or I will destroy it!"

I dove for Matthew's legs, hoping to knock him down so I could get out of the room. I missed him as he scrambled backward, but a flame from the floor caught his pants leg on fire. He screamed and dropped the torch as he tried to beat the flame out by rolling on the floor.

I grabbed for the torch. He saw me move and tried to retrieve the torch for himself. We both grabbed it at the same time, each one attempting to pull it away from the other. I could feel the heat burning my hand and face. On the other side of the torch, I saw Matthew staring at me.

Suddenly, Matthew pushed the torch towards me. I wasn't able to resist in time, and I saw the flame coming right at my face. I let go of the torch and fell backward. Matthew stumbled forward but kept himself from falling.

I expected to fall against a wall, but there was no wall to catch me. I hit the window. It held for a moment. In fact, it seemed to actually bend outward without breaking. I had a flicker of hope that it would support me. Then with a crack of the glass shattering around me, I fell through the opening.

The sensation of flying for the few seconds I was in the air fascinated me. I was flying! I forgot about Matthew. I forgot about my house, which was quickly being engulfed by the flames.

I was flying.

Somewhere far from Boston.

Flying!

I was soaring up. Up. Up toward Heaven.

Fly...

I hit the paved path beneath my window. My head smashed hard against a stone in the ground and opened. One of my legs twisted itself beneath me and snapped like a dried stick.

Above me, I saw Matthew silhouetted by the flames in my room. He was looking out of the broken window at me.

Burn! I thought to myself. I wished for the flames to reach out and consume him and send him as a flaming fireball straight to Hell.

Burn!

Matthew chose that moment to look behind himself. A wall of flame had blocked him off from the door to my room. The flames steadily consumed my house. He was trapped! I would have laughed if I could have.

Die, Matthew!

The rippling left me in search of another life to trade for mine. Moments later, I felt it return, and the itching, crawling sensation began as my body healed itself.

Matthew jumped from the window. No, he didn't just jump, he aimed himself at me. He wanted to wound me more while using my body to help cushion his own fall. I saw the fiery streak behind him and realized he was still holding the torch in his fist.

I tried to roll away, but my body hadn't completely healed yet. I felt light-headed as I exerted myself. My leg spasmed. Matthew was coming too quickly, and I had to move. I only managed to pull myself about a foot to my left before I collapsed.

It was enough.

Matthew hit the ground standing. I heard his leg bones snap as he pitched himself forward into a small, grassy area. He lost his grip on his torch, and it fell onto my still-healing leg.

I screamed. Oh, how I screamed. The touch of the flame in my bedroom had not prepared me for this agony. The torch seemed to incinerate my entire body in an instant. I could actually feel the flesh on my leg shriveling up.

I grabbed the end of the torch and threw it to the side, hoping it would land on Matthew.

I waited for the rippling to leave me again, but it didn't. For once, I actually tried to will it to leave me, so that the pain I felt in my leg would end. It wasn't any use, though. I could not begin the regeneration any more than I could stop it.

Then I felt something I had never felt before. I can only describe it as a screw. I felt it twisting into my chest. It bored right through me, and then it faded. It was such a faint feeling that I'm surprised I felt it at all with all the other sensations I was feeling.

Though I knew I had never felt it before, it seemed familiar. I looked over at Matthew. He was alive and staring back at me. I suddenly realized what I had felt. Matthew's body was searching for another life to restore his body. Now I knew what it felt like to have your life stolen.

Had Matthew stolen my life?

No. The feeling had gone through me and not returned to Matthew.

Matthew glanced at the burning torch between us.

"I'm going to kill you, Lazarus. I'll make certain of it this time. My time is at hand, and I won't be stopped. Not by you. Not by anyone. My power is too great," he said.

I could still feel my body regenerating from the fall. How badly was I hurt? Would I be able to heal myself before Matthew recovered?

He grabbed for the torch. He was already healed!

No! He was only moving his arms. His legs were quite still, but even as I watched, his left leg twitched. He was healing. His body had found a life.

I raised myself up on my arms and started dragging myself away. My injured leg trailed uselessly behind me. Why hadn't it healed yet? A wave of dizziness passed over me, and my vision blurred. I lost my balance and fell on my face.

I waited until the feeling had passed before I tried to stand up again. The tingling throughout my body had stopped. I was healed. I pushed myself to my feet and took a step. My burned leg dragged throwing me off balance, and I fell again.

"There he is," I heard someone say.

I felt a pair of hands under my armpits. They lifted me up, but I tried to twist away. I had to get away from Matthew.

"Steady, mister. I'm only trying to help you," the man said.

I looked behind me and saw the bearded face that the hands belonged to. I didn't recognize him as a man who lived in the house directly across the street from mine.

"Your house looks like a tinderbox," he said.

The street was filling with people as the fire became visible from the outside. The wooden shingles of the roof had caught fire, and a slight breeze was throwing flames twenty feet into the night sky. Already a line of men was forming a bucket brigade. They wouldn't be able to save my house, but at least they could keep the fire from spreading to neighboring houses.

I was standing again, but I had to support myself against a maple tree to keep from falling over.

I looked across the yard to where Matthew was lying. A man was helping him to his feet. More people crowded around the house, and I lost sight of him.

I couldn't let him get away. I didn't want to spend the rest of my years hiding away from him waiting for him to attack me again. I hobbled forward trying to reach him through the crowd.

The man who had helped me stand came up beside me and said, "What are you trying to do, mister. You're in no condition to walk."

I pointed across the yard. "I need to get..."

The crowd parted slightly. Matthew was gone.

19

January 20, 2016

Alexander sat down in his rocking chair and unlaced his left work boot. He pulled it off and let it drop to the floor with a loud thud.

"Did you lose your house?" Tim asked. He stood up and leaned across the table so that he could see what Alexander was doing.

"Yes. In those days, Boston favored wooden dwellings, and as you know, fire loves wood. Surprisingly, mine was the only house that burned that night. The bucket brigade concentrated on soaking the surrounding houses when they saw mine was a lost cause. I wasn't concerned too much about my house, though. A home I could replace. The fire had taken something more valuable from me," Alexander said.

"What?" Tim asked, leaning forward in his chair.

Alexander rolled up the pants leg of his jeans. His left calf and knee were a mass of pink scar tissue. Tim sat back down in his chair and put his hand on his stomach to try and quiet it down.

"The scar also covers part of my thigh," Alexander said. He touched a spot on his knee gently and then shook his head.

"Is that why you limp?" Tim asked.

Alexander nodded. "I've used a cane ever since that day. So you can see I am not invulnerable. I am only...hardier than everyone else."

Tim smiled. "That's like saying the sun is just a few miles away from the earth."

Alexander shrugged. "I suppose, but the point is, I can, and will, die eventually. I am not an immortal. Matthew reminded me of my mortality, but in doing so, he stole my sense of security from me."

"What about Matthew? Was he burned in the fire?"

Alexander shrugged as he rolled his jean pants leg back down to his ankle. "Not that I ever saw, but I have a theory about that. For Matthew to know that fire would cause irreparable damage to our bodies, he would have had to have been burned at some time in the past. Otherwise, he could not have known for sure that fire could kill us, but I never saw any scars on his body. Of course, you can understand that when we were together, we didn't chat about our wounds."

1809 A.D.

I learned the feeling of intense mortal pain that night. The fire didn't just destroy my leg, it overloaded my sense of touch. There was no shock associated with the fire to help prepare me for the pain. I felt every degree of the flame. My nerve endings were so overloaded that I was numb, literally numb, the next day. I couldn't feel anything.

Matthew had shown me the boundaries of my life by trying to push me over the edge of it. I had always said I knew I would die. I was not immortal, but they were just words. After nearly 2,000 years of life, I had begun to believe I would never die. Matthew quickly brought me back to reality. Alexander paused. Closing his eyes, he raised his hands to his head and massaged his temples.

When he had finished, he said, Father Halloran arrived just as the second floor of my house collapsed sending millions of glowing bits of debris into the sky. Silhouetted against the fire as he watched the house burn, his huge body was just a black dot against the flames. As I stared at him, he kneeled down on the ground and crossed himself.

"Father Halloran!" I called out.

Hearing his name, he looked around. When he saw me sitting on the ground near the street, he smiled and rushed over to me.

"What happened, Alexander?" was his first question.

"Matthew came to visit me in the house and tried to kill me."

"Buying Atlantic Importers must have upset his plans quite badly."

I shook my head. "I don't think so. He seemed angrier that I had interfered with his plans not that I had thwarted anything."

Father Halloran noticed my burned bed clothes. He squatted beside me and touched a blackened spot on my knee. "What happened to your leg?"

"It was burned in the fire," I said as I gingerly pulled back the burned wool. The charred remains of my night shirt stuck to my leg in a few spots. Pulling it free sounded like sandpaper being rubbed across a board.

Father Halloran touched my leg gingerly, but I was unable to feel anything.

"Do you need to see a doctor?" he asked.

I shook my head.

"Will the wound heal on its own?"

"I don't think so. If was going to heal, it would have done so already. The bones I broke in the fall have healed. Fire was Matthew's weapon. That is what can kill me." There was a panicked tone to my voice I wasn't used to hearing. Listening to myself talk was like listening to a stranger.

Father Halloran rubbed his chin. The flesh swung back and forth like a rooster's wattle.

"Why only fire?" he asked.

"I don't know. I suppose it might have something to do with the fact that fire consumes the flesh and cauterizes what it leaves behind. There might not be any time for my body to regenerate."

"Then you do need a doctor," he said, struggling to push himself upright.

"No!" I grabbed onto Father Halloran's cassock to keep him from walking away. I didn't want to see a doctor. I had never visited one in my life, and I was afraid if I did allow a doctor to examine me, he would be able to tell I wasn't normal, somehow. "I need to wash my burns and dress them with some bandages. Maybe a little salve wouldn't hurt, either."

Father Halloran looked skeptical, but he didn't leave. "Where will you go now?"

I held up my hand to him. He grabbed it, and with a grunt, helped me to my feet. I leaned my weight against a maple tree.

"There's a tavern that rents rooms on North Street, just a few blocks from St. Timothy's. Can you help me get there?"

Father Halloran nodded. "And you could probably use a good, stiff drink right now, I'll wager."

I nodded and smiled at him.

He helped me limp down to the tavern and rent a room for the night. After he helped me to my room, he left to get a jar of salve and bandages from the nearest doctor. He returned a half an hour later and did an excellent job of dressing my leg. He tried to get me to take a painkiller, but I refused to tell him that my leg didn't hurt.

He set the bottle on the small table near the window. "It will sooner or later. It's a bad burn. I wish you would let me fetch you to a doctor. The one who gave me the bandages and salve is an excellent one."

I sagged deeper into the bed, and Father Halloran stood up and stretched. He started to leave, but he paused at the door.

"What will you do now about Matthew?" he asked.

"I don't know. I haven't thought about it," I answered.

"Do you think he will run and hide somewhere?"

"It doesn't look like he will."

I put my hand over my mouth and yawned.

"Goodnight, Alexander. I'll come around in the morning to check on you and have a look at your leg."

"Don't worry, Father. I can make it to the church on my own. Besides, I'll be wanting something to eat, and I know how well they feed you at the rectory."

Father Halloran laughed as he patted his belly. "That they do. Mrs. Murphy does most of our cooking, and she's an excellent Irish cook, as good as my own mother." He held up his hand. "Tomorrow then."

"Tomorrow," I replied.

He closed the door behind himself as he went out. I leaned over to the table next to the bed and blew the lamp out. Then I pulled the thin wool blanket up to my nose. I was surprised at how easily I fell asleep, but my fatigue must have overcome any anxiety I felt about Matthew following me to the tavern to attack me a second time.

I woke up around eleven-thirty the next morning. I am usually a very early riser, often getting up with the sun, but my fight with Matthew had exhausted me. Everything I did that morning was almost as if I was watching it happen rather than doing it. I couldn't feel any part of my body. I pinched my cheek to see if there was a sensation of pain, but I felt nothing. My leg had swollen beneath the bandages, but it was also as numb as the rest of my body.

When I saw the time, I clumsily rushed to dress in the shirt and pants Father Halloran had borrowed from the tavern owner. I was surprised he hadn't been waiting for me at my door thinking I couldn't get out of bed on my own. He wouldn't have been too far from the truth. I was probably too late for Mrs. Murphy's breakfast, but I still might be able to get myself an invitation to supper in the afternoon.

It wasn't easy walking to St. Timothy's. I limped because of my burned leg, and since I had no feeling over my entire body, my balance was precarious. I felt like I was continually falling no matter whether I was walking or standing still. Somehow, I managed to reach the church, but if it had been any further away, I probably would have fallen on my face.

Father D'Armand, a young priest just recently arrived from France, answered the door to the rectory when I knocked. He told me

Father Halloran had given morning Mass, but he hadn't come back from the chapel yet. He expected him soon, and he invited me to wait for him inside the rectory. I declined and started across the yard to the chapel. I wanted to show Father Halloran I hadn't broken any bones on my way to the church.

I entered the church from the rear entrance that all the priests used. I expected to see quite a lot of people in the pews, praying and waiting to go into the confessional to ask forgiveness for their sins. I had thought that was the reason Father Halloran would still be in the chapel, but the chapel was empty. I walked down the center aisle to the vestibule at the front of the church. The doors had been locked from the inside. I had never known the church to be closed, and I wondered what the reason was.

I turned around to walk back out the rear door to the rectory. Covering my eyes, I fell to my knees. I was breathing hard with quick, sharp breaths.

I raised my head slowly, hoping I had only imagined what I thought I saw at the front of the church.

I screamed.

The plaster statue of Christ I had admired on previous visits had been taken down from the wooden cross and smashed into thousands of small, unrecognizable fragments. In its place, hung Father Halloran. His heavy body pulled against the nails that had been driven through his hands and feet. His palms and wrists were bloody, but no longer bleeding. His head was slumped against his chest and on it had been placed a crown of thorns.

I rushed to the front of the church as fast as I could in my condition. Father Halloran's feet were eye level with my chest, and I could see the large nail that had been driven through his feet.

I stood there wobbling unsteadily not knowing what to do. I wanted to scream again. I wanted to hit something. I wanted to cry. I could do nothing.

There was a large pool of blood on the floor that had mixed with the plaster pieces to form red clumps that had dried to the stone floor. So much blood.

I stepped back until I felt the pulpit against my back. Collapsing against it, I buried my head in my arms and cried.

Father D'Armand walked into the church through the back door and saw me crying. "I thought I heard..." His eyes locked on Father Halloran's body. "Dear Lord." He crossed himself and dropped to his knees.

I don't know how long we stood there immobilized with grief.

Me, crying in front of the cross in much the same way I had when Christ had given up his life. Father D'Armand kneeling across from me with his fist in his mouth as if he were stifling a scream.

He was the first one to regain his voice.

"How?" he asked very lightly.

I wanted to reply to him, but at the time, all I could do was shake my head back and forth.

How had it happened? Thankfully, I didn't believe Father Halloran was conscious when he was crucified. He would have screamed, and someone would have heard him and wondered what was wrong. Father D'Armand certainly would have answered his call for help as he had answered my scream. Father Halloran must have been unconscious at the time. At least I prayed he had been unconscious. I hoped he hadn't known any pain.

Who would have done it, though? Father Halloran had no enemies. That was apparent to anyone who ever attended on of his Masses. Who hated him enough to murder him?

Matthew.

Would he do something so sacrilegious?

Why did he continue to haunt me like a ghost, first in my dreams, then my house, and now finally my friends? Had he seen Father Halloran lead me to the tavern last night? Or had he recognized him from the description his driver would have given him about a priest asking questions about Peter Cromwell?

"Where is Father Davis?" Father D'Armand asked.

I pulled my attention away from the cross and looked at Father D'Armand. "Father Davis?"

"Yes." Father D'Armand's eyes darted quickly around the chapel. "He was helping Father Halloran with the morning Mass."

"There was no one else here when I came in," I told him.

Then I saw the confessional. The priest followed my gaze to dark box. He stepped slowly toward it as if he wanted to approach it silently. Pausing only a moment when he laid his hand on the door latch, Father D'Armand opened the center door. The booth was empty. He released an audible sigh and leaned against the door frame. The booths on either side of the center were empty also.

So where was Father Davis?

"Maybe he escaped and ran somewhere to hide," I suggested.

"Perhaps." His brow wrinkled.

Father D'Armand turned back to Father Halloran. "We need to get him down from there so that we can reopen the church. We don't want people to panic when they discover St. Timothy's is locked."

I nodded my agreement. It wasn't that I was anxious to reopen the church, but seeing Father Halloran hanging in such a humiliating pose made me feel sick. However, I was hesitant to move towards him.

When Father D'Armand reached the cross and looked at me, I finally moved up next to him. With his help, I pulled a bench up next to the cross and stood on it. I swayed slightly as my numb body adjusted to the new height. Touching Father Halloran's face was like touching wet mud. His skin was cold and very pliable under the touch of my fingers.

"I'm sorry, Father," I whispered.

I knew he couldn't hear me. He had probably been dead for an hour or more. I remembered my own experience with death, and I had to believe he would soon be happier than he had ever been on this planet.

"We'll need something we can use to pry the nails out. It would also be better if we broke the base of the cross so we could lay it on the ground," I said to Father D'Armand.

He nodded quickly. "There are tools in the rectory. Will a saw and hammer do the job?"

"Yes. Go get them." He didn't move. He kept staring at Father Halloran's corpse. "Is something wrong?"

"Obviously, much is wrong, but I was curious as to how they were able to mount Father Halloran's body on the cross. He is not a light man, you know."

"They?"

Father D'Armand stepped closer to the bench and looked up at me. "Yes, of course. You don't think one man could have done all this by himself, do you?"

I hadn't thought about it, but no. One man could not have held Father Halloran's enormous bulk pressed against the cross while nailing his palms to the crossbars. Not even Matthew. So who had helped him? And why?

Father D'Armand paused at the rear door. "I'm sorry you had to see this, Alexander. I know you and he were friends. He spoke quite highly of you." He shook his head in disbelief. "I've never heard of anything like this happening even in Virginia."

When Father D'Armand returned, we lowered the cross and pried the nails out of Father Halloran's hands and feet. For me, that was the hardest part. The only place to position the prying bar was against another part of Father Halloran's body, be it his fingers or toes. I heard at least three bones snap while I pried the nails from his body. The cracking sound made my stomach churn even though I knew Father Halloran was beyond feeling any pain.

Three words continued echoing through my mind while I worked, "Matthew did this. Matthew did this."

Father Halloran's funeral was two days later in the small cemetery next to St. Timothy's. Quite a lot of people showed up to pay their respects to Father Halloran. The memorial mass in the church saw every pew filled to capacity. Father D'Armand made the undertaker promise not to reveal how Father Halloran had died to anyone, so there were many explanations for his death from severe indigestion to suicide that circulated. However, most people, like me, showed up because they had genuinely liked Father Halloran.

I squirmed uneasily in my seat as I listened to Father D'Armand talk about Father Halloran's kind heart and devotion to God. My gaze kept drifting from the sealed coffin to the empty spot on the wall at the front of the church.

I could hear the ringing of metal striking metal in my ears. In my mind, Father Halloran hadn't been unconscious when he was crucified. I saw him being held against the cross by a faceless man while Matthew hammered a nail into his left palm. Father Halloran struggled, but he couldn't fight the combined strength of the two men. His body contorted in various directions as Matthew hit the nail with the hammer. Father Halloran screamed, but it only came out as a loud moan through the gag that covered his mouth. Matthew struck the nail again. Rivers of sweat rolled down Father Halloran's face. He shook his head violently back and forth. Blood dripped steadily from his palms, mixing with the plaster fragments and dust on the floor.

"Alexander," a voice said off to my right.

I blinked rapidly, and the scene slowly faded to be replaced with the empty spot on the stone wall. Tears ran down my face. I wiped them away with the back of my hand.

"Alexander."

I looked to my right and saw Elizabeth. She was one of the few people still left inside the chapel. Everyone else had moved outside for the burial.

"Are you all right?" she asked.

Wiping my eyes again, I nodded.

"Are you going outside for the burial?" she asked.

I stood up slowly, cast one final glance at the front of the chapel, and limped over next to Elizabeth.

"I didn't know you were going to be here," I said.

Elizabeth put on her black bonnet. It matched the plain black dress she was wearing.

"I know how much Father Halloran meant to you. I only met him the one time he came with you to the theater, but I liked him. He has...had such a wonderful sense of humor."

She laid her hand on my arm, but even her touch was not enough to bring me out of the falseness that I felt. I couldn't believe that what was happening to me was reality. Only weeks ago, I had thought I was the only person in the world who knew what immortality was like. Now another semi-immortal had tried to kill me and had killed my friend. It wasn't right. It had to be another dream.

I was destined to live my life in near solitude without friends or family. Even when my body didn't kill as it regenerated, I still killed those I loved.

I slowly walked outside with Elizabeth. The air was uncommonly warm for late March, and the sun was shining brightly. It was a spring day in the middle of winter. Almost. The trees and bushes in the cemetery yard were still bare except for the lone pine tree in the corner of the yard.

Standing off to one side of the grave, Father D'Armand began speaking. His words faded from my hearing as the undertaker lowered the coffin into the ground. I almost wished the ground would have been too hard to dig a grave. It would have spared me from having to look at the gaping hole.

The grave seemed to draw me down into it as it swallowed the coffin. I was following Father Halloran into the ground.

It was my fault he was dead.

Down deeper into the earth.

If I hadn't told him the truth...

Darkness covered me.

I pulled myself back with a sudden jerk. I hadn't realized I had started to lean forward over the grave. I looked around to see if anyone had noticed my action, but their collective attention was on the coffin at the bottom of the hole.

Except for Matthew.

He was standing away from the rest of the crowd next to the pine tree. I hadn't seen him there earlier. Our eyes locked over half a dozen yards, and neither one of us moved. His face was a mask showing no emotion at the unfolding event.

Had he actually killed Father Halloran?

Before I could stop myself, I was limping toward him. His gaze only broke with mine once when he glanced at my wounded leg.

When I reached him, I could think of nothing to say. I stared at him silently as if I thought I might be able to look into his heart and see the truth.

I broke the silence first and said, "Why are you here?"

Matthew smiled smugly. "Why to pay my respects, of course. Boston has lost an excellent priest but a poor investigator."

He did know Father Halloran had been asking questions about him!

"Father Halloran was murdered," I said.

Matthew nodded slowly. His eyes glanced over my shoulder, then back at me. "I know. You should not have brought outsiders into this, Lazarus. This disagreement is between you and me. Did you think I would not harm a priest? When others come between us, others die."

"You did..."

I clenched my fist and started to bring it up. I wanted to kill Matthew at that moment, though I knew it was impossible.

"Now, now, Lazarus. Is that any way to pay your respects to the dead? Besides, what would happen if you were to strike me with a fatal wound? Some innocent person would have to give up their life for me. It might even be that young beauty, Elizabeth Poe."

He pointed to the crowd, and I turned. Elizabeth was watching Matthew, and I talk. When she saw me turn, she started walking toward me.

I reached out to grab him, but he caught my wrist.

"Don't do anything foolish," he warned.

"If you hurt her..."

"I've made my point. I won't hurt her, but you will if you try to kill me now. Mrs. Poe is more useful to me alive. Our fight is between us, Lazarus. Don't let outsiders interfere or others may suffer as Father Halloran did." Matthew paused. "You should learn from the good father, Alexander. He knew how to live, not like you. He wasn't afraid to take a risk. You can't be afraid to live if you're afraid to die."

He turned and hurried off before I could reply. I was tempted to chase after him and kill him, but I refrained. It was not the time for such a display. Besides, with my wounded leg, I could never have caught up to him. When he disappeared down Winston Street, I turned back to Elizabeth just as she reached me.

"Who was that?" she asked.

"His name is Matthew. He is someone you don't want to have

any dealings with," I told her.

She cocked her head to the side as she looked at me.

"Why were you talking to him if he is such a bad person?" she asked.

"Unfortunately, our lives bring us into contact with each other more than I would like." I suddenly grabbed her hand and said, "Don't have anything to do with him, Elizabeth. Promise me if you see him approaching you, you'll head in the opposite direction as fast as you can."

Elizabeth smiled and patted my hand with her free hand. "You sound so worried. I'll probably never see him again."

I glanced over my shoulder toward Winston Street just to make sure Matthew wasn't watching the two of us. "Just promise me, please."

She sighed. "Fine. I promise. We should get back to the service now."

I nodded and started off in the direction of the open grave, following Elizabeth.

Would Matthew do something to hurt her? He had killed Father Halloran. What would stop him from killing Elizabeth? But what would be the point? To hurt me, of course. He could harm Elizabeth much more easily than he could harm me, and it would achieve the same effect.

I watched Elizabeth move into the crowd of mourners. She looked so frail and beautiful. This was the woman I loved. I didn't want to see her die. Yet, I couldn't watch her all of the time, especially with David's jealousy. As she walked away from me, I knew what I would have to do.

I would have to leave Boston.

I hated to do it, but my leaving would accomplish two things. If Matthew wanted to continue watching me so I wouldn't interfere with his plans, he would have to follow me wherever I went, in which case, he would be away from Elizabeth. My leaving would also cause him to believe Elizabeth was not as important to me as she actually was. I hoped.

I went home after the funeral and paced my room at the tavern. I certainly wouldn't have to worry about packing up my belongings if I decided to leave. Everything I had owned was hidden in China or in ashes in what had been my house. I had to go buy a whole new assortment of clothes the day before just so I would have something to wear besides what I had borrowed from the tavern owner.

Should I just leave Boston without telling Elizabeth? Would

telling her accomplish anything? I don't think she would have begged for me to stay. She had a husband and child to occupy her time. Nor would she have volunteered to leave with me. The theater was her life, and she depended on it even more when things were not as they should be between her and David.

I continued pacing well into the night. I asked myself questions and countered them in the same breath. I walked the floor so much I learned what spots on the floor to avoid because they creaked. When morning came, I was gone.

20

1809 A.D.

I hired a carriage and driver to take me to New York City. I planned to establish a new life for myself there far enough away from Boston so that Elizabeth would be safe. I needed to be around people and forget about Elizabeth, Matthew, and Father Halloran.

I bought a new house on Twentieth Street and concentrated on running Atlantic Importers, seeing as how I was the new owner. The ship captains and foreign managers that worked for me were all experienced men. I trusted their judgment in most of the business matters and learned from them, but I still insisted on making my own decisions.

Whenever Captain Jarvis was in port, I asked him if he had heard any rumors about Peter Cromwell. Since he sailed to Boston quite frequently, I thought it would be useful to know if anything out of the ordinary happened. I heard no news, though. If Matthew wanted to hide his identity from me, all he had to do was change his name. Unless he did something radical enough to draw attention to himself, I would never be able to find him.

Still, I hoped he had followed me to New York. If he hated me enough to try and kill me, he wouldn't want to let me get away from him. He didn't know how I might be able to interfere with his plans.

Over the course of my first year in New York, my entire life revolved around running my business and trying to locate Matthew. I made no friends because I was afraid of what Matthew might do to them if he had followed me to New York. I never even visited one of the theaters in town for fear that I might see Elizabeth.

That would have been too much to bear. Elizabeth already occupied most of my free thoughts. I wanted to see her and talk with her again. I dreamed about holding her and kissing her. My search for Matthew almost became an obsession as I grew to hate him for killing Father Halloran and separating me from Elizabeth and Edgar.

I wondered if Elizabeth missed me as much as I missed her. Did she wonder where I had gone and why I had left Boston without saying anything to her?

And what about Edgar? How was he doing? Was he healthy? Had David and Elizabeth finally left him with David's parents?

My time in New York stretched into two years. And in two years, I hadn't heard even a rumor about Matthew. Even the news Captain Jarvis brought me from Boston was worthless. No one knew of Peter Cromwell or any other rich man who fit Matthew's description. I knew Matthew wasn't dead, but I could not stand my loneliness any longer. It got to the point where I would talk to myself in the mirror and carry on a conversation. In isolating myself from Elizabeth, I hadn't hurt Matthew. I had only hurt myself.

My decision to find Elizabeth took longer to reach than my decision to leave Boston. Once I began thinking about finding Elizabeth, I debated with myself for two months whether it was the right thing to do.

I had panicked when I left Boston, yet I still felt the reasoning behind my departure was correct. However, I discovered one more reason I had left Boston during my time in New York City. I was afraid of Matthew.

I kept remembering how scared I had been when I woke up and saw him in my room with the torch in his hand. For one of the few times in my life, I hadn't wanted to die. Elizabeth had allowed me to forget what my future would bring, if only for a few weeks.

And I had run from it all. Over the time I spent in New York, I saw myself backsliding into my old ways. I avoided my future and conflict. I gave into more and more disputes with my captains and managers because I was tired of arguing with them. I willingly walked a longer route through town if I knew I could avoid someone I didn't want to see.

I had run after every one of my wives had died. I had run each time after my body regenerated. Yet, I had never outrun my problems. I had never come to terms with my life, and that had only caused more problems.

With Elizabeth's help, I had tasted life again, and it hadn't been taken from me. I had given it up. Knowing it was still possible to enjoy my life, I found myself longing for her company.

It took a few weeks to make the arrangements with my managers and ship captains to have business matters forwarded to Richmond. Once that was done, I left New York City with no regrets.

A theater owner on Broadway told me Placide's Acting Company was in Richmond, so that became my destination. I rented a room at the Exchange Hotel in Richmond. With the acting company in town, I was sure Elizabeth would be, too. What I wasn't so certain about was how to approach her. How would she react to seeing me again after two years?

The company was now performing *Abellino the Great Bandit*. Elizabeth played the beautiful Rosamunda. I watched the play every night for two weeks as I tried to choose the best way to reintroduce myself to her. Finally, I decided there was no best way. I was only stalling what I knew I had to do. Running away again.

I decided that night I would wait for her. I remember the date well. July 11, 1811; the day I came alive again.

I waited behind the theater for forty-five minutes after the performance had ended. The wait wasn't pleasant. The night air was a cool relief to the sweltering summer temperatures, but it certainly seemed like the longest wait I had ever made. I paced back and forth under a streetlamp. Twice, I almost left, but I told myself this had to be done. I couldn't run away again, not if I wanted to be with Elizabeth.

Finally, the rear entrance to the theater opened. The light from the inside of the theater backlit Elizabeth giving her an angelic glow. She stepped into the street and closed the door behind herself. She was wearing a light cotton dress. I was relieved to see that she was alone. David's jealousy was the last thing I wanted to deal with.

Suddenly, a wave of fear hit me as she walked in my direction. I stumbled back into the shadows of a store doorway and tried to catch my breath. My heart was beating fast doing its best to burst from my chest.

Elizabeth passed by the doorway so close I might have reached out and touched her shoulder. Instead, I pressed myself deeper into the corner hoping she wouldn't look my way.

In a moment, she was gone from my view, and I sighed with relief. Then I scolded myself for my cowardice. I couldn't continue doing this. Running had never helped me. It had only brought me more pain.

I stepped from the doorway and stood in the middle of the walk. My voice had left me, and I could only stare at her as she continued to walk away from me. Her hips swayed slightly beneath the dress as she made her way up College Street. Her hair was pulled up into a bun on the top of her head, and I could see the gentle slope of the nape of her neck.

"Elizabeth," I whispered.

She continued walking, and I felt myself trailing after her.

I took a deep breath and said her name louder.

She stopped and turned back. She couldn't see my face clearly in the dark, but she had recognized my voice. She moved a few steps closer and stared at me silently. Then she spun around on her heels and walked away.

"Elizabeth, wait!" I called as I hobbled to catch up with her.

She walked as fast as she could without breaking into a run. I struggled to catch up with her since I could only limp. I touched her on the shoulder, but she quickened her pace and pulled further away. I felt like an old man, not being able to keep up with her. With my good leg leading, I took longer strides until I was close enough to grab her by the arm.

She stopped and tried to pull her arm free, but I held it tight.

"Let me go," she said, jerking her arm away.

"I just want to talk to you, Elizabeth," I told her.

Elizabeth laughed. "You should have talked a long time ago, Alexander. It doesn't matter what you say now."

She turned and tried to run off, but I kept my grip.

"It matters to me," I said.

"Why? If it didn't matter in Boston, it shouldn't matter now! You could have told me goodbye or written a letter. Something!" She started crying. I tried to pull her close to me, but she pushed herself away. "I thought you were dead. I thought whoever had killed Father Halloran had killed you."

"I had to leave, Elizabeth, and I had to do it fast. I was afraid someone might try and kill me." It wasn't the complete truth, but it also wasn't a complete lie.

"You could have told me!" She dabbed her eyes with a handkerchief. "I had nightmares for weeks after you left. I thought we were friends."

"We are friends. I'm sorry. I didn't mean to hurt you. At the time, I believed I was doing the best thing for everyone concerned." She stopped crying finally. "Please forgive me. You're the reason I came to Richmond. I finally realized what a terrible mistake I made when I left Boston."

I slid my hand down her arm until it rested on her hand. It was so small in mine, like a child's hand, and I am not a large man. I placed her hand against my chest and held it there. She didn't try to pull it away.

She closed her eyes. I closed mine, too, and listened to the rhythm of her breathing.

"Alexander?" she said.

I opened my eyes. "Let's go somewhere and talk. There are

some things that you should know."

I nodded and started walking. I limped down the street beside this beautiful woman and wondered why she had reacted so angrily to my reappearance. I had expected indifference on her part, maybe even a little hostility, but not outright anger. I couldn't imagine that my leaving could have affected her so deeply. We didn't say a word to each other. Under the circumstances, I was happy that she was at least talking to me.

We came to a small two-story butcher's shop constructed out of stone. Elizabeth opened the side gate and passed through. I followed her down a short flight of steep steps that ran alongside the foundations of the building. My burned knee refused to bend more than an inch or two making it difficult to walk the stairs gracefully. I almost fell once.

At the bottom of the stairs, Elizabeth opened a door and went inside. Her home was one large room that had been partitioned off with blankets strung between the wooden supports. In the front area, there was a fireplace, a poorly constructed wooden table with two chairs, and a rocking chair. Various cans and bottles were stored on the shelves, which lined the wall on either side of the fireplace. In the back corner was a wooden staircase that I assumed went upstairs into the butcher shop. The room was cool, since half of it was actually buried beneath the earth, but the air was thick with the scent of blood from the beef sold in the store above.

A woman slightly older than Elizabeth sat in the rocking chair in front of the empty fireplace. She was stitching a quilt when we came in. She looked at me when I came through the door, and her eyebrows knitted together as she studied me.

"How are the children?" Elizabeth asked the woman.

Children? Had Elizabeth and David retrieved William from David's parents in Baltimore?

The woman stopped her stitching and set it aside. She had on a lovely light-blue dress that made Elizabeth's seem shabby in comparison.

"They're asleep," the woman said.

Elizabeth smiled and held the woman's hands. "Thank you so much, Frances."

Frances stood up, cast a glance in my direction, and then back at Elizabeth. "Is that..." she started to say.

Elizabeth shook her head. "This is Mr. Alexander Reynolds, someone I knew in Boston." I noticed she didn't call me a friend. "Alexander, this is Mr. John Allan's wife, Frances. Her husband is a merchant over on Fourteenth Street."

"Pleased to meet you, Mrs. Allan," I said.

She nodded curtly in my direction, then turned quickly to Elizabeth. "How did the play do tonight?"

Elizabeth started to answer, but her words turned into a violent cough. Frances put her arm around Elizabeth's shoulders and led her to the rocking chair.

"Is anything wrong?" I asked.

No one answered.

Elizabeth stopped coughing after a minute. Frances dipped an empty cup into the water bucket near the fireplace and brought Elizabeth a cup of water.

"Drink," she said gently.

Elizabeth sipped the water. When the cup was half empty, she set it aside.

"I'm all right now." She grabbed Frances" hand and patted it. "I'll be fine. Really. Thank you."

Frances looked at me, then back at Elizabeth. She picked up her quilt and folded it across her arm.

"I guess I'll be going then. I'll be by tomorrow," Frances said as she walked toward the door.

"Thank you again," Elizabeth said.

Frances smiled and waved as she went out the door. When she had left, Elizabeth motioned me to sit in one of the chairs. The chair legs wobbled slightly when I sat down on it because the legs were uneven.

As I looked around the room once again, Elizabeth said, "David's gone."

"Gone?" I repeated.

She nodded.

"He went out drinking one night while we were in Baltimore, and he never came back. No one knows what happened to him. He didn't say anything to his parents, either. Of course, I wouldn't expect him to, not really. He's never been very close to his father," she explained.

I hesitated. "Perhaps, I shouldn't say this, but I will. I think it is a blessing that David left you and the children."

"You should talk."

She crossed her arms over her chest, daring me to contradict her. My face flushed, but in the dim light of the lamp, I don't think she noticed.

"Elizabeth, David was a drunkard and too jealous for his own good. He hated me. He hated John Payne. He even hated you."

"He did not!"

"He knew you are more talented on the stage than he ever would be and that made him jealous. He couldn't stand to see your performances get praised while his got nothing," I explained.

"You're wrong, Alexander. You only saw one side of him, and it wasn't his best side. He could be very kind, too. He loved his children and me. He was a good husband and father."

I was tempted to tell her about the incident that had caused me to leave Richmond the last time I had been here. Her caring husband had tried to sell her as a whore. Of course, she probably wouldn't have believed me and only defended David more fiercely. He was gone. Hopefully, his memory would soon follow.

"How are the children?" I asked instead.

Her face beamed at the mention of her children. "They are doing wonderfully. Edgar is growing more handsome by the day. Frances positively dotes on him. And Rosalie..."

"Rosalie?" It was a new name to me.

Elizabeth nodded. "You don't know Rosalie. You were *gone* when she was born." She put such an emphasis on the word "gone" that I felt ashamed. "She's only two months old and such a quiet child. She never makes a sound most of the time."

"So you're all alone with the children now?" I asked.

She looked over at the blanket wall. "I guess no man wants to stay with me for long. My father died. Charles died. You ran off. Then David ran off. What's wrong with me?"

I couldn't bear to meet her stare. There was such a look of accusation in her eyes. There was nothing wrong with her; nothing at all. But for some reason, I didn't have the courage to tell her.

"But I came back," I said in my defense.

"Have you?" she asked as she took another sip of water.

I nodded.

"Why?"

Why? How could I have answered that? I could have said I was in love with her and risked being rejected since she apparently no longer considered me even a friend. Or, I could have told her I needed a friend, and she probably would have laughed and told me I was the one who had abandoned our friendship.

As it was, I never had to answer.

"Mama, mama," I heard a child say from behind one of the blankets.

Elizabeth stood up and parted the blanket that was furthest to the

182

left. There was Edgar. He was now two-years old and sitting motionless on a thin mattress laid on the floor. His brown hair had large curls giving him an almost feminine appearance, and his eyes looked exactly like Elizabeth's large eyes.

"Mama, mama," he said again, holding up his arms as he did.

Elizabeth bent over and picked him up. She walked over to the rocking chair and sat down with him in her lap. He tugged at a lock of her hair and popped his free thumb into his mouth. As Elizabeth rocked, he sat quietly in her lap staring at me.

I smiled at Edgar, but he just stared blankly at me.

Elizabeth continued talking. "Attendance at the theater is falling off, and I'm not earning much money right now. That is why I am renting this room from Lucas. It is the only place I can afford. Thankfully, Frances is always willing to watch the children. She loves them as if they were her own."

I nodded as she said all this, but I wasn't really listening. I was staring into her eyes hoping to read some emotion into them. Was she glad I had returned? Was there a chance that she felt the same way for me that I did for her?

We talked a while longer about the new life she had built for herself and the children in Richmond. When I finally left around ten o'clock, I was happy that I had made the decision to find her. I slept comfortably that night, dreaming of Elizabeth and the life we might be able to make together now that David had left her.

We spent the next five weeks getting to know each other better. There were tense moments, I admit, where either she or I would start talking on a subject that the other did not want to discuss. For her, the subject was David. For me, it was my past. We eventually learned to work our way around those topics.

I believe we were both quite happy during this time. I would have even asked Elizabeth to marry me if she still hadn't legally been married to David. As I said, she didn't want to speak about David, so I wasn't able to ask her what she intended to do with regards to her marriage. I was content to wait. For some reason, I had no fear that David would return and spoil the relationship that Elizabeth and I were nurturing. I suspected the reason for his leaving, but I kept my suspicions to myself since Elizabeth, and I never talked about him. He was a jealous man, though, and he practiced the same profession as his wife. I think seeing his wife win all the glory finally became too much for him, and he left to try and find a line of work where he could be the star and not just average.

Also during this time, I took an occasional turn watching the children at night while Elizabeth performed. Edgar was a bright boy who loved to listen to me tell him stories. I would sit in the rocking chair and rock with him on my lap. I told him stories from the Bible and from my travels around the world. Rosalie would usually sleep in her cradle. She was such a quiet child. It was a relief to Elizabeth that her daughter was so well-behaved, but it disturbed me. A baby shouldn't be so quiet. In all the time I was around Rosalie, I only heard her cry three times.

At night, Elizabeth would come home from the theater exhausted and depressed. Audiences were unusually small, which meant her meager salary was becoming even smaller. The papers were giving the play good reviews, but no one was going to see it. If the trend kept up, by the end of September the company would be playing to an empty house. Louis Placide was already talking about moving the company to Charleston two months earlier than he had originally planned. If he had moved the company, I would have followed it to be with Elizabeth. I wasn't going to let anything come between us again.

Elizabeth refused most of the financial help that either her friends or I offered her. I hated to see her in a state of constant poverty. Oft times, it almost seemed as if her eyes swelled as she tried to hold back her tears when a bill came that she couldn't pay or she saw something for one of the children that she couldn't afford. It's at those times I tried my best to comfort her. It was precisely those times, though, that she pushed me away the hardest.

One afternoon, I went to meet her for supper after her rehearsal at the theater. I got to her room at three o'clock, but she didn't answer the door. Frances Allan did. She was a very different woman from Elizabeth. Frances was about two inches taller with a slightly heavier build. She had very light-blue eyes and black hair, which she usually kept tied on top of her head.

"Come in, Mr. Reynolds. Elizabeth said you would be stopping by," she said as she held the door open for me.

I walked into the room. Edgar was rolling a ball against the wall and letting it roll back to him. He looked up when I came in, and I waved. He waved back and continued to play with the ball.

"Elizabeth's not here?" I said.

Frances shook her head. "She stopped by my house after rehearsal and asked if I would watch the children until she came home. She had to go see a priest."

"A priest?"

Frances nodded as she sighed. She grabbed my arm and said,

"You're not Catholic, are you?"

I shook my head as I patted her hand. "Don't worry."

"Good, then you won't be offended by what I'm going to say. I just don't like this man, and it goes beyond the fact that He's a Catholic. He is always talking about Jesus Christ being on the earth now and gathering up his chosen children. I don't like it at all."

I wasn't sure whether Frances didn't like the fact that she wasn't considered one of Jesus" chosen or if she thought the priest was lying. I knew he was lying, though. If Jesus had been on the earth, I would have been able to die.

"He sounds like he is overzealous," I said.

Frances let go of my arm and shrugged. Then she walked over to the table and began folding her quilt so she would be able to carry it home. "He just sounds crazy to me." I didn't reply. "Well, since you're here now, I guess I can go on home. I have to get supper ready for John when he comes home." She glanced over at Edgar. "He's been playing with his ball for most of the afternoon. Rosalie's sleeping in her crib." I nodded that I understood everything. "Tell Elizabeth Ruth will be by tonight to watch the children, and I'll see her tomorrow."

When she had gone, I sat down in a chair and watched Edgar play with his ball. Upstairs, I could hear movement in Lucas Douglas" Meats. Footsteps passed back and forth overhead as Lucas waited on his customers. I opened the window next to the door to let in some fresh air that wasn't tainted with the scent of blood.

Turning from the window, I saw Edgar standing behind me. I stopped myself so quickly to keep from tripping over him that I almost fell anyway.

Edgar held up his hands to me. "Renose," he said.

Reynolds.

I picked him up and sat down on the rocking chair. His fingers traced one of the brocaded flowers on my vest.

"Do you want to hear a story?" I asked.

He shook his head and moved his attention to one of my brass buttons.

"What would you like to do then?"

He shrugged. Then he reached up, wrapped his arms around my neck, and laid his head against my chest. I continued to rock the chair, but he didn't fall asleep as I thought he would. He just stared quietly out the window while I rocked.

That was how Elizabeth found us. Edgar clinging silently to me, and me with my eyes closed and head tilted back as I rocked.

"Hello, you two," she said as she opened the door.

Edgar slid off my lap and toddled over to his mother. Elizabeth scooped him up off the floor and hugged him tightly.

"How's my boy?" she asked, kissing his cheek.

"Good," he answered as he threw his arms around her neck.

She looked over at me. "Hello, Alexander. I'm sorry I'm late. I promised someone I would stop and see him after rehearsal."

"Frances told me," I said.

She set Edgar down, but he remained at her side. "I'm sure she did. She's Protestant," she said as if that explained her actions.

Elizabeth walked over to the water bucket and dipped herself out a cup of water. She offered me a cup, but I refused.

"Why do you need to see a priest?" I asked.

She sat down at the table, and Edgar climbed up on her lap.

"I don't need to. I'm not Catholic, either, but I needed to talk to a religious man about some things. I remembered how nice Father Halloran was, just like someone's grandfather, so I thought a priest would be as good a person as any to talk to. There's also been a priest I've seen around the theater a few times after rehearsal has ended. I spoke with him yesterday. He seemed almost afraid of me when I approached him. He is such a timid man, so unlike Father Halloran. Anyway, I asked him if I might speak with him. He told me he heard confessions in the afternoon, and that we could talk afterward. After rehearsal today, I went to the church and talked with him."

"What did you have to talk about?" I asked the obvious question.

Elizabeth looked away from me to the floor. "I talked to him about David, and asked him what I should do."

"Do?" I asked, not sure of what she meant.

Elizabeth nodded still not looking up. "I asked him if I should still consider David, my husband."

That caught my attention. I had thought she still believed David would return. Now I learned I might actually have a future with her.

"What did he tell you?" I asked anxiously.

"He really wasn't sure what to tell me. He said that I had an unusual case, and he would have to consult another more-experienced priest and pray about it before he would be able to make a decision," Elizabeth said.

"From what Frances said, this priest teaches some very un-Catholic doctrine. I don't know how much I would rely on his judgment."

She finally looked up. "Not Father Davis. He's very good. He may be shy, but he cares, Alexander. He really does."

I took her hand in mine. "That may be, but what does it matter what a Catholic priest thinks? You're a Protestant." Elizabeth didn't say anything. "When are you supposed to talk with him again?"

"Tomorrow. He'll have another priest with him, and they will talk with me. I saw Frances on the street on her way home. She said she would watch the children again. She's such a dear."

I leaned back in the chair and crossed my arms over my chest. "Well, it's your decision."

"You don't approve?"

"I think it would be hard for anyone to tell someone else how to live their lives. And priests have no experience with women. I don't know how they could correctly advise you as to what is right for you," I said.

"God will tell them." She said it so easily that I knew she believed that God would enlighten the priest to the correct solution to her problem.

I sighed and pushed the chair further back so that it was sitting on its rear legs only.

"I believe part of the reason we are on earth is to make decisions for ourselves about what is right and wrong. God has never made anyone do anything. It's all a matter of choice. So don't blindly follow whatever this priest tells you. Make your own decision about your life," I advised.

"Of course I will," she said and smiled.

I looked at her and wondered, but I said nothing.

I left after we ate supper. Elizabeth took a short nap before she had to go back to the theater for the evening show. As I walked back to my room, I decided to take a longer route that wound through the forest outside of town. I didn't want to return to my room yet.

The priest that Elizabeth had talked to seemed odd, especially if he believed the things Frances told me he preached. I was sure it wasn't Catholic doctrine, and yet this man was a Catholic priest.

It wasn't until the next morning that another puzzling thought occurred to me. The priest's name was Father Davis, the same name as the priest who had been with Father Halloran the morning he was killed.

21

1811 A.D.

Coincidence, I thought, thinking about the priest's name.

Davis was a common name. Certainly, the Catholic Church had more than one Father Davis. I wondered if the Father Davis of St. Timothy's had ever reappeared after Father Halloran's funeral. If he had, where had the man been when Father Halloran had been murdered?

By noon, curiosity had gotten the better of me, and I had decided I would visit the priest myself and talk with him. Even if he wasn't the Father Davis from St. Timothy's, he might know him and where he was living. I wanted to ask questions about Matthew's and Father Halloran's final confrontation that the Father Davis of St. Timothy's might be able to answer.

I walked to Frances' house first to ask her where Father Davis preached. Since John Allan was a successful businessman, I had expected the Allans to live in a large house, but they lived on the floor of rooms above John Allan's store.

"The Society of St. Ananias," Frances told me when I asked her about Father Davis.

I had never heard of a church called St. Ananias and said so.

"It's not the church. The church is St. Paul's," Frances said. "The Society of St. Ananias is a large study group that meets at the church."

St. Ananias was an odd name to use in relation to Paul. Ananias not a saint. In the Bible, two men share that name; the man who had baptized Paul the apostle and the man who persecuted Paul during his ministry.

Frances noticed my reaction to the name and said, "Odd, isn't it? So many people are now part of the study group that they usually call it St. Ananias rather than St. Paul. Even Father Davis and Father Halloran do."

I grabbed her by the shoulders. "Father Halloran?"

I saw fear in her blue eyes as she tried to pull away from me.

"Yes. You don't see him as often as Father Davis, but..."

"What's he look like?" I shouted.

"Alexander, I don't..."

"Frances, what does he look like?" I said more calmly.

She was trembling, but I didn't care.

"Black hair. Gray eyes. A little taller than you."

Matthew!

I released Frances and bolted off the landing and down the stairs to the street. I nearly fell because I was moving faster than my burned leg would allow, but I had to get to the church before Elizabeth did. Now I knew why Matthew hadn't followed me to New York. He had been waiting for me to return to Elizabeth. I hadn't fooled him at all!

I ran with my hobbling gait toward the church. I kept thrusting my walking stick out in front of me to help keep me from falling.

Matthew was using Father Halloran's name. He was imitating a priest. Why?

I ran across Broad Street, without bothering to look around me. A man trotting his horse up the street yelled something. I turned just in time to get knocked broadside. I hit the road on my back and rolled over twice. I shook my head to clear it, then got up and continued to run. The man who had hit me called to me, but I didn't slow down or even look back.

And Father Davis? It had to be the same Father Davis. He must have been the one who helped Matthew mount Father Halloran's body to the cross. Why would a man devoted to God do something like that? How could he?

I turned sharply onto Tenth Street nearly falling. My back was beginning to hurt now from the fall on the road, but I ignored the pain and continued running.

How much further was it?

People turned to watch me as I ran by. It wasn't often they got to see a limping man running as fast as he could. I saw the church in the distance, and I quickened my pace as much as I dared.

I stumbled on the second step of the four that led into the church. My burned knee struck the stone, but I felt no pain.

I slowed my pace to a quick walk and entered the church. It was larger than St. Timothy's with stained-glass windows and a gold chandelier. I wondered how much of this had been a part of St. Paul's and how many were acquisitions of St. Ananias. I limped to the front of the church, my walking stick clicking on the floor to count my paces.

As I neared the front, a priest emerged from a side room. He was my height, but much younger than I appeared, probably in his early twenties. His blond hair was beginning to grow longer than most priests allowed their hair to grow.

He stopped halfway to the pulpit when he saw me. He stared at me with wide eyes and a slightly open mouth. I wondered if I knew him from somewhere or if he knew me. I started to say something, but he turned and quickly went back the way he had come out.

I continued to the front of the chapel intending to follow after him. When I was about ten feet away from the door, it opened. The priest came out again, but this time he wasn't alone. Behind him, walked Matthew!

I backed away a few steps. The two of them separated. Matthew stayed in front of me while the young priest moved off to the side. I hadn't truly believed I would actually find Matthew in a priest's cassock, but there he was standing in front of me and looking like a very holy man--a holy man with the heart of a devil.

I wanted to rush at him and kill him, but the only thing that could kill him was fire. I had learned that lesson all too well.

He held his arms open as if he expected me to walk into his embrace. "Alexander, my son. Welcome to St. Ananias," his said, smiling.

"Which Ananias is that?" All I could think to say. "St. Paul's baptizer or persecutor?"

His smile never faltered. "Which do you think?"

"I wouldn't know, Father Halloran," I said.

The sarcasm in my voice didn't bother the new Father Halloran. "It offends you, does it? It shouldn't. I am only carrying on your friend's work, as well as his name."

I winced at the comment. "Father Halloran's work and yours have nothing in common."

He held his hands clasped in front of him. "Alexander, you judge me too harshly. I am performing God's work here. I have a strong following in Richmond. The poor and neglected are receptive to my words of salvation," Matthew said.

I looked around at the gold chandelier and the pulpit inlaid with rubies and onyx. "This is not a church for the poor."

Matthew rolled his eyes. "You judge by appearances, Alexander. This is a church for all those who seek the truth."

I couldn't help but laugh, and Matthew gave me a hurt look. "What do you know about truth, Father Halloran? You aren't even using your real name." I turned to Father Davis. "And you? What sort of priest are you to aid Matthew in murdering Father Halloran?"

"The old man tried to stop the Savior," he said.

I turned away in disgust. Elizabeth was standing at the back of the church in the doorway.

"Alexander, what are you doing here?" she asked.

"He's been seeking my counsel on spiritual matters," Father Davis said as he moved toward Elizabeth.

She walked up the aisle to meet him. I hurried past him and intercepted her before he could get near. I grabbed her by her arm and tried to turn her around.

"Let's leave, Elizabeth. You don't want to talk to him. He won't help you," I told her.

She pulled her arm away from me and stopped walking. "Wait. I came to speak with Father Davis," she said.

I grabbed her by the shoulders and turned her in Matthew's direction. "Elizabeth, look at Father Davis' superior." I pointed to Matthew. "Do you recognize him?"

She stared at Matthew for what seemed a long while. I don't know whether it was because of his cassock or the two-year time difference since she had last seen him, but she didn't recognize him at first.

"That's the man from the funeral," she said when she finally remembered him. I nodded. "The one you told me to stay away from." She paused. "But he's a priest. How can he be as bad as you said?"

"That's right, Mrs. Poe. I am a priest. You have nothing to fear from me," Matthew encouraged her.

"He's no priest, Elizabeth. Let's go!" I shouted.

Matthew started speaking quickly. "You came to this church seeking the truth. Let us show you the truth."

I couldn't believe that she was actually listening to him, but his robes and manner seemed to be influencing her. Besides, he was remaining calm and in control, while I was the one getting upset.

I started to say something, but I felt a sharp pain in my back. Spinning around, I saw Father Davis standing behind me smiling. I had forgotten to watch where he was standing, and he had been able to move around behind us while we were talking with Matthew.

"Die, devil," he said.

Elizabeth screamed. I turned to her, but my movement felt sluggish, and my back hurt even more.

"What!" I shouted at her.

"There's...There's a knife in your back."

Father Davis had stabbed me! I turned and started running as fast as I could away from Elizabeth. Father Davis had stabbed me in such a way as to not immediately kill me. He wanted to give himself time to get away so that my body would steal Elizabeth's life. What an appropriate punishment for me. I was going to kill Elizabeth to preserve my life.

I staggered after Father Davis, wanting to get as far away from Elizabeth as possible. It was hard to gain any ground on him because he had two good legs to run on. I had only one.

Desperate to stop him, I threw my walking stick at his legs. It struck him in the back of the thighs and tangled itself in between his legs. He threw his arms out and fell forward, hitting the floor hard. As I rushed to catch up to Father Davis, he scrambled to his hands and knees and started crawling away from me. I jumped on his back and pushed him onto the stone floor.

I reached behind my back to try and pull the knife free and felt the rippling go out of me. Father Davis screamed, and I guessed he had felt the ripple steal his life. Groping along my back, my fingers finally found the haft of the knife and pulled it free. It came loose with a sucking sound that I assumed was my flesh resealing itself.

Standing up, I tossed the knife into a dark corner at the back of the church. Father Davis rolled over on his back. He was crying like a small child who hadn't gotten his way.

Elizabeth still stood in the aisle between Matthew and myself. Matthew hadn't moved from his position near the pulpit.

"Elizabeth, let's get out of here," I said, retrieved my walking stick from Father Davis" feet.

She didn't move.

I stepped closer to her and touched her on the shoulder. When she turned to face me, I saw a confused look in her eyes.

"Elizabeth," I said.

"The hole in your back...it's gone," she mumbled.

I took hold of her wrist and pulled her toward the main doors of the church. She shuffled complacently behind me. Not resisting, but not aiding me, either.

"I saw the knife in your back," she said after a few moments.

"I'll explain it to you later. Now we have to leave before anything else happens," I told Elizabeth.

Reminding myself of the danger, I looked back over my shoulder. Matthew was holding a long knife in his hands. His arms were raised above his head, but the knife blade was pointed toward the floor. He was no longer looking at either Elizabeth or me. His concentration was fixed on his knife.

Suddenly, I realized what he was going to do. I saw the dream that Father Halloran and I had shared in Boston of the woman who had had her life stolen by Matthew in his white priestly robes. Dropping Elizabeth's hand, I started running toward Matthew.

"No!" I screamed.

Matthew glanced at me and smiled. "An eye for an eye! Tooth for a tooth! So it says in the Good Book, and so shall it be!"

He waited until I had almost reached him. Then he plunged the knife into his stomach while he laughed at me. I remembered what the confessing sinner Father Halloran had heard said about Matthew laughing as he impaled himself upon his attacker's knife, and I understood why they had been so afraid. Matthew's laugh was an unsettling mix of low pitches and gurgles. Matthew enjoyed stealing life. It was a game to him.

The ripple bored into me, leaving me with an empty feeling once it had passed through me. I knew whose life it would take, and there was nothing I could do to stop it. No one was closer. Father Davis had already surrendered his life to sustain me.

Elizabeth gasped when the ripple struck her. Looking around the church, I think she expected to see someone near her.

Turning back to Matthew, I managed to hold back the tears forming in my eyes. Matthew held his hands out to the sides as if waiting for the ripple to return to him. When it did, he lowered his hands and sighed. The bloody hole in his stomach knitted itself closed. Smiling, Matthew turned and left the chapel.

I was tempted to pursue him, but I heard Elizabeth fall behind me. She was of such a frail nature that I feared that she had already died. I ran to her side and patted her hand. Putting my ear to her chest, I still heard her heart beating, and I knew she had only fainted.

Father Davis was no longer laying on the floor. He had crawled off into some corner to die like the dog he was, I hoped.

I sat down beside Elizabeth and lifted her head and shoulders gently into my lap. I patted her cheeks gently and called her name as she began to revive.

As I waited, I wondered about the church Matthew had formed. Though it called itself Catholic, it was nothing of the sort. How many people had Matthew killed as a sacrifice so that he could live? How many people would yet die thinking they were being delivered into the hands of God?

Elizabeth's eyes fluttered open. "What happened?" she asked.

"You fainted," I told her as I helped her stand.

"I know, but why? I don't faint. But I felt so funny. It reminded me of when I sailed to America, and there was a storm on the ocean. I felt so sick then. I thought I would vomit."

I put my arms around her shoulders and led her to the door. "Let's get you back to your room."

"What about you?" she asked.

"I'm fine," I said, which was the truth.

"But I saw..."

Shaking my head, I turned and showed her my back. Blood stains soaked the back of my torn coat and shirt, but no scar or scab marked that I had ever been stabbed.

"But I saw the knife," she insisted.

I glanced at the front of the church at the closed door where Matthew had gone and said, "We need to leave before he comes back."

She looked again at the spot on my back. Taking her by the elbow, we walked through the door into the chilly December air.

"What happened in there, Alexander?" she asked once we had started walking down the street.

I couldn't answer her. A chill ran through me that had nothing to do with the winter temperatures. My whole body shook, and I had to stop walking until it passed.

"What's wrong?" Elizabeth asked.

I looked into her green eyes and wondered if they were duller than they had been an hour ago. How long would her final spark of life last?

Feeling the tears from my own eyes slipping down my cheeks, I turned away from her. I wiped at my eyes with the cuff of my shirt sleeve. Deep breaths helped to control my tears and to eventually stop them.

I felt Elizabeth's hand on my back as she leaned around to look at my face. "Alexander, what's wrong?" she asked again.

Turning to face her, I said, "Nothing." It was an obvious lie, but I was unwilling to tell her that she was going to die. No one should know that information until the time was upon them.

If I had told her, she would have wanted to know how I knew. My answers would have only lead to more questions which I did not want to answer. I would have had to tell her the truth about my life, which she wouldn't have been able to accept. Eighteen-hundred-year-old men weren't the type of people she frequently encountered.

For my sake, I think she chose not to pursue my weak answer and break it down. I was obviously upset. It was equally obvious that something had gone wrong in the church. Though I doubt she realized to what extent things had gone badly.

At Elizabeth's room, Frances had a fire burning in the fireplace. When we entered, she stared at me quietly through narrowed eyes. I expected her to make a comment about my outburst at her home earlier, but she didn't. As I turned to the fire to warm my hands, I heard her gasp when she saw my bloody coat and shirt.

"Mercy, what happened to him?" Frances asked Elizabeth. She was going to ignore me.

Looking over my shoulder, I saw Elizabeth shrug as she took off her coat and sat down in her favorite rocking chair. She was going to leave it to me to explain what had happened. Not that Frances wanted to talk to me.

"You were right about the priest, Frances," I said, hoping that feeding her ego by telling her she was right would end any questions about what had happened. I didn't want to explain things to her any more than I wanted to explain them to Elizabeth.

"He is crazy, isn't he?" I nodded. "I knew it. I knew it. But what did he do to you?"

"He didn't do anything to me," I lied. "This is his blood."

Elizabeth's head snapped up.

"Did you kill him?" Frances whispered as if there was someone around who would haul me off to the jail if I confessed. "You were awfully mad when you came by my house this afternoon. I thought you were a might crazy yourself."

I shook my head. "No. Father Davis wounded himself, but he might have hurt Elizabeth if I hadn't gotten to the church in time. I knew him in Boston. He was an evil man." I glanced at Elizabeth. She didn't say anything to contradict me. I wondered if it was because the details of the incident were confused in her mind, or if she was just supporting my story. "Thank you for your help, Frances."

Turning away from me with a smile on her face, Frances hung a pot of soup over the fire to heat it up.

"You're welcome. I'm just glad Elizabeth is all right," she said.

I didn't contradict her.

When Frances left a short time later, I turned my full attention to Elizabeth.

"How do you feel?" I asked.

"Fine." Now I knew I wasn't the only one who was a poor liar. "Where are the children?" she asked, changing the subject.

"Frances already told you. Edgar is upstairs playing with Lucas's son and Rosalie is in her crib."

"Oh," she replied, still looking slightly confused.

Elizabeth coughed. It began gently at first, but it quickly turned into a violent, hacking cough. I remembered what Frances had done the one other time I had seen Elizabeth in the midst of a coughing spell. I went to get her a cup of water from the bucket by the fireplace.

By the time I turned back to bring the water to Elizabeth, she was on her hands and knees coughing. On the floor beneath her was a pool of blood.

I dropped the cup and rushed over to her. Her coughing had stopped, but now she was crying. Pulling her from the floor, I set her back in the rocking chair. I tried to wipe her tears away, but she just kept crying.

After she had stopped, I asked, "How long have you been sick?"

She shook her head. "I don't know. I've been coughing for a long time, but I've never coughed up blood. I went to see a doctor in Baltimore last year. Louis made me go because I started coughing in the middle of a performance one night. The doctor told me I was consumptive."

Consumption. Such a nice way to say such an evil word. Tuberculosis. Elizabeth had been dying slowly even before Matthew had stolen her life. He had only accelerated her illness.

She grabbed my hand and squeezed. "It's never been this bad before, really. I've never coughed up blood before."

Putting my arms around her, I held her tight to my chest. "I know, Elizabeth. I believe you," I told her.

I was surprised she couldn't feel the intense heat emanating from my body. Or maybe she did and simply thought it was the heat from the fire. It wasn't. From inside my chest, I could feel my anger swelling and consuming my thoughts. It burned hotter than any flame could have burned.

I was going to kill Matthew.

Pulling away from Elizabeth, I said, "I must go. I need to do something." There is someone who must die, I said to myself silently.

Elizabeth clutched at me even tighter, wrapping her arms around my waist. "Alexander, no! Don't leave me! Please! Don't be like him!"

"I'll be back," I said, trying to calm her.

With her eyes red and swollen from her crying, she looked up at me. "No. No, you won't. You'll leave me because I told you I'm sick. Well, I lied. I'm not sick. I was just acting. I can have more children, Alexander. I can keep on working. I'm all right. Just don't leave me!"

She rested her head against my chest and cried while I ran my hand through her hair. Unsure of what to say, I said nothing.

She stopped crying after a while and wiped her eyes. Quietly, she stood up and walked over to the fire and took off the pot of soup Frances had put on earlier. She set the pot on the table and dished out two bowls of the vegetable soup. After begging for me not to leave, now she wouldn't look at me.

I walked over beside her.

"Elizabeth," I said.

She turned, so her back was toward me. She stirred the soup in the bowls with a spoon trying to cool it down.

"Elizabeth," I said again as I grabbed her by the shoulders and forced her to face me.

She still refused to look at me. Cupping her chin in my hand, I tilted her head up. She continued to keep her eyes downcast.

"Elizabeth," I said a third time.

She finally looked up, and I almost cried myself.

"Why did you say all that?" I asked.

She sniffled and closed her eyes. When she opened them, she said, "David left me the night after I told him I was consumptive. He didn't want a dying wife. I just know he didn't. That's why he left me."

"Did he say so?" I asked. She shook her head. "Then maybe there was another reason."

"There wasn't. I know," Elizabeth insisted.

So that was why she refused to give into her sickness. If David ever came back, she wanted to prove she could still be a fit mother and wife.

"You're fine just the way you are," I said as I leaned over and kissed her on the lips.

My anger with Matthew evaporated the moment our lips touched. It was hard to stoke a fire of hate when I was so happy. It was the moment I had dreamed of for years, and it was everything I had expected it to be.

I slipped my arms around her waist and pulled her to me. She laid her head on my shoulder. I couldn't leave her now, not yet. My fight with Matthew would have to wait for a few days.

And so I stayed with her. Determined to make her last days happy, I rarely ever left her side. We went on carriage rides through the countryside. I took her to expensive restaurants for dinner. I even took her on a cruise to Charleston on one of my ships.

To my delight, the few days I thought she would live lasted a week and a half. I began to think that maybe Matthew hadn't stolen her life. Then I awoke on Sunday and felt the coldness in her hands. I put my hand under her nose, and I couldn't feel her breath.

I laid beside her in bed and cried for half an hour. When I finally managed to get control of myself, I leaned across the bed and kissed her lightly on the forehead.

"Goodbye, Elizabeth," I said.

Part IV:
A Descent into the Maelstrom

It may appear strange, but now, when we were in the very jaws of the gulf, I felt more composed than when we were only approaching it. Having made up my mind to hope no more, I got rid of a great deal of that terror which unmanned me at first. I suppose it was despair that strung my nerves.

Edgar Allan Poe
A Descent into the Maelstrom

22

1811 A.D.

Edgar and Rosalie were still asleep in their portions of the room. I parted the blanket curtains and saw Edgar curled into a tight ball under two thin blankets. A wisp of his curly brown hair had fallen in his eyes, and it jiggled slightly with each breath he took. Rosalie was in her cradle lying on her stomach. Her arms and legs were spread out forming an X.

Feeding three more logs into the fire, I warmed the room up to a comfortable temperature. Then I dressed and left the house.

I stopped at the Allans' house and told Frances what had happened. Handing her a bank draft for one-hundred dollars, I asked her to handle all the funeral arrangements for Elizabeth.

"I think she would have rather had you do it, Mr. Reynolds," She said as she tried to hand the bank draft back to me.

I pushed it back to her. "I won't be staying in Richmond any longer," I said with some regret.

She was quiet for a few seconds. She folded and unfolded the draft as she stared at me. Finally, she slipped the bank draft into a pocket in her skirt.

"I think I understand. You were good for her, Mr. Reynolds. I hope you know that. I knew her before you came to town, and then after. She was much happier after."

I smiled. "Thank you."

"What about the children? Are you going to be taking them with you?" she asked me as I turned to leave.

"I think not." I felt ashamed saying that, but I wasn't sure if I would be alive tomorrow. If not, the children would only be in the same situation they were in now.

"Then could I...I mean, my husband and I, could we take care of Edgar?" she asked timidly.

"Of course. Elizabeth knew how much you loved him."

She smiled. "Oh, I do. He's a very special boy."

"What about Rosalie?" I asked.

"I think Mrs. MacKenzie will take her in. She's good people. You don't have to worry about that baby wanting for anything. She'll take good care of her."

Lightly shaking Frances" hand, I said, "Thank you for your help. I am not prepared to deal with this too well."

She nodded her head quickly. "I understand. Really I do. God bless you and good luck, Mr. Reynolds."

I left her then and walked down the street until I reached the forest at the edge of town. I found a sturdy oak sapling at the edge of a field that showed a lot of resiliency. Pulling my knife from my boot, I shaved away the thin trunk until I had cut it through. Once it was free, I shaved off the few limbs so that I had a four-foot piece of the sapling. If I had had the time, I would have chosen an oak branch for my bow. Then I would have shaved it clean, shaped it, and greased it so that it would bend easily.

Before I went back to my room, I gathered half a dozen pencil-thin and relatively straight pieces of wood that were all about three-feet long. I wouldn't have time to straighten them, but I would be able to shave some of the bends off the twigs.

In the 124 years that I had lived in the mountains, I had learned more than a few things about survival and hunting. Once I was back in my room, I strung a strong piece of thin twine, instead of sinew, between the two ends of the sapling. I tightened the twine until there was a slight bend in the wood and tied it off. Pulling back on the string, I tested the bow to see if the sapling would hold or break. When it held, I breathed a sigh of relief. It was a crude construction, but I didn't need the bow to last me more than six shots.

I shaved the half a dozen pieces of wood to a point on one end, and I notched them at the opposite end. I didn't have time to fletch the notched ends or mount a stone arrowhead on the pointed ends. Besides, arrowheads were meant to kill mortals. These arrows were meant to kill an immortal.

I went to St. Ananias on Sunday night after the final Mass of the day. The chandelier and sconces were all lit, and the church was bright with light...and fire. Walking up the side aisle between the pews and the wall, I entered the church. Mass had ended an hour ago, and the chapel was empty.

I carried my collection of arrows in one hand and my bow in the other. About two-thirds of the way toward the front, I set the arrows down in a pew. I used the end of the bow to reach up to the glass chimney on the nearest sconce and knock it off. Falling to the stone floor, it smashed with a loud crash.

"Matthew!" I yelled at the top of my voice.

My voice echoed slightly in the old church. It was the only answer to my call.

"Matthew, come out, or I'll burn down your beautiful church!"

The side door behind the pulpit opened, and Matthew stepped out. He didn't seem surprised to see me.

"Lower your voice, Lazarus. This is a house of the Lord," he said in his well-modulated priestly voice.

I kept my bow at my side so that it appeared to be my walking stick.

"Not anymore it isn't," I said.

Matthew smiled. "But it is. It just depends on your definition of the Lord."

I shifted my weight from the bow to my good leg.

"Goodbye, Matthew," I told him.

I reached down and snatched the first arrow from the pile. Matthew seemed undisturbed at the sight of the arrow. I don't think he realized what it was, or if he did, he simply wasn't afraid of it. I touched the sharpened tip of the arrow to the open sconce flame. Since I had soaked it in coal oil earlier in the afternoon, it flared up easily.

I notched the flaming arrow in the bow, drew it back, and let it fly. Perhaps, I should have taken another moment to aim the arrow more precisely. Maybe, I should have fletched the arrow. I had aimed for Matthew's chest, but it struck him in the side just above his right hip.

I would like to think Matthew screamed worse than I did when the torch fell on my leg. It was probably because his agonizing yell was amplified when it echoed off the walls of the church. I enjoyed it just the same. As well as burning his skin, the small flame from the arrow ignited his robes. I smiled as he danced frantically around trying to tear off his cassock.

When he turned away from me, I notched another arrow. Then I quickly lit it and loosed it. Although I took more time to aim the second arrow, it missed because of Matthew's frantic jumping. It hit the front wall behind the pulpit and ignited a tapestry hanging there.

By the time I had notched my third arrow and lit it, Matthew had pulled the first arrow free from his side and ripped off his robe. Just as I was prepared to let the third arrow fly, he saw me and dove behind the first pew. The arrow missed him and stuck in the back of the pew.

My advantage of surprise was lost now. Matthew would continue to stay hidden until he could find a way to safely escape. I thought about his scream and laughed. I had done some good.

I grabbed my three remaining arrows and began backing out of the church. I kept one arrow notched and lit in case Matthew made an appearance before I left the church. If he did, I intended to get a final shot at him.

As I reached the main doors of the church, I noticed the wooden ceiling in the church. I glanced around once more looking for Matthew. He was still hiding somewhere among the pews. I tilted the bow up and let the arrow go.

It struck and held in the roof. The small, yellow flame licked at the wooden shingles. I left before I saw if it caught or not.

As I hobbled from the church, I tossed the bow and my remaining pair of arrows off to the side. A carriage and driver I had hired earlier were waiting for me in front of the church. I climbed into the coach and ordered the driver to take me to the wharf. One of my ships was scheduled to sail for France with the tide, and I intended to be on it. And I was. As the sun rose Monday morning, I watched Richmond slip away from me.

I spent two years in France running Atlantic Importers from there. I also managed to arrange a trade agreement between Portugal and Atlantic Importers.

By the end of 1812, the news had reached me of the second war for American independence being fought across the ocean. I wrote Frances expressing my concern over her and the children's safety. I offered to bring them all to France if she so desired. Reaching me three and a half months later, the return letter said that both she and Edgar were fine, as were Rosalie and Mrs. MacKenzie. Neither family required my assistance. That didn't stop me from worrying, though. Each time one of my ships docked in Virginia, I had the captain verify the Allans' and MacKenzies' safety.

In June of 1815, after the war in America had ended, Frances wrote me a letter in care of Atlantic Importers. The letter was delivered to me in Italy where I was living at the time. Frances, her husband, and Edgar were sailing for Britain to reopen trading between them and John Allan's business.

In the five years the Allans lived in England, I managed to see Edgar just once. I had given into the opinions of my managers to reopen trade routes with the English. While in London, I met with the Allans for supper. They were pleased with the way their trip had gone up to that point. John had negotiated several contracts with various manufacturers to ship their goods to Richmond. Edgar wasn't with them, though. They told me that nine-year-old Edgar was attending the Manor School in Stoke Newington Village.

The next day, I hired a carriage and driver to take me to the school. It was located on a beautiful elm-shaded street. The school itself was a huge Tudor-style building with Gothic windows. Inside, the school was just as impressive. The ceilings were high with staircases that twisted in all manner of directions.

The headmaster led me to Edgar's classroom and allowed me to sit in the rear of the class to watch how Edgar behaved in the school. Staring at the back of fifteen children's heads, I was unable to recognize Edgar.

The children began standing at their desks and reading passages of *The Canterbury Tales*. When the fourth boy stood up, the headmaster said, "That's him speaking."

All I saw was the back of Edgar's head which was a mass of dark-brown hair. His curls were gone, and in their place was a natural waviness in his hair. He read the passage easily and with a sense of familiarity.

"He reads well," I said to the headmaster with a slight bit of pride in my voice. Not that I was responsible for his reading ability or even his creation. But I had helped bring him into the world.

The headmaster nodded his agreement. "Not only English but French and Latin, as well. He's one of our brightest students."

As Edgar finished reading and sat down, he turned slightly to find his seat. At that moment, I saw his profile. He was a handsome boy with his mother's wide, deep-set eyes. The general shape of his face was beginning to resemble David's in which case he would become a handsome man.

I left without saying anything to him. My name would have meant nothing to him. It was enough for me to see him happy.

In 1824, I was in Charleston when I heard that Thomas Jefferson had started a new university in Charlottesville, Virginia. The urge to teach came upon me again. I sailed north and applied for a position teaching history. My credentials from my year at Harvard made it quite a bit easier for me to be offered the position beginning with the upcoming term.

Once more, I was truly happy. I was sharing my knowledge with people again. I wasn't struggling to become richer. Though my wealth allowed me freedom in the way I lived, it also left me feeling empty. It felt to me as if I was helping no one but myself.

Not only was the teaching position one in which I felt

comfortable, but the campus was beautiful. The university was near the Blue Ridge Mountains and barely seemed to disrupt the natural beauty of the area. After my classes, I would hike the trails through forests of spruce and maple to keep my mountain-living skills intact. I did not want to forget how to survive in the wilderness, in case I found myself needing to return there. Besides, my skills had already proven themselves useful in helping me not only defend myself against Matthew but to launch an offensive attack, too.

I had heard almost nothing about Matthew since I had attacked him. The church had burned, or at least the roof had caved in rendering it useless. No one had come forward to begin repairs, so it had been abandoned.

Three weeks after I had attacked Matthew, the Richmond Theater burned to the ground killing seventy-two people. At first, I had thought Matthew was responsible for it. It was his way to exact his revenge for my burning his church. That sort of indiscriminate killing was not his style, though. He only killed when he could gain something from the person's death. That was why he preferred killing by stealing a person's life force.

On returning from a trip to Baltimore, Captain Randall, one of my ship captains, told me he had heard of a Monsignor Halloran preaching in Baltimore. From his description of the man, there was little doubt in my mind that the monsignor was indeed Matthew. It disturbed me to see that Matthew had risen in power and authority in the church.

In fourteen years that was all I had learned about him.

At the beginning of February, a list was sent around to all the faculty of the new students arriving for the spring session. I usually gave the list a cursory glance and passed it on. I was seldom concerned about who a student was before he came to the University of Virginia. I only wanted to see him do well while he was at school.

On this particular morning, I was drinking coffee in my office, and I had no paperwork to look at. Since I had nothing better to occupy my eyes with, I picked up the list and read the names to myself.

Nestled in between, "Nolan, Phillip" and "Porter, John" was a name I knew all too well. "Poe, Edgar."

1826 A.D.

So Edgar was going to be attending the University of Richmond! Elizabeth would have been proud that her son was intelligent enough to attend a university. She probably would have been even more proud that he could afford it financially because she would have never been able to provide it for him, not as a traveling actress.

I immediately went to the registration office and obtained a copy of Edgar's schedule. I scanned down the list of classes quickly, hoping to see my name among his instructors. Unfortunately, he wasn't in any of the classes I taught. He had enrolled mainly language classes. He already knew French and Latin. In addition to those subjects, he was taking classes in Greek, Spanish, and Italian.

He arrived on campus a week later around the middle of February, but I couldn't bring myself to go see him. I continually found reasons to avoid him. The truth was I wasn't sure of how I should introduce myself to him. How much had Frances told him about me?

At seventeen, Edgar had fulfilled the promise he had shown when I had watched him in the Manor School. He had a small build, much like his mother's, but he was not weak. A fellow professor had told me he had seen Edgar swim six miles upstream in the James River just to answer a dare.

I made weekly visits to his instructors without him knowing to check on his performance in class. His instructors said much the same things that the headmaster at the Manor School had said. Edgar was a bright young man. He was a quick learner with a memory with a vast recall.

However, by May, the reports began to change somewhat. Edgar was distracted in class. His grades had slipped from As to Bs and even Cs. He had failed to turn in an important paper in his Greek class. His instructors couldn't believe that they had been so wrong about a student.

Neither could I.

Something had to be wrong with the boy. Edgar was too smart to be failing his classes. I finally overcame my excuses and wrote him a letter asking him to meet me in my office at the end of the week. It was surprisingly easy to do. By using my position as a professor, I had found a way to introduce myself to him.

On the day of our meeting, I spent an unusual amount of time grooming myself. I greased my hair down and combed it straight back. I wore a suit that I had only worn at meetings with business associates when I had lived in Italy. Everything had to be perfect.

I spent most of the morning straightening my office, putting away papers, cleaning the window, getting a warm fire burning. Then I sat back and waited. In minutes, I was pacing the floor and looking out my door every few moments to see if Edgar was coming.

When I finally heard a knock on my door, it startled me. I hesitated a moment to give my office one final, quick inspection before I opened the door. I was facing a young man about seventeen-years old. He had wavy, brown hair and sad, gray eyes. His clothes looked threadbare. It was hard to picture him as a university student.

"My name is Edgar Poe, sir. Your letter said you wanted to speak with me," he said. As soon as he finished speaking, he dropped his stare from my face to the floor.

I invited him inside and had him sit down. Then I sat down at my desk and just stared at him. He looked up from the floor occasionally, but when he saw me staring, he looked away again. I knew I was making him uncomfortable, but I didn't care. I wanted to look at him. It had been over eight years since I had seen him.

"Is something the matter, sir?" he asked.

I shook my head. "No. Everything is fine. In fact, everything is wonderful." He looked at me oddly as if he thought I was a lunatic. "You look like your mother," I said finally.

His eyes widened. "You knew my mother?"

"Very well. I saw you when you were born."

His eyebrows arched. "You must not have been much older than me then," he guessed.

I remembered the last regeneration of my body had been when Father Davis had stabbed me in the back in St. Ananias. I must have only looked in my early thirties at the time. However, Elizabeth would have nearly been forty if she had still been alive. I couldn't have imagined what she would have looked like at that age. She would always be the twenty-year-old girl that I had first seen on the stage in Baltimore.

I smiled at Edgar and nodded. "Yes, I was younger then."

Edgar leaned forward resting his forearms on his thighs. "What was she like? I can't remember her. All I have is a locket with her picture in it. Mrs. Allan gave it to me when I left Richmond."

He fished the small brass locket from beneath his shirt and held it out toward me. Bending forward, I snapped the locket open. Inside was a small painting of Elizabeth. I closed my eyes and turned away to keep from crying.

"She was very beautiful," I said.

Edgar nodded as he looked at the portrait.

Could it have really been fifteen years since she had died? How much longer would she have lived if she hadn't known me? Two years? Three years? Maybe, even four? It would not have been a significant amount of time, certainly, but it would have given Edgar a stronger memory of his mother. He might have been able to recall her face if nothing else. He wouldn't have to swoon over a picture in an aging locket.

"Your mother loved you, and Rosalie, and William. She did everything in her power to provide for the three of you, even down to making sure you were cared for when you died."

I knew I was exaggerating somewhat, but I felt had she been given time, Elizabeth would have made the arrangements. I had helped cut her time short, so I made the arrangements instead.

"Mrs. Allan said she was an actress," Edgar said.

Nodding, I told him, "Your mother was a gifted actress on the stage. I saw her play Juliet, Cordelia, and Rosamunda. She was wonderful as all of them. Your mother had a way of truly convincing the audience she was the person she played. And, it is not just my opinion, either. All of the newspapers said the same thing, too."

He glanced at the locket portrait again and smiled. Looking up, he said, "And my father? Did you know him?"

I paused and looked away from the boy. I didn't want to lie to him. That was no way to start a friendship. And I did hope we could become friends. He reminded me much of his mother whom I had killed. Just to look at him pulled my heart apart.

So how could I tell him what I truly thought of David Poe? His father was a drunken and jealous man. His father had abandoned Elizabeth to make due on her own. He hadn't even tried to take Edgar with him.

I looked at Edgar. He was still leaning forward with his eyes focused on me waiting for his answer.

"Do you know where your brother is?" I asked.

His brow wrinkled. "In Baltimore with my grandfather. Why?"

I ran my hand over my chin as I considered my answer to his original question. Did I know his father?

"It would be better if you asked your grandfather about your father. I didn't know him," I lied.

Edgar's smile fell. He leaned back in his chair and gazed out the window. I waited anxiously for him to say something.

Without turning from the window, he said, "I have written him regarding my father."

"And?" I prompted.

"And," Edgar turned to face me, "My grandfather wrote back and told me to forget I ever had a father because He's forgotten he ever had a son."

Harsh words. Probably harsher than anything I might have ever said about David. At least I knew that despite my biased view of the man, I hadn't been alone in the way I felt.

"What do you think about that?" I asked.

He shrugged trying to lead me to believe that it didn't matter, but I could see the pain in his eyes. "It's one man's opinion. No one else seems to have known him. Mrs. Allan never knew him, but she doesn't like him. She says he left my mother while she was pregnant with Rosalie." Before snapping the locket shut, he glanced at the small portrait once more. "I guess I can accept that my father didn't love me. At least I know my mother did."

"That she did, Edgar. That she did," I said as he slid the locket back down his shirt so that it rested close to his heart.

He stood up and held out his hand. "Thank you for talking with me, sir. I always enjoy hearing about my mother, though it is infrequent that I do."

I grabbed onto his shirt sleeve and pulled him back down. "I'm not through talking with you yet."

His eyebrows arched. "Oh?"

"While I have enjoyed telling you about your mother, I called you here to talk about your grades," I told him.

He closed his eyes and sighed. His hands dropped to his side. He reminded me of a prisoner being positioned in front of a firing squad.

"Sit down, Edgar."

He did as he was told. I could tell by his change in attitude that the relationship between us had undergone another change. We had begun as strangers, become friends, and now we were student and teacher.

"I was told that you were one of the most-intelligent young men attending the University of Virginia." He didn't look up. "However, your grades no longer support this statement."

I let the silence hover between us like a guillotine blade as I waited for his reply. After a minute had passed, I began to wonder if he would answer at all. Would I have to coerce the information from him?

"I find myself with less time for my studies, nowadays. And the time I do have is usually split between not thinking clearly and not thinking of my studies at all," Edgar said finally.

I frowned as I leaned forward in my chair. "This is a university, Edgar, an institution of learning. To learn is your primary purpose for being here," I told him.

"I know, sir."

He still didn't look up, which I found quite annoying. Besides, I wanted to look into his face and see the traces of Elizabeth in his eyes and mouth and hair. Then I made the mistake of saying something that totally erased any trace of Elizabeth from his face.

"Your father is paying a lot of money to send you here. Surely..."

Edgar's head snapped up. I wished he had kept it down. I saw a fury in his eyes backed by a hardness that made me pull away from him.

"John Allan is neither my father nor is he paying for me to stay here!" he shouted.

I dropped the pen I had been twirling unconsciously between my fingers. It tumbled to the floor leaving a small ink spot on the wood. I bent over, picked it up, and sat it on the desk.

"I think you need to explain yourself," I said.

Edgar stood up. For a moment, I thought he would leave rather than explain, but instead, he began pacing the floor.

"The Allans never adopted me. The MacKenzies adopted Rosalie, and William is with family in Baltimore. But me?" He tapped himself on his chest with his fist. "I am still an outsider with the only family I have known."

"But surely Frances..." I started to say.

"Mrs. Allan is sweet and caring, everything a mother should be. I have no doubt that if it were up to her alone, she would have adopted me the moment she took me in. It's John Allan's fault. He hates me because I have no interest in his business. I don't want to be a merchant. I want to read, and travel, and write. He can't tolerate it."

He was so much like his father without even realizing it. David had wanted to act, to allow his creativity to flow. His father, though, had had other ideas. Acting was not a profession of men, but of failures.

"So John Allan is not paying your tuition," I said when he had finished his tirade.

Edgar nodded. "I think he found out I was studying language rather than law or medicine."

"How are you paying for your tuition?" I asked.

Edgar focused his attention on a loose thread on his pants leg and pulled at it. He wrapped it around his forefinger and gave it a sharp tug.

"I'm not paying for it," he said finally.

"What?"

Edgar drew back. "I don't have enough money to pay for it on my own. Besides, if I don't eat, I certainly won't have any need for school. I've cut back on my spending as much as possible. I'm eating one meal a day and not much of one, at that. I borrow books from my classmates. I continue wearing clothes that are too small or threadbare or both."

I could see that much even without him saying it. He pointed out two poorly sewn patches on his shirt. It also looked as if the buttons would pop off if he breathed too deeply. His pants had holes worn in the knees. He looked no better than a vagabond. His size resemblance to his mother was probably due more to malnutrition than genetics.

"There's nothing else you can do?" I asked.

"I can starve and go naked to class. I haven't tried that yet, but I've tried everything else. I can't even win the money," Edgar answered.

"Win?" I repeated.

"I've played cards at Hubner's, trying to win myself tuition money," he explained.

"How much have you lost?" I asked slowly as I tried to hold back the traces of anger in my voice.

Edgar hesitated. I think he sensed my anger, but finally, he said, "Everything I managed to save doing everything else."

I threw my hands up in the air. "How could someone so smart be so foolish?" I shouted.

Edgar's face flushed with shame. He turned away from me, and I thought for a moment that he might cry. I had to do something to help him stay in school. He had more to deal with than he could handle. If only for Elizabeth's sake, I had to help him.

"If you had the money to pay for your tuition could you, and would you, stop gambling?" I asked him.

He stared at me as if I had struck him. I was sure he knew what I was going to say next.

"Of course," he said, "I only gambled in the first place to make enough money so that I might stay here."

I nodded that I believed him. "I'll make arrangements with the finance office to have your tuition taken care of then," I promised.

Edgar's face brightened. "You mean you'll..."

"I'll take care of your tuition, but you must take care of your grades," I warned him. "If your grades fall too low, I won't be able to help you at all."

He grabbed my hand and shook it furiously. "Thank you, sir! Thank you. You don't know how much this means to me. I don't want to leave here. I love learning. This is an excellent school."

He left my office smiling. There was a springiness in his step that hadn't been there earlier. I grinned just to see him so happy.

I kept my word and paid his tuition that afternoon. As the treasurer wrote out my receipt, he glanced at me as if I was doing something wrong. He kept quiet, however. I had no doubt he would do his talking as soon as I left. What did I care? It was my money, and I could do with it what I wanted. Let him wonder where I had come by such a large sum of money and why I would spend it on a failing student.

I continued my weekly check-ups with Edgar's instructors. It wasn't that I didn't trust him. I just wanted to be aware if he needed any help in his subjects so that I might be able to offer my assistance where needed. After all, I could speak most of the languages of the world, including a few that had long- since become extinct.

The first week after our meeting, his instructors told me that his recovery was amazing. He had suddenly become attentive in class, answering questions as well as asking them. His assignments were submitted early and were excellent.

The second week, however, the situation was worse than it had been before our meeting. His Latin instructor, John Montgomery, said Edgar had staggered into the middle of class one morning half an hour late. Afterward, John had approached Edgar to remind him of a critical paper on the origin of language. John described Edgar as a drunkard with bloodshot eyes that were glazed over, poor balance, and the odor of beer on his breath.

I took it on myself to find out what had happened. My note for a meeting was ignored this time, though, and I had to set out to find him on my own.

I found him in a tavern at the edge of campus called Hubner's. Francis Hubner had converted his small home into a pub two months after the university had admitted its first students. A month before he had earned himself enough to buy a new, larger home next to the tavern. He had had the foresight to see that the students at the University of Virginia would need an occasional escape from the stresses of college life in the form of liquor and gambling. Hubner's was a small place whose sole patronage was students. It was a two-story cottage with the first floor acting as the bar. The second floor had been set aside for gambling. Cards, dice, betting on the outcome of grades. The gambling was all done on the second floor of Hubner's.

Amazingly enough, I didn't find Edgar on the second floor as I thought I would. He was sitting at a corner table on the first floor sipping a tankard of beer. Seeing him gave me a sense of deja vu´. He resembled his father enough that for a moment, I saw David nursing his drink at The Corner Stop eighteen years ago.

I moved up beside the table and waited for him to see me. He stared at the bottom of his empty tankard as if he was surprised that it was empty. He finally sensed my presence and looked up. He saw me, grunted, and looked away.

"What do you want?" he asked, slurring his words slightly.

I pulled out a chair and sat down. I tried to pull the beer tankard away from Edgar, but he clamped onto it and held tight.

"I thought we had a bargain," I said as I gave up trying to take the tankard from him.

He laughed as he waved his mug at the bartender. The bartender nodded, and Edgar set his tankard down.

"I'm not upstairs, am I?" he asked.

He refused to meet my gaze. The bartender brought over a fresh tankard of beer, and only then, did Edgar relinquish his grip on the empty one.

"That wasn't our deal. You were supposed to improve your grades," I reminded him.

"It doesn't matter. Things have changed," he said.

"How so?" I asked.

"If you were such good friends with my mother, why did you kill her?" he asked.

24

1826 A.D.

An awkward, thick silence fell between us. I was so shocked that I had heard Edgar mention his mother being killed that I couldn't say a thing. He slowly raised his head. Behind his bloodshot eyes, I could see his anger, and it was directed at me.

How did he know about how his mother had died? About how I had led her to her death?

I ran my tongue over my lips to moisten them, but my tongue was as dry as my lips. "What do you mean?" I asked finally.

Edgar slammed his hand on the table shaking it. "Don't play dumb! My father told me how you killed her!"

His father? How did David know about what had happened at St. Ananias, and why had he decided to reintroduce himself to his son?

I tried to stay calm, but I could feel my hands shaking. I reached across the table and put my hand on his wrist. Edgar quickly pulled his arm away.

"Your mother died in her sleep," I told him.

"Not according to my father."

"Your father had abandoned you a year before your mother died. You were only two," I told him.

"He's not the one who saw you," he said impatiently, "A priest did and told him about you. Monsignor Halloran."

Leaning across the table, I shook my finger in Edgar's face. "Stay away from him. He's dangerous."

"He's a priest," Edgar said.

"That's what your mother thought, too, and look what happened to her. He's no priest. He's a murderer."

"Now if that isn't the pot calling the kettle black," Edgar said.

He pushed himself to his feet and swayed uneasily. For a moment, I thought he would topple over. He grabbed the back of the chair to steady himself.

"My father is bringing Monsignor Halloran to see me tonight, and then maybe I will hear the truth."

He tried to grimace. I don't know whether it was his drunkenness or his gentle nature, but his face couldn't hold the expression.

He turned and quickly staggered from the tavern, weaving from side to side. I followed behind him. I had to convince him not to see Matthew. It would be a dangerous meeting.

"What are you doing, Reynolds?" he asked when we were outside. "Are you going to kill me like you did my mother?"

"I didn't kill your mother!" I shouted as I continued to follow him.

He walked to his room which, unfortunately, was only a quarter mile away from Hubner's. The location gave him easy access to the tavern, and I wondered how many times he had visited it. His room was just one room among many that a landlord rented out to students. They were the only ones foolish enough to pay his inflated prices. There was a fireplace, a small desk and chair, an armoire, a chest of drawers, and a low bed that looked as if it might collapse.

Edgar entered the room and closed the door behind him. I opened it and followed him in. He was sitting on the bed with one shoe in his hand.

"Can't you see I don't want you in here? I am expecting company soon!" he yelled at me.

"I am here to prevent that," I said.

Edgar shook his head in disbelief. "Don't you understand? I don't care what you did for me to keep me in the university. It's not going to bring my mother back to me, you bastard!"

He lunged off his bed swinging his arm that was holding his shoe. There was a fury in his eyes that I had seen once before, but not in him. It was anger that could no longer be contained and had to be vented. I had seen it on the faces of the Egyptians who had stoned me after Callames had died. It was a heat that burned through their normal inhibitions to allow them to strike out and kill me.

I ducked under his arm barely in time as the shoe brushed across the top of my head. The momentum of Edgar's swing carried him around in a circle. As I stood, I saw the surprise register on his face that he had missed me.

I don't know if had originally come knowing I would have to do what I did or not. I only knew I reacted very uncharacteristically. I slammed my right fist into Edgar's side. His mouth dropped open. I swung my left fist up and around. Just as he started to yell, I hit him on the side of the face.

His yell ended abruptly as his knees buckled and he fell. I managed to catch him in my right arm before he hit the floor. I didn't want him to be hurt any more than absolutely necessary.

Laying him on the bed, I wondered how long he would remain unconscious. It would only be a few minutes at most. Not nearly long enough. I rifled through the drawers in his dresser pulling out a clean, white shirt and two sets of suspenders.

Pulling open Edgar's mouth, I stuffed it with as much of the shirt as possible. Having gagged him, I rolled him onto his stomach and tied his hands behind his back with the suspenders. Following his hands, I tied his ankles together so that he would be unable to move.

Then I sat down and waited. Edgar was unconscious for nearly fifteen minutes. That surprised me. I hadn't realized I had hit him so hard.

His arms jerked slightly as he regained consciousness, but he was unable to move in order to push himself up. Next, his eyes blinked open. His eyebrows knitted together as he realized his shirt was in his mouth. He tried to yell, but it only came out as a muffled groan.

He started rocking back and forth trying to roll over on his back. He reminded me of a fish out of water flopping around on the ground.

"Don't make me hit you again, Edgar," I warned.

He stopped rocking and turned his head so he could see me. Even though the anger still burned in his eyes, it was only a secondary concern of mine. He could hate me as much as he wanted as long as it lasted a long time.

"After Monsignor Halloran and your father are convinced you're not here and leave, I'll release you," I told him.

He tried to say something, but I couldn't understand what it was through the gag. And I wasn't going to take the gag out and give him a chance to scream.

About twenty minutes later, I heard a knock on the door. Edgar had drifted off in a daze. At the sound, he blinked away the glazed look from over his eyes. He tried to scream through the shirt again, but at the first sound, I sprang on him.

Pushing his face into his pillow, I whispered in his ear, "If I hold you like this long enough, you will lose consciousness. I don't think you want that to happen so I'm going to let you breathe."

I released the pressure on his head. I hated being so brutal with him, but it was necessary to keep him alive. He turned his head to the left and started taking deep breaths through his nose.

There was another knock at the door. "Edgar. Edgar, are you in there? It's your father."

I almost laughed when I heard David say that. He had never been a father to Edgar. I was sure the reason he had reappeared had something to do with Monsignor Halloran, not parental love.

Edgar glared at me, but he didn't make a sound. I was relieved because I hadn't wanted to carry through on my threat.

I heard a muffled conversation behind the door. Too muffled to make out more than a few words, but I was sure I knew the gist of it. Of the two voices, one belonged to David Poe. The second was Matthew's. There was some argument going on between them. Every once in a while, Matthew's voice would rise, and I could make out a word or two. "Unrighteous." "Wasted." "Lazarus." He was obviously annoyed with David that Edgar was not in his room. David, whether out of fear of being overheard or respect for Matthew, kept his voice low.

When the voices faded, I realized they were walking away. The faint glimmer of hope Edgar had held faded, and he turned his head away from me.

I limped over next to the window. Keeping my back against the wall, I peeked around the edge of the window frame just in time to see Matthew and David leave the building.

Matthew paused on the walk and looked up at Edgar's window. I pulled back and resisted the urge to look again to see if he was still watching. Did Matthew suspect Edgar was still in his room and not answering the door? Could he sense that I was nearby? No, if that were true, I would have felt his presence also, and I felt nothing. What if he did and tried to burn down the house to kill me? Could I get Edgar and myself out in time?

The clopping of hooves on the road pulled me from my thoughts. I chanced a look around the window frame again. I saw the back end of Matthew's covered carriage as it turned onto Jefferson Street and disappeared from my view.

I leaned my head against the window and sighed. Edgar was safe for now, but how long would that last?

I turned back to the boy. He was staring at me again.

"They're gone. I'll keep my part of the bargain now," I said.

I grabbed him under his arms and pulled him into a sitting position. He didn't bother resisting. I untied his wrists, then backed away.

Rubbing his wrists, he restored the circulation to his hands. Never taking his eyes from mine, he pulled his shirt from his mouth. He ran his tongue over his lips a few times to moisten them. Then he bent over and undid the suspenders from around his ankles.

"You have assaulted me, as well as murdering my mother. Vengeance is mine. I demand satisfaction."

I stared at him for a while trying to figure out what he meant. He had suffered some personal embarrassment. Certainly. Every young man thinks he is invincible, but this particular young man had been beaten by a man who appeared twice his age.

I couldn't help but smirk. How would Edgar feel if he knew he had been knocked out by a man 110 times his age?

But how could he consider himself assaulted when he began the attack?

"Don't laugh at me!" Edgar yelled as he stood up. "I am challenging you to a duel to the death."

Now I did laugh out loud. "A duel? Edgar, you're a student, not Aaron Burr or Alexander Hamilton."

"I know precisely who I am, and I am demanding your presence at a duel.

Saturday at ten in the morning. McCarron Field."

I shook my head. "Saturday morning you'll be shooting at the squirrels in the trees because I won't be there."

Besides, I wanted to tell him, you'd never win. I can't be killed.

"Then I will shoot you in the back at the first opportunity that arises. Did you think you could buy my silence?" Edgar promised.

I panicked. If I showed up at the duel, I would kill him. There could be no other outcome. Either I would shoot him, or he would shoot me. And if he shot me, I would kill him when my body regenerated. Yet, if I didn't show up, he would shoot me anyway, and I would still kill him when my body regenerated.

I moved back to the window and looked out just to make sure Matthew hadn't returned. "I never tried to buy your silence because there was never anything to buy," I told him.

"Then why did you knock me out so I wouldn't be able to talk to Monsignor Halloran? You were afraid of what he might tell me how you murdered my mother, weren't you?" he yelled.

"I was afraid he might kill you!"

Kill me?" He laughed a sarcastic laugh. "He's a priest. Murderers don't become priests."

What could I say to convince him? Matthew had found himself the perfect alias. No one would believe a priest could be a murderer or even dangerous. He could steal their lives to continue his own, and they would never know he was doing it.

"The choice is yours, Reynolds," Edgar said. "You can face me like a man Saturday morning or die like a dog Saturday night."

I heard the words I spoke, but they seemed distant to me as if someone else had said them. "I'll be at McCarron Field at ten o'clock."

1826 A.D.

Edgar smiled and nodded when I agreed to be at the dueling place. "I see you have a little courage left, Reynolds, and do not confine your attacks only to women."

I left him alone in his room and walked back to my house, wondering what I had gotten myself into. How could I face him in a duel? Either way it went, Edgar would lose. Yet, I couldn't let him shoot me in the back at his leisure. He would surely die then. All I had managed to do was to postpone the confrontation by a day. I had given myself twenty-four hours to think of a way to save Edgar from me.

From Edgar's room, I walked to the nearest Catholic church. The priest there was named Father Newberry. He was a middle-aged man who wore thick glasses.

"Father, I have heard that Monsignor Halloran is in Charlottesville. Do you know where I might find him? I would like to speak to him," I told the priest.

Father Newberry shook his head. "I'm afraid you've been misled. Monsignor Halloran is in the Maryland Archdiocese."

"Really?" I acted surprised even though I wasn't. "Maybe my friend simply got the name wrong. Is the monsignor for this archdiocese in town?"

Father Newberry shook his head again. "Monsignor Trout won't be in Charlottesville until next month, but if you want someone to hear your confession..."

I held up my hand. "No, it's nothing quite so important that it can't wait until next month. Where will the monsignor be staying?"

"The Ashton's. Henry Ashton and his wife are wealthy members of this congregation who host any visiting official from the church since their home is many times nicer than the best hotel in Charlottesville. They live on Montgomery Road on the north side."

I thanked him for his time and left. I walked over to the Ashtons' house, and I was tempted to knock on the door. I didn't know if

Matthew was there or not, but I thought he would be if only to maintain the appearance of a regular church official. Besides, it wasn't Matthew I wanted to see.

A man passed me on the street. I stopped him and asked, "Excuse me, I'm new in this area of town, and I'm awfully thirsty. Where can I find the nearest tavern?"

The man took a moment to get his bearing, and then he said, "If you go to the end of this road, and make a left. The Lion's Head is only a few hundred feet further down the road."

I smiled. That is where I would find David Poe.

The Lion's Head looked almost the same as Hubner's, except the drinkers and gamblers there were businessmen, not students. It was crowded and noisy. I stood in the doorway for two minutes before I saw David. He was standing by himself at the bar drinking. He looked much the same, except now his hair was gray, and his eyes sagged with what appeared to be chronic fatigue.

I walked up beside him and stood staring at him without saying a word. He finally felt my presence and turned to look at me. He stared at me for a moment and then frowned and shook his head.

"So the priest was right, after all, you are immortal," he said.

"Not quite," I told him as I put my hand on his arm. "Let's go outside. We need to talk." Not only that, but I didn't want him telling everyone in the bar I couldn't die. Someone might try to test his theory.

He shrugged off my hand. "We don't need to talk about anything. I know all about you."

"I doubt that," I told him.

"You killed Elizabeth just so you could live longer!" he shouted. Luckily, the bar was so crowded and noisy no one noticed.

I shook my head. "Matthew did."

"Who the hell is Matthew?"

"Matthew is an evil man impersonating a priest who was a friend of mine also. Matthew killed my priest friend even more horribly than he did Elizabeth. Of course, Monsignor Halloran wouldn't tell you that seeing as how he is the one who did it."

David laughed. "You can't expect me to believe that."

"Didn't Elizabeth ever tell you about a friend of mine named Father Halloran?"

David thought for a minute and then said, "Yes, she went to his funeral, didn't she?"

I nodded. "Father Halloran had brown hair, and he was fat. Does that sound like the man you're with?"

"No, but that doesn't mean anything. There could be more than one Father Halloran in the Catholic Church." He took a sip from his glass.

"Why are you here, David?" I asked.

"Because Father Halloran said you were going to kill my son like you killed Elizabeth. I knew you were dangerous when I saw you, but she wouldn't believe me. At least it's not too late for Edgar," David said, and I actually felt he was telling the truth. He did have paternal concern for his son.

"Edgar has challenged me to a duel," I told him.

David slammed his glass down on the bar. "What?"

"Because he believes I killed Elizabeth, and because I stopped him from meeting you and Matthew earlier."

"But he can't kill you," David said.

I nodded my agreement. "I know, and if he tries, Edgar will die. If you really want to be his father, you'll stop him from killing himself."

I turned away and left David standing at the bar. It would do him good to think over what he had involved his son in by associating with Monsignor Halloran.

On Saturday morning, I nearly didn't go to face Edgar. I seriously considered hopping aboard one of my ships and leaving Virginia forever. That wouldn't have solved the problem, though. It would have only delayed the resolution until a later time, but I'm sure it would have come, eventually. Instead, I kneeled down and prayed that David had decided to save his son.

I arrived at McCarron Field shortly after ten in the morning. It was a large clearing a half mile outside of town that was surrounded by maples and oaks. John McCarron had once built his home and raised his family in the clearing, but the Iroquois had burned him out two decades ago, killing one of his sons and his wife. All that was left of the home were a few fire-blackened boards in the western corner of the field showing where the foundation of the cabin had been.

Edgar was already waiting for me with two other men when I arrived. He walked up to me, calmer than he had been the day before, and sober. His eyes were clear, though still a little red. I hoped it would be to my benefit that he could think clearly.

"Where is your second?" he demanded.

"I don't have one. I am still hoping you will forget this foolishness before it's too late," I told Edgar.

He spun on his heels and turned his back to me. As he walked

221

back to the other two men, I followed.

He pointed to the man on his left. "This is Paul Barker. He will act as the neutral judge and counter. Any objections?" I shook my head. He shifted his hand to the right. "And this is Sam Newton, my second."

I nodded to both men.

Paul stooped over to pick up a box from the grass. He flipped open the lid and held the box in front of me. Inside the case were two finely matched dueling pistols that looked as if they were rarely used.

"Choose your weapon," he said.

I hesitated, first glancing over at Edgar, but he was talking to Sam. I took the pistol nearest me. I am not a man used to dealing with guns, but I can tell a well-balanced weapon when I feel it. This was it. It was a small, .36-caliber, ball-and-powder pistol with an ash grip.

Edgar took the remaining pistol. He shifted it in his grip until he found a comfortable position to hold it. Then he aimed the pistol at my head, pulled the trigger, and said "bang." Sam Newton laughed like it was the greatest joke he had ever seen. Both of them pretended not to realize that Edgar had come to kill another man or die in the attempt.

Besides me, Paul was the only other person who seemed to acknowledge the gravity of the situation. I wondered if he had served as a dueling judge at other duels.

"If you both are ready," Paul said, "Let's finish this business."

Both Edgar and I nodded. Paul grabbed both of us by the shoulder and turned us, so we were standing back-to-back. He and Sam stepped away from us out of the line of fire. Sam wasn't laughing anymore.

"Do either of you wish to end this matter peacefully before it goes any further?" Paul asked.

"I do. This is foolishness," I said.

"Coward," Edgar said. "Let's proceed."

Paul was hesitant. He looked at Sam, then at me, and finally at Edgar.

"I will count off the steps you are to take," he said, "When I reach ten, you will turn and fire your pistols. Your pistols will have only one load. If both of you miss, I will reload the weapons, and you will repeat the process."

When Paul finished speaking, Sam took Edgar's pistol and loaded it. Since I had no second, Paul loaded my pistol. He measured in the black powder, then followed it with wadding and the small, lead ball. He tapped them deep into the barrel with the barrel-long, wooden rod that was attached to the pistol. That finished, he cocked the hammer and positioned the cap. He passed the weapon back to me for my inspection. I took it and waited.

Sam and Paul moved off to the side once again. Paul paused for what seemed hours but was probably no more than a few seconds. Then he began to count. I felt Edgar step away from me as we paced further and further apart. My mind rushed ahead of my actions still trying to decide what I should do. Should I shoot him or let him shoot me? Could I run? Should I...

"Wait! Edgar, don't!" a voice yelled from my right. I turned and saw David stepping out of the woods. His clothes were disheveled as if he had been sleeping in them all night. "Edgar, this isn't the way to solve this. You don't know what you are doing. You could be killed."

"But he killed Mother. You said so. How can you tolerate seeing him stand there alive while she's dead?"

"Because I don't want to see you..."

"Mr. Poe, I believe you should let Edgar make his own choices. Just as I have allowed you to make your own choices," Matthew said as he appeared behind David.

"But you didn't tell me that my son would be in danger," David protested, turning to the monsignor.

"Unforeseen things happen sometimes. We made a deal, David. I have kept my side of the bargain. I expect you to keep yours. After all, Edgar is an adult now." Matthew turned his attention from David to Edgar. "I saw Alexander Reynolds murder your mother, Edgar. Since I am a man of God, I believe you should follow the advice of the Bible and take an eye for an eye. He killed your mother. Kill him."

Edgar looked at me.

"Don't do it," David pleaded.

Matthew turned to David. "You and I will speak later on this matter. I am disappointed in your conduct here. It requires punishment."

David's face went pale, and he actually seemed to shake. He looked at Edgar, then to me. "Don't kill him," he said.

Before I could reply, he turned away and ran into the woods. Matthew smiled.

Edgar turned his back to me. I looked over at Matthew.

"It seems you have a duel to complete, Professor," Matthew said.

"You heard your father, Edgar. You don't have to do this, I called.

Edgar didn't answer. Paul said, "He wishes to continue, Mr. Reynolds. Please turn around, and I will finish my count."

I did so, slowly. When we were both in position, Paul finished his interrupted count. "Seven, eight, nine, ten!

The word was still ringing in my ear as I turned to face Edgar. I was moving too slow. He would fire before I was completely turned around. I wouldn't have time to make a decision. I finished my turn, and no shot had struck me. Edgar was still turning.

I felt my arm that was holding my pistol rising on its own accord. The weapon was heavier than it had been before. I was amazed I had the strength in my arm to raise it at all. But rise it did.

I don't want to kill him, I thought. *I want to save him from being killed.*

My arm came level with my eye just as Edgar completed his turn. His eyes went wide as he saw he was about to die. He had been too slow.

Then my arm continued to rise past my face until I was holding the pistol straight over my head. I pulled the trigger. The explosion shook my arm, pushing my arm bone into my shoulder.

For a moment, everything froze, except for the echo of my shot which continued to ring in my ears.

Then everything began moving again. Sam was yelling something in Paul's ear about cheating. Edgar brought his pistol up so that it was level with my chest, and he waited.

Paul glanced nervously at me. "You are within your rights to fire, Edgar," Paul told him.

I hoped he wouldn't. I was counting on his basic decency to keep him from shooting me. He wouldn't be saving my life but his own.

His hand wavered slightly as he pondered the choices.

"This is for my mother," he said as he pulled the trigger.

I heard the loud explosion from the gun and saw the smoke leaving the barrel moments before I felt the lead ball strike my chest. It tore into my ribcage and lodged itself somewhere inside of my chest.

I was lifted off my feet and flung backward onto the ground. I could feel the blood pumping out of my chest. Someone was going to die. I rolled over onto my stomach and tried to push myself to my knees. My left arm refused to move. I struggled for a short distance then collapsed on the grass.

The ripple went out of me quickly and returned a few seconds later. I heard one of the boys yell in surprise, but I couldn't tell who it had been. I was facing away from them at the time.

"Please don't let it be Edgar," I prayed. "I led his mother to her death. Don't let me do the same thing to him."

As soon as the feeling returned to my arm, I rolled over and sat up. The three of young men had started walking toward me but stopped. Matthew had left during the shooting.

"You're supposed to be dead," Sam said.

The tingling stopped. I was fully healed. "I'm not, though. Edgar must have only grazed me."

"That's a lie!" Sam yelled. He pointed at my chest. "Look at the blood all over him and on the grass! Look at the hole in his shirt! Eddie didn't graze him! He hit him dead on!"

"Then why am I still alive?" I asked.

Sam's face flushed red as he tried to think of something to explain what had happened. He couldn't.

I pulled my shirt up to my neck and showed them all that there was no scar on my chest. Sam stared intently at my chest as if in looking for some sign of a wound would make it appear. As he looked, I stared over his head at Edgar who hadn't said anything about the duel.

When Sam had finished looking, I tucked my shirt back into my pants. "Are you satisfied now?"

He snorted and turned away from me. He stomped back toward the university. Halfway across the field, he looked over his shoulder and said, "I don't know how you did it, but you cheated. I know you did."

Paul looked at Edgar and me. "Do you want to reload and continue?"

I looked over at Edgar. He was staring at the blood on my chest. "No, I don't think we'll be doing that."

"I think that's a good idea," Paul said. He collected both of his dueling pistols and left us standing alone together in the field.

"Who was standing closest to me when I fell?" I asked.

Edgar was still staring at my chest. His head snapped up when I spoke to him. "Paul was, I guess."

Paul Barker would soon be dead. I was sorry that it had to happen, but I was glad that at least it hadn't been Edgar.

"What are you?" Edgar asked.

"I'm not a thing. I'm a man," I corrected him.

"You're not a man. I know that now. I did shoot you squarely in the chest. You bled more blood than I have ever seen, and yet, you still live. You don't even show a sign of the wound."

"I'm lucky I suppose."

Edgar shook his head. "Luck had nothing to do with it. I saw you when you tried to sit up. There was a hole in your chest the size of a plum. Now there's nothing. That is not human. That's why my father was trying to warn me about you."

I unconsciously put my hand on my chest to cover the hole that was not there. "I would tell you the truth, but you don't seem to believe that anything I might tell you is the truth," I said.

He stood in front of me shifting from one foot to the other and kicking nonchalantly at the grass. He reminded me of a young boy who had just been scolded by his mother.

When he looked up, he said, "What do you have to tell me? I'll listen to what you have to say. I may even believe you."

So we sat down there in the grass, and I told him the story of my life. At several points in the early part of the story, he almost got up and walked off angrily. I always was able to calm him down, though, and continue with the story. I told him about his father. I could see in his eyes he doubted what I said, but he had to be remembering that his grandfather, David's very own father, had said much the same thing. Besides, David had run off to let Edgar fight a duel in much the same way David had abandoned Elizabeth when she told him she was sick.

I told him about his mother and how much I had loved her. Finally, I explained to him about Matthew and Father Halloran.

By the time I finished my tale, Edgar was lying on his back in the grass. His hands were behind his head, and he was staring at the clouds in the sky.

I ended my story by saying, "And so I believe that Matthew, the present Monsignor Halloran, will try to kill you if he has the opportunity. Not out of any malice toward you, but because he wants me to know that he is in charge. Matthew doesn't want me to interfere in his rise to power. I don't want to give him the opportunity to kill you like he did your mother. He was probably hoping either I would kill you or my regeneration would kill you in this duel."

Edgar rolled his head to the side and said, "How can I believe what you're telling me? Do you know how fanciful your talk of eternal life and Christ sounds? You're telling me tales."

"I know, but how can you not believe me? You saw the hole in my chest. You put it there yourself. And you saw it disappear," I reminded him.

"So you're saying someone will die now because your body stole that person's life?" I hesitated, unsure if I should tell him. "Well?" he asked.

I nodded. "It should be Paul Barker. You said he was the closest one to me when you shot me."

Edgar sighed and rolled over on his side so that he was facing away from me. I thought I heard him sob, but I couldn't be sure.

"I'm sorry, Edgar. I didn't believe that you would shoot me if I fired my pistol in the air. I didn't want anyone to die."

"It's not all your fault," he said without turning to face me, "I shouldn't have overreacted so badly, but when my father told me about my mother..." He paused and took a deep breath. "I couldn't stand the thought that she might have lived longer and I might have known her or at least been able to remember her. I love her, Reynolds. She's my mother. But I hated her for dying and not being around when I woke up in the nights with bad dreams. Then to hear that she was killed, well, that meant it wasn't her fault for dying. It hadn't been anything she could have prevented, and I felt guilty for hating her."

"She loved you, Edgar, and I know she would have done anything she could have to be with you today."

He rolled over, and I saw he was indeed, crying. "But she's not here. She left me alone without even my brother and sister with me. And why would my father lie about my mother?"

I shrugged and began to pace. "I don't know. Somehow Matthew convinced him to help kill me. Maybe Matthew lied to him, and your father believed I actually did kill your mother. I don't know, but I do know that when David found out you might be hurt, he tried to help."

Edgar smiled slightly. "He did, didn't he?"

I nodded. "Yes, he did," I agreed.

Edgar put his elbow on the ground and propped his head up. "What will happen to him now? Will Matthew try to hurt him because he tried to stop the duel?"

"I don't know. I'll try to find your father when I go back to town. Maybe I can send him away from Matthew," I told him.

"Thank you," Matthew said as tears formed in his eyes.

I sat down in the grass beside him and let him cry himself out. After he had finished, he lay still in the grass for a while not saying anything. Yet, even though nothing was said, I felt a bond had been formed between us. It was a comforting feeling to me. I imagine a father feels this way with his son. When we finally walked off toward town, the sun was going down.

26

1826 A.D.

I didn't see Edgar again until the following Wednesday, four days after our duel. As I was sitting down to a hot supper of stew and biscuits, I heard a knock at the door. I pulled the linen napkin out from where it was tucked into my shirt and tossed it on the table alongside my bowl.

Opening the front door, I saw Edgar. His clothes were wrinkled, and he reminded me of how David had looked when he had interrupted our duel. Edgar's eyes were bloodshot. I suspected he had been drinking, but I couldn't be sure.

"Paul Barker died today," he said.

Without saying anything more, he turned and started walking across my front yard toward the road.

"Edgar, wait!" I called. I stepped out of the house to chase after him.

He paused and turned back to me. "I need to be alone, Reynolds. Can you understand that? Paul was my friend."

"Then why come to me?"

"I wanted you to know that you had killed someone else," Edgar said harshly.

I stepped back inside. "I'm sorry," I said.

He acknowledged my apology with a slow nod, then turned away and continued walking. He crossed the street and headed east on University Street, probably back to Hubner's. He shoved his hands deep into his pants pockets and kicked at the stone that was in his path across the street. But he did not look back to see if I was still watching him from my door.

Paul Barker's memorial service was a sad affair. Sixty students and a dozen faculty members gathered in the campus chapel to hear Reverend Harvey eulogize Paul. His parents had arrived in town the day before to take his coffin to Annapolis to be buried in the family cemetery. Paul had been a promising medical student until I ended his dream. As I sat in the chapel, I saw Sam, the boy who had been

Edgar's second, staring at me. I think he suspected that I had had something to do with Paul's death. Either that or he was still angry at me because he believed that I had somehow cheated during the duel. Edgar attended the service, too, but I hadn't gotten close enough to talk with him.

As I stood up to leave after the service, I saw David standing in the vestibule. He saw me and nodded. I thought he would leave, but he waited for me as I limped over to him.

As I approached him, I saw the worried expression on his face. "I heard one of the students died. Was it..." His voice trailed off as he choked down a sob.

I put my hand on his shoulder, surprising even myself that I did it. "It wasn't Edgar. It was the boy who was officiating at the duel. He was closest to me when Edgar shot me."

"Thank you for not killing him. I know you could have," David said.

"He may not be my son, but I love him, too," I said.

He looked over my shoulder into the chapel. "He looks just like Elizabeth, doesn't he?" I nodded. "She was too good for me, and I did her a great wrong. I deserve whatever Monsignor Halloran decides to do with me," he said.

"What do you mean?" I asked.

"When Monsignor Halloran found me in Baltimore, I was drunk, of course. He sobered me up and told me that if I helped him, he would make me a great actor. I said 'yes' without even asking what he wanted me to do. Monsignor Halloran helped me get a leading role in a play at the Baltimore Theater. After three months, he came to me and told me it was time for me to help him. When I asked him what I had to do, he said he wanted to meet my son and that I would help him catch you," David explained.

"Is that when he told you about what happened to Elizabeth?" I asked him.

David nodded. He leaned closer and looked into my eyes. "Are you really Lazarus?" I nodded. "And he is really the widow's son from Nain?" I nodded again. "Why did Christ resurrect him? He scares me."

Why did Christ resurrect him? It was nearly the same question Father Halloran had asked me long ago in Boston, and I still had no absolute answer.

"I don't know why, but the real Father Halloran thought there might be more than one spirit in Matthew's body." David nodded as if he understood, but I doubted he did. "Do you know where

Matthew is now?"

"Who?" David asked.

"Matthew. Monsignor Halloran."

David shook his head fiercely. "No. I haven't been back to the house since the duel. I'm afraid of what Monsignor Halloran will do to me for breaking our deal. I wanted to stay around until I knew what had happened to Edgar, though. Now, I think I will be leaving. I think I'll go back to Boston. I always liked it there." He turned to leave, but he stopped at the door and turned back toward me. "If you love my son, don't let Monsignor Halloran near him."

"I won't," I promised.

David gave me a curt nod and then turned and left.

Though Edgar and I didn't talk to each other, I continued my weekly visits to his instructors to follow his progress in class. His grades had risen slightly after Paul Barker's death, but not nearly to the point they had been at the beginning of the semester.

I toyed with the idea of trying to meet with him and discuss his grades, but I doubted it would have done any good. None of our previous meetings had affected his grades except for the worse. If he was going to pull his grades up, it was better that he do it on his own.

Using that reasoning may have only been an excuse of my own so I could avoid Edgar. Although I was relatively sure I would not experience another regeneration for a few more years, I did not go to see him. I didn't want to endanger him any more than I already had. I was ashamed because he knew the truth about me. I was as great a murderer as Matthew.

It was Edgar's grades that convinced me to go see him. A month before the semester ended, his grades soared. His final examinations in French and Latin were near perfect. I was so excited and proud that he had turned himself around that I decided to visit him and congratulate him on his performance.

There was no answer, though, when I knocked on the door to his small room. I was about to leave when the young man in the next room opened his door and looked out.

"Have you seen Edgar?" I asked.

"He's not in," the boy said.

"I can see that. Do you know where he went?"

The boy frowned. "I can't say, sir."

"Why can't you...," I thought for a moment, "Never mind, I know where he is." Edgar had gone to Hubner's.

When I looked in Hubner's, I saw him sitting alone drinking a beer and staring at the locket portrait of his mother. I walked into the tavern and sat down at the table across from him. He looked up when I sat down, but didn't say anything.

"What are you doing in here, Edgar? Don't you know that the faculty is beginning to think you're an alcoholic?" He sighed. "Let me take you home. You've had too much to drink," I said.

"I'm not ready to leave yet," he said with slightly slurred words. "My father left, you know." I nodded. "I was so excited to finally meet him. I thought I finally have a father. I finally have a family. When I first talked to him, I just knew my grandfather had been wrong about him. Then my father ran off just like he did to my mother."

I discreetly slid the mug of beer away from him. "He was afraid of Matthew, and he was right to be. Matthew is a dangerous man."

"But I would have gone with him. Anywhere he wanted to go. All he had to do was ask." Edgar slammed his fist on the table.

"He knew that, but he wanted you to learn. You've done a good job of that so far, but if you don't stop coming here, you won't be able to keep up your grades."

"I..." Edgar's eyes clouded over, and his head slid forward onto the table.

"Edgar," I said as I shook him.

"He's just passed out again," someone said from behind me. I looked around and saw a tall man with a blond mustache looking at Edgar. "I guess you're elected to take him back to his room tonight."

"Tonight? You mean he's passed out here before?" I said.

The man nodded slowly. "Probably a dozen times. The first person that checks on him to see if he is all right gets to take him home. Otherwise, he'll be sleeping in the yard when I close up."

I stood up and walked around to the other side of the table. I certainly wasn't going to allow Edgar to be tossed outside like a sack of flour. I pulled his chair back and pulled him off the table. Then I leaned forward and let his body fall over my shoulder. I hefted him up and carried him back to his room. After I had put him to bed, I thought about waiting for him to wake up. Instead, I decided to leave him his dignity, and I left him alone.

The conversation about his father was the last time we spoke for years. At first, I thought he was embarrassed because he had passed out in front of me, but I soon realized it was more than that. Several times, I saw him outside or in the halls only a few feet away from me. He would have seen me if he had only looked up, but he didn't. At the time, I thought he was just absorbed in his own thoughts trying to keep up with his studies. Considering what I learned later, I doubt that was the case.

He was afraid of me. He thought I was going to kill him like I did Paul. He didn't want to be anywhere near me for fear that I might experience another regenerative attack.

Perhaps, I should have confronted him, but I still believe it was better that I did not. As I feared, his drinking and gambling became known by the university administration. Despite my pleas on his behalf, by December it was decided that Edgar should not be invited to return to the university the following semester. Although I hadn't talked with Edgar in over six months, it still broke my heart to know that he was being forced to leave. I remembered how excitedly he had expressed his love for learning when we had met that first time. I nearly went to him then and talked to him. I don't know why I didn't. I made pitiful excuses to avoid facing him much like I had when he first arrived at the university. By the time I did get around to visiting him, he had been gone for a week, and his room had been rented by a young man from Savannah.

I remained on the faculty of the university. Eventually, my work went beyond the framework of a job. I lived only to teach. Students came to me ignorant in the history of the world and even their own country, but I taught them. I took them on a journey through Christ, Caesar, Shakespeare, and Napoleon. When they left me, they knew more than when I had received them. That was all I could ask of them. If Elizabeth had been alive to ask me again if I was a good teacher, I could have told her definitely, "Yes."

After his expulsion, Edgar began his career as a writer. I read his biting reviews and haunting stories in the *Southern Literary Messenger*, where he was an assistant editor. His writings were very much enjoyed by the faculty, but few of them realized this was the same person they had expelled nearly a decade before. To me, it seemed ironic that he became such a harsh critic of the theater since it had been the workplace of both his parents. After 1837, he left the magazine much to the dismay of my colleagues, but his writings began to appear in other newspapers and magazines around the country. He even published his work in books. His short story collection, *Tales of the Grotesque and Arabesque*, was a particularly frightening work.

In 1844, Edgar became an overnight phenomena when he published his poem, *The Raven*. However, my favorite stories of his were those that featured C. Auguste Dupin, an early version of Sherlock Holmes. Dupin was featured in *The Murders in the Rue Morgue*, *The Mystery of Marie Roget*, and *The Purloined Letter*. The character was an incredibly logical detective who seemed to be able to deduce explanations out of the most unexplainable of circumstances. How I would have liked to have met such a man and ask him some questions of my own to see if he could explain them logically.

During this time, I almost forgot about Matthew. I heard little of him from either my faculty associates or the ship captains who worked for me. There was only one instance I can remember hearing about him. Cardinal Halloran came through Charlottesville in the spring of 1842. He gave Mass that Sunday at the Catholic Church on First Street, which was oddly enough named St. Matthew.

I went to hear Matthew because I wondered how someone who loved to kill as he did could preach of love and hope. I sat in the rear of the chapel where I could be furthest from Matthew's view. I was surprised at the crowd he attracted. It seemed that everyone in a twenty-mile radius had come to hear Cardinal Halloran preach.

He approached the podium dressed in his purple robes and the quiet murmur that could be heard in the crowd disappeared. With narrowed eyes, he looked over the congregation and smiled. It wasn't a smile that I had ever seen before from Matthew. It was open and friendly and appeared genuine. For the first time, I wondered if perhaps Matthew might have changed. Then he began his sermon.

In English, he talked about the love God had for each of us. He said a person should look forward to death because it would free his soul from the confines of the body to be with God.

In Latin, he said that he was the one, true God. He alone could set a person free, and that if you gave your life for him, it was an honor. Within him, existed the power of life and death. From the looks on everyone's face around me, they didn't understand the Latin version of his sermon. If they had, they wouldn't have been smiling. Yet, the young priests that were in attendance had to have understood his Latin sermon, but they didn't do anything, either. They just nodded their agreement as he spoke.

Matthew was the hunter, and these people were his prey. He could pick and choose among the lives he would take, and his followers would welcome their death as a chance to be with God.

The congregation at the Mass loved him. When he finished his Mass, I heard people saying how moving and spiritual Cardinal Halloran was. I could have told them otherwise, but they wouldn't have believed me. Matthew looked like the perfect priest. His hair was trimmed short, and he had a relaxed pose at the podium. His voice was commanding, but not overpowering. It compelled people to listen and almost hypnotized them into believing him.

That Sunday night, I had the same dream I had had years ago after I had left Father Halloran—the real Father Halloran. Matthew in white robes stabbing himself so that he could steal the life force from a woman. Only now instead of waking up screaming when the woman's face crumbled to dust, I saw more. The people bent over, touched their hands to the ground, and then raised them to Heaven.

"Oh, God. We are your children. Oh, God. Thy will be done," they chanted as one voice.

I woke up Monday morning with the odd feeling that I should do something to alert the world of Matthew. Matthew had to be stopped. It was the same thing I had felt when I had originally had the dream, but I didn't see how I could stop him. The time to have halted him was long past. It should have been done when his influence in the church was minimal or even before he had taken on Father Halloran's identity. I had been too unsure then to do anything, and my indecision had only strengthened his position. He was a cardinal of the Catholic Church. Who would believe that such a man could be an 1,800-year-old murderer? And who was his accuser? A teacher. Which one of us would be believed?

No, if there were accusations to be made, they had to come from above Matthew and not below him.

Then an idea I hadn't even imagined occurred to me. The thought was so foreign that it seemed more likely someone had whispered it in my ear than for me to think of it. I could write a letter to another church authority.

When I sat down at my desk, my hand seemed to almost write the letter independently of my thought. I wrote to Cardinal Franieu who served the Catholics of the southern United States. In the letter, I wrote that I was a Latin scholar and that I had attended one of Cardinal Halloran's Masses. I described to him the content of both the English and Latin versions of the Mass. I encouraged him to send someone, unknown to Cardinal Halloran, to attend a Mass at his church to hear for himself the discrepancies. I also wrote that I had once heard of a Father Halloran in Boston years ago. Were the two men the same? If so, they had changed very drastically in physical appearance over the years. I ended the letter by saying, "Considering the Catholic Church's precarious foothold in this new country it would be quite destructive if the newspapers found out about this discrepancy in Masses being preached. Something should be done about this before it gets out of hand if it hasn't already."

I posted the letter and forgot about it. Hopefully, calling

someone of equal authority's attention to the problem would help solve it.

A month after I posted the letter, I received one. It wasn't from the Cardinal Franieu, though. I hadn't given him a return address. This letter came from Edgar. He was in Fordham, New York.

The letter read, "Reynolds, I know it has been nearly twenty years since you and I have last spoken. To tell the truth, I had intended for that time to continue until my death. But circumstances have changed, and you are the only person I know who may be able to help.

"My wife Virginia is very ill to the point of death. Five years ago while entertaining at a party, she burst a blood vessel. From that point on, we both knew her time on this earth was limited. Still, she seemed in such good health for the last few years that it was easy for the both of us to ignore the fact that she was dying.

"I cannot say that any longer. In the past weeks, she has continually worsened. Her usually healthy skin is now pale, and she has lost a great amount of weight. The doctors say there are few things they can do except to ease her pain with various drugs.

"I think there is something I can do, though, and I have done it. I have written you. I know you can help her, Reynolds. Perhaps, I should not even be asking you this after all that has passed between us, but you are literally my last hope. When there is nothing science can do, one turns to religion. Please help me, Reynolds.

"Please."

Part V:
The Fall of the House of Usher

I shall perish, said he, I *must* perish in this deplorable folly. Thus, thus, and not otherwise, shall I be lost. I dread the events of the future, not in themselves, but in their results...In this unnerved, in this pitiable, condition I feel that the period will sooner or later arrive when I must abandon life and reason together, in some struggle with the grim phantasm, FEAR.

Edgar Allan Poe
The Fall of the House of Usher

1846 A.D.

After all the misery that I had caused Edgar, leading his mother to her death and killing Paul, Edgar had asked for me. He had asked for my help. How could I refuse him? I owed him some happiness after all the pain I had caused. I resigned my position at the university with the excuse that I was going to England to research the myth of King Arthur and I wasn't sure how long I would be away.

My fleet now numbered thirty-five ships. Two were docked in Richmond at the time. One was off-loading a shipment of wine from Spain. The second was preparing to sail to London. I added an extra port of call to Captain Jennings" voyage to England. Instead of sailing directly to England, he would sail to New York first before proceeding to his final destination.

In New York City, I rented a carriage and drove out to the Poe house in Fordham. They were living in a small Dutch cottage that they rented from a wealthy farmer. It sat on a small rise that provided an excellent view of the area. The house was surrounded by half a dozen bare cherry trees. The cottage had four windows, two of which looked out over the front porch.

I hesitated before knocking on the front door. I wasn't sure coming to Fordham the right thing to do. Edgar expected something from me that I might not be able to deliver, but I couldn't abandon him, either. I had to do what I could to help him. I suppose part of this feeling was due to the guilt I felt over his mother's death. It was too late to help her. Any chance I had of making amends to her had to be made through Edgar if only in a small way. Like helping his wife regain her health.

I knocked on the door.

When the door opened, a chill shot through my body. I was looking at a ghost. I unconsciously held my breath and took a step back. The heel on my left boot slipped off the edge of the porch, and

I almost fell. I was staring at the ghost of a child with skin the color of pearls and with the same luminescent glow. Her violet eyes appeared black and sunken. Her black hair hung limply below her shoulders.

I was even more frightened when I realized I was not looking at the ghost of a child, but a very ill young woman.

I regained my composure and asked, "Mrs. Poe?"

"Yes." Her voice was soft, and I had to strain to hear it.

I sighed with relief that she spoke. I wasn't facing the supernatural. I stepped forward and held out my hand. She took it with a light grip, and I kissed the back of her hand. She smiled, and I saw the traces of the woman she had been before she had taken ill.

"My name is Alexander Reynolds. I am here to see your husband. He asked for me to come," I told her.

She stepped away from the door. "He's taking a walk right now. It helps to ease his mind. He worries so much about me. He should be back shortly, though. Won't you please come in and wait?" she offered.

I stepped through the door into the main room, which covered the front half of the house. Two doorways led off the main room to a kitchen and bedroom.

As Mrs. Poe closed the door behind me, an older woman who shared Mrs. Poe's hair and eye color stepped into the main room from the kitchen. An angry expression crept into her face, and she put her hands on her hips.

"Virginia, what are you doing out of bed?" she scolded.

Virginia cast her eyes to the ground. "I'm sorry, Mother, but you were so busy in the kitchen, I didn't think that you heard the knock."

Her mother pointed to the bedroom. "Back to bed with you," she ordered. When Virginia had climbed back under the sheets, the woman closed the door to the room. She turned to me and said, "And who might you be?"

"Alexander Reynolds, ma'am. I'm here to see Edgar," I said once again.

Well, have a seat over there," she said as she pointed to a wooden chair by the empty fireplace. "I'm sorry we can't offer you any heat. Edgar will be along soon, I suppose."

I did as she told me and sat down in the chair. I kept my coat on because the house was freezing in the cold December air. Virginia's mother left me alone and went back into the kitchen to continue whatever she had been working on.

The room was only barely furnished. A writing table and chair sat next to the window nearest the fireplace. A small eating table and three chairs sat at the opposite end of the room from me. On the walls were shelves filled with books, magazines, and newspapers. I assumed many of them contained stories which Edgar had written.

About ten minutes after Virginia's mother had left me, Edgar walked in. He was considerably older than when I had seen him last. His face had filled out somewhat, but his eyes seemed as large and sad as ever. He had grown into a handsome gentleman. At least David had given his son some of his better qualities as well as his negative ones.

He closed the door behind himself and rubbed his arms, furiously trying to warm them by friction. He had foolishly gone out into the freezing temperatures without wearing a coat. I stood up and faced him. At first, he didn't say anything. He only stared at me as if he had never seen me.

"You look older," he said finally.

"So do you," I replied.

"But I am older," he added.

He walked over to the bedroom door and looked in on his wife. She had quickly fallen asleep once she went back to bed.

"So am I," I assured him.

He looked confused. "What about your power to heal your wounds and live continually?" he asked.

I sat back down. "That doesn't stop me from aging. In fact, it is what keeps me aging. I don't stay forever thirty-five-years old. I have lived many lives, although I hope I will not steal another life for many years to come."

Edgar pulled the chair from his desk up next to my chair and sat down. "How do you do it?" he asked.

I shifted uneasily in my chair, disturbed by his curiosity of something I would have rather tried to forget. "I told you before. I don't do it. My body acts independently when it needs a life to keep me alive and healthy," I explained.

"Alexander, I want to thank you for coming so quickly. I really wasn't sure that you would come."

I shrugged. "You said you needed my help. I'll do what I am able." I glanced at the bedroom. "What is wrong with your wife?"

"She's consumptive," Edgar said, looking toward the bedroom.

Consumptive. I had grown to hate that word more and more each time I heard it spoken or whispered. Consumption. Tuberculosis. I don't care what people called it. To me, it still meant death.

I stared absent-mindedly at a spot on the floor. "Just like your mother," I said barely above a whisper.

"And Mrs. Allan," Edgar added.

My head snapped up at hearing the name. "Frances?" I said.

Edgar nodded. "She died in 1829. I was in the army when it happened. I had known she was sick for weeks. I tried to get home to her to help, but I had to fight through all the army bureaucracy to do it. I didn't get to Richmond until the day after her funeral." He wiped a stray tear away from his eye.

"I'm sorry. She was a good woman, and I know she loved you very much." It didn't seem like I was saying enough, but at least I knew I hadn't been responsible for her death.

Edgar clenched his fists. "It's like the damned thing follows me killing whomever I love." For someone famous for his macabre stories, he didn't deal with death any better than I who had lived with it for so long. "First, my mother died. Then Mrs. Allan. And now it wants to take my Virginia. Well, it can't! I won't let it!" he shouted. He jumped to his feet, and I thought he might strike the stone fireplace. Instead, he leaned against the mantle and cried.

I put a hand on his shoulder and led him back to his chair. "Do you have a choice? What do the doctors say?" I asked.

He rubbed his tear-swollen eyes with the back of his hand. "They say Virginia will die soon. They can do nothing except feed her useless pills and potions. You are my last hope, Reynolds."

"How so?" I asked.

"You have a power only one other person on the earth possesses. Instead of that power being a curse to you, you can turn it into a godsend," he explained.

I have to admit I was curious. I would do anything not to have a condition that stole the life of my friends and family, as well as those of total strangers. But I was skeptical. How could things change? After 1,800 years, I had not found a way to alter the way my body acts. How could my curse be a benefit to others?

"How?" I asked.

"Let me draw a cup of blood from you and feed it to Virginia," Edgar said.

I jumped to my feet. "No!

Edgar was on his feet beside me. "But it will work, Alexander. I know it will, but you are the only one who can do it. Please help her. Don't let her die like my mother," he pleaded.

I leaned over so that I was only inches from his face. "You're talking nonsense, Edgar. This is an idea for one of your stories, not a way to save your wife's life," I told him.

He kneeled down in front of me and grabbed my right hand between his two hands. "You saw her, Reynolds. She's dying, and you can help her. Only *you*. Don't let her die. I love her."

"But I can't help her, at least not in that way," I insisted.

His grip on my hand tightened. "Why? Why?"

"It won't work."

"Do you know? Have you tried it before?" he asked.

"No, but..."

He cut me off before I could say anything more. "You told me you would do what you could do to help. This is it. Even if it doesn't work, at least try it. Then we can know for certain that we tried everything."

He was crying just like a small child. What he was suggesting was ludicrous. Drinking my blood wouldn't heal Virginia. It was ghoulish. It would probably only make her sick to her stomach. My blood wasn't what carried my curse.

Or was it?

I didn't know. I had never experimented with my body to know what caused of my curse. Christ had told me my body would never release my spirit. What had he done to give my body such power over my soul? Was it a blood-borne disease as Edgar thought?

"Please," Edgar said once more.

If she dies, she kills part of him, I thought. *He won't ever be the same. I had to try to save her to save him.*

"We will try," I conceded.

He bowed his head and kissed my hand. "Thank you. Thank you," he said.

"I will need bandages to wrap my wound when it is done. I don't know how quickly it will heal," I told Edgar. My body allowed non-fatal wounds to heal at a natural rate.

He nodded and hurried off toward the kitchen. When he returned, he had three towels, a bowl, and Virginia's mother.

"We don't have any bandages. I brought towels instead. I hope they'll do," Edgar said as he laid the bowl and towels on his desk.

"Eddie says you can help my daughter," Edgar's mother-in-law said.

I looked at her and saw the same worry in her face that I saw in Edgar's. "I don't know, ma'am, but I am going to try," I told her.

"Do you need a knife?" Edgar asked.

I shook my head. "No thank you. I have my own."

I spread out one of the towels on top of the desk so no blood would stain it. Then I set the bowl on top of the towel. Edgar moved up next to me, but Virginia's mother stayed near the doorway to the kitchen.

"Do you know what you're doing, Eddie?" she asked across the room.

I looked at Edgar wondering the same thing. What was happening? We were trying to save Virginia by cursing her.

Edgar walked over to his mother-in-law and put his arms around her. He led her to the chair I had been sitting in and helped her sit down.

"No, I'm not sure what I am doing," he said. "I need to do something, and this is the only thing I can think of to do. I don't want to sit around and wait for Sissy to die. I have try and help her. Otherwise, she will die. That's what the doctors have said all along. You don't want that do you?" His mother-in-law was crying now. Edgar wiped away a pair of tears from her cheek as she shook her head. "Neither do I," he said.

He hugged her and turned back to me.

I pulled my knife from my boot and laid it across my palm. I took a deep breath and paused. Then I sliced a straight line across my palm. It wasn't deep enough to be fatal, which would have started the rippling. However, it was enough to start my blood flowing in small rivers down my palm.

I tilted my hand perpendicular to the desk and let the blood run down my hand and drip into the bowl. My hand throbbed, but I ignored it. I laid down the knife and pressed the fingers of my uninjured hand into my bleeding palm to increase the blood flow. When the bottom of the bowl was covered, I grabbed another towel and wrapped it around my hand as tightly as possible so that the bleeding would stop.

Edgar picked up the bowl and stared at the ounce of blood in it.

"Is it enough?" he asked.

I shrugged. "I don't know. I've never done this before, but it should be. Besides, I don't believe I'll get her to drink more than a swallow. Before I go into her bedroom, though, I think you and your mother-in-law should go into town for an hour or two," I told him.

"Why?"

"If this works, a ripple is going to leave your wife searching for a life to restore her fading one. You don't want that ripple to take your's or your mother-in-law's lives, do you?" I asked.

Edgar closed his eyes as he ran his hand through his thick hair. He turned to Virginia's mother and said, "Muddy, why don't you go to the market? You said you needed to go earlier today."

"But what about..." She saw the concerned look on Edgar's face and stopped. "I guess we could use a pound of coffee. Is there any money?" she asked.

"Take what's in the fruit jar," Edgar replied.

She looked from Edgar to me. She continued staring at me, and I looked away, not knowing why I felt embarrassed.

"You're not going to hurt her, are you?" she asked.

I looked at Edgar and waited for his answer. "She hurts already, but she won't hurt anymore."

He sounded so sure that this would work. It has been written that faith the size of a mustard seed can move mountains. With the size of Edgar's faith, I should have had no doubts.

But I did.

I was actually trying to pass on the power of my body, the very thing I considered a curse, to another person. It was the thing that had ruined my life and separated me from the ones I loved. So why was I trying to infect someone else with it? What right did I have to inflict that torment on anyone?

The answer was simple. Because Edgar had asked me. I would do anything for him.

After Virginia's mother had left, I turned to Edgar and said, "You should leave, too. It will be just as dangerous for you."

He shook his head. "I'll stay. If anyone is to give his life so that Virginia may live, it should be me. Let's begin."

"I wanted to protest, but he seemed determined to continue. I think, perhaps, if I had truly believed it would work, I would have voiced a stronger protest.

Edgar picked the bowl of blood and handed it to me. Then he started across the room to the bedroom door.

"Edgar," I said from behind him, "This could kill her as easily as it could save her. We don't know what powers we are dealing with."

He shook his head. "Blood never kills. Only the lack of it," he answered.

I followed him into the bedroom. Virginia was lying on a bare mattress with two thin sheets and her husband's overcoat thrown over her to keep her warm. Now I knew why Edgar had gone walking without a coat. He had given his coat to Virginia so that she might stay warm. Even so, she was shaking in her sleep.

"She should have blankets covering her in this weather, especially since there's no fire," I said when I saw her.

Edgar looked down at his wife. "I wish she had both blankets and a fire, but we can't afford it. Before William McDougal gave us the sheets, all she had to keep her warm was my coat and a stray cat."

He leaned over the bed and kissed his wife lightly on the forehead. He put his hand on her shoulder and shook her.

"Sissy, wake up," he said gently.

Virginia seemed to fight her way back to consciousness. Her chills became more violent as she struggled, then gradually subsided as she awoke. Her eyes fluttered open. They were cloudy as if the violet and white areas of her eyes had mixed into one color. After she had blinked a few times, they cleared up.

Edgar put his hands under her arms and helped her sit up in bed. He turned to me and took the bowl out of my hands and passed it to his wife.

"I want you to drink this, Sissy. It will make you better," he said confidently.

Virginia looked at it. Pushing the bowl away from her, she closed her eyes and turned her head away.

"It looks like blood," she said.

"It will taste like blood, too, but it certainly can't taste any worse than some of the medicines the doctors have been giving you."

Virginia smiled faintly. "No, I doubt that." She glanced at my hand wrapped in the towel. "Is it Mr. Reynolds' blood?" she asked.

Edgar looked at me, then back at her. "Yes, and it will help you get better so please drink it all."

Virginia took the bowl from his hand. Holding it in both of her hands, she looked at it again and wrinkled her nose. She closed her eyes, tilted her head back, and drank the small amount of blood in one gulp.

Almost immediately, she started coughing. Edgar sat on the edge of the bed next to her. He pulled her to his chest and hugged her tightly.

"You were wrong," she said once she had regained her voice. "It was worse than the medicines."

Edgar laughed, and even I chuckled.

"Do you feel any different?" he asked.

She shook her head throwing her black hair back and forth from one shoulder to the other. "My stomach feels a little upset, that's all."

"You'll feel better soon," he said, and he hugged her again.

He was so sure and so wrong.

Virginia died at the end of January slightly more than a month after she had drunk my blood. It hadn't done any good at all. Edgar's faith in my ability to save his wife had been placed in the wrong man.

Edgar interred his wife's body in a tomb in the graveyard of the Dutch Reformed Church in Fordham. From that day on, I don't think

I ever saw him wear any color clothes other than black. He was in perpetual mourning for his dead wife.

At the cottage, he seemed to be forever crying. He would wander off for hours at a time to be alone. After two months of this sort of behavior, I decided to follow him. He walked directly to Virginia's tomb and stayed there for three hours sitting next to the door to the tomb, alternately crying and mumbling to Virginia. As I watched him, he pulled a bottle from his coat and drank a quarter of it down quickly. He held the bottle up and looked at it, then he tossed it aside. A few moments later, he collapsed against Virginia's gravestone.

I rushed forward from my hiding place and picked up the bottle. It was laudanum, a cocaine and whiskey mixture some doctors used as medicine, but it was addictive and could kill just as easily as cure.

I grabbed Edgar by the shoulders and shook him. He was unconscious. He had drunk too much laudanum. I opened his mouth and shoved my fingers deep into his throat. His body's reflexes took over, and he gagged. His body twitched, but he remained unconscious. I kept my fingers in his mouth. I could feel his throat muscles contracting until finally, he vomited.

When he finished emptying his stomach, I lay him on his back and waited for him to wake up. It took about five minutes, but he eventually came around.

I held up the bottle. "Edgar, you don't need this. It nearly killed you," I said.

He stared at me for a moment, then started crying. I dropped the bottle and grabbed him by the shoulders and pulled him to his feet.

"You can't keep doing this to yourself, Edgar. Virginia is dead. You're alive," I told him.

"I don't want to be. I would have gladly given my life for hers if it would only have worked. It should have worked, Reynolds," he said.

"I know, and you tried everything there was to try to make her well again. You can't blame yourself that she died."

He pulled away from me. "Then why did my love die if I did everything I could do to help her?"

"I don't know why certain people die and others don't, any more than I know when I'll die. But people do die. Everyone at some time will die. Even me. You've got to start thinking clearly. You haven't written a word in weeks. You need to start working again, not drown yourself in something that will kill you."

He hit his fist against the stone wall of the tomb. "I can't!"

"You can. You just don't want to. You would rather let all that pain that is inside of you consume you. Don't you think I know how you feel? I've had ten wives, and I've had to bury them all. Do you think I loved them any less than you loved Virginia? Do you believe I hurt any less that you hurt now? I cried. I grieved, but I didn't try to follow them into their deaths like you're doing. You've got to continue working," I urged him.

"I can't. It will hurt too much," he said.

"Put your pain on paper. Write another poem like *The Raven*. Do anything, but don't torture yourself."

He had stopped crying. I only hoped he was listening to me.

"I'll try," he said finally.

He tried. Indeed, he tried.

It wasn't easy, but he never gave up. The first few times he sat down at his desk to write, he managed to write no more than a line or two. He continued coming back to the desk, though, and eventually he finished a poem. It wasn't one of his best, but it was the first thing he had written and completed since Virginia's death. The next time he returned to his desk, it was much quicker and easier to write.

In the next year, he wrote some of his best works. *Ulalume, Annabel Lee*, and *The Bells* were all published. I was pleased when I realized he was using his writing as therapy. When I read *Eureka*, I knew he was trying to come to an understanding of life and death. *Eureka* explored the origin of the universe, it's purpose and Edgar's version of God.

Maria, Virginia's mother, and I were also busy during the year following Virginia's death. We continued writing Edgar's friends and publishers hoping to sell some of Edgar's work. We had a two-fold purpose in this. Edgar desperately needed the money, and the publication of his poems and stories encouraged him to write more.

After what seemed a long climb back to sanity, Edgar started lecturing and giving readings again. He was even beginning to notice the beauty of other women. Though his engagement to Sarah Whitman was short-lived, it showed me that Edgar was finally getting over his grief. He could love again, as well as grieve.

It was when he prepared to leave Fordham and leave Virginia behind that I decided it was time for me to depart. When he left for New York City in the summer, I left for Charlottesville to reapply for my former job at the University of Virginia. That was where I felt most at home in this young country.

I wish I could say we parted as friends, but we did not. I felt more like a father who was watching his son leave home for the first time.

28

1849 A.D.

It was in Baltimore that I had the dream. Now it seems so much more than a just dream. It is closer to a premonition, but at the time a dream is all I considered it.

I was burning.

I don't know how it happened, or whether it was an accident or not. All I knew was that I was on fire. Ever since the night Matthew had shown me I could be killed by fire, I had feared it. The yellow flames around me were all I could see. I screamed from the pain and the heat as my flesh bubbled and blackened.

"You will not die until I return to the earth," a voice said. It took a moment to recognize the voice through the crackle of the flames. It was Jesus" calm voice, but I couldn't see him or even determine the direction the voice had come from.

"Help me! Please!" I screamed.

I did not want to live. How would I appear if I lived? Would I be a mass of puffed, pink scar tissue? Or would I be a charred skeleton? Living in those conditions would be worse than dying.

"Fire will not burn you," Christ said. "Have faith."

But the fire was burning me. I opened my mouth to tell Matthew so, but only my scream came out.

When I woke up, I was sweating, and I still imagined I could feel the heat. I threw my sheet back and looked at my burned leg. The scar tissue was no longer pink, but bright red. It throbbed and pulsated as if there was a wave of fluid beneath it rolling back and forth. I had never seen this happen to my leg before if it ever did. Was the ripple going to occur now after forty years? Had the fire only delayed the reaction? After a few minutes, it stopped and the imagined heat I felt vanished. The scar tissue faded to its normal pink color.

I touched my knee unsure of what to expect. There was no sensation within the scar tissue. It was like touching something that was not a part of my body.

Being resurrected certainly hadn't stopped Matthew from burning me in Boston. I was still alive, but the fire had burned me. I wouldn't want to be alive if my entire body looked like my leg. My state of existence had already forced me to live like a pariah. Why should I look like one, too?

The dream unsettled me so much I wasn't able to fall asleep again. I spent the remaining hours of the night lying in bed and staring at the ceiling of my room in the Calvert Manor House on Calvert Street.

I went outside before breakfast and bought a newspaper and read it while I ate my meal. Most of the news didn't hold my interest. Fells Point had held a town meeting to decide how their area's needs could best be represented to the mayor of Baltimore. There was an article about the on-going trial of John Stover who had been accused of poisoning his neighbor's stud stallion.

The article that did catch my attention was on page three at the very top. The headline read: "Cardinal and 12 priests excommunicated." After receiving a letter from a concerned church-goer, Cardinal Franieu, of the southern United States archdiocese, had been moved to investigate the teachings of Cardinal Halloran of Baltimore. Cardinal Franieu had asked Bishop John Carroll to investigate the matter and determine if Cardinal Halloran of Baltimore was teaching a false doctrine. Bishop Carroll was chosen, the article said, because of his efforts to keep peaceful relations between the Roman Catholics and other religions. Discreet inquiries from Bishop Carroll showed the papal advisor, though popular, had grossly veered from approved Catholic doctrine. His falsehoods included saying that Christ had returned to the earth and that he was taking up the righteous while striking down the wicked. Upon Cardinal Franieu's recommendation to Pope Pius IX along with the reports of other investigations being conducted into Cardinal Halloran's behavior, the cardinal and twelve priests, who were considered more loyal to Cardinal Halloran than the church, were excommunicated the week before. But Cardinal Halloran had not ended his religious career with his excommunication. He had bought and converted the Howard mansion on Charles Street in which he would hold services for his new church. Presently, it appeared to the writer that many of the same people attended his services in their new location as they had done in the old. Until another Bishop could be appointed to oversee the Maryland archdiocese, Cardinal Franieu was assuming both the duties of not only his archdiocese, but of Cardinal Halloran's archdiocese also until a suitable replacement could be found.

I wadded the paper into a ball and threw it across the room. My letter hadn't really helped. Excommunication hadn't stopped Matthew. It had only opened up other options for him. He was no longer under oath to obey the Pope and the teachings of the Roman Catholic Church. In essence, he was now at the top of his own church and could openly teach whatever doctrine he wished.

How many people had he led away from the Catholic Church? How many people now worshiped him thinking they were worshipping God? How many worshiped him expecting God to appear and take them to Heaven? Matthew was obviously quite persuasive, or he wouldn't have been able to rise to such a high position in the Catholic Church or take as many people away from the church with him when he was excommunicated. Because of Maryland's religious tolerance, Baltimore was the ideal place to center his new church.

I'm not sure why I did it, but I walked out to the mansion on Charles Street. I wasn't alone, either. I saw dozens of people walking into the mansion when I arrived. It must have been approaching the time Matthew held morning Mass or whatever he called services in his church.

The mansion had three floors and seemed to be as large as many of the hotels I had seen. The front walk was paved with red brick. It ran between two rows of dogwood trees. At the very beginning of the walkway, near Charles Street, was a larger wooden sign that read:

HE IS RISEN!

THE CHURCH OF ST. MATTHEW

ALL ARE WELCOME

I read the sign and almost laughed. It was so obvious to me what his intent was that I couldn't see how anyone else could have been so blind to it. Of course, no one else knew Cardinal Halloran's real name was actually Matthew of Nain.

A young couple stepped around me and started up the walk. I followed a few feet behind them curious to see how Matthew had altered his approach to religion now that he was in charge of his own church.

The walk was about 150-feet long. With each step that brought me closer to the mansion, I seemed to grow smaller. The mansion's immense size dwarfed me in comparison. The young couple in front of me had been talking gaily when they started up the walk, but by the time they had reached the double doors to enter into the Church of St. Matthew, they had fallen silent. The young man looked somber and stern-faced when he turned to open the door for the woman.

A young priest stood on either side of the doorway greeting people as they entered. They must have been two of Matthew's disciples that had been excommunicated for being more loyal to Matthew than the church. I could see how that would have happened. Matthew, as a cardinal, was an advisor to the Pope and the spiritual leader of his archdiocese. He had the advantage of being a physical presence to the priests while the Pope was only a faceless name. They still wore their priestly garments, but they allowed their hair to grow longer than most priests. Matthew was apparently not as strict on appearances as the Catholic Church.

I shook the priest's hand on my left. He smiled and welcomed me to morning Mass at St. Matthew's.

As soon as I entered the chapel, I felt uneasy. The room had once been a ballroom. It occupied the north wing of the first floor. Fifteen rows of pews had been added which took up most of the floor space. The windows were covered first with a thin, cream-colored sheer, then with an expensive set of red-velvet curtains held back by gold cords. The unlit chandeliers and sconces appeared to be made of gold.

I took a seat in the middle of the chapel hoping that Matthew wouldn't notice me among the other worshippers when he made his appearance. By the time the doors to the ballroom closed signaling the beginning of the Mass, I was sitting shoulder-to-shoulder with about two-hundred people.

The silence that filled the room deepened, if that was possible. I stared at the front of the church at a pulpit set on a slightly raised platform and behind it was a large set of black curtains nearly covering the entire wall. Nowhere in the church did I see any pictures or statues of Christ. Nor did I see any crosses or pictures of the saints or disciples. And the priests, I remembered, had not been wearing rosaries.

The black curtains parted in the middle about three feet, and Matthew walked from behind them up to the pulpit. His black hair was tied back in a tail that touched his left shoulder. He wore a simple white robe tied at the waist with a piece of rope. It was similar to the outfits we had both worn in our first lives.

He stared at the congregation silently. His eyes seemed to lock on mine for a moment, but I tilted my head down.

When he had finished his inspection of the congregation, he began talking. "My brothers and sisters, I welcome you here this morning. I am here to speak with you today on the things that are troubling to the savior."

Matthew continued for another forty-five minutes. He talked

about how Christ was appalled that the established churches had not accepted his return to earth and the beginning of the Second Coming. He told the congregation that at a time in the future, they would be called upon to devote their time and material goods to the spreading of the Lord's word among the people. Those who believed would be taken up to Heaven, and those who rejected his word, would die.

There was no holy communion at the Mass of St. Matthew's. I wondered why, but I said nothing because I didn't want to give away my ignorance of the customs of Matthew's church.

As the congregation filed out of the chapel after the service, I felt a hand on my elbow. I looked around and saw a brown-haired priest standing at my side.

"Please come with me," he said.

"Why?" I asked, even though I knew the answer. Matthew had recognized me when he saw me from the pulpit.

"I don't know. I was just sent to fetch you," the young priest said.

I considered running, but I thought that might only lead to someone else being hurt if I tried to escape. I broke away from the crowd and followed the priest to the staircase at the end of the hall.

"Why do you follow Cardinal Halloran?" I asked.

"He is not just a cardinal. He has power," he answered without turning his head to look at me.

We started up a staircase to the second floor. Hanging over the landing was a life-size painting of Matthew in his cardinal's robes. It had been painted in such a way that Matthew's eyes seemed to follow me wherever I walked.

"Cardinal Halloran has only the power to kill," I said.

"He has the power to live," the priest replied. "He cannot die. He is the Savior, and his word will spread to all the people. The righteous will join us, and the wicked will perish. Armageddon approaches."

We began climbing a second set of stairs to the third floor. It appeared deserted. We walked down the hallway to the third door on the left. The priest knocked.

"Enter," a voice said from inside.

The priest opened the door and motioned for me to go inside. I stepped into a bright room that seemed to stretch the entire length of the east wing. The door closed behind me. The young priest had remained outside. The room had only one piece of furniture. It was a throne-like chair set at the far end. Except for the throne, the room was empty of furnishings. The windows didn't even have draperies.

And on the throne, sat Matthew.

"So you have returned, Lazarus," he said.

I slowly walked forward.

"I was curious as to how much further you had separated yourself from the man who made you. Now I have seen," I told him.

"Come forward, Lazarus. You should have stayed away. You had your opportunity to kill me, but you failed. Now you will learn what it is to face a god. Experience how it feels to incur his wrath!"

Matthew rushed from his throne tackling me in my mid-section. I fell back on the wooden floor with him on top of me. His fists pummeled me relentlessly in the side and the face. I tried to protect my face with my hands, but a few of his punches still slipped under my guard and hit me.

I tried to push him off of me, but he was too strong. I started hitting back. Compared to his punches, my punches seemed weak and ineffectual. I am not weak, but his strength was more than natural power. His fury added to the power of his blows. I felt something in my chest crack. I felt pain with each breath I took.

Then amazingly, he backed off. I lay on the floor not wondering why I had been granted a reprieve but enjoying it. I could feel my face swelling and my chest burned with pain. He had to have broken at least one of my ribs. I wondered if it would heal without the aid of the rippling.

I sat up in time to see Matthew coming at me again. This time he held a sword. I don't know where he had been hiding it. It must have been next to his throne.

He swung at me as if he was trying to slice me in two from head to toe. I rolled to the side, and the blade only nicked me on the backside of my shirt sleeve. I rolled over once more and started crawling away as fast as I could. I was breathing harder and that only made my chest hurt worse.

Matthew chased after me holding the sword over his head. As he drew near, I pulled in my good leg and kicked it out as hard as I could. The heel of my boot struck Matthew's right knee. He screamed and fell to the floor holding his leg.

I hurried out of his reach and scrambled for the door I had come in. I grabbed the handle and pulled. The priest had locked it behind me. I saw the row of windows off to my right and for a moment I saw myself jumping out of one of them. Then I remembered how close Matthew had come to killing me when I had fallen through my window in Boston.

Matthew staggered to his feet, favoring his right leg. At least we had equal disadvantages.

What was he trying to do with the sword? It wouldn't kill me as far as I knew unless Matthew knew of a certain way to use it that would keep me from regenerating. He had known fire would kill me before I had even suspected it. What if fire wasn't the only way I could die?

Dismemberment?

If that was what he was attempting, I didn't want to experience it. I remembered all too well how badly the fire had hurt.

Matthew picked up his sword and swung it around. I think he wanted to scare me, but I showed no reaction to his theatrics.

"I will not have a watchdog, Lazarus. My one mistake in my quest was revealing myself to you. Any usefulness I thought you might have had to me once is gone. It is time for you to die," he said.

I reached down and slid my knife from my boot. Instead of holding it point out, I turned it inward and held the blade flat against my forearm.

Matthew rushed at me swinging his sword. Actually, I think hobbled might be a better word. His sore knee slowed him down considerably. He wasn't as used to accommodating his disability as I was.

As he drew near me, he swung his blade at my neck trying to behead me. I threw up my arm to block it. His sword struck the blade of my knife. The force of the impact drove the point of my knife into my forearm, starting it bleeding. I felt a trickle of blood running down my arm inside my sleeve. It hurt, but I'm sure having my head separated from my shoulders would have hurt more.

Matthew threw his weight onto the sword as if he thought it would slice through my knife. I let him press me down until he was almost directly over me, then I rolled out from under him. His own weight threw him forward, and his sword chipped the thick oak door.

He screamed out of anger and turned to face me. Holding the sword in both hands, he pointed it at me.

"I won't let you haunt me. You can't stop me! No one can! Do you hear me!" he screamed.

Haunt? Watchdog? Did he think I was spending my entire life in an attempt to undermine him? I wanted to do so much more with my life besides haunt him.

But what could be more important than saving someone from a meaningless death?

Matthew charged thrusting his sword in front of him. He was trying to pin me against the wall like a butterfly in a collection.

I dove to the side. The sword struck the wall with a dull thud.

How was I going to get out of the room? The door was locked, and diving out the window would only give Matthew the chance to find me. If I didn't get out quickly, he would eventually catch me. There were only so many places I could run. I was running around in circles. Sooner or later, I would tire, and he would be ready to kill me.

Where had Matthew come into the room? He couldn't have come up the stairs I had climbed with the priest. Too many people would have seen him and tried to stop him to talk with him. So where had he come into the room?

Matthew pulled the sword from the wall and swung it wildly at my head. I ducked and moved backward.

Then I saw the throne. The only section of wall I couldn't see was hidden behind the throne. There had to be a private entrance behind it.

I turned to try and run for the throne, but I slipped and landed on my side. I put out my hand to right myself and Matthew swung the sword.

The blade sliced through my wrist as if it were nothing more than paper. I saw the blood start to pump from my handless arm. Then I fell again because I had no hand to push myself up with.

Matthew raised the sword to strike again, but I kicked his legs out from under him knocking him to the floor, also. The sword flew out of his hands and landed a few feet away.

I felt no pain, only the sensation of the ripple leaving my body. Without thinking, I grabbed my hand and held it against my wrist. The ripple returned, and I felt my wrist beginning to tingle and itch. The blood flow stopped, and after a few seconds, I could feel some sensation in my hand. My hand had reattached itself to my body.

Matthew grabbed his sword and charged at me again. I picked up my knife, which I had dropped when I grabbed my hand and threw it as hard as I could. It struck Matthew squarely in the chest. His mouth dropped open in surprise. He staggered back a step.

Pulling the knife out of his chest, he laughed as he tossed it back to me. It clattered on the floor near my wounded hand. Unconsciously, I reached over and grabbed it. My hand was completely healed.

The ripple from Matthew bored through me as his body searched for a life to steal. As the hole in his chest started to heal, I lunged off the floor toward the throne. I heard Matthew scream behind me, but he was too late.

I grabbed the arm of the throne and swung around behind it. I saw the door. Grabbing the handle, I prayed that the door wouldn't be locked. The handle turned, and the door swung open easily. Apparently, Matthew had thought he would be able to kill me quickly with the sword.

I was halfway down the first flight of steps when I heard Matthew come through the door above me. It slammed open with a loud crash.

"I will kill you, Lazarus! I know how! But first I will make you suffer! Remember how Elizabeth Poe died? It can happen again! It will happen again!" he yelled from behind me.

I turned on the second-floor landing and started down toward the first floor. A priest came up the stairs to aid Matthew, but he stepped to the side when I pointed my knife at his face.

I stepped onto the first floor behind the black curtains draped behind the pulpit in the chapel. I limped through the chapel and out the door I had first entered the church through.

Running out to Charles Street, I hobbled away from the mansion as quickly as I could. I had expected to be followed by Matthew and a dozen priests, but none came. They wouldn't want to be seen outside the church chasing a man down in the street. It would destroy their religious image.

When I got back to my room, I collapsed on my bed and caught my breath. I tried to keep my body from shaking, but it was impossible. Holding my arm up, I studied my wrist and hand. I could see no scar at all from where the sword had severed my hand. I made a fist and unclenched it. I shook my hand from left to right, then back and forth. It was perfectly normal.

What if I hadn't been able to grab it and put it back on my wrist?

What would have happened then? Would I have been left with an amputated stump or would my hand have regenerated itself on my wrist?

I looked at the calendar I carried with my records for Atlantic Importers. It was June thirtieth. Edgar would be in Philadelphia for a reading and negotiations for investors in the magazine he wanted to start. After that, he would be heading to Richmond. I had told him I would attend his reading at the Exchange Hotel there.

I had intended to head south for Charlottesville, but after what I had just seen, I couldn't leave Edgar unaware of the dangers. I had to tell him what had happened and warn him of Matthew.

29

1849 A.D.

Getting to Philadelphia was a simple matter. Finding Edgar once I got there was more of a problem. I only knew of one person that he knew in the city and that was John Sartain. He was the man who had arranged Edgar's reading at the Independence Hotel and one of the men Edgar hoped would lend him money to start his own magazine.

I arrived in Philadelphia late Tuesday night, and it took me to Wednesday night to locate where John Sartain lived.

Mrs. Sartain greeted me at the door when I knocked. She was in her early forties, but she looked even older. Her hair had grayed early, and her skin sagged at her chin.

"Hello, ma'am. I'm looking for Edgar Poe. I was hoping your husband might be able to tell me where he is staying," I said.

"My husband is still at work at his magazine. He spends late hours there the week he has to print an issue." She saw the disappointment on my face and asked, "Is something wrong?"

"I need to find Edgar Poe. I have no idea where to locate him," I told her.

"I don't know where he is staying, but Edgar stopped by here when he arrived in town yesterday. His reading is at the Independence Hotel on Market Street. You might look for him there."

I climbed into my carriage, wondering how I was going to contact Edgar. Knowing how quickly Matthew acted when he was angry, I didn't want to put the meeting off. As I trotted the horse up the street, a carriage passed mine going in the opposite direction. The odd thing I noticed was that the carriage was driven by a priest. Something made me turn around and watch where the it went. It pulled up in front of the Sartain house.

Matthew!

It had to be. He was going to try and hurt me through Edgar. I started the horses moving into a trot. I needed to get to the Independence Hotel as quickly as possible.

"Is Edgar Poe staying here?" I asked the clerk as I rushed in from the street.

"Yes. He is giving a..." the clerk started to say.

"What room number?"

Two-oh-four. It's..."

By then I was already running up the staircase as fast as my bad leg would allow me to run.

I banged on the door to his room, not caring whether I woke everyone else in the hotel up. Finally, Edgar opened the door rubbing his eyes.

"Reynolds, is that you?" he asked.

I pushed my way into the room. "Lock the door behind me and blow out your lamp," I said.

"What's this all about? I thought you would have been back in Charlottesville by now," he said groggily.

I drew the curtains closed. "I was on my way there, but something happened," I said.

"What?" he asked as he blew out his lamp.

The room was thrown into total darkness. I stopped moving until my eyes adjusted enough so that I could see shadows moving.

"I was spending the night in Baltimore, and I heard that Cardinal Halloran was excommunicated by the Catholic Church," I told him.

"That's why you knocked me out that time in my room while I was still enrolled in the university. You didn't want me to talk to him." Edgar added.

His voice was off to my left. I thought I could make out his shadow sitting on his bed.

"Yes. Only now He's started his own church. I'm still not sure why I went. Curiosity, I guess. Maybe, I wanted to see how Matthew preached. Anyway, it was the wrong thing to do. He saw me and tried to kill me, but he also said he would cause me pain like he had when he killed your mother. Since you're the closest person to me, I assumed he was threatening you, and I was right. As I was driving away from John Sartain's house, I saw a priest also stop at the house. I didn't see who got out, but I would assume it was Matthew," I explained.

"So he's going to try and kill me?" Edgar asked, trying to hide the edge of panic in his voice.

"Yes. You had better get a pair of pants on. We need to get out of here before Matthew traces you here. Mrs. Sartain will certainly tell a priest that your reading is at this hotel," I said.

I heard movement around the room, and I assumed Edgar was dressing in the dark. Then I heard footsteps in the hallway not far from the door.

"Be quiet," I whispered. "I think I heard them coming down the hall."

Edgar was instantly still. There was a knock at the door.

"Mr. Poe?" It wasn't Matthew's voice. "Mr. Poe, this is Father Harrison. I need to speak with you."

I moved as quietly as I could toward the window. Pulling the lock back, I silently slid the window open. I tugged on Edgar's arm, pulling him toward the window.

There was another knock at the door. This time Matthew spoke. "We know you're in there, Mr. Poe. The clerk said he saw you come up a while ago. He also said Mr. Reynolds is with you. He can't protect you, Mr. Poe," Matthew said.

"Hang from the ledge, then drop to the ground. It should be no more than a six- foot drop," I whispered in Edgar's ear.

He nodded that he understood and climbed out of the window. I watched his silhouette fill the window, then disappear below the sill as he dropped to the ground.

Someone rattled the doorknob trying to get inside.

I looked out the window. Edgar was standing in the street waiting for me. I climbed onto the window sill.

I heard a thud against the door as they tried to break in. The door wouldn't hold Matthew and his priests for long, either.

I held onto the wooden sill and let my body slide over the edge. When I had stretched out as far as I could, I let go. It was a short drop, but my bad leg gave out, and I fell on my backside.

Edgar held out his hand and helped me to my feet. I quickly brushed the dirt from my back.

"My carriage is over there," I said, pointing to the front of the hotel.

As we started toward the carriage, I heard wood splintering above us. Matthew had broken in. The sound of the door giving way was followed by anxious, muffled voices.

"Hurry!" I urged Edgar, putting my hand on his back to push him along.

We climbed into the carriage, and I hurried the horses into a fast trot. We rode away from the Independence Hotel in silence. Edgar kept glancing behind us expecting pursuit from Matthew and his priests.

After nearly five minutes of silence, I said, "What will you do now?"

He turned from looking out the rear of the carriage to face me. "What do you mean?" he asked.

"You can't go back to the hotel or John Sartain's. They'll be watching for you in both places," I explained.

Edgar was quiet as he thought about his options.

"I'm going to do my reading tomorrow," he said.

"You can't. That's one place they'll definitely be waiting for you. You can't go back there. These men are trying to kill you, Edgar," I warned him.

"But being in a crowd is the best place for me. If Matthew tries to kill me like he did my mother, and that's what you seem to think he wants to do, he'll have a high risk of failure if I am in a crowd. He'll have to make sure I'm the closest person to him, and that will be hard to do at the reading. It would be too easy for the crowd to shift, and then I would no longer be the closest to him. It's only when I am alone that I am at risk." He paused. "Besides, I need the money."

"I can give you money, Edgar, but if you take it, I want you to leave the state," I offered.

"And do what? I'm a writer. I have to write. As soon as I publish something, no matter where I am, he would be able to find me. I won't spend my life running away from him," Edgar said emphatically.

It was my turn to be silent.

"I'm not afraid of him, Reynolds. I won't mind dying. I've written the greatest work I'll ever write with *Eureka*, and I've loved the greatest love I'll ever know with Virginia. If what you say about Heaven is true, then she, and my mother, and Mrs. Allan are all waiting for me to join them. Why should I be afraid to die?"

"You can't seriously be thinking about letting him kill you, are you?" I said.

Edgar shrugged. "Sometimes, I think why should I go on living? But I will do my reading tomorrow night," he said.

The rest of my arguments urging him to cancel the reading still did not change his mind. I took him to the hotel where I was staying and paid for a room for him. I don't know how he slept, but I was awake most of the night wondering if Matthew and his priests would find us.

The next evening, Edgar had me drive him back to the Independence Hotel. I put a chair behind the podium where he was speaking so that I would be able to scan the audience and watch for Matthew. Three-hundred people filled the room, and each one had paid four dollars to hear Edgar speak for an hour. He collected thirty percent of the total. John Sartain took in thirty percent of the total, and the rest went to pay for expenses such as renting the ballroom in the hotel.

With the famous words, "Once upon a midnight dreary...," Edgar began his most-popular poem, *The Raven*. Halfway through the poem, I saw Matthew. He walked in through the rear door and stood at the back of the room. Edgar saw him, too. I could tell it in the way his voice faltered for a moment.

He quickly recovered, but Matthew had noticed. He smirked and moved off to the side. Two other priests moved in after him. They all stood at the back of the room listening to Edgar speak.

Edgar's reading pace picked up slightly. Sweat broke out on his forehead and rolled down his cheeks. He paused to wipe his face with a handkerchief.

I moved my chair next to an end table with a lamp sitting on it. It was unlit since it was still light outside. I took the chimney off and lit the wick. A small flame flared, and I let my hand rest near the base.

I met Matthew's stare and didn't turn away.

Edgar finished the poem. The audience clapped loudly and rose to their feet. Edgar looked back at me, and I smiled. He raised his hand to move the top sheet in his pile to the bottom, and I saw his hand shaking.

Matthew started to walk forward up the side of the room. Edgar saw him move and looked around quickly.

The crowd quieted down and waited for the next poem.

Edgar turned to me.

"Don't worry," I said as I tapped the base of the lamp.

Edgar pressed his lips together tightly and wiped off his damp forehead.

Then he ran. He turned and darted out the rear door that led into the street behind the hotel. It happened so quickly that he was out of the room before I could even get out of my chair. Luckily, he also caught Matthew off guard.

Matthew and his priests started running forward up the aisles. I grabbed the lamp and stood up. Matthew stopped abruptly when he saw the open flame.

The crowd started standing wondering where Edgar had gone. A few rose to leave. Most just complained loudly about Edgar's rudeness at leaving so abruptly. For my part, I was also wondering where he had gone.

I backed away from Matthew still holding the lamp in my hand. I actually saw fear in his eyes every time he glanced at the flame. I jabbed it at him a few times to give him a reason to be cautious.

I reached the door Edgar had run out and stepped outside into an alley. Throwing the lamp to the ground, it shattered and spread a line of flame between the hotel and me.

I hobbled away to my carriage as quickly as possible while the two priests with Matthew tried to put out the fire in their path.

I had no idea why Edgar had run, or even where he had run. He had said he wasn't afraid of Matthew as long as there was a crowd around him. There had certainly been a crowd in the room. So why had he run? It was something his father would have done.

The first place I searched was the hotel we had stayed at the night before. The clerk hadn't seen him since we had checked out an hour earlier. Next, I looked into a few of the nearby taverns without any success. I found a slight measure of relief in the fact that Edgar wasn't drinking.

Finally, I decided to ask John Sartain if he had seen him. When I knocked on the door to the house, Mrs. Sartain answered the door again.

"I'm looking for Edgar Poe, ma'am. I was wondering if he stopped by here to talk to your husband?"

Mrs. Sartain nodded vigorously. "I should say so. That man is crazy, absolutely crazy."

"Why do you say that?" I asked.

"He rushed in here an hour ago in total hysterics." She waved her hands wildly in the air. "He told John assassins were searching for him who wanted to kill him."

"So what did your husband do?" I asked.

"He tried to calm him down, but he didn't have much luck. Edgar asked him for a razor to shave his mustache off. Now John was not going to give that crazy man something as sharp as a razor. There was no telling what he might have done with it. If John had tried, I would have stopped him. Anyway, John told Edgar he would shave his mustache off for him. He only trimmed it a bit, then lied to Edgar and said he looked completely different. Edgar believed him, too. Then Edgar wanted to go out. Well, he was in no condition to drive a carriage so my husband said he'd take him to the rail station."

Edgar left town?" I asked.

Mrs. Sartain nodded. Then he should have been heading for Richmond. I thanked her and left for my hotel.

I considered not following him, but he was still in danger from Matthew. If Matthew had discovered Edgar was in Philadelphia, he might also know of his reading in Richmond.

It took me three days to get to Richmond, but I saw no sign of Edgar. I couldn't decide whether he had gone into hiding after all, or if he had merely gone to another town instead of Richmond to hide from Matthew as well as me.

30

1849 A.D.

A week passed, then two. Still, I hadn't heard from or seen Edgar. If he was in Richmond, he certainly wasn't making his presence known to me.

I also did not see any sign of Matthew or his priests, either. That, at least, was a relief. I thought that they might not have followed Edgar to Richmond, but I couldn't see them giving up. Then I happened to read an article in the paper about a priest causing a disturbance at Edgar's Philadelphia reading. The article was drawn from second-hand knowledge and largely inaccurate, but it did point out one thing. The priest in question had been the former Cardinal Halloran who had started his own church in Baltimore.

After I had read the article, I realized why I hadn't seen Matthew in Richmond. It was too dangerous for him to make an appearance. If he tried to attack Edgar again, he might be seen by many people as a renegade priest persecuting a beloved poet. Most Americans were all too eager to believe the worst about Catholics or former Catholics. Matthew might even abandon the idea of harming Edgar to avoid anymore poor publicity for himself or his church, or so I hoped.

The day for Edgar's reading at the Exchange Hotel arrived, and I wondered why I hadn't seen a notice that it would be canceled. I asked the clerk at the hotel if the reading was still scheduled as originally planned, and he told me yes.

Edgar wouldn't come out of hiding and risk his life for a reading, I thought. Then I remembered how adamant he had been about continuing his reading in Philadelphia.

The rented ballroom was filled to capacity the night of the reading. I had purchased a ticket earlier in the week and took a seat near the back so that I would not only be able to watch Edgar dramatize his reading, but I could see if Matthew attended the reading.

At six o'clock, a murmur went up from the crowd. Where was Edgar? I began to wonder if the hotel had canceled the performance in the hopes that Edgar would show up. Five minutes passed, and I began to think that Edgar would not show up and risk facing Matthew.

At ten past, a side door opened, and Edgar walked across the floor to the podium. This was not the Edgar I had seen in Philadelphia. This man was well-dressed in a new broadcloth suit. His hair and mustache had been neatly trimmed, more than likely by John Sartain. He even seemed to have regained his health to some extent. His eyes appeared to be not as deeply sunken as they had been.

He stepped up to the podium and paused. He turned to the wall and lifted one of the oil lamps from its brace and set it on the podium. Then he removed the chimney from the lamp and let the flame burn openly. He hadn't forgotten about Matthew. He knew he was taking a chance at appearing at a public event.

He opened his book of notes and began reading from *The Poetic Principle*, a piece about creativity that he had written before he left Fordham. I noticed when he looked up occasionally, his eyes always sought out the rear door of the ballroom before anything else. Although he appeared calm, he was still afraid that Matthew might show up like he had at the Independence Hotel.

When the hour had passed, and Edgar concluded his reading, he moved to the side of the podium and took a long, sweeping bow in front of the audience. They rose to their feet and clapped loudly. Edgar smiled and walked back out the side door. I think that his smile was partly due to his relief that Matthew hadn't appeared during the reading.

I hurried out of the hotel as quickly as could. I had to push my way through members of the audience who had already begun to leave. Outside, I hurried around to the side of the hotel I thought the door that Edgar had exited through was on. As I came around the corner, I stopped and pulled back suddenly.

Edgar was still in the alley. He was standing with his back against the wall of the hotel just staring up at the night sky. I peeked around the corner every few seconds until he finally began to walk away.

I followed him as stealthily as I could trying to call on the wilderness skills I had not used for so many years. He walked up Broad Street until he turned onto Twelfth Street. As he neared Duncan's Lodge, he turned off the road and started onto the path that ran behind the lodge. He stopped at the side door of the lodge and picked up a lantern so that he would be able to see the path. Then he continued on.

Keeping pace with him was hard. He would walk very slowly for a few feet, then suddenly speed up, only to stop completely. After following him along the wooded path for five minutes, he turned around and said, "I don't know who you are, but you had better show yourself. I'm armed, and I just might decide to shoot you if you continue to follow me any further."

I stepped from the shadows into the small circle of light Edgar's lantern cast.

"Reynolds! What are you doing following me?" he asked when he recognized me.

"I wasn't sure if you would want to see me," I answered.

Edgar lowered his head. "I'm sorry I ran out of the reading and left you alone with Matthew. But when I saw Matthew...well, I guess I'm not as brave as I thought I was. I'm sorry."

I waved my hand. "It doesn't matter. I wasn't hurt, and neither were you. I guess we were both lucky," I said.

Edgar nodded. His deep-set eyes were only two black holes in his head. "Well, I am for now. Is there something you need to talk to me about?"

"Let's walk," I suggested. "I feel more comfortable nowadays staying on the move."

We started across the path that ran behind Duncan's Lodge. Edgar held onto the lantern as if it were a charm that warded off spirits.

"I cannot stay long," Edgar said, "I am expected at the Weiss" shortly. I sail for Baltimore tomorrow to see Muddy. Then from there, I'll go to New York. I need to finish certain unfinished matters before I get married."

I stopped walking. "Married?"

"Yes. Sarah Royster, the woman I told you about during one of our conversations in Fordham, the one whose father and John Allan conspired to keep us apart, is now a widow, and she has agreed to marry me on my return from New York. Life has been good to me since I've returned to Richmond, Reynolds. I don't know why I didn't return sooner. I've always considered myself a Virginian, and this is my home. I gave a reading of *The Poetic Principle* at the Exchange Hotel. Three-hundred people showed up paying five dollars each to hear me speak," Edgar said proudly.

"I know. I was there," I told him.

"Really? Then you saw how well I did."

I nodded. "I saw a lot of things," I noted.

"Was..." he started to say.

I shook my head. "I didn't see Matthew. I just meant that I saw how confident you were. I also noticed the burning lamp you kept in front of you on the podium," I explained.

"How long have you been in town?" Edgar asked.

"Two weeks," was my reply.

"Two weeks? And you've not tried to talk with me before now?" he said.

I could tell by the tone of his voice that I had hurt his feelings.

"I couldn't find you," I told Edgar. "No one that I knew seemed to know where you were or if you were even in Richmond."

"I stayed off the streets and kept myself indoors as much as possible. If I did go out, it was at night when it was harder to recognize. I wasn't sure if Matthew had followed me or not, but apparently, he didn't."

"He may still be after you, though," I said.

Edgar stopped walking. "No! He can't be. It's not fair!" he yelled.

"What's not fair?" I asked.

"Everywhere he goes, he ruins my life. I am happy here, Reynolds. I don't want to lose this," Edgar said.

I grabbed Edgar by the shoulders. "You won't lose this. Since Matthew has been excommunicated from the church, He's going to have to be extremely careful about what he does and how he is perceived. Catholics and non-Catholics alike will be very suspicious of his church for years to come. He can't risk drawing any critical attention to himself, or it might ruin his church. Even a small incident, like when I blocked him from pursuing you out of the Independence Hotel, was made a note of in the papers. That's probably why he didn't follow you here. He doesn't want to be seen right now. He has no power, Edgar," I said.

Edgar shook his head fiercely. "You're wrong. He still has power. Don't you see that? His power comes from within, from the evil that animates his body. That is not contained, nor will it ever be."

"You're wrong. I can't destroy it, but I can contain it," I promised.

"How?" Edgar asked.

"Matthew's anger is directed at me right now. Although he attempted to kill you, it was only because you knew me and I had told you the truth about Matthew and me. I was the one who arranged his excommunication. I caused him to alter his plans. Even though I haven't been able to defeat him, he also has not been able to beat me. If you are right about the evil in him, he will realize that I must be destroyed before he can begin to rebuild his external power in the form of his church."

"He will come for you then," Edgar said.

I nodded. "Yes, and I will be far from here. I think I will lead Matthew into the canyons in the west. Somewhere along the way, his apostles will refuse to follow him any further. Once he has lost them, I will capture him and imprison him. We will spend the rest of our lives together. He as the prisoner and I as his jailer."

Edgar ran his hand over his mustache. "You'd be giving up your life," he said.

I shrugged. "I've already lived my life and many others. This would be a way to make sure other people have a chance to live theirs without having to die prematurely," I said.

Edgar shook his hands in front of my face. "Why not kill him? You could burn him with a torch. Then you wouldn't have to give up your life, also."

I must admit the thought had crossed my mind more than once, but I had always come up with the same answer. "I once thought that I could kill Matthew. Now I am no longer sure. It is bad enough that I take life unintentionally. I could never take it purposefully even if I believed that person deserved to die. I tried once, but I had been pushed beyond my limits of tolerance at the time."

"So you've made your choice," Edgar said.

"Yes." I held out my hand to him, and he shook it. "I wish you much happiness and love, Edgar. I know it has eluded you for far too long."

Edgar smiled. "Thank you, Reynolds. But what about you? Is this the elusive purpose for your life that you have been seeking?"

I smiled slightly. "I believe it is," I said.

And so we parted on that path behind Duncan's Lodge. Edgar went to be with his friends on Broad Street, and I went back to my room to prepare for my next confrontation with Matthew.

The next day I went to the wharf and saw Edgar off on his journey to Baltimore. We shook hands and wished each other well. I honestly felt like we were friends at that moment. After the boat had sailed, I felt an empty feeling inside me. I knew I would miss him, but I hoped he had finally found happiness.

I walked back into town to the cemetery where Frances had had Elizabeth's body buried. The gravestone was a simple one that just listed Elizabeth's name and date of her death. I suppose Frances hadn't known when she had been born. There was a pile of dead flowers in front of the stone. I wondered how many years they had lain there, and who had set them there. I stayed there for nearly an hour just sitting in the grass next to the grave and staring at the headstone. I didn't try to talk to Elizabeth because I knew her soul was not under the ground, but somewhere in Heaven where she was living a happy life.

On my way back to my room, a priest walked up beside me as I crossed Ninth Street.

"Good evening, Mr. Reynolds," he said as he drew near me.

I turned to look at him. When I saw he was a priest, I was immediately cautious. I quickly scanned the crowds on both sides of the street looking for more, but he was alone.

"Do I know you?" I asked.

"No, but you are known to my master. He calls you the Devil," the priest said.

The man was one of Matthew's disciples.

"Your master lies," I told him.

"Blasphemer! You are the spreader of lies and filth, but my master will survive you as he always has," he shouted.

I pulled away from him and left him standing on the side of the street next to John Washington's Store.

I hadn't gotten four-feet away when he said, "We have your servant, the one who writes the stories of evil to spread your message of hate."

I stopped.

Edgar. They had Edgar, but he had left Richmond. His boat should have nearly reached Baltimore by now. They couldn't have taken him. He was safe.

I turned around to face the priest. "Edgar is gone," I said.

The priest smiled. I had grown to distrust that smile. It was a copy of Matthew's evil smile.

"Yes, he is gone. He has gone right into the lion's den. Baltimore is where we are strongest. We shall make an example of your servant and show him the error of his ways. He will accept the true God of the world before we kill him," the ex-priest said.

I grabbed the man by the folds of his cassock and pulled him close to me. A few people stopped and stared, obviously wondering why I was attacking a priest. Of course, most of them didn't care one way or the other what happened to the Catholics. They were Protestants by and large.

"What have you done with him?" I demanded.

The ex-priest smiled Matthew's smile again, and I wanted to break his teeth. Let him try to smile then.

"Nothing, yet, but I cannot say how long that state will last," the ex-priest said.

I shook him trying to stop him from smiling. "Where is he in Baltimore? Did you take him to your church?" I demanded.

"I do not know. I wouldn't tell you if I did know. I was told only to contact you this evening and tell you that your servant was being held by Master Halloran." Master must have been the new title Matthew had created for himself in his new church. "The servant will die soon as all devils and witches do in the atoning fire of repentance."

I pushed the ex-priest away from me. He stumbled backward and fell onto the roadway. I scowled at a man who tried to help the priest up, and he backed away.

I left Matthew's disciple sitting in the road and ran down the street to William Randolf's Livery on Eighth and Broad Streets. I bought an overpriced stallion from Randolph's without even dickering over the price. I could have bargained him down to a reasonable price, but I didn't have the time. As soon as he told me it was the fastest animal he had, I said I'd take it. I could guess by the size of his smile how much he had overpriced the beast.

As I threw a saddle on the horse, I patted his muzzle and whispered in his ear, "Get me where I want to go, and I may not kill you. Throw me, and I will make you a gelding," I warned him.

I rode that horse hard all the way to Washington D. C., and he must have taken my words to heart because he didn't try to throw me once. In Washington, I found the first livery I could and traded him for another, fresher mount. It was a red roan, and I rode him hard until we reached Mrs. Clemm's house in Baltimore.

I pounded on the door of her house until I heard her walking down the steps to answer it. I could hear her muttering to herself as she opened the front door.

"Alexander?" Her surprise was evident even through her sleepiness. "What do you want? And why are you making such a racket at four o'clock in the morning? The sun's not even up yet."

"Marie, is Edgar here?" I asked frantically.

"Edgar's in Richmond. He had a reading two nights ago," she said.

"No, he left Richmond yesterday by boat. He should have been here by now," I told her.

"Well, He's not here. Maybe he decided to stay in a room in

town because the boat came in late. Edgar's considerate that way. He wouldn't wake me up at four o'clock in the morning," she said sarcastically.

I understood her implication and turned away from the door. Behind me, I heard Edgar's mother-in-law closing the door.

Where was Edgar? Had the priest in Richmond sent me on a false trail to get me out of Richmond?

I turned to retrieve my tired horse from where I had tethered him. I saw a blur of movement in the dark before something was thrown over my head. I tried to shake it off, but before I could, someone grabbed me from behind. I felt a loop of rope tighten across my arms and then another and another. Then I was hit over the head with something hard, and I lost consciousness.

When I awoke, the first thing I saw was a heaping pile of wood at my feet. Then I felt the ache in my shoulders and wrists. I tried to move them to a more comfortable position, but I couldn't. My arms were tied behind me, and I was tied to a pole.

I stood up slowly and leaned back against the pole. The pain in my shoulders and wrists subsided a little, but I still felt like my arms had been pulled from their sockets.

I realized I was standing in the middle of a pyre.

I was in a large yard surrounded by high, brick walls. I looked over my shoulder, and I could see a mansion behind me. I turned myself around so I could see it without straining.

It was a three-story homemade of red brick. I recognized it as Matthew's church, although I was on the side that faced away from Charles Street. I thought I saw a face inside one of the second-floor windows, but it was a brief, fleeting glimpse.

It was daylight now. I assumed it was still morning, but I couldn't be sure. I had no idea of how long I had been unconscious.

I could do little but wait.

I couldn't see any other buildings surrounding the mansion or over the wall. It seemed like this place was an isolated home somewhere in the country even though we were just north of Baltimore.

I pulled at the ropes that bound my hands, but they held tight. My effort only served to chafe my wrists further and send dull pains through my arms.

The back door to the house opened, but no one came out. I stared at the gaping black hole, wondering if someone was watching me from the shadows that congealed inside the doorway.

After a few minutes, a priest walked out carrying two buckets.

The weight of the buckets pulled his shoulders down and caused him to lean forward. He had to hurry his pace to keep from falling over. His stance, along with his black cassock, gave him the appearance of a large ape, like the murderer in Edgar's story *The Murders at the Rue Morgue*.

Now I knew who had attacked me. Not this priest, perhaps, but a group of them, definitely. This was one of Matthew's disciples.

"Where is Master Halloran?" I asked as the priest drew closer to me.

He didn't answer. He didn't even look at me. He set one the buckets down. Holding the second bucket with both hands, he splashed the contents over the pyre. The scent of coal oil reached my nose.

"Where is Edgar Poe?" I asked.

Again, he said nothing. When he had emptied the first bucket, he set it aside and began splashing the second bucket of oil over the pyre. Once finished, he picked up both buckets and walked back into the house.

He hadn't said a word or even looked at me.

He reappeared a minute later pushing Edgar in front of him. Edgar's clothes were torn, and I could see purple bruises on his exposed skin. His head nodded as he shuffled ahead of the priest.

The priest picked up a ladder that was leaning against the wall and laid it across the pyre. Then, with Edgar still leading the way, they climbed to the top beside me.

"Edgar," I said.

He looked up. I saw a flicker of hope in his eyes fade when he saw that I was also tied to the post.

The priest turned him around so that he was standing back to back with me and the pole was between us. It reminded me of the time Edgar, and I had fought our duel at McCarron Field. Only this time, we were not opponents, but comrades. The priest tied Edgar's hands to the pole below mine.

When the priest had gone back inside the mansion, Edgar asked, "Reynolds, will Matthew kill us now?"

"I suppose he'll try," I said honestly.

"No!" Edgar screamed.

"Edgar, calm down. They haven't lit the fire yet. There's still a chance we can escape." I immediately felt him struggling against the ropes that bound his wrists. "How did they capture you?" I asked.

"I was walking to Muddy's from the harbor and three of Matthew's priests stopped me. I tried to run, but they caught up with me. They tied me up, but not before they beat me. For priests, they are brutal."

"They aren't real priests anymore," I reminded him.

"I found that out. How did they get you?" Edgar asked.

"I was at your mother-in-law's looking for you. A priest in Richmond told me that Matthew had captured you and was going to kill you. When I turned to leave Maria's house, they jumped me and knocked me unconscious," I said.

"How are we going to get off this pyre?" Edgar wanted to know.

At that moment, I didn't know, but I was saved from telling him that when the rear door to the mansion opened. Matthew's twelve disciples filed out of the mansion and encircled the pyre standing about six feet away from it. The priests all turned to look back at the open door. Matthew stepped into the light holding a lighted torch.

I felt Edgar pull against the ropes again, but it was of little use. The priest had bound us tightly to the pole.

Matthew stopped in front of me and smiled. He moved up close to the pyre and held the torch near my face. The heat burned my face, and I tried to turn away as far as possible.

"So it comes to this, Lazarus. This is how immortals die," he said.

"How's your side, Matthew?" I asked, reminding him that he could also be hurt by fire.

"Don't kill us, please!" Edgar yelled.

"Don't waste your time begging, Edgar. A man needs compassion to be moved to mercy. Matthew has neither," I said.

From behind me, I heard Edgar sob.

"After all these centuries of wondering when you would finally die, the time has finally come," Matthew said.

"It has not. Christ said I would live until he returned to the earth," I told him.

"He did not!" Matthew yelled.

Why was he disturbed by that comment? The same thing was said to him. Wasn't it? I decided to press my advantage. "How do you know, Matthew? Were you there? I will not die today, not until Christ is risen," I said.

"He has, Lazarus. Don't you listen to my Masses?" Matthew said, smiling.

I should have been as frightened as Edgar, but I wasn't. I felt calm and oddly safe standing atop the pyre.

"Tell me one thing, Matthew. What is your true name?" I asked.

I am Matthew of Nain."

I shook my head. "No, not the name of your body. *Your* name."

Matthew's smile faltered. "I am Abapai."

He spun away from me to face his priests. "Brothers, the demon and his servant have been taken. You have done well. Now they must be cast down into the fires of Hell to free the world from their evil. Only then will I be able to walk the world in my pure form as your savior."

He turned back to me. Lowering the torch until it was only inches from the pyre, he said, "Goodbye, Lazarus."

He touched the fire to the base, and the flames licked at the wood. Edgar screamed again.

31

1849 A.D.

The fire will not burn you.

I remembered the voice from my dream. I wanted to believe in the words, especially now, but fire could burn me. It already had. My leg was proof of that.

Have faith.

I closed my eyes and leaned my head back against the pole. Did I have any hope left in me? Was my faith as strong as Edgar's had been when he believed I could heal Virginia by allowing her to make a sacrament of my blood? If I had had as much faith, would she have lived?

"Edgar, hold onto my hands," I said.

He continued screaming, although the fire had not reached us yet.

"Edgar, hold onto my hands," I ordered him. I felt his fingers interlock with mine. "Good, now be quiet and close your eyes." He fell silent, and I assumed he had closed his eyes.

"You must believe, Edgar. Believe that you will not die." The bottoms of my feet felt hot, and I shifted them to an area of the pyre that hadn't begun to burn. "Believe that the fire will not burn you." I was saying it as much for my benefit as for his. I could feel the heat from the nearby flames on my lower legs, but I refused to open my eyes. "Believe that I will live until Christ returns," I said.

What would happen now? I could hear Edgar whimpering, but he didn't scream.

The ripple started to leave me but then stopped. I could still feel it connected to my body, but it wasn't moving any further out. It rolled from my fingertips and onto Edgar.

Was I stealing his life before the fire did?

Suddenly, the heat vanished. I slowly opened my eyes, not knowing what I would see. The flames were waist high all around me and growing larger. They should have been burning my body, throwing me into death spasms, but I felt nothing.

"Reynolds?" I heard Edgar ask.

"Keep your eyes closed, Edgar. Keep telling yourself that you believe, and don't let go of my hand," I said.

"But I don't feel anything." He paused. "Am I dead?"

"No, you are very much alive. Just do as I told you," I said.

In another minute the flames had engulfed us as the pyre turned into an inferno, and still I could not feel the heat. I couldn't see Matthew or his priests through the flames and smoke. I waited patiently until I felt the ropes that bound my hands fall away.

I stepped through the flames, pulling Edgar by his hand. Amazingly, there was no hesitation in my step as I passed through the flames. My feet found sturdy footholds even as the logs around us turned to ash. Edgar kept his eyes clenched shut and totally relied on my guidance. If my eyes had also been closed, I would never have known I was in the middle of a raging fire. I could feel no heat from the flames. Nor could I hear the crackle of the wood or the roar of the fire. It was as if Edgar and I had been enclosed in a fireproof bubble. I wondered if the ripple I could still feel connected to my body was somehow protecting us.

As we emerged from the fire and jumped to the ground, I could feel the heat once again at my back and hear the flames consuming the logs. Edgar sighed behind me. His hand pulled away from mine as he fell to the ground.

Embrace your enemy as your friend.

There were startled looks on the faces of Matthew's priests as they backed away from me. They had been accustomed to seeing Matthew's miracles of self-healing, but they had never seen a man walk through fire. Even Master Halloran would not attempt that.

"He controls the flames of the earth as he does the fires of Hell," one of the priests said.

Matthew stood outside the ring of priests that surrounded the pyre. I slowly walked toward him, and he stood his ground. The priests parted to let me through their line.

"How could you..." he started to say.

"You don't know everything there is to being a god, Abapai, and you never will. You aren't even supposed to be mortal," I said.

His eyes widened with fright. "Yes, I am. I am Matthew of Nain."

I held open my arms.

"Yes, do it," said a young voice from Matthew's mouth. The real widow's son who I had assumed dead for many years was making his last wishes known.

Matthew walked into my embrace. I could tell from the expression on his face that he was fighting every step, but for those few moments, at least, he was not in control of the body. Or at least the demon was not in control of the body; the widow's son from Nain was.

"Reynolds, no!" I heard Edgar shout from behind me.

I clasped my arms around Matthew. All the heat that I should have felt in the fire rushed out of my body into his. He trembled. I wasn't sure if it was a reaction to the heat or if he was making a last attempt to escape.

I stood face-to-face with him as the heat entered his body. His skin shriveled like a grape left to dry in the sun. As I watched, his face paled and began to crumble like a dried sand castle. When it was over, all that remained of Matthew was a pile of white dust at my feet.

I turned to Edgar who was shaking his head.

"You shouldn't have done it," he said.

"Why not? I've ended Matthew's chance to establish Satan's church on the earth," I said.

"No, you haven't. You've given him the opportunity to go forth in a way he never could have while he was locked into a body. His spirit is free to roam the earth creating whatever havoc he wishes," Edgar said.

I reached down and helped Edgar to his feet. "Matthew is now just a shadow. With the faith of man being as weak as it is, he is less likely to be accepted now. His evil will still grow, unfortunately, but it would have done that even if he had stayed in a body. Now it will be harder for Matthew, or rather the spirit that possessed Matthew's body, to rally people against the righteous. The righteous will stand on their own and face their adversary. In the end, they will prevail. In the end, the son of man will still come," I explained.

Edgar stared at the pile of dust and shook his head again. "What did you do to him?"

I told him the truth. "I don't know. I just felt I should embrace him. When I did, I felt heat surge from my body into his. He burned up from within. I saw him age and decay within seconds after I had touched him."

Edgar looked back at the still burning fire. "Reynolds, why didn't we burn up in the fire? It should have killed us."

"No, it shouldn't have. I was promised by Christ I would see him walk the earth again. It was not my time to die, nor yours because you held onto my hand," I answered him.

"Wasn't Matthew promised the same thing, and yet he died?"

I looked back at the pile of ash that had once been Matthew. "That promise was made to Matthew, not Abapai. I think when he possessed Matthew's body, he must have altered whatever Christ did to it to resurrect it. It was similar to mine, but not the same as mine.

That is why my regeneration felt like a ripple, and his felt like a screw. It was one of the subtle changes that manifested itself."

Edgar grabbed at his head. "This can't be real!" He pulled at his hair. "I'm dreaming again. This is all another story that I am dreaming!"

I grabbed him by the shoulders and shook him. "This is real, Edgar, but it is over," I told him.

"No." He covered his eyes with his hands and pulled away from me. "I want this dream to stop. I want to wake up."

I didn't know what to do. He was hysterical.

"Edgar," I said calmly.

"Leave me alone! You're only part of the dream. You're a spirit! I'm going to wake up!"

He turned and ran off into the mansion. I tried to chase after him, but my best run was nothing more than a fast walk. I stopped at the back door when I heard the front door slam shut. He would be long gone before I got through the house to the other side.

I turned back into the yard. Matthew's apostles were gathered around his ashes staring at the pile. They looked up at me as I approached. They would separate and return to their homes. Matthew had been their leader, and with him gone, no one would urge the priests to do evil.

I thought a warning from me might help them forget quickly about Matthew and his church. "Repent, lest the fires of Hell consume you as they did Master Halloran," I warned them in my most-solemn voice.

"But they did not burn you," someone said.

"I was not the evil one."

The priests began murmuring among themselves as they backed away from me. The nearest one to the house turned and ran. When the other eleven saw I wasn't going to stop him, they turned and ran also. Two of them got tangled in their cassocks and fell. They quickly scrambled to their feet and rushed into the mansion.

I was left standing alone in the garden with the pyre still burning at my back.

I stooped down to pick a handful of the ashes that had only minutes ago been Matthew. I rubbed my fingers in it. I smelled it. It had no particular qualities that would differentiate it from talc or that told me these ashes had once been a man.

So this was Matthew. Eighteen-hundred years of stolen life had caught up with him, and all his power couldn't prevent it.

I dropped the dust and brushed my hands off. Not even bothering to look back on the pyre, I left also.

32

1849 A.D.

Four days after Edgar ran off, I began to hear the talk in the taverns. Edgar had been found unconscious in an alley and taken to Washington College Hospital in Baltimore. Most people thought he had gone on a drunken binge. Others thought he might have been attacked because they had heard his body was bruised.

My first thought was that one of Matthew's priests had attacked him seeking revenge for Matthew's death. Then I remembered Edgar's face in the moments before he had run from Matthew's house. I kept hearing him scream his denials about what had happened. If he had gone on a drunken binge, I had driven him to it.

I ordered a bottle of scotch and drank it dry, trying to forget the look of disbelief and horror on Edgar's face. By the time I left the tavern three hours later, I had drained two more bottles.

I staggered onto Calvert Street and slowly oriented myself. Then I started off for Washington College Hospital. Somehow—and don't ask me how I can't remember—I made it to the ward room. I don't know how many beds I stumbled over and how many poor souls I woke up before I finally found Edgar. I was surprised that a doctor or a night nurse didn't chase me out of the hospital. They must have thought I was a patient fumbling with a chamber pot.

Edgar looked awful. His skin was so pale that it almost glowed in the darkness. Beads of sweat dotted his face, although the room was slightly chilly even with the wood stove burning. As I watched him, he murmured something incoherent in his sleep.

I shook him lightly on the shoulder, and he opened his eyes. He stopped murmuring and stared at me.

"Reynolds?" he asked.

"It's me," I whispered.

"I must not be too sick, you look worse than me," he said with a weak smile.

"At least I can walk on my own," I said.

Edgar tried to speak, but his words turned into a violent cough.

When he regained his voice, he said, "I'm not too sure about how well you walk. Those men you fell over trying to get from the door to here might have something different to say on that matter."

"What happened, Edgar?" I asked.

His expression went blank. "I can't remember too well. I was so upset after everything that happened at the house. I took a lot of laudanum and..."

"Laudanum! Are you stupid? That so-called medicine nearly killed you before," I shouted, not caring who I woke up. Of course, he said he later said he had only taken the laudanum to ease a pain in his back, but neither Maria nor I believed him.

"I know, I know, but I didn't care. I didn't want to be a part of this, Reynolds. I was pushed into it because I knew you," he said.

I leaned my head into my hands and said, "I know, and I'm sorry. I never meant for it to happen that way. That's why I wanted to draw Matthew away from you."

"It didn't work. They were waiting for me."

"But it's over now," I said.

"Is it? What if you're wrong? What if Matthew can rise like the phoenix from his ashes?" he asked. He tried to push himself into a sitting position, but he fell back against the bed.

"He can't," I assured him.

"How can you be so certain?" Edgar pressed.

"My leg has never healed from the fire that Matthew started in my house just after you were born."

"Maybe the damage to your leg wasn't severe enough for your body to regenerate. Besides, you were able to survive the fire at the mansion. Why shouldn't he?" Edgar asked.

"I explained that to you," I reminded him.

"You gave me your theory. You are no more sure that Matthew is dead than you know why you are alive." I started to say something, but he held up his hand. "The point is: I'm tired of wondering from which direction death will come at me. I don't want to have any more nightmares. Touch me and heal me," he said.

"You're talking foolishly, Edgar. My touch has never brought health, only death. I couldn't even help Virginia."

"Only death will heal me now. I'm dying, Reynolds. Everyone is, except you." I wanted to tell him that I too was dying, but he kept talking with renewed energy. "Your battle with Matthew has taken everything from me. My mother is dead. Virginia is dead. My father is missing. Now it's my turn. Kill me," he pleaded.

I shook my head. "You're delirious. You know I couldn't," I told him.

He grabbed my hand with both of his. "But you can. You kill now with no direction to the deaths you cause. All I am asking of you is to direct your power for once. Take my life and not some innocent's."

"No," I said.

I turned away from his bed.

Edgar kept pleading. "Reynolds, don't desert me now. You gave me life, now take it back. I don't want it!"

"Goodbye, Edgar," I said.

"Reynolds! Wait, Reynolds!" he yelled.

I could hear the other men in the ward room waking up and telling Edgar to be quiet so they could sleep. He ignored them. He kept screaming my name even after I had left the wardroom. I could hear his voice through the walls as I walked down the hall. A nurse rushed by me, I suppose, to quiet Edgar down.

The next day I went to the hospital again to ask if Edgar's condition had improved any.

"I hope you're not a family member," a doctor told me.

"Why?" I asked.

The doctor shook his head. "He is a pitiful sight to see. He's not eating a bite, and all he does is scream "Reynolds!" No one knows who he is talking about or we'd try and help him just the give the man some peace when he dies."

I thanked the doctor and left.

Why couldn't Edgar be quiet? Why did he want to die so badly?

That evening I sat in front of the fireplace and tried to write a letter to Maria Clemm explaining Edgar's condition. I just couldn't get my thoughts from my head onto the paper. I scratched out a useless line and wadded up the page into a small ball. Throwing the paper into the fire, I watched it blacken and crumble. My body should have done the same on the pyre.

I stared at the yellow and orange flames watching them vibrate back and forth. Closing my eyes, I let the heat spread over my face warming it. I reached out my hand and brought it close to the flames.

How easy it would be.

Just reach out a little further, and it could be over like it should have been so many years before. Like it should have been at the mansion.

What about the pain?

I still could remember how it had felt when the torch touched my leg. The jolt of heat that numbed my body was a thousand times greater than the warmth I was feeling from the fire.

I pulled my hand away.

Leaving my room, I walked back to Washington College Hospital. Now in a private room, Edgar was still screaming my name.

When he saw me, he stopped yelling. I hoped no one would come to investigate his sudden silence.

"How long have you wanted to die?" he asked me in a hoarse whisper.

"Too long. Far too long," I answered.

"And you've never killed yourself?" I shook my head. "Why?"

"I can't die," I said.

"But you can now. Throw yourself into a fire. Lay your neck on a rail track and wait for a passing train," Edgar said.

"I'm afraid of the pain. I might have been able to do it once, but now I know how painful it would be for me to kill myself. I have never felt much physical pain in my life, except for when the torch damaged my leg. It's not a feeling I am willing to magnify," I explained.

"As a mortal, I can tell you, there's not much difference in physical pain and emotional pain except where they leave their scars," Edgar whispered.

"How long have you wanted to die?" I asked.

"Since Sissy died," he admitted.

"What about Sarah? What about the wonderful life you told you had found in Virginia?" I reminded him.

Edgar shrugged. "I lied. Life is very empty for me. It will be that way for as long as I live. As for Sarah, I did love her once, but we have both changed since then. She thinks she is marrying Edgar Allan Poe, the great writer. I am not the man she imagines. I am afraid to live," he told me.

"And so you want to die?"

Edgar nodded slowly. "I've tried laudanum, but it hasn't worked. It's too slow, and it gives doctors the chance to counteract the effects. Like you, other methods are too painful for me to use. My body won't consciously allow me to inflict pain on it. You can kill me without the pain, though. Help me, Reynolds. If you care, help me," he said.

I slid my hand down the side of my leg and pulled my knife out of my boot. I looked at the blade and hesitated. I knew stabbing myself wouldn't hurt me. I had experienced worse wounds. But, could I allow my regenerative power to take a life unnecessarily?

"If you can't help yourself, Reynolds, at least, help me," Edgar said from his bed.

"How could you have grown to hate life so much after only forty years?" I asked him.

Edgar said nothing. He stared back at me anxiously waiting.

"I can't do it. I may be afraid of life, but running to death is not the answer," I said.

I slid the knife back into my boot.

"No, Reynolds, no." Edgar began to cry.

"It's not right," I told him.

Suddenly, Edgar rolled over, snatched the knife from my boot and slashed a deep gash across the inside of my thigh. Then he fell against me plunging the knife into my stomach.

I didn't have time to react. I barely had time to grunt when Edgar stabbed me. He grabbed me by the hips and fell against me. The rippling went out of me almost immediately and returned just as quickly.

I heard Edgar yelp as he pushed himself back onto the bed.

"God have mercy on my soul," he whispered.

"And mine," I said.

My blood stained the front of my shirt. My leg had healed quickly, but the wound in my stomach, because it was deeper, took slightly longer. I could feel the tingling as my stomach knitted itself closed, and I knew that I had stolen what remained of Edgar's life.

"What have you done?" I said to Edgar.

He rolled away from me as if to dismiss me and lay quietly. I looked at him for a moment, then turned away to leave. It would do no good to argue with him about it. The outcome couldn't be changed.

"Reynolds?" he said.

I turned back. Edgar still wasn't looking at me.

"What?" I asked with a slight trace of irritation in my voice.

"Don't blame yourself. This is what I wanted. Remember, I made the choice, not your body," he told me.

After that, he said nothing else, and so I left. Nothing more was left to do but wait. It wasn't even a long wait. Edgar died the next day.

Nearly every magazine and newspaper in the world carried an article about his death. The Great Edgar Allan Poe was dead, and no one knew how he had died. I tried to fool myself into believing he would have died whether or not I had interfered. I told myself the laudanum had killed him, and I had only hurried him along.

I've never been a good liar.

At times, I wonder how much better his writing would have gotten had he lived. How many more melodic verses would he have left to enchant readers? How many more horrific nightmares would he have put on paper?

Unanswerable questions, I know, but one still wonders.

After his burial at the Westminster Cemetery, I left Baltimore. I went back into the mountains and purchased the land we're sitting on now. And here I have stayed for the last 167 years. Of course, at the time I bought it, this area was still wilderness. Now, it seems as if civilization is reaching out to find me.

My body still steals life, but it does it much less frequently. In fact, I appeared quite old before it happened the last time. Maybe that will truly have been the last time.

January 20, 2016

"And that is my story," Tim.

Tim looked up from his notes. "What about the years between then and now?" he asked.

"I've been living on this mountain, except for my brief trips into Cumberland for supplies, and of course, my annual visit to Baltimore to remember my old friend."

"Why do you bring cognac to Edgar's grave?" Tim asked.

"It was his favorite drink when he could afford it. Though, I doubt he could really taste much after the first sip. The first half of the bottle I always pour onto the ground to allow it to soak through to him. I figure it can do him no harm now to drink, and it certainly helps me forget my guilt for a few minutes."

"And the roses?" Tim continued.

"I once described his mother as a woman of frail beauty like a flower that has been cut from the ground. The roses are for three women of such frail beauty and also the most-important women in his life. Elizabeth, although he could barely remember her, he still loved her because she was his mother. Frances, because she was the mother he did know, and she loved Edgar as if he were her own flesh and blood. Virginia, because she was his wife and the woman he had pledged his eternal love to," Alexander explained.

Tim nodded. "You've shown a lot of dedication to him. Some might even call it an obsession," he noted.

Alexander nodded his agreement. He walked over to the wall and stared at an oil painting of Edgar Allan Poe. "Oh, it is. Edgar was the only good thing my life has ever produced. I take pride in his accomplishment, probably greater than David ever did."

"What about stopping Matthew? That was a good thing. As you said yourself, you saved a lot of people from dying prematurely. Maybe worse."

Alexander shook his head. "That was a necessary thing. Murder is never good, even the murder of an evil man, but it is sometimes necessary. I killed Matthew because I was the only one who could have done it."

"I believe Jesus suspected something went wrong with Matthew's resurrection. He may have even known for certain, and simply not been able to cast out the demon because Matthew's body had been altered with his resurrection. That would have explained why Jesus did not rush to help me when I was ill. He wanted me to die so he could resurrect me. I was the fail-safe in case his suspicions proved correct and he wasn't around to stop Matthew himself," Alexander theorized.

"Are you still afraid to die?" Tim asked.

Alexander shook his head. "No. I can die peacefully now knowing I have played out my role in life. I welcome the day when I will be alone no longer."

Part VI:
The Premature Burial

The tortures endured, however, were indubitably quite equal, for the time, to those of an actual sepulchre. They were fearfully - they were inconceivably hideous; but out of Evil preceded Good; for their very excess wrought in my spirit an inevitable revulsion. My soul acquired tone - acquired temper. I went abroad. I took vigorous exercise. I breathed the free air of Heaven.

Edgar Allan Poe
The Premature Burial

33

Alexander sat on the front porch of his house, reading the story of Moses in the Bible. The February air was a relatively warm sixty-five degrees. A warm front had moved into the mountains that morning, melting the frost on the ground and the windows. The weatherman on channel seven had said to enjoy it because it would only last until the weekend. Then the bitter cold of winter would return. Taking the weatherman's advice, Alexander had slipped on a sweater and moved his rocking chair outside to enjoy the sun and warmth.

From his stereo in his upstairs bedroom, David Lanz's melodic piano playing of *Cristofori's Dream* came. Alexander had opened the upstairs window so that the relaxing music could pierce the silence of the mountain.

As he read Exodus, he felt an odd tightness in his chest. He ignored it, as he did most of the aches and pains he felt, and read on.

"Lazarus."

Alexander looked up. A man stood in front of him. No, not a man, a god. Jesus Christ. He appeared not to have changed in the centuries since Alexander had last seen him. He was even clothed in the same white robes.

Christ smiled at him.

"Is it truly you?" Alexander whispered as he slipped from his rocking chair onto his knees.

Jesus held out his hands so that Alexander could see the nail prints in his palms. Alexander clenched his eyes shut and turned his head away.

"I don't need to see them, my Lord. I was at Calvary when they killed you," he said.

"I know, my friend, but look. See that I am who I say that I am," Jesus said.

Alexander obeyed and slowly opened his eyes to look at Christ's hands. The puncture wounds seemed freshly scabbed over as if Jesus had healed himself yesterday, not a million yesterdays ago.

Alexander felt the tears welling up in his eyes. He grabbed Jesus' hands and kissed them. Jesus freed one of his hands and stroked the back of Alexander's head.

"Do not weep. Lazarus, for the time of my return has come."

Alexander looked up. "It's too late for me."

"Do not fear. In my first resurrection, you were given the power to repent and receive the celestial glory. The deaths that your body has caused were not done with any purpose or malice on your part. You were my chosen instrument to combat Lucifer and his follower. You grieved for your actions and did your best to forsake them. You were forgiven. Today you will walk with your parents, sisters, and wives through the gardens of Heaven," Christ said.

"What about you, my Lord? Will you be there with me?"

"Not yet. I must walk among my brothers and sisters here. I will teach them again and show them the way to righteousness."

Alexander continued to cry. Christ grasped him gently by the shoulders and raised him up.

"Are you ready, my friend?" Christ asked.

Lazarus nodded.

February 19, 2016

"The old man took you for a ride, and you fell for it hook, line, and sinker," Brad told him from the other end of the telephone line.

"He wasn't lying," Tim insisted.

"How do you know? Did you put him on a polygraph machine while he told you his story?"

"Of course not."

"So how do you know?" Brad pressed.

"Gut feeling, I guess," Tim admitted. He trusted his gut feelings a lot more than he did some of the things he was told by so-called sources.

Brad laughed at him.

Tim couldn't believe that Alexander had lied to him. "You had to be there, Brad. He was genuine. He had paintings of himself in other eras. He had old documents in his name and old photographs of himself."

"I would have been there, but I wasn't invited. Remember? Tim, this guy is a con man who protected his privacy by feeding you that line of bull about living forever. Listen, pal, I know this guy must have been really convincing to sucker you in, but a 2,000-year-old man? Come on, Tim. Think about it."

Brad started laughing again, and Tim blushed. Thankfully, Brad couldn't see him.

"Besides," Brad continued, "if you turn that story into Conklin, he would toss it in the circular file and never give you another assignment."

"I guess you're right, but if I could only write the story and let you...," Tim started to say.

Brad cut him off. "No one would believe it. You know that, Tim. You need to focus on something other than the old man."

"I know," Tim answered.

"So what are you going to write about?"

"I don't know yet, but I'll come up with something."

"Don't let me down, pal."

"Have I ever?" Tim's voice held no enthusiasm.

"That's what I'm counting on."

Tim hung up the phone and tried to forget Brad's laughs. He couldn't, though. Brad's deep, rolling, belly laugh continued echoing through his head.

Tim stared at the digital recorder filled with hours of his interview with Alexander Reynolds. The man had been so detailed in his descriptions and the ancient conversations. Everything he had said coincided with facts that Tim already knew about history and Edgar Allan Poe. How could Alexander have been lying?

The old man fed you a line, pal.

Did Tim have nine hours' worth of lies on tape? He pushed the play button on the recorder and listened to Alexander's voice. I could feel my body regenerating. The feeling was a cross between... Tim switched the recorder off.

Alexander definitely spoke with an accent, but was it actually Israeli? Even Alexander had said it probably wasn't. It was so faint that nearly any nationality could have been read into his voice.

I know this guy must have been really convincing.

Tim had wanted to believe in Alexander. He was a miracle, and Tim wanted to believe in miracles again. He liked Alexander. He didn't want to believe that the old man could have slipped over the edge and taken born-again Christianity one step too far.

Alexander was obviously wealthy, judging by the land he had fenced in on the mountain. But was he sane?

Did Alexander live in a fantastical dream? Had he built himself a life history that rivaled any work of fiction? If so, the photos and papers might have been faked. Alexander could have had them made not only to convince anyone who might question his history but to convince himself as well.

Tim felt his face flush with blood as he grew angrier with himself. He flung the recorder against the wall. It dented the drywall and fell to the floor.

February 20, 2016

The gate to Alexander's land was closed. That didn't surprise Tim. Alexander was definitely the type of person who preferred being alone and didn't invite many guests.

Tim jabbed the button on the console and waited for Alexander to respond. After half a minute, he jabbed the button again.

"Alexander, this is Tim. I know you're up there. Let me in. I need to talk to you," Tim said to the silent console.

Still no response.

Was Alexander avoiding him now like he did everyone else? Tim pulled his head inside the car and rolled up his window. The weather had turned cold yesterday, and the warm temperatures of three days ago had dropped twenty degrees.

He was going to get the truth out of Alexander one way or another. He turned the engine off and left his car blocking the gate in case Alexander tried to leave. He climbed out of his car and opened his trunk. Tucked behind his spare tire was an old army blanket he had bought at a military surplus store when he was in college. He pulled it out and closed his trunk.

He didn't see any way he could climb the gate. There was nothing he could get a handhold on. The chain-link fence off to the sides offered slightly easier access onto Alexander's land. Once inside the fence, the house was probably no more than a half a mile away if walked in a straight line. Of course, that straight line would be all uphill.

Tim carried the blanket with him as he walked into the woods. The iron gate turned into a chain-link fence about fifteen feet from the driveway. The fence was eight-feet-high topped with three strands of barbed wire that leaned out from the fence at a forty-five-degree angle.

Tim touched the metal weave lightly and quickly pulled his hand away. He wouldn't put it past Alexander to electrify the fence to keep people away from him. Fortunately for Tim, he hadn't.

He zipped up his coat to his neck. He was going to need as much padding as he could get. He slung the blanket over his shoulder and began climbing the fence. When he reached the top, he held on with one hand and hung the blanket over the strands of barbed wire.

Letting go of the fence, Tim grabbed the outermost strand of barbed wire through the blanket. He had folded into quarters before he threw it over the barbed wire. Yet, he could still feel the pointed barbs even through the four layers of the blanket. They were too well covered to hurt much, though. They only pricked at his hand like thorns. He moved his hand to the side so that it rested on an area without barbs, and pulled on the wire to see if it would snap under pressure.

It held.

Tim let go of the fence and let his full weight hang from the wire.

It still did not break.

He reached up with his free hand and grabbed another clear area of wire. Then he rotated himself so that he was facing away from the fence.

He started swinging his body by thrusting his legs high out in front of him and letting them drop. It was hard to get any momentum going because he kept hitting the fence on his back swing, and it slowed him down. When Tim was swinging as high as the fence would allow him, he kicked his legs up as hard as he could and pulled down on the wire at the same time.

His legs rose over his head, and suddenly he was looking at the ground rather than the trees. As his thighs fell on top of the covered barbed wire, he felt a dozen barbs in his legs. He bit down on his lip to keep from yelling.

Careful to avoid any further barbs, he pushed his upper body on top of the barbed wire also. That done, he shimmied himself off the wire until he could climb down the opposite side of the fence.

Tim walked back to the gate hoping to find a way to open it so that he could get his car through it. He would rather drive up to the house than trudge through the woods and risk getting lost. He saw no switches on the inside of the gate. It was apparently controlled either by a remote control in the house and probably one in Alexander's jeep, too.

Tim turned and looked up the mountain. It was a steep path through the woods, and the road was scarcely less steep. However, the road was clear. It would be better to take it even if it did take longer.

He started walking up the road.

He was determined to get the evidence from Alexander that would either prove or disprove his story. He had made certain to bring a camera with him on this visit. He also wanted to bring back the old daguerreotype and the earliest letter back with him. He wasn't sure Alexander would want to part with them, but he would argue with him until Alexander gave in. He had to have proof if he wanted to publish the article.

It took Tim forty-five minutes of uphill climbing to reach Alexander's house and walk into the quiet front yard. When he stood in the yard, he heard no outdoor sounds. The area was utterly silent.

Tim started toward the porch when he saw the pile of Alexander's clothes. He picked up the wool sweater and a cloud of white dust fell out. He dropped it and stepped onto the porch.

Knocking at the front door, he called, "Alexander, It's me. Tim. I need to talk to you."

There was no answer, not even a sound of movement from inside the house. Tim knew Alexander still had to be on the mountain. His Jeep was in the garage. Alexander might have walked off into the woods, but he wouldn't have walked off the mountain. It would have taken too long to get anywhere.

Tim knocked once more, and there was no answer a second time. He opened the door. He wasn't surprised it wasn't locked. Alexander lived alone on a mountain. The nearest people were twenty-five miles away. Most people didn't even know there was a house on the mountain, and if they did, the fence would keep them out. Alexander's living room was empty.

He walked into the dining room. The pile of documents Alexander had shown him during their interview was still on the dining room table. Tim sorted through them picking out the old daguerreotype and the letter Edgar Allan Poe had written Alexander asking him to come to Fordham to help Virginia.

Tim looked over his shoulder expecting to see Alexander at the door at any moment, but he remained alone. He went upstairs wondering if Alexander might be sleeping. In Alexander's bedroom, the bed was made. Tim noticed the open window when a slight breeze ruffled the curtains. Now, why would Alexander open a window when it was forty degrees outside? As he shut it, he noticed that the old stereo next to the window was on, but the cassette player had turned off. It looked like Alexander had been listening to a tape but hadn't turned it over or off when the side had finished.

Tim went back downstairs. He picked up the letter and picture and started for the door. He would take them and leave before Alexander returned. That way he would avoid an argument with Alexander. He didn't consider it stealing because he planned on returning them once he had their authenticity verified or denied.

Tim shut the front door behind himself as he stepped onto the porch. He noticed Alexander had moved his rocking chair from the living room to the porch. The old man had probably been listening to his tape player while he sat on the porch. That would explain the open window in Alexander's room, but Alexander wouldn't have been sitting outside on a day as cold as today.

Then he noticed the Bible lying on the porch next to the chair. Odd that Alexander would have left it lying there. It was one of Alexander's most-prized possessions. Tim stepped off the porch and saw the pile of clothes again. That really struck him as odd.

He picked up the sweater and the jeans. More of the white dust that had fallen out of the sweater fell out of the jeans. Alexander's work boots also had piles of the dust in them. There was a complete outfit. It was as if Alexander had totally undressed and thrown his clothes in a pile.

What was all the white powder?

All those I have known are dust in their graves.

Tim picked up a handful of the dust and looked at it more closely. Could it be? Was this what happened to a body after two-thousand years. He let the dust trickle between his fingers.

Ashes to ashes. Dust to dust.

It was the only line from the service he knew, and now he knew what it meant.

Alexander's wish had come true.

35

January 19, 2017

A solitary car, badly in need of a tune-up, rumbled down Fayette Street past Tim's Corolla, which was parked on the street a block from the Westminster Church. Tim's head snapped up as he heard the noise. He had been dozing again.

He was surprised he was able to sleep at all. His car seat was uncomfortable, and the January temperature was in the teens. He hadn't been able to keep his engine running because he didn't want to draw attention to himself.

He glanced at his watch. It was nearly two o'clock in the morning. He had better leave soon. If he fell asleep again, he might not wake up again until morning.

Well, Alexander wasn't going to show. Tim had entertained a small grain of hope that his friend might surprise him and show up. But he had known what the white dust in Alexander's clothes meant. Alexander wouldn't visit Edgar's grave again. The responsibility now fell to Tim because he was the only one who knew the truth.

Just him and no one else. Tim had written his book about Alexander's life, and it had been the best thing he had ever written. When it came time to mail it, though, he couldn't do it. It didn't seem right somehow. It almost felt like a betrayal of confidence even though Alexander had known Tim wanted to publish the story.

Instead, Tim had driven back to Alexander's house last month. He had climbed over the fence the same way he had the February before and walked up to the house. Everything was much the same as it had been the last time Tim had seen it. Rains had washed away the last remnants of Alexander and there was a thick coating of dust over the furniture, but everything else remained the same as it had been— the only remaining tribute to the man who killed Edgar Allan Poe.

Tim had taken his manuscript from his backpack and set it on the cherry-wood table where he had sat and listened to Alexander's life story. At least whoever found the house in the future would know what sort of man had lived in it. In place of the manuscript, Tim had taken two items. Alexander's Bible and a bottle of cognac.

The Bible now sat next to his bed in his apartment. He was in the middle of reading through it.

Now it was time to use the cognac.

Tim looked outside the car. The street was deserted. The windows in the row homes were dark. No one was even walking home from a bar after a late night. The street wouldn't get any more deserted.

Opening his door, Tim shivered as the cold night air rushed in and dropped the temperature in his car by five degrees. He reached across the seat and picked up the brown-paper bag laying in passenger's seat. As he climbed out of the car, he reached behind his seat and took out the oak cane.

He walked to church, hesitating for a moment by the front gate. He pushed on the front gate, and it swung open. Leave it to Nelson to make things easy on the Toaster.

Tim pulled his hat lower on his face, then limped through the gate. He turned right and made his way toward the grave at the front of the cemetery. He made sure not to walk on any of the other graves that crossed his path.

When he reached the six-foot grave marker in the corner of the cemetery, he kneeled down in front of it. He reached into the brown-paper bag and pulled out three red roses. He separated one from the bunch and laid it on the grave.

"This is for Elizabeth, who loved you as a baby," Tim whispered.

He set the second rose on the grave.

"This is for Frances, who loved you as a boy."

He laid the final rose down.

"This is for Virginia, who loved you as a man."

Tim reached into the bag again and pulled out the bottle of cognac he had taken from Alexander's house. He uncorked the bottle and took a gulp from it. The liquid warmed his cold body as it slid to his stomach. He poured half the bottle over the grave.

Holding up the bottle to the engraved image of Edgar on the grave marker, Tim said, "A toast, to Edgar and to Lazarus of Bethany, may they rest in peace."

It wasn't quite the same toast Alexander made. Tim had added the part about Lazarus. It just seemed right. Someone who knew the real toast would know he was a fake, but then, he also knew the real toast and had added to it. So the toast wasn't fake, just different just as Tim wasn't a fake Toaster, just a different one.

Tim recorked the bottle and sat it down next to the roses.

As he stood to go, he turned toward the church. He saw the pale face of an old man in the corner window. It was Nelson Bennett. Nelson stared at him without moving, and Tim wondered if the old man recognized him.

Nelson nodded. Tim smiled and returned the nod. Then Tim limped out of the graveyard until next year.

About the Author

J. R. Rada is a pen name for award-winning writer, James Rada, Jr. He has written five books of fantasy and horror. These include *A Byte-Size Friend, Welcome to Peaceful Journey, Kachina, and Kuskurza.*

He works as a freelance writer who lives in Gettysburg, PA. James has received numerous awards from the Maryland-Delaware-DC Press Association, Associated Press, Maryland State Teachers Association and Community Newspapers Holdings, Inc. for his newspaper writing.

If you would like to be kept up to date on new books being published by James or ask him questions, he can be reached by e-mail at *jimrada@yahoo.com.*

To see James' other books or to order copies on-line, go to *www.jamesrada.com.*

DON'T MISS THESE BOOKS BY J. R. RADA

KUSKURZA
Contains "The Path to Kuskurza" and "White Indian" as well as a sneak peek to "Kachina." These are stories of the ancient gods of the Hopi and Third World in which they lived before emerging in this world.

KACHINA
David Purcell was on his way to meet his girlfriend when he fell into a cave. When he next comes aware of things, he is in a hospital recovering. He has been missing for five weeks and has no memory of his time in the cave. He soon realizes that something followed him from the caves, something dark from the ancient legends of the Hopi.

WELCOME TO PEACEFUL JOURNEY
Welcome to Peaceful Journey Funeral where the journey from life to death can be anything but peaceful. The viewing rooms bear the names of heavenly glory as found in the different religions of the world, but it is a long-forgotten religion that controls Peaceful Journey. Owner Bruce Godsey tries his best to be comforting to mourners, but he has seen a lot more than he can admit.

Made in the USA
Middletown, DE
20 October 2020